BETRAYED

BETRAYED
ANNA SMITH

Quercus

First published in Great Britain in 2014 by

Quercus Editions Ltd
55 Baker Street
7th Floor, South Block
London W1U 8EW

A CIP catalogue record for this book is available
from the British Library

PB ISBN 978 1 78087 124 0
EBOOK ISBN 978 1 84866 627 6

10 9

Printed and bound in Great Britain by Clays Ltd, Elcograf S.p.A.

Typeset by Ellipsis Digital Limited, Glasgow

For my sister, Sadie, the most selfless woman I know.

'Those who will not reason, are bigots,
those who cannot, are fools,
and those who dare not, are slaves.'

Lord Byron (1788–1824)

PROLOGUE

Glasgow, July 1999

They belted the song out to the beat of the Lambeg drum.

'Do you know where hell is, hell is in The Falls . . . Heaven is the Shankill and we'll guard those Derry's walls . . . I was born under a Union Jack . . . A Union, Union Jack . . .'

'What a night, Jimmy boy! Fucking rocking!' Eddie McGregor stood at the bar, his arms folded across his chest as Jimmy Dunlop came up beside him.

'Aye. Class, man.' Jimmy winked to the barmaid whose face lit up as she smiled back.

'You'll be a proud man tonight, Jimmy, eh?' Eddie dug him in the ribs with his elbow. 'Your da's well made up over there. Look at him.'

Jimmy smiled, squinting through the fug of smoke where his father was leading the sing-song at his table, whisky in hand, face crimson from drink and exuberance. Two of the guys next to him stood on chairs, swaying, arms around each other's shoulders as one song followed another in a medley of the sectarian hate they'd all grown up with.

'That's your wee bird there, isn't it? You giving her plenty, you rascal?' Eddie jerked his head towards the barmaid as she stretched up to the optics on the gantry. He grinned, his tongue darting out to lick his lips as she bent over in her skintight jeans. 'She's well fuckable. I'll tell you that.'

Jimmy caught a whiff of Eddie's sweat and felt a little disgusted. He said nothing, but forced a smile because he knew he was expected to. After all, Eddie was his commanding officer now. He hoped his face didn't show the stab of resentment he felt at Eddie's remark. Wendy was *his*. He couldn't get her out of his mind. One of his mates had told him Wendy was easy – and maybe she was. But he'd been seeing her for nearly two months now and he felt different when he was with her. When he'd told her he was determined to hold onto her, tears had welled up in her big brown eyes and she was suddenly so unlike the brash barmaid, quick to slap down a smart-arsed customer despite her skinny frame. It was there and then that Jimmy saw where he wanted to be for the rest of his life.

He took a long drink of his pint, rolled up his shirtsleeves and tried to relax for the first time all evening. The hall was heaving. It was billed as an all male smoker night for Rangers football supporters. But everyone who'd bought a ticket knew it was in fact a fundraiser for the Ulster Volunteer Force. It was nights like this that Loyalist hardliners lived for, and Jimmy had been to plenty of them. It had kicked off with a bit of stand-up by a famous Glasgow lawyer, ripping the pish out of Catholics and Celtic. But the highlight of the night was the parade around the hall led by the 'colour party' of UVF heroes in balaclavas, who'd come all the way from Belfast. They'd made their entrance in dramatic fashion as a hush fell over the room. Once the outside doors had been locked and secured, they emerged from a side room, in full paramilitary uniform, bearing rifles on their shoulders as they marched beneath the UVF flag. Then followed a rousing call-to-arms speech by the Belfast brigadier. And there, among the official stewards, in their black trousers and crisp white shirts, one Jimmy Dunlop, the newest recruit to Glasgow B Company, Number Two Platoon, proudly wearing his new UVF tie – the badge of honour that put him a cut above the rest.

On the stroke of midnight, with a brisk drum roll and flutes at the ready, the Portadown Sons of William Flute Band assembled in the centre of the hall for the national anthem. The crowd of three hundred revellers, sweating like horses in the heat of the sweltering summer's night, stood with their chests bursting with pride as they sang 'God Save the Queen'. And on the final line, a chorus of lusty roars of 'No Surrender' and 'C'mon, the Rangers' rang out around the hall.

'All right, Jimmy boy?' Mitch Gillespie staggered up and slung an arm around his shoulder.

'Great, Mitch. Couldn't be better.' Jimmy drained his pint and placed the tumbler on the bar.

He was a little light-headed, having already downed half a dozen pints in quick succession after staying sober for his stewarding duties earlier. He kept one eye on Wendy clearing up behind the bar. He wouldn't be able to go back to her place, as his da was so blootered he'd have to see him home. But he was hoping to get a snog at her round the back of the pub before she left. Big Eddie was giving the barmaids a lift home, as he'd only had three pints the whole night.

'C'mon, we'll go to the dancing,' Mitch said, dragging him away from the bar. 'I need a ride, man. Make up for lost time.' He grinned.

'Yeah, sure you do,' Jimmy grinned. 'But don't start getting fresh with me. Your arse must be like a ripped-out fireplace, after all that any-port-in-a-storm stuff in the nick.' He shrugged Mitch's muscular arm from his shoulder and slapped him on the back.

'That'll be fucking right,' Mitch snorted derisively. 'No' me. Even when I was gagging for it, I wasn't going to let some big randy fucker in the boys' gate.' He chuckled. 'Mind you, once or twice I nearly let somebody blow me.'

Jimmy laughed, part of him full of admiration for Mitch being able to handle six years banged up for culpable homicide. But a bigger part of him was still revolted at what he and his mate witnessed seven years ago during a mêlée after an Old Firm match. They'd been sent to the East End by big Eddie to find Mitch, and when they got there, he was coked out of his nut, jumping on the head of a Celtic fan, the guy's face like something from a butcher's dustbin. It was fair enough to give somebody a hiding in a fight, but this was bang out of order. They dragged Mitch off and bundled him into a car. But the cops caught up with him within twenty-four hours and he was locked up. Mitch, or Mad Mitch, as the newspapers dubbed him at the trial, had only been released from jail five weeks ago after his sentence was reduced on appeal. He'd come through the prison doors of Barlinnie like a prize fighter, arms like hams and muscles rippling through his skintight T-shirt, and a wide grin across his face as he strutted towards Jimmy's waiting car. Then he turned and pumped his fist defiantly at the building and shouted, 'It was a fucking walk in the park, you cunts!'

'Nah, Mitch. I can't go anywhere tonight. Look at my da. He's blitzed. I'll need to get him home. Maybe tomorrow night, mate.'

'Right, okay, pal.' Mitch walked away, giving him the two thumbs up. 'You're the man, Jimmy. I love you, man.'

Jimmy watched as he went unsteadily towards a group of young men, who were all drunk and who knew Mitch well enough by reputation not to object to him barging in on them.

*

Half an hour later Jimmy struggled up the tenement stairs with his father hanging onto him. He was still singing the 'Billy Boys' at the top of his voice.

'Sssh, da. You'll get us fucking shot.' Jimmy knew that at least two of the downstairs neighbours were diehard Celtic fans.

'Aye. That'll be fucking right. Them pikey bastards can fuck off back to the bogs,' big Jack Dunlop slurred, his Belfast accent still as strong as the day he left his home city for Glasgow forty years ago. 'Any shooting to be done round here, I'll be doing it.' He stood on the landing, swaying as Jimmy put the key in the door. 'You just remember who you are, Jimmy. You've got a fucking pedigree that goes all the way to the Shankill.'

His father burst into song as Jimmy gently wrestled him inside the doorway. 'Follow, follow, we will follow Rangers . . . up the stair, down the stair, we will follow you . . .'

The mobile ringing on his bedside table woke Jimmy with a start. He looked at his watch. He must have dropped off, because it was only one thirty in the morning and he still had his clothes on. He saw Wendy's name on the screen and cleared his throat.

'Hiya, Wendy. Still up? You missing me?'

Silence. Then Jimmy thought he heard sobs.

'You there, Wendy?' His stomach lurched.

'Oh, Jimmy.' Her voice was a whisper.

'Wendy. You all right? What's wrong?'

'Oh Jimmy.' More sobs. 'He . . .'

'What's wrong? Calm down.' He was on his feet. 'You been in an accident or something? Are you hurt?'

'No . . . Oh . . . Yes . . . He . . .' Wendy sniffed. 'He raped me, Jimmy.'

'What? Who? Who raped you?'

'Eddie.' She dissolved into sobs. 'Eddie raped me . . . In his car.'

'Aw fuck! Aw fuck no, Wendy! Eddie raped you? I'll fucking kill him.' Red-hot anger burned from his stomach to his throat. 'You in the house?' He shoved his feet into his trainers.

'Uh huh . . .'

'Wait there. I'm coming over right now. I'll get a taxi.'

But when he got there, Wendy was gone.

CHAPTER ONE

The marching season. All human forms are here, Rosie thought, judging by some of the rat-arsed, drunken knuckle-trailers on the sidelines. She stood for fully ten minutes in the sunshine, watching the Orange Walk in its swaggering stride through Glasgow city centre, like a conquering army with a jaunty tune. Then she weaved her way through the Bath Street hordes on the pavement till she could find a place to cross the road without cutting through the march-ers. That was more or less a hanging offence. Or at the very least you'd get your face wasted if you dared to barge through the parade of flute bands, or the well-dressed ladies in straw hats, or, worst of all, the strutting men in bowler hats and brollies, resplendent in orange sashes – no doubt the very ones their fathers wore.

Rosie needed this like a hole in the head – especially on a Saturday morning with a hangover. She walked briskly until she reached the head of the parade and made a dash across the road. Her mobile rang in her bag and she rummaged through, fishing it out.

'That you, Rosie? I'm in the bar waiting for you.'

'I'm there in two minutes, Liz. The city centre's mental, with the walk being on.'

Rosie recognised the voice of the woman she'd met yesterday, the woman who had shut the door in her face when she told her she was working on the story of the missing barmaid, Wendy Graham. It was now over three weeks since she vanished after finishing her shift in the bar that had been hosting a Rangers supporters' smoker night, and the story was falling so far down the news schedule it barely got a mention. The media very quickly lose interest in a missing person unless it's a child or a celebrity, or unless there is some glaring sense that the missing person is about to turn up dead. The police would tell you that their files are chock full with people who just disappeared into thin air, but Rosie had pushed the editor to keep a line in the newspaper, hoping she'd get a call that might open the story up. She was even more intrigued after her Strathclyde Police detective friend tipped her that Wendy Graham's sudden disappearance might be more than just a missing person.

When Wendy's pal Liz had refused to talk to her, it only added to her interest in the story. Rosie had slipped her business card below the door as she left the tenement, but she didn't really expect a call. The knockback had been fairly emphatic, laced with a few expletives. So when the call did come last night as she was out at a farewell party for one of the *Post*'s feature writers, Rosie knew she would have to be available any time, any place. Even on a Saturday morning. It should have stopped her carrying on for a full house and ending up at a nightclub till three. But it didn't. She was feeling a little fragile as she went downstairs to the basement bar for her meeting. She hoped it wouldn't last too long.

The Unit Bar was empty and the air was thick with the reek of stale cigarette smoke and alcohol, mixed with last night's sweaty bodies. Bars the morning after were always lonely, depressing places; a kind of stiff reminder that there was always the cold light of day to bring you crashing back to reality, despite the hopes and possibilities of the night before. And the Unit was one bar where the possibilities were endless – ecstasy tablets that were circulated like sweeties; or some speed; or if you were hard core and past caring, a few grams of crack – the latest lethal fix with more terrifying implications than the heroin explosion of the last decade. But like every form of refuge, there was a price to pay. So whoever was here last night off their face on drugs was now probably festering in some housing scheme, or city centre flat, or student digs, coming down to earth with paranoia and loathing crushing their head. And, of course, the pressing urge for more.

Rosie felt a little nauseous and took as deep a breath as she dared, squinting across the dingy room where she spotted Liz at the fake leather seating in the far corner. She walked across, feeling her feet sticking to the carpet. Classy joint.

'Liz,' Rosie stretched out her hand, 'thanks for coming.'

Liz shook her hand and gave her a sheepish look.

'Sorry about yesterday.' She shifted in her seat. 'I mean, shutting the door in your face. I'm just under a bit of pressure. You know. Wendy going missing and that.'

Rosie sat down.

'No worries, Liz. If I'd a pound for every time someone shut the door in my face, I'd have chucked work years ago and retired somewhere sunny.' She looked at her almost empty glass. 'Let me get you a drink.'

'Vodka and diet Coke,' Liz said, swirling the remains of her drink. 'I'm only having a couple. It's not often I'm on this side of a bar.' Then she looked up at Rosie as though attempting to justify being on her second vodka before midday. 'I haven't been drinking much in the past month . . . Since Wendy disappeared.'

Rosie nodded. 'I'll get the drinks in and maybe we can have a chat, if you're all right with that.'

She returned to the table with a glass of mineral water for herself and watched while Liz poured the dregs of her glass into the fresh one and took a swig. She was built like a pit pony, and looked like a thirty-something bottle-blonde who had been around the course a few times. Rosie imagined that she wouldn't take any crap from customers on the other side of the bar. She hoped she wasn't as hard as she looked.

'I'm surprised there's not been a lot in the papers,' Liz said, lighting a cigarette and flicking a glance at Rosie. 'A lassie's gone missing. Nearly a month now. You'd think the papers would make more of it.'

There was a tone of reprimand in her voice.

'Yeah,' Rosie said. 'I've done a few pieces myself but I get the sense that the story is slipping off the news agenda. I'm trying to keep it alive, look for new lines.' She gave Liz a look that let her know who was running this meeting. 'Which is why I'm here, and what I was trying to do yesterday.' Rosie paused and pushed her hair back. 'Do you want to tell me a bit about it? All I know is that Wendy and you were friends and that she was working in a bar at some Rangers smoker night and then went home with you. I think the two of you got a lift home with someone called Eddie McGregor, according to what the cops put out? He was one of the organisers of the night? That about right?'

Liz rolled her eyes upwards and blew air out of her ruby lipsticked lips. 'Well you're not wrong about some of it. Eddie did give us a lift home.' She leaned forward. 'But it wasn't a smoker night. That's just a load of fanny they tell the council so they can get a licence.' She furtively glanced around even though the bar was empty. 'It was a UVF fund-raiser.' Her voice dropped to a whisper as she inclined her head to the side. 'You know. From across the water.'

Rosie nodded, deadpan, as if she heard this every day. A little nudge of adrenalin in her gut pushed her hangover away. It wasn't news that the UVF had fundraisers in Glasgow and elsewhere, under the guise of a Rangers football supporters' night. They were no different from the IRA who ran certain Celtic supporters' nights, where tins got rattled among the Republican faithful, and all the proceeds went across to the hardmen paramilitaries in Belfast. That was part and parcel of what Glasgow had become – more so in recent years. Even if the truth was that most of the punters spouting sectarian bile could fit their knowledge of Northern Ireland's bloody history on the back of a fag packet. The fact that they were raising funds here wasn't a huge story, but nobody from the inside was ever willing, or brave enough, to spill the beans. A barmaid going missing after one of these nights just cranked it up.

'I gather that they have a few of these fundraisers, but nobody ever talks about it.' Rosie screwed up her eyes. 'So who's this Eddie McGregor then?'

'He's UVF,' Liz whispered. 'High up. A commander or something.'

Rosie scanned her face, trying to work out why this woman who had shut the door on her yesterday was now singing like a canary, and giving her a rundown of who's who in the UVF. Either she had a death wish or was already five vodkas in. But she didn't look drunk. Not by any stretch.

'Look,' Liz said, as though she had read Rosie's mind, 'I'm

not some nutcase, who's going to fill your head with a load of shite about the UVF. I know stuff. I know what they do. I sometimes hear things in my job.'

'What kind of things?'

'Like for instance how they get their money.' She shrugged. 'I don't really give a damn about that.' She took a mouthful of her drink and raised a hand towards the muffled sound coming from the flute bands as they passed by the bar. 'In fact I used to walk in the Orange Walk. Most of my life. Born and bred. Queen and country. Rangers fan and Unionist through and through. It's how we're brought up here. You're either Orange or Green. But this is different. There's something not right about Wendy just disappearing like that.' She paused, looked Rosie in the eye and half smiled. 'You a Prod or a Tim?'

Rosie looked back at her, wondering just how loaded the question was. In certain parts of Glasgow you answered that one very carefully, depending on where you were and who was asking. Rosie didn't feel like giving this complete stranger the lowdown on her spirituality, or how she'd more or less given up organised religion when she woke up to the fact that the Catholic Church had been running it like a multinational organisation, for their own ends. And that she believed all religions were the same – from the Muslims to the Mormons – it was all smoke and mirrors. But she hated the bigotry that ran through the very heart of Scotland, and she despised the way Northern Ireland's troubles had crept into the terraces at football grounds, turning almost every Old Firm match into a bloodbath.

'I was brought up a Catholic.' Rosie decided to be honest. 'But I'm not really anything now. I have lots of friends of all religions. But I don't like bigotry.' She pointed her thumb in the direction of the bands outside. 'I dislike that walk out there every bit as much as the Hibs walk from the other mob next month. None of them have any place in this country.' Stuff it, Rosie thought. She called a spade a spade and if it offended Liz's sensibilities, then so be it.

Liz said nothing for a few seconds, then stubbed her cigarette out.

'Aye. Fair enough.' She smiled. 'At least you're honest.'

Rosie was relieved, and the iciness between them had been broken. Her mind was a blur of questions and she felt now Liz was ripe for talking. Whether any of it was provable was another story.

'So, Liz . . . What do you mean you know how they make their money? You mean from the fundraiser nights?'

'No. Well. That as well.' She raised her eyebrows. 'It's all drugs. Coke. Ecstasy. They make a fortune from that. The UVF run it big-time in Scotland – mostly Glasgow and the west.'

Saying that Loyalist and Republican gangs were organised, drug-dealing criminals was like revealing that a bear shat in the woods. But Rosie decided to let Liz talk and see where it took them.

'The UVF run all the coke, you're saying? How exactly do you mean?'

'They bring it in. In football buses. In the Rangers supporters' buses, when they go abroad. Spain, Holland. Germany . . .'

Rosie hoped her eyes hadn't lit up.

'You serious, Liz? You mean on buses when the fans travel to European Cup matches? With ordinary fans?'

Liz nodded. 'Aye. Most of the fans don't know anything about it. But I used to go out with a guy who goes on one of the supporters' buses from the pub I worked in down on London Road. I still see him now and again. I could maybe find out. But they do it in other pubs too.' She paused. 'But he told me that Eddie McGregor is the money man. It's him who goes with the cash for the deals.'

'You know a lot of stuff about an organisation and a criminal activity that's supposed to be top secret.' Rosie tried not to sound sarcastic.

'Over the years I've got to hear a lot.' She crossed her heavy thighs and glanced down at her chunky wedge sandals. 'It's never really mattered to me until now. But something stinks about Wendy going away, and I'll do anything to find out.' She paused. 'Right now I want to know if you and your paper are going to do anything to try to find her.' She stopped and swallowed. Suddenly her eyes filled up. 'Wendy didn't do a runner. I'm telling you that for sure. She had no reason to run away.'

'Do you think something has happened to her? Is it possible she was mixed up in the drugs and you didn't know?' Rosie asked.

'No, no,' Liz said quickly, shaking her head. 'Definitely not. I would know if she was involved in that. But I think something's happened to her. And I think Eddie knows about it. Okay, I know I'm telling you stuff that could get me done in, and I'm sure the coke runs on the bus have got nothing to do with Wendy's disappearance. But one thing I feel sure of is that Eddie McGregor is behind her going missing, and I've got no other way to get to him than get somebody like you to expose him.' She shook her head. 'But I'm terrified just being here, if I'm honest.'

She shook her head and put a hand to her lips, looking vulnerable for the first time, and Rosie watched as she tried to compose herself.

'Do you think something has happened to her? Have you told the police?' Rosie asked.

'I told them some stuff. Like how Eddie drove us home that night. But I didn't tell them everything.'

Silence.

'Why not, Liz?'

Silence. Rosie watched her as she wiped tears from the corners of her heavily made-up eyes.

'Because I thought she would turn up. I didn't want to do anything that would get them digging around on what the night *really* was – you know, the UVF fundraiser. I didn't want to be the one who grassed that up to the police. So I just said Eddie dropped me off, then took Wendy home to her house.'

'And is that not what happened?'

'No. Not quite.' She wiped under her eyes where the mascara had smudged. 'We went to a flat Eddie uses in the city centre – he keeps the place very quiet, so nobody knows he's got it. We just had a couple of drinks.'

Rosie nodded.

'We weren't drunk. Just tipsy. Then Eddie dropped me off at my flat.'

'So the only thing you didn't tell the cops is that you went back to Eddie's for a drink?'

Liz bit her lip.

'Well. No.' She paused. 'The next day, I got a phone call from Eddie saying to keep it quiet that we were at his for a drink. He said it was because Wendy was going out with Jimmy Dunlop and he didn't want him to get to know about it. I didn't tell the cops about that. I tried to phone Wendy all day, but couldn't get her. I thought she'd be sleeping. Then I was working at night, so I didn't go round to her house till the next day. There was still no answer. Her mum and dad were away on holiday, so she was in the house by herself. I spoke to Jimmy, and he was upset because he couldn't get her either. It was only when her parents came home the next day that they called the cops because there was no sign of her anywhere.'

'Jimmy Dunlop?' Rosie said, hoping she was remembering all the details. She didn't want to take a notebook out as the barman kept glancing over at them. 'Do you know him?'

'Yeah. He's UVF too. Wendy told me he was in Belfast last month taking the oath at the Shankill. They've been going out for nearly three months. He's all right, Jimmy. Hard, but a good guy. He's nuts about Wendy and she's really into him too. That's how I know she wouldn't just up sticks and leave home. She was staying with her ma and da. She's the only one in the family. She wouldn't leave them like that.' Tears came again and she shook her head. 'Something's happened to her. I just know it. It's been a month and we've heard nothing. That's not Wendy.' She looked at Rosie. 'Can you help? Can your paper do something?' She took a tissue out of her pocket and blew her nose.

'We can write something, Liz. I need to work out exactly what, though. I need to talk to the editor and see what we can do. But maybe you should have told the cops what you've told me.'

'No fucking way. And get my throat cut?'

Rosie took a deep breath.

'But you're telling me.'

'That's different.' She looked Rosie in the eye. 'You won't tell anybody it was me who told you stuff, will you?'

'Listen, Liz. Nobody will ever know you talked to me. But you must never tell anyone you spoke to me. It would be dangerous for you if the kind of people we're dealing with thought you were talking to a reporter. You know that, don't you?'

'Don't worry. I'm not stupid, Rosie. I know I'm taking a risk just sitting here. But I didn't know what else to do. I didn't want to go to the cops. Then when you came to my house yesterday, it got me thinking.'

'Have you told Jimmy Dunlop anything?'

'No. Nothing.'

'Would he talk to me?'

Liz shrugged. 'You could try. He's not a bad guy. No way is he involved in Wendy's disappearance though. But he's a UVF man through and through now.'

'What about her parents? Would they talk?'

'No. They haven't said much. They're nice people. But I don't think they'll know anything.'

Rosie asked for Liz's mobile number and stored it in her phone.

'I'll be in touch in the next couple of days, and we'll meet again. Meanwhile, say nothing.'

'I know.' Liz finished her drink and stood up and looked at her watch. 'I need to go. I hope you'll help find Wendy. I don't care what you do with any of the rest of the information I gave you. I don't care if you blow the whole thing sky high. I'll even help you. Wendy and me have been pals from school. I need to find her.'

'I'll do what I can,' Rosie said.

She watched as Liz walked across the carpet, and as she

pushed open the swing door, the sound of flutes and drums drifted into the bar. Rosie looked at her watch. Give it a few more hours and it would be the screams of police and ambulance sirens, as the Orange and the Green that had split the city down the middle for generations descended into the annual mayhem.

CHAPTER TWO

Jimmy's gut was in a knot as he waited in his car outside
Eddie McGregor's house. He was well used to going on jobs
with Eddie, and it never mattered to him whether it was a
punishment beating or a routine robbery – he was up for
anything he was asked to do. At twenty-four, he was already
a known hardman, fearless but disciplined, and Eddie had
used him more and more to assist on jobs, earmarking him
for the UVF when the time was right. But this would be Jimmy's first ordered hit that had come all the way from UVF
command in Belfast, and now that he'd been sworn in, he
wanted to be sharp as a tack.

He stared out of the windscreen. It had been nearly a
month, and every day that passed, it was becoming clearer
that Wendy wasn't coming back. If she'd just disappeared
he would have lived with it, even though he was crazy about
her. But he was haunted by her phone call, her sobs as she
told him Eddie had raped her. He knew she was telling the

truth. Even though he hadn't known her long, in the weeks since the first time he'd taken her home from the pub, they had clicked. It wasn't just the sex – they'd become best mates, and he saw a side to her that you didn't see in the bar. With him she was softer, vulnerable, and he was sure they could have made a go of it.

Jimmy had considered talking to his father about Wendy's phone call, but he didn't want to place him in an awkward position, having to go against another UVF man on the word of someone who wasn't even here any more. Big Jack Dunlop was one of the most respected Loyalists in Belfast, notorious after he bombed a Glasgow pub – a known haunt of IRA men – at the height of Northern Ireland's Troubles. He took a back seat these days, but he still had clout. It would be a loss of face if his father took the rape claim to Belfast, which he would have to do by UVF rules. The top brass there would hold their own inquiry, haul Eddie over for questioning. But it was all based on a phone call from a woman who wasn't there to back it up. It was pointless. Maybe it was time to move on. He let out a sigh, wishing he hadn't got drunk a couple of nights ago and told Wendy's pal Liz about her phone call. That was stupid, because Liz was a bit of a piss artist. He'd phoned her the following day to warn her not to mention it to anyone. He knew she'd probably be too scared to go to the cops. But if she did, there would be all sorts of shit flying around, and he was sure to be the guy pulled in as a suspect.

He felt miserable, his mind drifting back to his first face-to-face talk with Eddie, after Wendy vanished. He recalled how nervous he'd been as Eddie looked right through him as they stood outside the pub.

Eddie had got in first.

'How you doing, man? That's weird about wee Wendy, isn't it? Just disappearing like that.'

'I know, Eddie. That's what I wanted to ask you about.' Jimmy felt uncomfortable.

Eddie gave him a cold look.

'Me? Fuck has it got to do with me? I just dropped her off at the house. Dropped Liz off first, then Wendy. Then I went home. Fuck all to do with me where she went to after that.'

His tone was aggressive and Jimmy was on the back foot.

'I know,' Jimmy said, feeling disarmed and already regretting approaching him. 'What I mean is . . . Well . . . When you dropped her off, what kind of mood was she in? Was she all right?'

Christ! Whatever he was trying to do here, he was fucking it up royally.

Eddie, a head and shoulders taller, looked down at him. He smirked and spat on the ground.

'I'd say she was a bit horny, mate. You should know. You were dry humping her outside the bar before she got in the car.' He looked Jimmy in the eye. 'Did you not go round and give her one after she got home?'

'No. I didn't, Eddie.' He clenched his jaw and looked at the ground.

'But you spoke to her on the phone, did you not?'

'Aye.'

Jimmy let the silence hang in the air and looked up at Eddie's face for any sign of guilt. There was none. He glowered back at him, his blue eyes narrowing.

'So what did she say?'

Jimmy took a deep breath and swallowed his rage.

'Nothing.'

Wendy's sobs were ringing in his ears. He knew Eddie was lying. But he was backed into a corner. If this had been anyone else, Jimmy would have broken his legs by now. He would have hit first and questioned later. But Eddie was his company commander, feared and respected from London Road to the Shankill. He had seen it with his own eyes when he went over to swear the oath last month in the back room of a Loyalist pub in north Belfast beneath the flag and in the presence of the brigadier and two masked, armed UVF paramilitaries. Eddie's word was gospel in every quarter. You didn't even think about taking him on.

Eddie's eyes seemed to soften a little. He took a pack of cigarettes out of his pocket and handed one to Jimmy.

'Look, son.' He gave him a perplexed look, lighting both their fags. 'I know you were shagging the wee bird. But fuck's sake, man. It's only a shag. Wee Wendy has seen more cockends than bookends, from what I hear. So don't get yourself all hung up about it. It looks like she's just fucked off somewhere and didn't want anybody to know. Including you. So get over it. People have all sorts of shit going on in the background, and maybe she was owing money or something and did a runner.'

'I liked her,' Jimmy said, disconsolate. 'I'd been going out with her for a couple of months and she seemed all right.'

Shit! He sounded like a fucking teenager being disciplined by the headmaster.

Eddie shook his head slowly.

'Jimmy. Listen. You never know what's going on in somebody's head. Especially a fucking woman. Look. She might turn up. She might not. But you don't need to be getting your balls in a lather over it.' He started to walk away. 'If you want a ride, I'm sure they'll be lining up for you, man.' He gave him a playful punch on the shoulder, grinning. 'Especially now you've got a bit of status. UVF he-men don't need to look far for a fuck.' He walked off then turned around. 'Come on. I'll buy you a drink. I want to tell you about a wee job we're lining up anyway. You've got more important things going on than a fucking woman.'

Jimmy followed him into the bar, rage burning through him.

Now, as Jimmy watched Eddie striding towards the car, he tried to focus on the job ahead.

The contract, Eddie had told him and Mitch yesterday,

was on two heroin dealers who had to be taken out of the game. The request, from a medium-ranking Glasgow hoodlum, had gone to the UVF top brass in Belfast for approval. It was common knowledge among the troops that gangsters, from Liverpool to Manchester to Glasgow, often used the UVF to bump someone off. It was secure and tidy and there was never any comeback. Nobody with half a brain would grass up the UVF. The rules were simple; the UVF in Belfast named the price for the contract, and it was non-negotiable. There was no room for sentiment. Anybody had a price, and once the money was put up, the person they wanted wiped out was as good as dead.

The pair about to be dealt with were small-time thugs who'd got too big for their boots. Not only had they moved in, punting heroin on someone else's turf in the north of Glasgow, they were also stupid enough to stiff the local godfather for twenty grand.

'Awright, Jimmy,' Eddie muttered out of the side of his mouth. It was more of an order than a question.

He got into the front seat and shot Jimmy a sidewards glance, thin lips tight in his lean face. Two-day stubble made his pale skin look pasty. He put a black holdall at his feet and unzipped it. He took out a revolver and handed it to Jimmy.

'Stick it in your waistband. But make sure the safety catch is on or you'll blow your dick off.'

Jimmy quickly checked the standard nine millimetre

automatic pistol. From his weapons training, he could strip any weapon down and put it together blindfolded. He stuck the gun into the waistband of his jeans. He'd used it before, and feeling the cold metal against his bare stomach gave him a feeling of power. He drove off as Eddie rolled down the window, hawked and spat.

They went out of the housing estate, dubbed Millionaires' Row with its massive detached properties, and drove down towards the main road where Mitch was waiting at the traffic lights. He pulled over and Mitch got in the back seat.

'Evening, chaps,' he said cheerily, giving Jimmy a friendly dig on the shoulder.

'All right, Mitch.' Eddie didn't turn around. He went into the holdall and handed him a gun. 'Make sure the safety catch is on.'

'Where to, Eddie?' Jimmy asked.

'The M8. Out towards Lanarkshire, then down the M74. About half an hour. Near Stonehouse,' Eddie said, looking at his watch. 'I should get a call in about fifteen minutes to say these cunts are on their way. They're driving a silver Mondeo. I'll get told the reg. So keep your eyes peeled in the back, Mitch, once we get to an area where we can see the cars coming off the motorway onto the Stonehouse road.'

'Okay, boss.'

The air was crackling with tension. Jimmy felt sweat break out on his back, and he rolled down the window.

'Now when we get there,' Eddie shifted his body so he

was addressing both of them, 'just do exactly as we talked about, the way we planned it. We can't afford to make any fuck ups, because these guys will be tooled up. It has to be clean and quick. Classic ambush. Understood? Just do everything I tell you.'

Eddie liked to give the impression of a crack soldier who had seen a bit of action. The fact was he'd never actually been a regular soldier, but he had been in the Territorial Army as a sergeant and he'd adopted the military demeanour. Nobody had ever been brave enough to call him a weekend soldier.

'Sure, boss,' Jimmy and Mitch both said at the same time.

From where they were sitting, they had a clear view of the motorway slip road. The evening traffic was quiet, only a trickle of cars coming off at the junction.

After a few minutes, Mitch piped up.

'I see a silver Mondeo, Eddie. Look.' He squinted through binoculars and read out the registration number. 'That has to be them. Two guys.'

'Right, I see the car.' Eddie strained his eyes. 'There's about three cars coming off at the same time. But ours is the Mondeo. Get ready.' He turned to Jimmy. 'When they come off here, hang well back until they cut up the country road. I know where they're headed. They've been told they've got a meet outside Coalburn to hand the gear over.'

Jimmy reversed his car and took off up the road, arriving

at the junction just as the third car came off. They drove behind it for a few hundred yards, then it indicated and went left.

'Shit,' Eddie scowled. 'I'd hoped for a couple of cars in front to keep us covered. Just slow down a bit, Jimmy, so we're a good distance behind. They'll be turning off in about a mile or so. We'll wait till they're well up the lane before we go. Then we hammer it.'

Jimmy dropped back then followed the Mondeo as it turned off the main road and into the narrow country lane.

After a few seconds, Eddie spoke. 'Right, let's go now, Jimmy. You got the stuff in the back there, Mitch?'

'Got them, boss.'

In his rear-view mirror Jimmy could see Mitch fiddling with the pickaxe handle and the expandable police batons. His close-cropped blond hair made his neck look even thicker on his chunky shoulders. His eyes sparkled with adrenalin, or he'd snorted a couple of lines of coke before he left his house. He handed two batons over to Eddie who flicked his so it was twice the length. He gave the other to Jimmy, which he rested on his lap. They turned into the lane, so overgrown with bushes it made the road narrow and difficult for cars to pass. There was no sign of the Mondeo but they knew it had to be up ahead around one of the tight bends.

'Right, lads. Showtime.' Eddie pulled his balaclava over his face.

Jimmy and Mitch did the same.

'Now do it exactly as I said.' He turned to Jimmy and barked, 'Right. Get the fucking boot down. Let's go!'

Jimmy dropped a gear and shoved his foot to the floor as the car surged forward, sending up clouds of dust. Within seconds the Mondeo was in sight, and it seemed to slow down, pulling over to the side as they approached, to make way for them to pass.

'They probably think we're boy racers out for a spin,' Eddie sniggered, cocking his gun. 'They're in for some shock. Now, Jimmy! Right in front of them! Just as we planned. Wedge the fuckers in!'

He sped up to the car that was now almost stationary. Just as they were about to pass, Jimmy pulled in and slammed on the brakes, the car spinning so it was in front of the Mondeo, blocking their path. He caught a glimpse of the stunned looks on the faces of the two guys in the front seat. Before they had time to register what was happening, Mitch was out of the back seat and rushing towards the car with the pickaxe handle, smashing the windscreen. Eddie was instantly at his side, and fired a shot through the side window. Jimmy pulled out his gun and jumped out of the car. Mitch was already dragging the driver out, smashing him on the side of the head so many times with the baton that he lost consciousness quickly. The passenger jumped out and fired off a couple of shots at Mitch who was only about three feet in front of him. But he missed. He then stumbled over the ditch and tried to escape across a field. But Jimmy was after him, and when he got close swung his baton, striking the back of his head and knocking him off his feet. He stood over him and, as the guy looked up, defenceless, Jimmy hit him hard on the face, making blood spurt from his mouth. Mitch arrived at his side.

'Get him up, Jimmy. Take him back to the car.'

They lifted him by the shoulders and dragged him the few yards to the car, where Eddie was attempting to shove the barely conscious driver into the back.

'Stick him in,' Eddie said.

Jimmy went back to his own car and started the engine. He drove on, just as they had planned, to the edge of the lane and then down towards the forest where the road ended and became a dirt track, towards the quarry.

In his rear-view mirror, he could see Mitch driving the car; Eddie's body was half turned so he could keep a gun on the guys in the back. Not that they would need much guarding, Jimmy thought, judging by the state of their faces.

The dirt track road opened onto a flat expanse and Jimmy drove his car to the edge of the quarry. He got out and took a couple of steps towards the cliff. It looked like a steeper drop to the murky water than it had when they'd done the recce a few days ago, as they meticulously planned every step of the hit. The other car arrived, also driving right up to the edge, and Jimmy walked towards it. He reached into the back and along with Mitch hauled one of the guys out, shoved him into the front seat and closed the door, then helped Eddie pull the other one from the back and into the driving seat.

'Right. Check the car. Get the stuff out and take what they've got in their pockets. Take everything.' Eddie stood back.

Jimmy and Mitch opened the boot and brought out a grey holdall and took it to Eddie. He opened it and brought out one of four bricks wrapped in masking tape, tearing open a corner of one of them with a knife.

'Fucking smack.' He held it up to them. 'Fuckers deserve all they get. We'll send it to Belfast and let them shift it. I don't want to touch that fucking stuff.'

Jimmy moved the passenger roughly so he could get into his jeans pockets. He only had two tenners and a bank card. He held the card up to Eddie then handed it to him. Mitch said there was nothing in the driver's pocket, but he put his hand under the seat and pulled out a small bag and handed it to Eddie.

'Fuck! There must be ten grand here.' He grinned at them. 'We better hand this into the police station. Maybe we'll get a reward if someone comes to claim it.' He tossed the bag to Jimmy and told him to put it in the car.

For what seemed like an age the three of them stood silently in the fading light. All they could see were each other's eyes behind the balaclavas. Jimmy saw Eddie's eyes fixing his, and for a moment he thought he was going to ask him to finish them off. He steeled himself, ready to do it. If he needed any justification, it was the fact that they were heroin dealers – the scum of the earth. It would be no problem for him to put a bullet in them if he was asked, even though he had never killed before. But Eddie said nothing. He took a step towards the driver's door and opened it. Jimmy and Mitch watched as the guy raised his blood-smeared face and looked at Eddie as he took the gun from his waistband. For a split second the driver's lips seemed to move in protest. Then Eddie fired, the driver's head exploding, sending sprays of blood and bone across the windscreen. And as the gunshot echoed in the vastness of the gully, Eddie leaned across and shot the passenger in the side of his neck, blood gushing out like a burst pipe.

'Right, boys.' Eddie jerked his head in the direction of the quarry.

Jimmy and Mitch got behind the car and pushed it slowly towards the edge. They watched as the front wheels went over, then with one final push the car dropped down the eighty-foot ravine as if in slow motion. All three of them stood as it plunged, bumping off rocks, then hitting the water with a splash before disappearing beneath the blackness.

Eddie pulled his balaclava off and wiped the sweat from his face.

'Well done, lads. Let's go. I'm choking for a pint.'

CHAPTER THREE

'If I'm really honest, Rosie, I'm more excited about the UVF bringing drugs in on Rangers supporters' buses than I am about the missing barmaid.' McGuire gave a mischievous grin over the top of his reading glasses.

'I knew you were going to say that. To hell with the poor missing girl!' She rolled her eyes sarcastically.

'Yeah, sure, Gilmour.' McGuire took off his glasses and sat back, shoving his feet up on the desk. 'You'll be telling me next it never occurred to you. A Loyalist drug-smuggling exposé is worth five missing barmaids – and you know it!' He wagged his finger.

Touché. Rosie half smiled, feeling a little ashamed that he wasn't far from the truth. She was prepared to chip away at the missing barmaid story for as long as it took, but her heart only really started pumping when Liz opened up about the drugs on football buses.

'Well, you have a point,' she conceded. 'But it might all

be connected. Maybe Wendy has vanished for a reason – like she's involved with the drugs and had to disappear.'

McGuire nodded slowly, tugging at his cufflinks, then smoothing his pristine pink shirt and navy spotted silk tie as though congratulating himself on how immaculate he managed to look when he arrived at the office each morning. He was a fastidiously sharp dresser, and it wasn't unusual for him to pull up a young reporter who arrived on the editorial floor looking shabby.

'Possibly,' he said, steepling his hands under his chin. 'But then again, she might just be shacked up somewhere and doesn't want anyone to find her.'

'Or she could be dead, Mick. The cops said her passport and bank cards are still in the house.'

'Well . . . Nothing to suggest she's dead yet.' He shrugged. 'So we have to assume that she might turn up. And if she *is* dead, she'll turn up sooner or later. We can't wait around for that. Right now, we have to look at how we can get to grips with the drugs story. That's a belter. We need to find a way inside this.'

'I've been thinking about it all weekend, actually. Ideally, we'd want to be on a supporters' bus, but that's just not going to happen. That'll be as tight as a drum. They'll all know each other. And the thing is, most of the Rangers fans on the bus will know nothing about drugs. They'll just be travelling to see their team.'

'You think so?'

'Yes, I do. Not every Rangers fan is up to their knees in Fenian blood. Lots of them are just football fans who worship their team. Same as loads of Celtic fans are disgusted at the IRA slogans and chants that have taken root in the terraces.'

McGuire glanced at his computer screen as an email pinged. 'Well, if you say so. I think they're all nutters anyway. I'm sure the rancid bigotry runs through the lot of them. Bred into them down the generations.'

He got up from his desk and came around to sit on the leather armchair opposite Rosie on the sofa.

'What about this Eddie McGregor character? Any way to find out more about him?'

Rosie sat back and folded her arms, gazing at the ceiling.

'What I'm thinking, Mick, is that if we go trampling around the undergrowth anywhere near McGregor, the pub where the barmaid worked, the parents, or the boyfriend, we'll blow any cover we have if we want to properly investigate the drug smuggling.'

'Agreed. We need to tread softly, see if we can discreetly find out when they go, what pub the bus leaves from.'

'There's more than one bus brings drugs, Liz told me. But she only knows of the McGregor connection and the bus he travels with. She says she'll find out what pub it leaves from. Really, what we have to do, Mick, is follow the bus from here. Tail them by car to wherever they are going in the next

Champions League match.' She checked her notebook. 'They play Eindhoven in two weeks. We should go there, establish who McGregor is, and follow him everywhere. If nothing happens, then we just put it down to experience. Their next match after that is in Seville, two weeks later. We do the same again. If we want to look seriously at it, we have to put the time in. If they're doing it in Eindhoven, they'll be doing it in Seville. With a bit of luck we'll get them doing it in two places.' She paused. 'But we might end up with bugger all. It's a chance we take.'

McGuire nodded. 'What about this Liz bird? The pal. Do you trust her? She seems to be all slack-mouthed about the UVF without much encouragement. I'm not sure I trust that.'

Rosie puffed. 'Who knows? Nothing we can do right now but trust what she says. I have a couple of contacts I can speak with who might throw a bit of light on who's who in the UVF in Glasgow and the west of Scotland. See if McGregor's name comes up. Also, I'll try to find out about the coke dealing and how deep he's into it. Treading carefully, of course.'

McGuire looked at her. 'Yeah, Rosie. And I mean very bloody carefully.' He went back behind his desk.

Rosie stood up and walked towards the door.

'Oh, and don't go pissing off any UVF men, for Christ's sake. I don't want to have to check under my car for bombs every morning,' he said, pointing a finger. 'And I want to be kept informed. Or I'll get very annoyed.' He raised his eyebrows for emphasis. 'And I mean it.'

'I'll be discreet. Discretion is my middle name, Mick. You know that.'

'Yeah. I've got an ulcer now, and I'm sure it's all your fault. Every time you come in here with stuff like this, it starts acting up.' He went into his drawer, took out a tablet and popped it into his mouth. 'Now go. I've got a paper to put out.'

Rosie glanced at her watch as she ordered a gin and tonic from the silver-haired barman at O'Brien's. Six thirty. In New York it would be just before midday. She pictured TJ lounging around his Manhattan apartment, drinking coffee, gradually easing himself into the day after gigging in the jazz club till three in the morning. The familiar ache in her stomach niggled as she reran little scenes of places they'd been and things they'd done during her recent trip to see him. It had been perfect. And she'd been surprised at how totally relaxed she'd felt, how for the first time in as long as she could remember, she'd managed to switch off completely. Even when Rosie went on holiday with her friends to chill on a beach, she was always taking phone calls from contacts, planning to see people for stories when she got back. Midway through a two week holiday, if she did manage to relax enough, there might be one moment when she'd become so accustomed to being away from the office that the thought of going back filled her with dread. But every time, the moment she stepped back onto the editorial floor, it all clicked into place; this is what she did – that two weeks of fun wasn't actual real life. But in New York with TJ she had felt different. It *had* felt like real life. She'd missed him from the moment they kissed goodbye at the airport. And it had made her lonelier than ever when she returned, especially when it now looked like TJ was going to be there for at least another couple of months. She took a mouthful of her gin and tonic, enjoying the kick as it hit her empty stomach.

'That's more like it,' Don said, as he sidled up to the bar without her noticing. 'Proper drinking. What happened to the skinny lattes?'

'Sometimes I can be a bit of a rebel.' Rosie smiled, glad to see her old friend.

'Good. I'm always deeply suspicious of people who don't drink.' He ordered a pint of lager and leaned closer. 'So, howsit going? You're looking well. We need to go for dinner some night, Rosie. A proper night out. Get *really* rebellious.'

'I couldn't keep up with you over a whole night.' Rosie handed the barman a tenner.

'Yeah, but you could have fun trying.' He lit a cigarette and offered her one, but she declined. 'So did you get any joy with the Wendy story?'

'Little bit. I talked to her pal, Liz.'

'Oh yeah? The barmaid. Hard as nails. Takes a right good drink, I'm told. How was she? Talk much?'

'A bit.' Rosie had decided to be economical with the truth. 'She's upset that there hasn't been much in the papers for the past few days.' She spread her hands. 'Newspapers just lose interest after a while, unless there's a good line being punted every day. You know what it's like. Are you getting anywhere your end?'

He drew on his cigarette and blew a stream of smoke out of the side of his mouth. 'We get the feeling we're not getting told the truth. We think Eddie McGregor – the guy who dropped her and Liz off – knows more than he's saying. Just a feeling. But we can't turn him over because we've got no solid reason to.' He took a long drink from his pint and loosened his tie. 'Then there's the boyfriend. Dunlop. Jimmy Dunlop. We've checked Wendy's mobile out with the phone company and the last call she made was to him. We know it was Glasgow. Probably her house, given the timeline.'

Rosie raised her eyebrows. 'Really? And the phone hasn't been used since?'

'Nope. Hasn't turned up. Hasn't been used. And neither have the bank cards.'

'What about the boyfriend? What's he saying about the phone call?'

'Admits he took a call from her, saying she was at home. That's all. He says he was in his bed.' Don ran his hand across his chin. 'Not sure he's telling the truth though.'

'So what's the thinking? Does he know more? Has he done something?'

He puffed. 'Don't know. I don't believe him though. He's holding back. But we can't really put him under any pressure either because we've only got the final phone call to him and nothing more. He was in the house with his father who he said was drunk in bed and sound asleep. So we don't know if after the phone call he went out of the house and went to see her. He says he didn't, but he's got no real alibi.'

'So is he a suspect?'

'Suspect of what? We haven't even got a crime yet. We're keeping an open mind. But that McGregor's a dodgy bastard. He's got some kind of building and plumbing business – houses, conversions and stuff – but it's all drug money. Coke mostly. He was below the radar for so long he was able to build up quite a little empire. Now his drug money is so well laundered nobody has ever been able to get him on anything. Clean as a whistle. Smart bastard accountants see to that.' Don lowered his voice. 'He's also UVF – which has made him fairly untouchable among the rest of the drug-dealing pricks in this city. Special Branch know about him. He's back and forward to Belfast a lot. But he's got no convictions.'

'So how come nobody pulls him in – for the UVF in itself?'

'Can't prove it. It's not as if they have coffee mornings

to discuss their business,' Don said. 'But that aside. He was the last to see Wendy.'

'Do you think she's going to turn up dead?' Rosie scanned Don's craggy features that had seen too many late nights and too much booze over the years. But at forty, he was still attractive, in a lived-in kind of way.

'I'd say it's a safe bet.' He looked at her almost empty glass. 'Another drink?'

'Sure,' Rosie said, draining her gin. 'But just one for the road. I need to get an early night.'

She didn't tell him that even the early nights weren't bringing her the sleep she needed these days. Since the stabbing in Glasgow two months ago that had left her hospitalised and off work for weeks, Rosie had been plagued by nightmares, waking up unable to catch her breath, gasping until she got it under control. Her GP friend, who'd known her for years, told her it was the stress of the attack on top of everything that had happened to her in Belgrade during her last big investigation, where she'd been kidnapped and managed to escape, running for her life. Rosie's dreams had always been frightening, vivid affairs, mostly dominated by images of her mother and the childhood trauma that continued to haunt her. And the doctor said that lately there had been one ordeal after another, and her subconscious mind was having trouble trying to arrange them into some manageable order. It would get better in time, but he warned her not to seek sleep by drinking alcohol.

That would only make it worse. She'd already proved that to herself.

'So what did Liz tell you, Don?' Rosie fished. 'And what do you know about her and Wendy? She told me they'd been pals since school.'

Don played with the beer mat. 'Not much, really. All she said was that McGregor gave them a lift home. Dropped her off then dropped Wendy at the house where she lives with her parents. She didn't say much more, just keeps telling us we're not doing enough. She said the boyfriend Jimmy is crazy about Wendy, and would never do anything to harm her. Didn't say much about McGregor at all. Also, the parents. We spoke to them, and the mum was in a right old state. They'd been up north for a week on a bus tour. But the dad's not saying much. They won't play for making an appeal to the media even though we told them that's the best way to get it in the papers.' He paused. 'Though the mum did tell us that when Wendy was a teenager she ran away for a few days over some daft family row. Then after that she was shacked up with some guy they didn't like, so she basically didn't get in touch with them for a while. So I'm not sure that Wendy is the kind of girl you'd like to take home to your mother, if you get my drift.'

'Don't be so judgemental,' Rosie said, giving him a dig in the shin. 'Whatever she is, she needs finding – even if only to put her family at ease.'

'Of course,' Don said, smiling, and rubbing his shin.

'Liz didn't mention about Wendy running away and stuff to me. Does she get on okay with her parents now?'

Don shrugged. 'So it would seem. She's living with them . . . Was.'

Rosie looked at him. 'Was?'

Don puffed. 'Well. Put it this way, Rosie. I'll be surprised if we see this bird alive again.'

'Why do you say that, Don? You've nothing to go on.'

'Just a hunch. I don't trust McGregor. I think he's a bad one. The DI wanted to bring the boyfriend in and give him a bit of a grilling, but I talked him out of it. I don't think he's telling the truth either, but I don't think he's harmed the girl. If anything's happened to that lassie, it's McGregor we should be looking at. From what I hear, he's a bad bastard.'

Rosie finished her drink and got off the bar stool. They both walked out of the door, past the early evening movers and shakers that could be found in O'Brien's oyster bar any night of the week.

'Time to go,' Don said. 'Can't stand all that pinstripe suit brigade. Champagne and a line of charlie on the side. Bunch of pricks.'

They stepped out into the warm night air, and Rosie found herself automatically turning to look for TJ playing his saxophone in the side street as he had done for so long. She smiled to herself, remembering how the friendship had been forged, and everything that had gone on between them since then.

'Penny for them.' Don gave her a whimsical look.

Rosie sighed and shook her head. 'A penny wouldn't begin to cover it, Don.' She gave him a hug and he kissed her cheek then left.

Rosie flagged down a black hack, almost reluctant to leave the atmosphere of Royal Exchange Square, awash with people enjoying those rare moments when you could sit in a pavement cafe in Glasgow and watch the sun dip behind the city centre buildings. She climbed into the taxi and closed the door, a wave of loneliness washing over her as they pulled out of the street and up towards her home in St George's Cross.

Her mobile rang, but no number came up.

'Rosie?'

'Yeah.' She thought it sounded like Liz's voice but it wasn't her number.

'It's Liz. Sorry to disturb you.'

'No problem. You're not disturbing me, I'm just on my way home. Something wrong? This isn't your mobile.'

'No. Phoning from my house and I always hide the number. Listen, Rosie. I've got something to tell you.'

The relaxing effects of the couple of gin and tonics instantly vanished and Rosie was razor sharp.

'You want to meet?'

'No. Can't. About to go to work. But I was with Jimmy a

couple of nights ago. We had a few drinks. Actually we got pissed. He told me something.' She paused. 'Christ. I can't believe this. I can't fucking believe it.'

Rosie could hear the tension in Liz's voice.

'What is it, Liz? What did he tell you?'

'He told me that Wendy phoned him after Eddie dropped her off. He said she was crying ... sobbing. He said that Wendy told him Eddie raped her.'

'Christ!' Rosie saw the driver looking at her in the rear-view mirror, as if he was earwigging. She shielded the phone with her hand. 'Jimmy said that?' She whispered.

'Aye. And he said he went straight round to her house in a taxi, but she wasn't there. No sign of her.'

'Did he go in the house? How did he get in?'

'He had a key. She gave it to him while her mum and dad were away, so he could nip in any time. He went into the house, and she was gone.'

Silence. Then Rosie could hear Liz sniffing.

'Something's happened to her, Rosie. I know it. I knew it from the start. Eddie's done something to her.'

'So what happens now? Is Jimmy going to the cops?' Rosie already knew the answer to that.

'No way. He can't. He's already told them a different story. He can't go changing it now. Plus, he can't grass Eddie up.'

Rosie didn't know what to say.

'So is Jimmy just going to live with it? Keep the

information to himself? Wendy may be in danger.' Wendy was dead. It didn't need saying.

'I don't know. I'm only telling you because I had to tell someone. I don't know what to do. That's why I didn't phone sooner. I can't go to the cops.' She paused. 'Look. I need to go to work. I'll call you tomorrow.'

The line went dead.

CHAPTER FOUR

Rosie had been waiting nearly half an hour and still no Liz. She ordered another mug of tea and sat tapping at her mobile, resisting the urge to phone or text to see what the hell was keeping her. Last night Liz had called her again, halfway through her shift at the bar, and told her not to use the mobile number she'd given her. The longer she waited, the less faith Rosie was beginning to have in her. She'd been quick to rattle off the information about the UVF drugs and Rangers fans, but she'd managed to leave out the personal details that Don had touched on. She had painted a picture of Wendy's troubled life, but it wasn't the full picture, and it crossed Rosie's mind that she was playing games. But despite her reservations, the call last night about the rape was enough to bring her stampeding – she still would have, even if Liz had claimed she'd once scored a hat-trick for Rangers.

Rosie looked out of the window, her mind buzzing with

the possibilities of chasing the drugs story. She'd already had a chat with Matt in the *Post* canteen, and he was bristling with excitement at the prospect. But they both knew how much of a long shot it would be without an inside track on what buses went where. Eddie McGregor was the key, if Liz was to be believed. He was the money man. And he wouldn't be the kind of guy who'd be careless.

Just as Rosie was beginning to feel deflated, the door of the cafe opened. Liz briefly scanned the room, then raised her eyebrows when she saw Rosie at a table in the very back. She came trotting up, her high heels clicking on the tiled floor.

'Sorry I'm late, Rosie.' She sat down heavily, her face flushed.

'No problem,' Rosie said, relieved to see her.

'I'm totally fucking wound up today.' Liz rummaged in her handbag and brought out a packet of cigarettes.

Rosie noticed her hands were trembling a little. She wondered if she needed a drink, and hoped not. She waved the waitress over, and Liz ordered tea.

'I need something to eat,' she said quickly to Rosie. 'I'm starving.' She turned to the waitress. 'A bacon roll, please.'

Rosie watched as Liz lit up a cigarette and sat back swallowing the smoke as though her life depended on it.

'You look shattered, Liz. What's the matter? Late night? Work too hard?' Perhaps she had a drug habit. She was certainly jumpy enough today.

Liz shook her head, biting the inside of her jaw, deep in thought. Her bust was squeezed into a skintight black blouse and she pulled at it, attempting to make it long enough to cover her bare midriff poking over the top of jeans that were a size too small. She leaned forward so she was closer to Rosie across the table.

'Listen.' Her voice was a whisper. 'I don't know what the fuck I'm doing. I don't know whether I'm coming or going with all of this. But I've been thinking and I've made a decision.' She took a breath. 'I need to know that I can completely trust you. I need to know that no matter what, you never tell anyone that I'm talking to you.'

'Of course,' Rosie frowned. 'I told you that when we met. Look, I've been doing this job a long time. I've never betrayed a contact in my life. I never would. It doesn't matter what you tell me. Whatever I do with your information, if it leads to me being able to run down a big investigation, the one thing that nobody will ever know is that any of the information came from you. Nobody will ever drag that out of me.' She reached across and touched her wrist. 'You need to trust me on that. That's all I can say. It's up to you.'

Liz nodded.

'Right. okay, Rosie. I do trust you.'

The waitress came and put down a mug of tea and a roll. Liz tore off a piece and stuffed it into her mouth, washing it down with a mouthful of tea. Rosie waited as she hungrily took another chunk then swallowed.

Liz sighed and dabbed the sides of her mouth with her finger and thumb, ignoring the napkin on the plate. 'I feel better now. I can't cope if I'm hungry, and I haven't eaten since last night. Rushing around like mad.'

'I know the feeling.' Rosie watched her patiently.

'You know when I called you last night, about what Jimmy said,' she whispered, 'about Wendy getting raped by Eddie? I want to talk you through the whole conversation.'

Rosie nodded.

Liz told how they'd met for a drink after her shift was finished in the pub, and had ended up in a late bar in the city centre drinking until three in the morning.

'Jimmy was on a real downer. He wasn't saying too much about Wendy in the beginning – just that he really missed her and couldn't get his head around why she hadn't contacted anyone. At first I just listened to him and we kept the drinks coming. But after a while I said to him that I really have a feeling something bad has happened to her. He looked right through me and asked what I meant. I said that I didn't trust Eddie.' Liz looked beyond Rosie. 'I don't like Eddie. He's a bully and a dangerous bastard. He's the kind of guy who could put a bullet in you and not turn a hair. I'm sure he's done plenty of people over. That's why he's untouchable with the coke. People are scared of him. He's a cold bastard.'

Once more, Rosie was surprised at how easy Liz was with her information – and she wasn't even drinking.

'Do you have any personal experience with Eddie?'

she asked. 'Has he ever done you a bad turn? Or harmed you?'

Liz shook her head.

'No. But he scares me. That's all.'

'Go on with your story. How did Jimmy come out with the stuff about Wendy phoning him?'

Liz lit another cigarette and took a deep draw.

'He went quiet after I was saying what a psycho Eddie was. I asked him what was up, and did he think the same as me. I know Eddie is his boss, and didn't expect him to say anything against him. But I felt he was holding back. Then suddenly he comes right out with it. He looked me in the eye and grabbed hold of my arm, squeezing it so hard it hurt. He made me promise I wouldn't go to the cops with what he was about to tell me, and I promised him. Then he said to me that Wendy had phoned him that night. Jesus, Rosie. I nearly died. I couldn't believe my ears. Jimmy's a really tough guy but he was on the verge of tears. He told me that Wendy had phoned him sobbing. And that she said Eddie had raped her in his car.' Liz shook her head. 'I didn't know what to say. I know Jimmy was drunk. But I know he was telling the truth. He wouldn't make a thing like that up.'

'And did he tell you anything else?'

'Yeah. He told me he went round to her house immediately and she wasn't there. That's what he said. And I believe him.' She sighed. 'The next day, after we were drunk, Jimmy phoned me and made me vow again not to tell anyone. He said he shouldn't have told me, and if I did anything crazy like go to the cops then I would be signing my death warrant . . . And probably his. But I'm not that stupid.'

Rosie looked at her and said nothing.

Liz puffed her cheeks and shrugged. 'Then again, maybe I am. I'm sitting here talking to a fucking reporter about it.'

Rosie watched her, trying to work out how she was going to tell McGuire this one. Just being in possession of the rape information was dangerous, whether there was any truth in it or not. Passing it on to the police, which is what she should do, would be even more dangerous for Liz, and for Jimmy. And who knows, maybe even for Wendy – if she was still alive somewhere. Keeping it to herself could have consequences for everyone, including the paper.

Rosie drummed her fingers on the table.

'This is dodgy, Liz. To be honest, right now, I'm not sure where we go from here. I want to have a think about it.' She lowered her voice to a whisper. 'But I definitely want to pursue the story about the drugs on the football buses. I want to nail that down.'

'Aye. And nail big Eddie down with it.' She stabbed a finger in the air. 'I'd pay good money to see that bastard locked up. Poor Wendy. She's a skinny wee thing and that slimy bastard climbing all over her.'

Rosie nodded sympathetically.

'There's more than one way to skin the cat, Liz. Did you

find out any more information for me? Like where the bus leaves from?'

Liz nodded.

'I did. As I told you, there's supposed to be a few Rangers buses that do it, but the one Eddie will be on is leaving from the Tavern. You'll know the pub. On the London Road. Big 'Gers pub. But it's more than that. It's a UVF pub as well. They have meetings there. Upstairs, so I heard.'

'How do you know all that?' For a barmaid she was pretty clued up.

'My ex-boyfriend. He knows a lot of the boys. I still see him now and again. For a shag. He was over yesterday afternoon and I was spearing him for information about the bus that's leaving from the Tavern. He's going too. He says big Eddie's on it. He didn't say anything about the coke, but he told me once before that's what Eddie does when he goes abroad. He always brings a few kilos back.'

'Okay. Liz,' Rosie changed the subject, 'you didn't tell me that Wendy had some problems years ago with her mum and dad. She ran away. Stuff like that?'

Liz said nothing. She looked at the table and pinched her bottom lip.

'Yeah. She went a bit nuts a couple of years ago. Went through a bad patch. She was doing a lot of coke.' She looked shamefaced. 'To be honest, we both were. We got caught up in some stupid things, and did a runner to Spain – Costa del Sol – for a while.' She shook her head, her lip curling a little. 'Wild days. We carried on with it over there. Got to know quite a few people. Bad company and all that.'

'It's not smart to get mixed up in the coke scene on the Costa del Sol,' Rosie said, beginning to wonder what Liz was going to come out with next.

'You can say that again. But that's also how I know a bit about big Eddie. There's UVF men over there too. A couple of bar owners. I know where he goes.'

Rosie said nothing. Even if Liz knew half as much as she seemed to know, the fact that she was talking about it so freely worried her. The last thing she needed if they were going to track a UVF drug story across Europe was a mouthy contact waving her arms around.

Liz gave her a knowing look.

'You don't believe me, do you? I can tell.'

Rosie put a hand up.

'No, no, Liz. I do believe you.' She spread both palms, trying to choose the right words. 'But, cards on the table. I'm having a little problem here with the fact that you are talking about it so easily.' She saw Liz's eyes look downwards, then said quickly, 'Don't get me wrong. I totally appreciate what you're doing, and I'm really impressed with the level of information. But you and I both know how dangerous it is to talk freely about anything involving these people. They are not just drug dealers and gangsters. This is the UVF. People pay them to get rid of people.' She paused. 'Look. I need to know that if we go into this story, and start a full investigation, I can rely on you. No matter who comes to you or how circumstances might change. Do you understand where I'm coming from? It's dangerous.'

Liz's expression was part irritated, part on the verge of tears.

'Rosie. I'm not stupid. I've told you that before. I know all about the danger. I've thought about this long and hard – agonised about it. I know that if Wendy phoned Jimmy and said Eddie McGregor raped her, then that is what happened. I have no way of knowing what happened to her after that.' She swallowed. 'But I'm worried sick that he's done something to her. I'm worried he's done her in and dumped her somewhere.' She bit her lip. 'So I have no way of getting to that bastard. Whatever he's done, right now he's getting off scot-free. Wendy had a lot of problems in the past. She's a bit daft. But her heart's in the right place. I'm going to make Eddie pay for what he did. That's all I can do. I can't go to the cops. I can't get anything done myself. So I've come to you and spilled my guts on it.' Her face flushed. 'To be honest, I'm a bit disappointed that you're thinking I might just start blabbing.'

Rosie could see where this was going. She had to rescue the situation and quick, before Liz got up and left. She'd been here before, with people who had come to her and trusted her with information. And they'd paid with their lives. Mags Gillick, the junkie prostitute, and Emir, the refugee with nowhere else to turn. Part of her wanted to walk away now, but she couldn't let it go.

'No. Liz. Listen. Please understand this. I absolutely believe you and I know why you are doing this. I'm honestly grateful.' She saw Liz's lip quivering and reached across the table and squeezed her wrist. 'I want to take a real run at this story. And I need you to help me. But you need to know what you're getting into. Are you prepared to do that? Are you prepared to get involved in it with us? Because I'm thinking of tracking this all the way to Europe and exposing the whole shooting match.'

Liz's eyes narrowed. 'Of course I'm in. And you don't have to worry about me. You don't know me. But once I've made my mind up to do something, nothing will stop me.'

They sat for a moment in silence, then Rosie smiled.

'Good. Then I'll talk to my editor, and we'll see where we go from here.'

They got up to leave, and Rosie went across to the counter and paid the bill, then followed Liz out of the door.

'Oh. Take this other mobile number, Rosie. I bought it so I can talk to you if I hear any information.' She gave Rosie a cocky look. 'I was thinking ahead. Trust me. I'm not daft.'

CHAPTER FIVE

'What you going to do with your cash?' Mitch asked Jimmy as they moved away from the bar with their pints and sat in a corner.

'Dunno,' Jimmy shrugged. He took a long drink of lager and licked his lips. 'Hold onto it for a bit, I suppose. Maybe go somewhere on holiday, after the Champions League matches.'

'You going on the bus?' Mitch looked at him. 'Eindhoven first next week, then Seville. I can't wait.' He grinned. 'Especially Holland, man. Them Dutch birds are filthy.'

Jimmy chuckled. 'Aye, Mitch. And they'll have been gagging for it all those years you were in the nick.' He handed Mitch a cigarette and took one himself.

'It'll be brilliant. It's party time all the way when you go with the boys to Europe on the bus. Totally mental.'

'I flew the last couple of times, but the bus could be a good laugh. I'll talk to the lads and see what the sketch is.'

'Good,' Mitch said. 'We could go from the Victoria Bar.'
He took his mobile out. 'I'll phone Billy Whyte and ask him
who's running the show from there.'

Jimmy sat staring into middle distance as Mitch talked
on the phone. They'd just come from making the drop to
the lorry driver who was going on the late-night ferry from
Stranraer to Belfast. Jimmy didn't know the guy's name and
had never met him before. He and Mitch were simply told
by Eddie where he would be and what they had to do. He
told them that truck drivers were used nearly all the time
by the UVF to take drugs, cash and weapons to and from
Belfast, as they seldom got stopped.

The heroin from the contract on the two boys lying at the
bottom of the quarry had to be delivered to Belfast where
the UVF would make sure it disappeared into the growing
smack market up and down the housing schemes. Jimmy
had learned fast that drugs went beyond any sectarian
divide. The heroin they were shifting to their UVF cronies
could just as easily end up in the Catholic Falls Road as
the Protestant enclaves of Ballymena or the Shankill. Same
applied to the cocaine that big Eddie supplied in Glasgow.
He had told Jimmy he didn't give a toss who was snort-
ing, any more than he cared about the punters who were
making the crack cocaine that was upping the demand for
coke. It was all money. Supply and demand. Just as long as
nobody was late with their payment.

His mind had kept replaying the latest job – and how

Eddie had calmly shot the two guys through the head. He'd never seen anyone do that before. Afterwards, they'd come to Eddie's house and stripped off the clothes they were wearing, giving them to his wife who he told to burn them in the diesel drum in the back garden. Then they'd got changed into clothes Eddie had bought for them, before going to a bar and getting drunk. Mitch had been high on the adrenalin kick that he got from violence. Jimmy tried his best to join in but was finding it hard to lift himself out of the downer he'd been on since Wendy disappeared. Late in the night, Eddie had insisted they go on to a club, where Mitch and he disappeared with two women. Jimmy eventually made his way home on his own. Eddie had given them two grand each, and they didn't ask where the rest of the wedge that was in the bag went. Jimmy had a feeling that the package that they'd just delivered to be taken to the Belfast bosses didn't contain much more than the heroin, plus the money that had been paid for the contract. He didn't ask and he didn't care. It was business, and he could deal with that.

He thought he might take his father on the Rangers matches to Eindhoven and Spain. It would be good for the old man. Since Jimmy's mother died last year, his da hadn't been out much, and the grief hanging over the house like a blanket was as raw and oppressive as the day his ma dropped down dead in the kitchen from a massive coronary. He missed her just as much as his father, though they'd not once had a conversation about her since her death.

Sometimes Jimmy still missed her so much it hurt. In darker moments, he tried not to dwell on how his father had often dismissed her as a half-breed. She'd been raised as a Catholic in Glasgow, but turned her coat when she fell for the big, brawny Belfast man who'd crossed the water to work in the Clydeside shipyards. His ma always hated the fact that he was filling their son's head with Rangers and the Orange Walk, telling him Catholics were thick, lazy bastards. His da took him to Belfast every twelfth of July to see the Orange Walk, so he could see for himself what he came from.

Most of the time, as he was growing up, his mother had been silent and accepting. Only once did she make the mistake of taking him to a Catholic church when he was six years old. She was spotted coming out by the wife of one of her man's workmates, who shopped her. When they got home, his father slapped her hard on the face. She knew what he was when she married him, he told her as he stood over her. She could walk away now, but she would never see her boy again. Jimmy had never forgotten the look in her eyes or the sound of the slap on her face. She never spoke about religion again to him, but he knew she hated his eagerness to follow in his father's footsteps.

But much as he loved his mother, she was just wrong, Jimmy told himself. You were either a Billy or a Tim in Glasgow. It was as simple as that. You stuck to your own people, because the other side hated you as much as you hated them. You joined a flute band and proudly marched, parading what you were. He remembered as a boy, the band practices in his local Orange hall, and always at the end of it a few of the older lads stayed behind for training. It was all kept hush-hush, but he later learned it was UVF weapons training. He dreamed of the day he would be one of these lads. This was about defending Queen and country. What had happened down the years in Northern Ireland, with the IRA bombing the fuck out of Belfast and the UK, had to be defended. It had to be financed. That's what they were doing. He didn't question it. Never had. They were fighting the fight, armed and ready.

Eventually, the door opened at the far side of the room and Eddie came in, followed by a couple of other UVF men who Jimmy knew to be platoon commanders.

'All right, lads,' Eddie said as he came towards them. 'Everything go okay with the drop?'

'Yeah, Eddie. Fine. No problem at all.'

'Good bloke that. Knows what he's doing.'

Jimmy and Mitch nodded.

'Listen, boys. Leave your pints there for ten minutes. Follow me upstairs. I need a wee word.'

Jimmy's stomach turned over. It flashed across his mind that Liz had opened her trap about Wendy's phone call to him. He felt his palms sweat. He'd been in back rooms before when a guy had been brought in and beaten to a pulp until he admitted whatever he was being accused of. Now he was terrified that this was his turn. They walked along the corridor until they came to a heavy padlocked door, which Eddie opened with a key. They went upstairs to the UVF function room, past the walls adorned with pictures of Rangers heroes down the years. Each print, Eddie explained, was sponsored by individuals who paid into the UVF coffers to have their names on a plaque below the photos for a year. There were hundreds of pictures and the sponsors changed every year, raking in a fortune. At the top of the hallway, they faced a door which Jimmy had never been through, even though he'd been in the main function hall many times. Eddie turned to them.

'Nobody gets to go in here, unless by invitation.' He gave them a look. 'So you boys are getting a wee privilege here – for doing a good job the last few days. You're shaping up well, lads.'

Jimmy breathed a sigh of relief as they stepped inside the room. It was a shrine with rows of glass cases full of memorabilia and handmade wall carvings by Loyalist prisoners in Belfast jails.

'Come. Look at this.' Eddie showed them a piece of twisted metal in a glass case. 'Bit of a car,' he said. 'It's from the explosion when the SAS boys got eight of them scum IRA pikeys back in eighty-seven. Fuckers didn't know what hit them.' He grinned proudly at both of them. 'And look. These are the war medals of men, real men who fought and died for the cause. They were British soldiers, the Thirty-Sixth Ulster Division, but they were UVF men first, right back to the First World War. That's what you're part of now, boys. A proud history.'

'Amazing,' Mitch said.

Eddie went behind a table. He motioned them to sit.

'Right. Here's the situation. We're going to the matches – Eindhoven then Seville in Spain. I've got a pickup to do. I'll be bringing back four kilos each time. Coke.'

Jimmy had never been on the coke run before with the Rangers buses, but he had heard about it.

'Great,' Mitch said. 'We were just talking about going to the games, Eddie. We were looking at the Victoria Bar bus.'

'No. Forget that. We're going on the bus from here. One of the crowd. Just fans. We keep the bag with the money in with us all the time, then we come back with a holdall and the coke. There's never a problem at the border. They don't go on and search every bag on the bus. It's a piece of piss. Been doing it for years. Deal with the same people.' He sat back. 'So that's the job. You two will be with me at all times. My wingmen. It's a big job for you.' He looked at both of them. 'You square with that, lads?'

Jimmy and Mitch nodded. They both knew they weren't being asked for their opinion.

'Definitely, boss.'

'And don't worry, Mitch. There'll be time for a bit of

rumpy.' He smirked towards Jimmy. 'You too, Jimmy. A blow job by some foreign bird is just what you need.'

Jimmy managed a half smile.

'Sure, boss. Sounds great.'

It was after ten by the time Jimmy got back to his house and he was surprised to find the living room almost in darkness, without the usual blare of the television. His father always had the sound up loud when he was watching. But tonight there was no sound, and Jimmy assumed he must have gone to bed early. He went into the kitchen, filled the kettle and stuck a couple of slices of bread in the toaster. The few pints had made him hungry, and he would polish off the remains of the chicken his da had made for dinner.

'That you, Jimmy?'

Jimmy turned around, puzzled. His father's voice was coming from the living room. He walked out of the kitchen and opened the living room door. He was sitting in the dark, staring into the fake flames flickering over artificial coals in the electric fire. Jimmy automatically pushed the light switch.

'What you sitting in the dark for, Da?' His stomach tightened. Something was wrong. 'You all right? What's wrong?'

'I had enough of that film I was watching.' He looked up. 'Just waiting for you.'

Something was definitely wrong. His da had never waited up for him since he was at school. Fear swept over him.

'Waiting for me? Christ, Da, I'm not fifteen.' Jimmy tried to make light of it, but he could see his father's face grey with worry.

'I want to talk to you. Go and bring us a cup of tea.'

Jimmy went into the kitchen as the bread popped up on the toaster. He looked at it, but his hunger had suddenly vanished. He poured water into the teapot and filled two mugs with black tea and went back into the room. He sat down softly on the couch opposite his father, still staring at the fire.

'What's wrong, Da?' Jimmy swallowed.

His father turned to him, his eyes fixing him.

'I'm not well, Jimmy.'

'Not well? Will I phone the doctor?' Jimmy handed him a mug of tea.

'Nah.' He shook his head, looking at the carpet. 'Done all that.' He paused. 'Listen. I was at the hospital today. I'm . . . I'm . . . Ach, fuck it! There's no easy way to say it.' He faced his son and their eyes met. 'I'm dying, Jimmy.'

Jimmy felt as though he could hear the words in the distance. He looked back at his father, the muscles in his massive hand around the mug suddenly looking pale and ropy. He had never considered his father to be in old age, and though he was now well into his sixties, he'd always been a fit strong man and had worked up until the past two years. But the chiselled looks that made him handsome even as he was knocking on suddenly made him look older, and for the first time in his life, Jimmy contemplated losing him. Even after his mother had died, the one constant in his life was the strength of his father. Sure, he could be a bastard. He was a hardman from Belfast. He had seen him lay two big men out with his bare fists. He was unbreakable, and Jimmy strived to be just like him. Everyone knew Jimmy as big Jack Dunlop's boy, the bomb-maker who brought the explosives over and masterminded the bomb plot in Glasgow, and Jimmy had always been aware of what that meant in the world they lived in.

'What is it?' he managed to say.

'Cancer. Stomach. You know how my gut has always bothered me. Thought it was my ulcer, so I never bothered with it. Then was doubled in two the last couple of months and I knew something wasn't right. I went to the doc and he sent me down to the hospital. They gave me one of them ultrasound things. Massive tumour. And then blood tests. It's been going on for over a week now. I've to go in for more tests. Maybe an operation. But it's not looking good.'

'Aw, but Da, they can't just say that without having a real look. Don't be so worried. It might be all right. I mean, there's loads they can do nowadays . . .' Jimmy's voice was running away with him. He felt his chest tight with emotion. 'Why didn't you tell me?'

'What's the point of that? It's me who's sick. You don't need to worry about it. Listen, son.' His eyes softened. 'I've seen the specialist this afternoon. He's told me they can do more tests, but there's no point opening me up because they can see from the scan and the blood tests that it's an aggressive cancer and it's already spread.' He shook his head. 'I'm fucked, Jimmy.'

'Don't say that, Da.' Jimmy swallowed his tears. 'Don't say that.'

They looked at each other and Jimmy saw this big six foot man, who had been the world to him, suddenly vulnerable, his eyes shining as though he was going to cry. He watched as his father stood up.

'I'm going to bed now, son.'

Jimmy felt his legs go weak as he got to his feet and they faced each other. For a moment, he thought his da was going to hug him and when he didn't, he resisted the urge to throw his arms around him. They just stood there, the wall of silence between them.

'I'm tired,' his father sighed, as he walked out of the door, leaving Jimmy in the stillness of the room.

CHAPTER SIX

'So what's happening with our Billy Boy friends, Gilmour?' McGuire studied his computer screen as Rosie walked into his office. 'You've not called me for a couple of days.'

'I know, Mick. I've missed you too.' Rosie gave him a sarcastic smile as she sat down. 'Actually, I've been out doing a bit of digging. Didn't want to talk to you till I had something to tell you.' She opened her notebook and flicked through pages. 'Oh, before I say any more – about the Rangers Champions League matches. We need to get booked on ferries and stuff. I know what bus I'm watching and what ferry it's on, so we need to get organised. And I also need to discuss the logistics of it with you.' She looked up. 'I might need some help.'

The thought of going undercover, tracking UVF drug dealers with just Matt, made Rosie a little nervous. She wanted to involve her Bosnian friend Adrian, and Javier for the Spanish end, if he could be persuaded. She was considering bringing both of them on the two jobs.

'But first . . . there's been a pretty shit-hot development.'

She'd toyed with the idea of not telling Mick about the rape but she knew the consequences if it came out later.

'You know Wendy's pal Liz?'

'Yeah, the barmaid with the big mouth,' Mick said, deadpan.

'Yes. Well. She called me the other night, and I had a meet with her yesterday. You'll never guess what she said . . .'

Mick rolled his eyes to the ceiling.

'Now let me think. No. You're right, I'll never guess. Just tell me, Rosie. I can tell from the look on your face I'm going to have trouble believing it.'

'Mick. Liz's all right. I had a long talk with her, and I like her. She does run off at the mouth a bit and I talked to her about that. But she seems to know the score.'

'So what did she say?'

'Well, she said that her and Jimmy were out getting pissed a couple of nights ago, and he told her that when Wendy phoned that night she disappeared, she was crying. Sobbing. Jimmy didn't tell that to the cops.'

'And?' Mick was suddenly interested.

'And, she said Wendy told Jimmy that Eddie McGregor raped her. In his car.'

McGuire was silent for a moment, then he put his head back and his hands went to his face.

'Oh fuck! That's all we need. Can you imagine what kind of shit will be flying around if we don't report *that* to the cops and Wendy turns up dead?'

'Yeah. But we can't report it, Mick. That's the problem. Neither could Liz, because she knows if she goes to the cops, she will have to bring Jimmy into it, and he can't report it because of his connection with the UVF. They don't go to the cops. They have their own people to investigate internal matters. He can't go to the cops. And if Liz does, then she's a dead woman.'

'Christ! What if this is just a smokescreen by Jimmy, and he's the one who's done something to Wendy? He was the last to talk to her, according to what he's told the cops.'

'But he wasn't the last to see her. Eddie was.'

'Well, we don't know that for sure.' Mick paused. 'Do you believe Liz? And more to the point, does she believe what Jimmy's saying?'

'Yes. To both those questions. Liz absolutely believes Jimmy. She says he was smitten with Wendy. We have to take that at face value. We can only work with what we've got.'

'Christ. So where does this leave us?'

Rosie took a deep breath. 'I think we just carry on with our investigation. See if we can get them in Holland and in Spain with the drugs, then get them busted. That's what Liz wants to do. She is convinced Eddie has done Wendy in, and the only way she can get him busted is by getting him done for the drugs. She's prepared to help us do it.'

McGuire stood up and walked towards the window, his back to Rosie for a moment.

'I don't like it, Rosie. I'm not comfortable with it.'

'But what happens if I get the cops and we report a rape allegation? They're going to ask who gave us the info, then we're up to our armpits in the usual shit with them saying if we don't give them the name we're committing a criminal offence by withholding information.'

'Which we are, Gilmour. We are withholding information. Crucial information.'

'Christ, Mick. You're sounding like that big DI who came in here trying to rough us up over the last investigation.'

'I'm playing devil's advocate. It's well risky, not telling anyone. What if that bastard McGregor has killed the girl?'

'I think he probably has. But we can't do anything about that. As I say, we can only work with what we've got.'

'Christ. I wish she hadn't told you that, though.'

'I know. I do too. But the thing is, Liz is well onside with us. She's got an ex-boyfriend who she still sees sometimes and he can give her an inside track on the buses. I know what bus McGregor's on. And I know what he looks like. And the Jimmy guy.'

'How do you know?'

'Matt and me have been sneaking around the last couple of days. Matt's got snatch-pics of him. That means we can follow him when they go abroad.'

'Hmm. We need to think about this.'

'I know. That brings me to my next suggestion.' She paused.

He glanced at her, eyebrows raised. 'This sounds like it's going to cost me money.'

'Well, yes, it is. I want to bring in big Adrian, you know, the Bosnian guy who's been involved in the last couple of jobs. The one who saved my life?'

'Is he here? I thought he was lying low in Sarajevo after hanging that Serbian from the gorge?'

'He is. But I know where to find him. Listen, Mick, I think we need some muscle and stuff on this job. Just in case anything unforeseen happens.'

'Unforeseen? Christ, Gilmour. It's all unforeseen with you. Every time you go away it winds up in some cluster fuck abroad.' He snorted.

Rosie smiled.

'At least I'm consistent.'

He nodded. 'Yeah, okay. Right. Agreed. Just talk to that big grim reaper geezer and see how much we need to pay him to work for us. It's only going to be a few days.'

'And I also want to ask Javier. For the Spanish side. Maybe even for Holland as well. He's smart and ahead of the game.'

'The guy who got shot in Spain? He got well compensated for that by our company insurance. He'll probably do it for free.'

Rosie smiled at the thought. She hadn't spoken to Javier

in a few weeks, but she knew he didn't ever get out of bed for free.

'No, he won't do it free. He might not even do it at all. But if he does, he'll definitely want a good few quid.'

'Fuck's sake, Rosie. I'm not going to break the bank paying anyone over the odds. Could you not take a couple of boys from here? Some of the younger lads?'

'No. I want these guys. Look how we did the job in Spain and Morocco.'

'You nearly got killed.'

'I know. But the fact that I didn't has a lot to do with the way they operate. They're a different class.'

McGuire sighed, shaking his head.

'Okay. Get me a costing and I'll run it past the bean counters. They're as tight as a duck's arse these days.'

'I know. But if we want to do proper investigations we need to spend money. Otherwise we can just chuck it altogether.' She stood up. 'This could be massive, Mick. And you never know what might come out during the exposé if we can get McGregor and Co. with their backs to the wall.'

'Yeah, I hear you,' McGuire said. 'I want this story, Gilmour. Leave the finer points like money to me. You just get out there and make it happen.'

Donna McGregor finished ironing and took the pile of clothes upstairs to the bedroom. She felt a little stab in her ribs as she walked, still sore from Eddie's hefty punch when he came home drunk last night and turned on her again. She managed to explain away the small bruise under her eye to her pals at the bakery where she worked part time. But she knew they had their suspicions from the way she was having difficulty lifting trays from the worktops to the ovens. She told them she'd strained her ribs doing a fitness workout from the telly, but was sure they didn't believe her.

'Make sure you pack that blue linen shirt I bought in Spain last year,' Eddie said as he emerged naked from the steamed up bathroom, drying himself with a towel.

She tried not to look at him as he put the towel around his neck and paraded across the bedroom, but she could see that he was aroused. Donna took the shirt from the pile and left it out on the bed. She bent down to his bedside cabinet and took out several pairs of neatly folded boxer shorts and left them beside his case. Then she felt his arms around her, his hand sliding her skirt up her thighs and touching between her legs. She could feel him hard pushing against her.

'Eddie. I'm trying to get some work done here. I'm trying to pack your things.'

He said nothing, turned her around and scooped the towel over her neck, pulling her towards him.

'I'm sorry about last night, Donna,' he said, his lips curling a little. 'But you'll need to learn to watch your mouth.' He touched her lips gently. 'That lovely mouth of yours will get you in trouble.'

Donna felt sick. She looked up at him as he put his hands firmly on her shoulders.

'Come on, darlin'.' His breath quickened as he put pressure on her, pushing her down. 'I'll be away for a few days. Come on now.'

Donna very carefully sank to her knees, grimacing at the pain in her ribs, and took him in her mouth.

'That's it, darlin',' he groaned. 'Oh fuck, I love the way you do that.'

His body jerked and he gasped as he came. She gagged and she swallowed, tears coming to her eyes. Then she got to her feet, managing to compose herself as she walked out of the room.

Downstairs in the bathroom she rinsed her mouth and retched into the toilet. She wiped her mouth with a piece of toilet paper and walked into the kitchen. She flicked on the television as the six o'clock news burst onto the screen. She could barely see the picture for her tears, but it looked like a car being pulled out of a quarry. Two drug dealers murdered in a Mafia-style hit, the newsreader announced. Pictures flashed up of the two men, whose bodies had been recovered in a car from the quarry somewhere in deepest Lanarkshire. There was something about turf wars but she wasn't interested. She shoved the kettle on and looked out of the kitchen window at the patio in the setting sun. Her stomach gave a little leap. Tomorrow, once she got rid of that bastard upstairs, she had plans. Andy would come over and she could be alone with him for an entire afternoon. If Eddie had the slightest notion of what they did, of how Andy made her life worth living, he'd put a bullet in him, and probably her as well. Donna's eyes went back to the television. The names of the two men. Tommy Ritchie and James Balfour. One sounded familiar, ringing a bell somewhere in her head. Ritchie . . . Richard. She went into the bottom drawer next to the cooker and pulled out the bank card she'd taken from Eddie's jeans the night he'd come home with Jimmy Dunlop and Mitch Gillespie. She looked at it – Thomas Ritchie. It was the same name. She should have burned it with the rest of the clothes they took off that night, but it had fallen out when she was emptying pockets and she didn't find it until a day later. She'd stuck it in the drawer without giving it another thought. Now she put it back in the same place, and covered it over with papers, knowing that he would never look there. She smiled to herself. Big Eddie McGregor didn't make mistakes. Oh yeah? He'd made one now.

CHAPTER SEVEN

It was stifling in the back of the van. They'd been sitting outside the Tavern for the best part of an hour in the dark blue works van Matt had borrowed from one of his mates. It was uncomfortable and grubby, but at least it wouldn't look out of place in the street. It was the first time Rosie had been in a van for a stake-out, as she usually left it to photographers. But she wanted to see this for herself.

She had taken a call mid-afternoon from Liz to tell her about a UVF monthly meeting that took place upstairs in the Tavern, which all the commanders throughout Scotland normally attended. Her boyfriend had let it slip that they were going to meet, and that he was going down to the pub afterwards to talk to a couple of the lads. Rosie thought it was a bit far-fetched, but she didn't want to take the risk. Even if nothing interesting happened, it might be another opportunity to get a snap of Eddie McGregor, if, as expected, he turned up to the rendezvous.

'I'm suffocating in here, Matt,' Rosie said as she shifted around on the floor of the van.

'I know. Me too.' Matt wiped sweat from his forehead as he adjusted his camera so that the long lens was fixed on the side door of the pub. 'This is what it's like if you're an SAS sniper. Just sitting for ages with your gun pointed at the target, waiting for the right moment to fire.'

'Aye,' Rosie sniggered. 'You're just like James Bond, you are.' She knelt up, so she could see out of the window.

'You know what snipers do if they need a crap when they're sitting with a target in sight for hours?' Matt said. 'They just crap where they're crouched. Into a crisp packet or something.'

'Christ,' Rosie chuckled. 'Please tell me you don't need a crap.'

'No. Luckily for you I don't, darlin'. But if I did, I could do it right into a crisp bag.' Matt was grinning, his eye still on the lens. 'It was part of that Special Forces training job I went on. It's easier than you think. You just open the bag . . .'

'Aye, right, Matt. I get the picture.'

It was nearly seven by the time a few cars and vans had driven up and one by one the men filtered in through the side entrance. If this was the UVF top brass, then they didn't resemble anything like the military. More like punters or football fans, and a pretty thuggish-looking bunch at that.

But at least Liz's information about the meeting seemed to be spot on. Another car drew up, and Rosie peered through binoculars.

'Look,' Matt said. 'It's McGregor. Brilliant. Face on, too. Bastard's looking right down the lens.'

'You don't think he can see us, do you?'

'No. No way. Relax. It's just a coincidence that he's looking this way.'

A couple of minutes later, another car – a smart black BMW – drew up. Rosie peered through her bins, as Matt adjusted his lens. It took a few seconds before the tall, well-dressed man emerged from the car.

'Wonder who he is,' Rosie said. 'Seems quite well groomed. Top car. Looks like he's about forty-something, would you say?'

'Yeah. It would be nice if he was a referee,' Matt smiled. 'It would prove to Celtic fans that the rumours are true.'

Rosie replied, 'Yeah. Make sure you snap his number plate anyway. I'll get someone to run it through for me.'

She wrote down the registration and took her mobile out of her pocket. She dialled Don's number.

'Hi, Don. What you up to? You're not working tonight, are you?'

'Hey, Rosie. No. Finished half an hour ago. What's up?'

'I was going to see if you could run a registration plate through for me. Any chance?'

'Yeah. No bother. My mate's still working. Give me the

number. I'm in the pub having a pint. I'll do it now, and get back to you.'

A couple of hours later, Rosie watched as Matt wolfed a vindaloo, mopping the plate with a chunk of naan bread, and washing it down with lager.

'I'm glad I'm not doing a stake-out in a van with you tomorrow, pal,' Rosie said, sipping her lager.

Matt grinned. 'No. You definitely don't want to be anywhere near me.'

They'd had a productive two hours outside the pub, Matt snapping every man who came out of the side door at the end of the meeting. They had no way of knowing who any of them were, why they were there, or even if it was a UVF meeting. But it was a start, Rosie told him, and it was good to have them on file.

They'd been intrigued as the man in the BMW emerged from the side door with Eddie McGregor, who handed him a black holdall. Matt reeled off some snaps as they shook hands and parted. Whoever they were, they seemed close, and that had to be worth a look in itself.

Rosie's mobile rang on the table and she picked it up.

'Hi, Don.'

'Listen, Rosie. That registration you gave me. You up to something sneaky?'

'You know me, Don. I'm always trampling around somebody's dirty secrets. Why? Is he interesting?'

'Not sure. All it gives is the owner of the car. He's from Ayrshire. Irvine, actually.'

Don reeled off the details and Rosie wrote them down on the back of a napkin.

'Well?' Matt said when she came off the phone.

'The guy in the BMW.' Rosie folded the napkin and put it in her bag.

'Please tell me he's a referee.'

'No idea. But I've got an address. Why don't we nip down early doors tomorrow and see where he lives. Maybe snatch a picture of him coming out of his house. Just in case he's a respectable businessman.'

'Or a church minister.'

'Yeah. In your dreams, Matt.'

The house was a semidetached job in a fairly new estate outside Irvine. Clipped lawns, patio furniture and this year's car in the tiny driveways of the little corner the residents had cleared for themselves, as they strived to be upwardly mobile. The place was dubbed Spam Valley by the hard-up tenants in the nearby council housing scheme. They'd feel vindicated if the folk in the fancy new estate couldn't afford to feed themselves, their hefty mortgages hanging round their necks. Rosie could see why bitter little jealousies reared their heads in what had once been a thriving new town, but now was lumbered with high unemployment and heroin creeping out of Glasgow like a cancer, spreading all the way down to devastate scenic little towns that had been jewels in the Ayrshire coastline. Saltcoats, Ardrossan, Irvine, Ayr . . . All of them brought back memories of bus runs with her mother on long summer days, fish teas in the cafe and sleepy journeys home among drunken day-trippers singing on the top of the double decker.

Rosie and Matt had found a good spot to park within shooting distance of Fraser Thomson's house. It was the kind of place you'd be rumbled if you asked questions, so they wouldn't hang around too long. It was interesting already, given that whoever he was, he didn't fit the profile that Rosie had expected.

'Are we going to follow him?' Matt said, yawning.

'Only if we can do it discreetly. It's definitely the right house though. The BMW's in the driveway. We'll just see what happens if he comes out.'

The houses in the estate were beginning to stir now that it was after eight thirty, and various people were coming out and getting into cars.

'Hope he's not having a long lie, because I'm going to need a crap soon,' Matt said.

'Thanks for sharing.' Rosie shook her head.

Just then, the front door opened.

'Here we go,' Rosie said, pulling the sun visor down to cover her face.

The tall, slim figure they'd seen last night stepped onto the threshold. Rosie's mouth dropped open.

'Holy fuck!' Matt fired off several shots. 'You're fucking joking. He's a cop!'

'Jesus! It's definitely him, isn't it, Matt?'

'Damn right it is. Same hair. Definitely same face. It's him. Fucking belter!'

Rosie's eyes nearly popped when she saw the hat wedged under his arm.

'Look, Matt. His hat. It's got scrambled egg on it. He's an inspector. Zoom in on his jacket. Get the buttons on the shoulder. I'll need to check, but I'm sure two buttons is an inspector.'

'Come in, Inspector Shiny Buttons, your number's up. You're nicked, big man.' Matt grinned as he twisted the lens. 'Oh I fucking love it when this happens.'

He fired off several more shots as they watched him put a black holdall into the boot of his car, then walk back round to the driver's door.

'Right. Just let him get out of the estate, and then we'll follow him. On the main road we should be able to keep him in our sights. See where he goes. It will either be Ayr cop shop or Irvine. Any one of them will do nicely.' Rosie smiled. 'It's a bit early to be going to a fancy dress party.'

They followed as he drove his BMW out onto the main road and up towards the edge of the town, then onto the A77 south.

They were still two cars behind him when he pulled off the road and into Ayr town centre. They followed until he turned up a street towards the car park at Ayr police station.

'Brilliant! Thank Christ we decided to come down. Come on, I'll buy you a celebratory bacon roll,' Matt said.

'I told you – I'm a lucky reporter,' she smiled as she headed back up onto the dual carriageway.

Rosie was surprised at how willing Liz was to take the risk. She'd agonised over the decision herself, part of her feeling guilty, the bigger part driven by the chance it might work.

Liz had phoned her as they were driving back from Ayrshire. Eddie McGregor had asked her to work behind the bar at a party in the Tavern tonight – a bon voyage party for the Rangers fans going off to Eindhoven tomorrow for the match. Rosie's mind went into overdrive. The bus was leaving in two days, and it would be a chance to get pictures inside the hall upstairs that was used for UVF functions. Risky, but possible, and Liz was up for it.

Now, as they sat in her car in the derelict industrial estate in the East End, she watched Matt attach the secret video camera to Liz's blouse.

'Jeez. It's tiny,' Liz said. 'Are you sure this will really take pictures?'

'Definitely,' Matt said, carefully securing the clip inside her blouse. 'I've used it before. It works great for what we need.'

Liz smoothed down her blouse.

'Can you see it?' she said.

'No,' Rosie reassured her. 'It blends in with the colours in your blouse. Can't see it at all. You'll be fine. Now let's see if you can move around, because you'll be busy behind the bar, and we have to make sure it stays on when you're working.'

'Christ. Don't say that, Rosie,' Liz snorted. 'All I'd need is for it to drop into Eddie McGregor's pint.'

'Don't even go there,' Rosie said.

Liz made as though she was pulling pints, then stretched her arms as though reaching for the optics, the way she'd have to if she was serving behind the bar.

'It's fine. Not moving at all.' She sat back down. 'Right. Tell me what you want me to do.'

'Okay,' Rosie said. 'You told us about the pictures with Rangers players on the walls up the staircase to the function hall. If you're in early enough before anyone arrives, there'll be nobody to see you going around there. So if you can, go slowly up the stairs and get the pictures captured on video.'

'We can also take stills from the video footage,' Matt says. 'So don't worry if you don't have time to do a lot of filming. Just the crucial pictures.'

'Yes,' said Rosie. 'And inside the function room, see if you can get any other pictures on the wall, the UVF emblems and stuff embroidered on the chairs and wall seating. Anything at all that has those connections. And of course, you'll be talking to Eddie McGregor as the night goes on, so you'll capture anyone who is talking to him on camera. Plus it's got audio, so you might get him and Jimmy.' Rosie looked at her. 'But only if it's possible to do it discreetly.'

'I'll try my best, Rosie.' Liz nodded.

'I know you will. But the main thing here is for you to remember that if there is any problem at all, or you're the least bit uncomfortable with it, just go to the loo and take it off. Are we clear about that?'

'Of course,' Liz said. 'I'll be fine with it. Honest. I can do this.'

'Okay. Let's have a practice with it. Make sure it works,' Rosie said.

Liz reached inside her blouse and switched it on and Matt spoke towards the camera. Then she opened the door and got out of the car for a second.

'Let's have a look,' Matt said, looking at it. 'Works. Brilliant.'

'Okay. Game on.'

Rosie glanced at Matt. Her stomach was in knots. Images of Gerhard Hoffman flashed into her mind, the dogged German investigative reporter who had helped her expose the scandal of refugees being killed for the illegal international tissue trade. Hoffman had been found murdered, suffocated with a plastic bag over his head in her hotel room in Belgrade a few months ago. She blinked his face away.

The three of them sat for a moment in the silence of Rosie's car, staring out of the windscreen at the drab council houses nearby with boarded-up windows and graffiti on every block. The rain sweeping across the streets made it look even more depressing.

'What do you think has happened to Wendy?' Liz shifted her body around, so she faced Rosie.

Rosie sighed. 'I don't know, Liz. That's the truth. I want to think she's done a runner somewhere, maybe was too scared to do anything about the rape, maybe too scared or sick about it to stay here.' She paused. 'But to be honest, I think if she'd done that she would at least have got in touch with you. Don't you think?'

Liz nodded, then gazed out of the side window.

'The longer it goes on, the worse it looks for her.' She shook her head.

CHAPTER EIGHT

It was after seven by the time Rosie left the *Post*, having spent the past half hour in McGuire's office with the picture editor, viewing Matt's shots of Inspector Fraser Thomson. McGuire was delighted, but it was nothing without proof of his UVF involvement. He wasn't convinced that Liz would be up to the undercover camera work, and they discussed other ways to investigate. He had agreed that the unmasking of the inspector was an unexpected bonus. 'But don't take your eye off the ball,' he told Rosie. The Rangers buses and the coke smuggling were the big one. No pressure there then, Rosie told him as she left.

Driving home to her flat, Rosie wished she could have dinner with TJ and offload all her worries – just relax, drink too much wine, and talk. She missed the friendship as much as she ached for his touch when she reached across the bed in the middle of the night. She longed to be against the softness of his neck, listening to his reassuring words when she was under pressure. She even missed watching how peaceful he was when he slept. She'd call him when she got home – it would make the night shorter.

Her mobile rang as she was getting out of her car behind her block of flats.

'Don. How you?'

'All right, Rosie. Where are you?'

'Just about to go into my flat. Why? What's up?'

'I would have phoned you earlier, but I was tied up out in darkest Lanarkshire. You probably saw that car pulled out of a quarry in Coalburn? I've been chasing that most of the afternoon.'

'I saw it. I was just glad it wasn't Wendy.'

'No, no. Two wee neds. Drug dealers. Not as big-time as they thought they were, evidently. Not much left of their heads.'

'Good.' Rosie was always glad when a scumbucket drug dealer was taken off the face of the earth. 'Executed, I guess.'

'Yeah. Point-blank. Forensic boys are doing the post-mortem now. Obviously there's been a hit on them.' He paused. 'Listen. Fancy a quick drink, somewhere near you? I'm heading up that way anyway.'

Rosie locked the car. She could walk to a pub in Charing Cross in two minutes.

'Meet you at the Bon Accord,' she said. 'I'm on my way.'

In the pub, Rosie looked at her watch, thinking how

nervous Liz must be feeling – she would be about to start work at the Tavern. She tried to push away the twinge of guilt.

'One glass of fine red biddy for the lady.' Don put a glass of wine down on the table and sat opposite her. He pulled his chair closer.

'So, what's the sketch, Don? Who are the guys from the quarry? I heard the names but they didn't mean anything.'

Don lit a cigarette and swallowed the smoke.

'Tommy Ritchie and James Balfour. They fancied their chances with the big boys. Moved in on Al Howie's turf and were selling heroin, with their eye on the main prize because big Al's not around. They thought they were just the boys to take over. But word is they were lured to a meet out in Coalburn by that wee bastard Bobby Gardner – he's the wanker who's looking after the shop while Al's gone to ground in Spain . . . Well, after your investigation, he had to disappear.' He smiled. 'Anyway. So it's obviously an ordered contract. Fuck them.' He raised a glass. 'To two more useless bastards getting what they deserved.'

Rosie clinked his glass.

'Any ideas?'

'Anybody's guess really. Too well done and kept really tight to be any of the pricks around wee Bobby. We're thinking UDA or UVF hit. Not IRA. Bobby's a big Rangers man. But it seems like a Loyalist hit. They don't leave any loose ends lying around.'

Rosie raised her eyebrows.

'Well, they must have, because the cops have found the car and the bodies. Surely they weren't meant to float back up to the surface of the quarry. Who found it?'

'Local guy, out walking his dog. He stopped for a pee and saw on the horizon what he thought was the top of a car. He got the cops.' He shrugged. 'But you're right. There shouldn't be any loose ends if it was a proper hit.'

'Why didn't whoever did the job not just set fire to the car?' Rosie asked.

'Too much smoke. Out in the country it's too quiet to start a fire. Would attract too much attention. They obviously thought the quarry would keep it forever. Might have seemed a good idea at the time, but it was a bad move. Especially in the warm weather. It hasn't rained for the past week, and nobody could expect that in our summer. Water level must have gone down a bit.'

'Any idea when it happened?'

'Dunno yet. But these two wee toerags haven't been seen for nearly a week. So I suppose it was on their last outing. We're going through CCTV to see if they were spotted on the M74. They're well out of their own patch, so they might have been coming up from down south with a stash. But there's nothing in the car. So whoever did it cleaned them out.'

'How sure can you be about an ordered hit, Don? You know what it's like. We always hear these rumours – a

Loyalist hit is a good newspaper headline. But are these guys still operating to that extent these days? With the peace process and all that?'

Rosie knew they were, but she wanted to hear it from an official source.

Don looked at her, surprised. 'Of course. You kidding? The Good Friday Agreement last year didn't make much difference to these guys. They were never really about the Troubles. Well, maybe years ago, but not now. It's all about thuggery and gangsters. It's the same over in Belfast. But you must know that yourself.'

Rosie nodded. She knew. She'd been to Belfast many times during flashpoints over the years, and had built up a handful of connections on both sides of the divide. On one occasion when the peace process collapsed, she'd persuaded someone to give her a glimpse into the men who stood in the way of peace. She'd been taken by Loyalists to a secret location in a house in East Belfast for what they loosely described as a photo opportunity. She and Matt had been blindfolded and driven through a warren of housing estates, so that by the time they'd reached the house they had no real sense of what area they were in. Once inside the council house, she was struck by how normal everything had looked in the family home – kids' school pictures on the wall, football trophies on the mantelpiece, and breakfast dishes piled up in the kitchen sink. Minutes later they were taken to a back room where two armed men in full paramilitary jerseys stood with rifles, as a commander sat beneath a flag and read out a UVF statement. It was the usual diatribe you got from both sides, whether it was defending the union or fighting for a united Ireland. When they finished, the men in balaclavas marched out of the room and probably went back to whatever day jobs they had, in whatever life they lived before they'd come in the back door.

But over the years, it was becoming more and more obvious that the armed struggle wasn't about Irish freedom or fighting to preserve Queen and country. It was gangsters, fighting to preserve their sordid little drugs empires under the banner of a cause.

'Yeah. I do,' she said. 'But I didn't think they were still at it so much over here.'

'Of course they are. They have to pretend to have something to fight for. The fight is drugs, Rosie. That's what it's all about. The rest is sheer fucking hypocrisy.' Don shook his head and ran a hand over his stubbly chin. 'I'd rather have an ordinary bastard of a drug dealer than any one of these fuckers trying to shove politics down my throat. Politics went out the window years ago. Coke is the new cause. And worse still – crack cocaine. We'd never heard much of that stuff before until a couple of years ago, but now it's here to stay. And that shit's going to fuck with people's heads big time. Tell you what. We get a crack cocaine problem here and it will be like an explosion. It's already starting to happen. We're getting a few more busts every other week. So it's here to stay. Doesn't bear thinking about. And most of the market is controlled by the UVF and the IRA.'

'Do you know who are the main players?'

'Special Branch would tell you better. But there's a few faces on both sides. That Eddie McGregor. He's a UVF man. Big enough player these days. Special Branch know about him and others.'

'I see. What about weapons? I take it weapons that get used across the water sometimes end up here, and vice versa?'

'Exactly. And the same with the money. Lot of it goes back there. The UVF and IRA top brass would tell you they're against drugs and work to clean up their areas. But it's all crap. They turn a blind eye as long as they get a kickback sent over. But it's all so well orchestrated, it's hard to get anything that would lead you to a conviction. Almost impossible in fact. There's so much traffic back and forth across the water. With both sides.'

'So what you going to do to get someone to talk about the dead guys?'

'Well . . . It'll be all over the papers for the next few days . . . Gangland killing. There'll be plenty of speculation, so hopefully it will throw up a few names. We've got a team out at Coalburn and the areas at the moment, trying to question a few people. But we're not holding our breaths over getting a conviction on this one.' He stubbed his cigarette in the ashtray. 'Anyway. Fuck them. At least they're dead.'

CHAPTER NINE

So far, so depressing, Rosie thought, as Matt pulled into the motorway car park. Tracking a ferry load of rat-arsed Rangers fans from Glasgow to Eindhoven wasn't her idea of a midweek break, but it had to be done. It was more of a fact-finding mission than anything else, Rosie and McGuire had decided. The whole exercise was to determine exactly where McGregor and his cohorts went and who they met during the run up to the match. They'd simply follow them and take pictures if the opportunity arose. It didn't prove a lot, but it would be enough for some groundwork.

The bus shook to the dull thud of stamping feet. Fists pumped against windows as they belted out the song: 'And the cry was No Surrender . . . Surrender or you'll die . . . DIE! DIE!'

'Christ.' Rosie stretched her legs as she got out of the car. 'Listen to that. They're well pissed. I'll be surprised if half of them actually make the match tomorrow.'

Matt had followed the bus south as it turned off the M6 to the motorway cafe. The singing had started by the time the fans had all piled out of the Tavern pub at seven in the morning and onto the bus. Rosie and Matt were at the end of the street watching discreetly as hordes of locals turned out to wave the bus off with the kind of reverence usually reserved for soldiers going to war. One of the cheeky fans dropped his trousers and mooned out of the side window, much to the hilarity of those left behind. Matt had kept a modest distance behind the cavalcade of cars and coaches bedecked with banners and scarves, blazing south towards Ramsgate to catch the ferry to Ostend. *Bears On Tour*, one of the red, white and blue banners read. Sure, Rosie thought – in more ways than one.

'They're a scary lot when you see them all together like that,' Matt said.

'I know. I hate all that sectarian shit. They're bad enough with it when they're sober. But when they get boozed up, you just know something's going to kick off.'

They watched as Eddie McGregor got off the bus with Mitch in tow and followed the crowd into the cafe. Jimmy Dunlop had dropped back a couple of steps and was walking with a man who looked like a taller, older version of himself.

'I wonder where he's left the money for the coke deal,' Rosie said. 'If this all stands up and he is picking up coke, it's not as if he's going to hit the bank in Holland for a few grand. He'll have it on him.'

'Look,' Matt said. 'The other guy. Mad Mitch. He's carry-ing a holdall. Maybe it's in there.'

As more fans filed off the bus, Rosie suddenly felt sick as she watched a pale-faced drunken man stagger and projec-tile vomit in the car park.

'Christ,' Matt grimaced. 'Glad I'm not sitting next to him all the way to Eindhoven.'

Rosie consoled herself with the fact that they'd already made some progress back in Glasgow. Liz had played a blinder at the farewell party in the Tavern. When she'd met them yesterday to return the camera, they were blown away with the pictures. The function room above the pub was like a shrine to the UVF. Even if nothing else happened, they already had a scoop with pictures and video footage of the UVF's secret rooms above the bar. The Tavern, on the face of it, was just another Rangers pub. But these pictures would expose it for what it really was. McGuire couldn't believe it as they pored over the images adorning the walls – photos of Rangers football stars down the years, alongside UVF flags and posters. Closer examination of the pictures showed printed names of those who had sponsored them for that year, and Liz had informed Rosie that she'd been told the fees for having your name up on the wall for all to see were almost a grand a year, all of it going straight to the UVF. Young Declan was already doing a trawl of the names to see if any of them flagged up an interesting pro-file. Crucially, there was also footage of Eddie McGregor and

Jimmy Dunlop talking quietly at the bar. The audio wasn't great, but there was a mention of a meet with the contact in Utrecht, around an hour's drive from Eindhoven. Marion had organised a hired car from Eindhoven for following McGuire. She'd also booked them rooms at the hotel where the bus load of Rangers fans were staying.

Inside the motorway cafe, Rosie sat at the window while Matt went to get them sandwiches. She looked at the text message from Adrian. He was already in Eindhoven, and had checked into the hotel. She was surprised at how much she was looking forward to seeing him. They hadn't spoken much in the last few weeks, not since his phone call informing her of the fate of the Serbian war criminal they'd tracked from Glasgow to Belgrade. But that was Adrian's way. He didn't do small talk. But still, she knew he'd be there for her if she needed him. She'd managed to screw a decent wedge of cash from the *Post* to pay him to work for them for as long as the investigation took, over the two legs of the Rangers Champions League matches. If she'd asked, he'd probably have done it for free, but she wasn't about to admit that to McGuire. She felt safer just knowing he'd be in Eindhoven when they got there. She'd decided to leave Javier until the Spanish end, when she could see how it was all panning out.

By the time the ferry pulled out of the terminal at Ramsgate, Jimmy had already intervened in two arguments between drunken fans. As he relaxed in the bar, Eddie sent him and Mitch across to sort out another rowdy table after two of the fans were on their feet poking each other in the chest.

'Sort them lads, for fuck's sake,' Eddie said. 'The last thing we need is a rammy drawing attention to ourselves.'

Jimmy and Mitch crossed to the table of drunken fans. He knew most of them from the Tavern, but more importantly, they knew him and Mitch.

'Right, boys.' Jimmy stepped between them. 'Sit the fuck down and behave yourselves. You're going to end up getting arrested.'

Both of the men sat down and the table fell silent. Fans from nearby glanced over and turned away. Jimmy leaned towards them.

'Eddie says you'd better screw the nut.' He stabbed a finger. 'There are a lot of families and youngsters on this trip as well as you, who just want to go and enjoy the match. Now there'll be plenty of time for you to get drunk and do whatever the fuck you like when you get to Eindhoven. But right here and now, just behave. Unless any of you want to go for a swim.' He made eye contact with each one of them. 'And I'm serious about that.'

'Okay, man,' they muttered as Jimmy turned and left.

He went over to where his father sat with three of his old workmates from the shipyards.

'All right, Da?' Jimmy said.

'Aye. Fine, son,' his father answered, but his gaze was forlorn. He had hardly touched his pint.

'Come on out and we'll get some fresh air.' Jimmy nodded towards the deck.

'I think I will.' His father got to his feet and walked behind Jimmy.

Out on the deck, Jimmy lit a cigarette as they stood staring out to sea at a watery sun behind a pale grey sky. His father held a roll-up cigarette between his nicotine-stained thumb and index finger and smoked it until it was almost burning his skin.

'Maybe you should chuck that, Da,' Jimmy said, glancing at the fag.

'No' much point now.' His father flicked the fag end into the sea.

They stood in awkward silence, Jimmy afraid to look at his father and see the sloping shoulders that used to carry him as a boy when he'd run to meet him coming home from his shift on a Friday night. Jimmy could just make out the fading tattoo on his still muscle-bound forearms, beneath the black hair. The red hand of Ulster and the letters *UVF* written in black ink beneath it. They leaned on the railings in the breeze, looking out at the white trail from the wake of the ferry, and Jimmy glanced at his father's face, seeing the haunted looked he'd had since he'd broken the news a few days ago. He thought he heard him sniff and when he looked straight at him, he was shocked to see tears welling up in his eyes. He didn't know what to do. He hadn't even seen his father cry at his mother's funeral, though in the weeks that followed he'd heard him sobbing through his bedroom wall in the middle of the night. The memory of it still broke his heart. He leaned across and tentatively put an arm around his father's shoulder.

'You're all right, Da,' he said, choked. 'I'll never leave your side. You know that, don't you.'

His father shook his head and looked down at the deck.

'Aw, Jimmy, son. I miss her so much. You've no idea.' He wiped his tears. 'She was too good for me, your mother. Too fine a woman.' He ran the back of his hand across his nose. 'I didn't treat her well enough.'

'Aye you did.' Jimmy knew he was lying. 'Don't be daft, man. My ma thought the sun shone out your arse.' He smiled, trying to make light. He wasn't equipped to deal with this.

For a few seconds they said nothing, then his father sighed, seeming to compose himself.

'All the same. I didn't give her everything she deserved.' He turned to Jimmy. 'Don't you ever make the same mistake, son.'

Jimmy said nothing.

'You see that wee lassie you were going out with,' his father said.

'Wendy?' Jimmy said, surprised. He'd only brought her to the house twice.

'Aye. She seemed all right. What did she disappear for? That was weird.' He shook his head. 'I thought she might have been the lassie for you. The pair of you looked good together. What made her up sticks and go like that?'

Jimmy felt his throat tighten as he swallowed, and for a few seconds he said nothing. But his chest was bursting.

'Eddie raped her.' It was out before he could stop himself, and just saying it brought back a sickening image of Eddie climbing all over her.

The words hung in the air, and they stood looking at each other, silent but for the drone of the engine and the swish of the waves against the boat.

'What?'

'Eddie. He raped her.'

'You're fucking joking, son.'

Suddenly the tired pallor was gone, and his father's eyes blazed.

'Tell me.'

Jimmy ran his hand through his hair and shook his head. 'Da . . .'

'Tell me, Jimmy. Tell me right now.'

His tone was calm but firm. Jimmy had heard it before, and he knew he had to answer.

'Da. Listen. I shouldn't have said it. I . . . I've been keeping it to myself for weeks. You see the night of the do?' His stomach fluttered, recalling the moment. 'Well, after I put you to bed I fell asleep. Then my phone went and woke me up.

It was Wendy, and she was sobbing. I couldn't get any sense out of her for a minute. Then she said to me that Eddie'd raped her in his car.' He shook his head in disgust. 'Fuck! I jumped in a taxi and went right over to her house . . . But she wasn't there.' He swallowed and shook his head. 'She was gone. Totally disappeared. And hasn't been seen since.'

'Fuck me, son. Why didn't you tell me?'

'Because . . . Well. What's the point? You can't go accusing big Eddie because Wendy's not here to back it up.'

'You should have told me. I'd have taken it to the provost marshal in Belfast. We'd have pulled that bastard over for questioning.'

'I know you would have, Da. Then maybe lost face. Look, there's nothing anybody can do about it. I don't even know where Wendy is or what's happened. I've been worried sick.'

'Did you ask big Eddie? I don't mean about what she said, but did you mention anything at all to him?'

'Yeah. Just asked how Wendy was when he dropped her off, but he said he'd no idea. All he did was drop her off. He wasn't pleased at me even asking. There's no way I could pursue it any more.'

'Do you believe her? Would she make something like that up?'

'No. No way. I believe her.' He paused. 'Da. Don't say anything.'

His father folded his arms and muttered under his breath, looking out across the horizon, his mouth tight with defiance.

'He's a manky bastard,' he said.

CHAPTER TEN

'Hello, Adrian,' Rosie smiled as Adrian looked up from the table in the busy pavement cafe outside their hotel in Eindhoven.

If he was pleased to see her, it wasn't written all over his face. But that was Adrian. The Bosnian wasn't big on expressive emotions. He stood up, his face as impassive as ever, and stretched out his arms in front of him.

'Rosie.' He took both her hands in his. 'My friend.' He scanned her face. Then he hugged her tight.

'So great to see you, Adrian. Thanks for coming.' She felt comfortable pressed against his muscular frame.

'But of course I come. Always, I am very glad to see you too, Rosie.' He pulled away then turned to Matt. 'Hello again, Matt. Good to see you.' They shook hands.

'You too, big man,' Matt grinned. 'Seems like yesterday we were traipsing around chasing all these bad boys over in Belgrade.'

Adrian shrugged. 'Well. They get what they deserve . . . in the end.'

An image of the Serb war criminal hanging over Paklenik gorge in Bosnia with his throat cut flashed across Rosie's mind, and not for the first time she was fascinated by how clinical Adrian was when it came to right and wrong. She'd seen him shoot and stab people with no compunction. His survival philosophy was basic – them or us. In all the years she had known him, since the day of their chance meeting in a cafe in Glasgow when he was a poor refugee in trouble, Rosie had never glimpsed behind Adrian's detached exterior. Until two months ago, in Bosnia. For the first time, he'd opened up his life to her and Matt, and she could finally see the scars that made him the haunted figure he was.

They sat down and ordered coffee from the waiter. Rosie glanced around – plenty of Rangers fans had already arrived, sitting at tables cluttered with drinks and bottles. The ancient, pretty town of Eindhoven wouldn't know what hit them. Rosie figured she and Matt were about half an hour ahead of the bus, having shadowed it from the ferry terminal in Ostend, in Belgium, then overtaken it on the final part of the journey towards Eindhoven. She wanted to check into the hotel and touch base with Adrian before the bears arrived.

'So, Adrian,' Rosie said, keeping her voice low so she wouldn't be recognised as Scottish, 'hopefully, this job will be less messy than the last couple.'

Adrian shrugged. 'For me is no problem. Whatever happens happens.'

'Yeah,' Rosie smiled as Matt rolled his eyes to the sky. 'Well, this is mainly just a watching brief. What we're trying to do here is track these particular guys. We think they're here to do a coke deal, as I explained to you. So they'll probably have a stash of cash – we've already seen them carrying a holdall that they haven't let out of their sight since they left Glasgow. So we just want to follow them, see where they go and if possible take pictures.'

Adrian nodded.

'And they are making contact with some person here?'

'Well, we don't exactly know yet. We think they might drive to Utrecht to meet the contact and pick up the drugs. If they're going to do that, then I'd imagine it will be fairly soon – like tomorrow morning. The game is tomorrow night, so they'll want to do their business and get back. They're here two nights in all. We just have to watch them from the moment they arrive until they leave.' She paused. 'It's very much flying by the seat of our pants, but we'll just hope for the best.'

'Okay,' Adrian said.

They sat for a while as Rosie filled Adrian in about Eddie McGregor and his background. As she recounted the story of the rape and what they had so far, Matt interrupted.

'Look, Rosie. We're in business. Here they come.'

They could hear the racket on the bus as it pulled up

in the street outside the hotel. The fact that the fans had been drinking for almost eight hours solid didn't appear to dampen their enthusiasm. They filed out of the bus, rummaging for bags as soon as the driver opened the huge luggage compartment. A few of them went immediately to the bar next door, dumping their bags on the floor beside them.

Rosie watched as Eddie McGregor came down the steps.

'Okay, Adrian. There he is.'

Adrian turned his chair slightly for a better view.

'The man with the thin face, carrying the black bag?'

'That's him,' Matt said. 'And the two guys behind him. Coming off now. That's Dunlop and Gillespie. The three of them have been together for the whole journey. There's always at least one of them with McGregor.'

Adrian stood up.

'I go into the hotel with the fans. See what rooms they are staying.'

Rosie didn't question him. She watched as he disappeared inside the automatic glass doors of the hotel, surrounded by a sea of royal blue football jerseys.

In the morning, it took three stiff cups of coffee to lift the grogginess and get Rosie ready for the trip to Utrecht. She'd hardly slept a wink for the noise in the hotel from the partying Rangers crowd. She was knackered, but glad to be away from last night's mayhem at Eindhoven. Dutch police had milled around the city centre bars and terrace cafes, trying to keep the atmosphere genial. But Rosie predicted it would descend into at least one punch-up before the end of the evening. When it did, the cops waded in as fans began fighting and throwing glasses, according to what she'd overheard from the talk in the hotel at breakfast. A few had already been arrested and would see the rest of their trip out in police cells.

Now, after the drive to Utrecht and with ice-cold beers in front of them, the three of them looked like any other tourists enjoying an afternoon in one of the colourful little bars fringing the canal in the old city.

'It's easy to feel as if you're on holiday here,' Matt said, gazing around him.

'I know.' Rosie looked out as a boat glided through the water and disappeared beneath an ancient bridge arched across the canal. 'It's like being in a watercolour painting. So peaceful. I could sit here all day and just stare into space.'

Two bars along, McGregor, Dunlop and Gillespie sat sipping beers. They had to be here for a reason. Rosie watched as McGregor took a call on his mobile, while Matt got up and went for a walk along the canal, which was bustling with the lunchtime crowd. He found himself a vantage point on the balcony of a bar where he could snatch pictures unnoticed.

'Someone is arriving now, Rosie,' Adrian said, his expression flat. 'He is carrying a bag. Black. Similar to the one they have.'

'What does he look like?' she asked.

'Like them, I think. The hair is very short. I don't think he is Dutch. I think he maybe is British or Scottish. Maybe he is around forty years . . . They are shaking hands . . . He is sitting down.'

'I'm going to the loo for a better look.' After a minute she stood up, put on her dark glasses and made her way across the bar.

She was close enough to get a good view of the three of them sitting at a table drinking beers. The man who had just joined them was well dressed in a white linen shirt and faded blue jeans. He looked wealthy and deeply suntanned, so if he was Scottish, he definitely didn't live there. They'd been having a decent summer back home but that was definitely not a Scottish tan. Perhaps he had travelled from Spain or Amsterdam and made his way down to Utrecht for the meet.

'I got some good shots there,' Matt said as he came back to the table and sat down. 'I got them exchanging the bags, and both of them looking like they're examining inside. It will mean something if it all works out.'

Rosie looked beyond him at the four men who seemed to be preparing to leave as the suntanned man paid the bill.

'It's not enough though, Matt. We need more.' Rosie felt a little deflated. 'I know we've got them together, and witnessed the handover of the bags. But number one – we don't know what's in them. I'm sure it's money and coke. But we can't use that unless we can prove it.' She sighed. 'And secondly, the guy with the tan. We don't know who he is.'

Adrian leaned across the table.

'Why don't I follow him? I just get in the car and go when he goes. If he drives to Amsterdam and takes a plane, I go with him.' He shrugged. 'What have we got to lose?'

Rosie looked at Matt, a little annoyed with herself.

'We should have thought about that before we left, and brought two cars,' she said. 'What do you think, Matt?'

'I'm with Adrian,' Matt said. 'To be honest, short of stealing that bag from McGregor and his two henchmen, we're never going to find out what's in it. I think we've done all we can do here. And it's only the start. We've still got the other match in Seville. They're bound to be doing this again in Spain. At least now we know roughly how they operate.'

Rosie nodded slowly. 'Okay.' She looked at Adrian. 'Let's do it. What about your bags back in the hotel room though?'

'I have no bags. Everything is in the boot of the hired car. I flew here, and always I travel light – in case I have to move fast, I have everything I need.'

Rosie looked across at McGregor's table.

'Okay. They're getting up, Adrian. You'd better move.'

Adrian stood up. 'I'll call you, Rosie. From wherever I end up.'

'Be careful,' she said, as he turned to leave.

'Of course.' He glanced over his shoulder as he walked away.

'I wonder what time the trains go from Utrecht to Eindhoven.' Matt chuckled. 'We could hire bikes. Or we could just stay here and get pissed.'

'Come on,' Rosie said, standing up. 'Let's try their public transport.'

Jimmy sat in the hotel bar having a quiet beer with his father while they waited for the arrival of the coach to take fans to the stadium for the match.

'Where were you all day, Jimmy?' his father asked. 'I was looking for you.'

'I was with Eddie and Mitch, Da. We had to go up to Utrecht.'

'What for?'

'Eddie had a bit of business to attend to. He was meeting somebody.'

Jimmy avoided his father's glare. He knew he would be well aware that if McGregor had business it would involve drugs. And he knew how much his father hated the fact that almost every section of the UVF was knee-deep in the coke market.

'I take it he was picking up drugs?' he said, disgusted.

'I don't ask. I just do what I'm told,' Jimmy lied.

His father shook his head and sighed.

'Everything's changed so much. It's all fucking drugs now, no matter what you do. Time was when the UVF would have sorted out any of the lads involved in drugs. In my day, we worked to keep the drugs out of the working-class areas. I've kneecapped a few of the dealers myself over the years. But now? Anything fucking goes.'

Jimmy didn't know what to say. As far as he knew, Belfast was aware of the coke deals and turned a blind eye as long as they got their cut. But he didn't want to get into an argument.

'It's the way things are now, Da. It's all money.' He saw his father glower at him. 'Before you ask, I don't do coke. Never have. But it's big business out there. Everyone's doing it.'

'Doesn't make it fucking right. Doesn't mean we have to sink to their level. The UVF was never like that before. That's not who we are – cheap bastard drug dealers. We're supposed to be fighting for something that's right. Defending the Union. I've made my feelings well known to the brigadier in Belfast. It's not where we should be.'

Jimmy said nothing.

'And that bastard McGregor. He's a chancer. Don't know how he got where he is.' He shook his head. 'I always knew he was a scumbag, long before you told me about him raping that wee lassie.'

Jimmy's stomach knotted.

'Da. You can't say anything about that. Just forget I told you.'

His father stood up.

'Fuck it. Come on. Let's go and watch the Rangers.'

CHAPTER ELEVEN

Donna slid open the patio doors and stepped outside with her coffee. She spread out the day's *Post* in front of her, and flicked through the pages to see if there was any more on the car pulled out of the quarry. When it had come on the breakfast news on television as Eddie was getting organised to leave for Holland, she'd watched him closely for some kind of reaction. There was none – but that didn't prove anything. It wouldn't have surprised her if he'd bumped them off and just got on with his day. She'd seen him disappear several times over the years on what he said was business, and she knew that meant UVF business. She didn't dare ask. But she knew how he worked, how he dealt with people who crossed him. Over time she'd picked up little snippets about some guy or other having the crap beaten out of him by Eddie and his cronies. He had respect, he continually told her, and she should be proud of him.

She adjusted the chair and pushed herself back, turning

so she could feel the sun on her face, and relaxed, relishing the fact that Eddie was gone for a couple of days. If only she had the guts to get up one morning and disappear, just keep on running. She'd fantasised about it enough, but she knew he would find her. He'd already made that clear to her when he beat her up for threatening to leave, soon after their kids went off to lead their own lives.

To the outside world, she had an enviable life, but in reality she was trapped. Eddie was a successful builder and plumber and their lifestyle had all the trappings of wealth. They holidayed on luxury cruises, lived it up in lavish hotels in Spain, and their two-storey house in the south side of Glasgow wouldn't have been out of place in a magazine shoot. She drove a smart 4 x 4 and spent a couple of days a week getting preened at the hairdressers. But she was utterly miserable. Being bored shitless was only half the problem. Her hatred of her husband grew every morning she faced him over the breakfast table. She knew he had other women. She could smell them on him some nights when he came through the door, but she kept silent. Donna had despised him for so long she couldn't even remember what it had been that first attracted her to him. He'd been brash and tough, but there had been a certain charm about his swagger when they were young. That had disappeared a long time ago. Over the years he became a bully, a boorish waster, who would pull her onto his knee on a night out, telling anyone who would listen how she was his possession, that he owned every single bit of her.

Donna had somehow managed to convince him to let her take a part-time job to get her out of the house once the kids flew the nest. And that's when her life got out of control, when she met Andy, one of the head bakers. He was like a breath of fresh air, younger and so different, a gentle soul of a man. They'd become friends and some-times would sit outside with lunch while she laughed at his easy humour and placid view of the world. The first time he kissed her took her totally by surprise. She'd been drop-ping him home because his car had broken down and as she stopped outside his flat he leaned over and kissed her on the lips. That was how it started. Now her life revolved around stolen moments when Eddie was at work, or she made some excuse to be out of the house so she could meet Andy. They were behaving like star-crossed teenagers. They had sex in his car, in a field, and one time on the banks of a loch during their lunch hour. Her body ached just thinking about it. He had coaxed her to leave Eddie, and she prom-ised she would, while deep down knowing she couldn't. She just didn't have the heart to tell him.

The card in the drawer flashed into her mind. She had to face facts. Not even that could free her. What if she took it to the cops? Where would that leave her? In the witness box, sending her man to jail. And not just any man – a UVF man. She might as well take a gun and shoot herself. She closed the drawer and looked up at the kitchen clock.

The doorbell rang and Donna checked herself in the hall

mirror, fluffed up her blond-streaked hair, and opened the door.

'I brought my tools.' Andy held up a canvas bag in front of him, a broad smile on his face. 'Make it look right.'

Donna glanced furtively outside to where his white van was parked in their drive, and then stepped back into the hallway.

Andy gave a soft whistle as he looked around him.

'Nice place, Donna. Pretty damn swish.'

'Yeah. Would be great if I was here by myself.' She took the tool bag off him and placed it on the floor. 'Come on, let's sit out in the garden for a little while.'

'Are you sure it's all right, me being here?' Andy said as he followed her through the kitchen.

She poured both of them iced tea and handed one to him. She knew the risk she was taking every time they were together, and bringing him to the house when Eddie was away was beyond reckless. But she couldn't help herself.

'Sure, you're a handyman, doing a bit of work. Anyway, this whole estate is like a graveyard during the day. Everyone's either working or old and rich. You can go a whole day and never see a person. That's one of the reasons I like to get out when I can.' She paused, thinking how attractive he looked, the shaft of sunlight coming in the window making his eyes an even brighter blue. 'One of the reasons I took the job at the bakery.'

'I'm glad you did,' Andy said, running his hand over her back as they walked into the garden.

Donna felt a little shiver at his touch. They sat at the table and he reached across and took her hand.

'Donna, I wish you'd leave him.'

Donna opened her mouth to speak, but Andy went on.

'I know what you're going to say. You're too scared he'll come after us. I know.' His fingers gently touched her bruised cheekbone. 'But we can't go on like this. I know how we could do it. I've thought about it every day and night. I've got some money saved up, we could go away somewhere. Another country. France, Spain or something. I could buy into a wee baker's shop or something. That's my dream. Have my own place. But it wouldn't mean anything to me without you.'

'But Andy, how can we just up sticks and disappear? I'd love to. I wish I could. I think about it every day too.' Her eyes filled with tears. 'Do you think I want to be part of what he's made me? He treats me like a slave. Every way. Mentally, physically – sexually. I can't stand it.' She stopped. 'But you know what he is. There's no hiding place for anyone who crosses them.'

Andy squeezed her hand and they sat for a long moment in silence. Eventually, Donna spoke.

'Listen. I want to tell you something.'

She told him about the card, and about the bodies in the quarry, and how she knew Eddie must be involved.

'Andy, if anyone ever found out I was telling you this, I'd

get a bullet in the head. No questions asked. I'm promising you that. Please don't tell anyone. Christ, I can't believe I'm even telling you.'

'Have you got the card? Can I see it?' He was calm.

Donna got up and went into the kitchen. She took the card out of the drawer and handed it to him. He held it very carefully, only touching the edges.

'I didn't pay much attention to the story on the telly when I saw it, to be honest,' he said. 'Are you sure it's the same name?'

'Look.' Donna opened the paper at the page where the story said the cops had no new lines in the quarry murder. 'See for yourself.'

'And that card was in his pocket the night he came back here and told you to burn the clothes?' He shook his head, incredulous. 'Jesus. That's heavy-duty stuff, Donna.'

'I know.'

'So Eddie's obviously forgotten about the card. Or he expected you to burn it with the clothes.'

'Yeah. He would have expected that. I think he forgot it was there. I didn't notice it at first. But when I'm doing a wash I normally empty the pockets in case there's anything in them. I didn't even see the card. I actually only found it below the bed when I was hoovering the next day. Then I realised I should have burned it. I just stuck it in a drawer.'

Andy sat staring at the card on the table. 'Can you give it to me?'

'What?'

'Can I have it? Then what I want you to do is forget about it. Completely.'

'What you going to do with it? You know you can't go to the cops and tell them the truth. First thing that would happen is they'd come battering on my door. Jesus, Andy, you can't do that.' She picked up the card and looked at him. 'If you did something stupid with this, you'd be a dead man. I'm telling you.'

'Look, just give it to me and forget you ever saw it. That's all I'm saying. Trust me.'

Donna handed him the card.

The sound of the doorbell ringing woke Donna. She turned to Andy and let out a gasp.

'Shit! We must have fallen asleep.' She leapt out of bed. 'There's someone at the door.'

Andy sat up, rubbing his eyes.

'Leave it,' he whispered. 'Maybe they'll go away.'

The doorbell rang again, and Donna looked out of the window. She saw Rod Farquhar's blue Mercedes outside their house.

'Christ. That's a friend of Eddie's. It's big Farquhar.' She stumbled around the room, pulling on her skirt and bra. She drew a vest over her head. 'I'd better go down. Don't move a muscle. I'll get rid of him.'

When she opened the door, Rod Farquhar had that smug

look she detested. His eyes roved up and down her body, stripping her naked.

'You in your bed?'

Donna was conscious that he was speaking to her breasts. Creepy bastard that he was.

'No,' she said sharply. 'Course not, Rod. In the middle of the afternoon?'

'I was ringing the bell.'

'I was in the back room. I'm clearing out cupboards.'

He nodded slowly, his eyes resting on her thighs.

'Eddie's away, Rod. Did you not know? He's in Holland.'

'Aye,' he said. 'I knew he was going to the match.' He licked his lips. 'I was just passing. Thought I'd call in for a coffee.' He took a step forward onto the threshold.

'No,' Donna said quickly, feeling herself blush. 'Actually this is not a good time, Rod. I'm really busy. You know what it's like. So many things you promise yourself you'll do when you get the house to yourself,' she gushed, pushing her hands through her hair. 'So I'd best be getting on with it. I'm going to be up to my eyes all day. Eddie's home later on tonight.' She started to close the door.

Rod's face fell, his eyes suddenly cold. He scanned her bare legs and again rested on her breasts. He stepped back and glanced at Andy's white van in the driveway, but said nothing. Donna felt her insides churn.

'Right,' he said, walking away. 'I'll let you get on with your work then.'

Donna closed the door and stood with her back to it as she heard his car door close and the engine start up.

'Christ!' she whispered.

'Who was it?' Andy was on his way downstairs, buttoning his shirt and carrying his shoes.

'Some arsehole mate of Eddie's.' She felt her hands shaking. 'He was calling in for a bloody coffee. He's a creep. He's made a pass at me once or twice. If Eddie knew he'd tear his head off, but I've never mentioned it. He obviously thought he'd chance his arm because he knows Eddie's away. Pervy bastard!'

Andy took her in his arms.

'You're shaking.'

'I know. I'm so scared we'll get found out. And he had a look at your van in the driveway.'

'Did he say anything?'

'No. Nothing. But he definitely clocked it.'

Andy sat on the stairs and put his shoes on.

'Just say I was pricing a job for you or something. Don't worry.'

'I can't help it.' She hugged him. 'Don't go just now. Give it a half-hour in case he's lurking around. That's the kind of creep he is.'

Donna tried to muster a smile as she walked into the kitchen.

'Come on. We'll have a coffee before you go.'

*

As Matt crossed the border into Scotland, Rosie was glad they were only an hour from home.

'I always feel a bit misty-eyed when I leave England behind and we're back home. Makes me patriotic,' Matt said.

'Yeah, right. You'll be quoting from *Braveheart* next.'

'They can take our women! They can take our freedom, and our deep-fried Mars Bars! But they'll never take our shitey weather,' Matt declared as the downpour started.

Rosie looked at the horizontal rain sweeping across the hills beneath the heavy sky.

'Good to be back.' She sighed. 'Though I don't feel we gained a whole lot from the trip.'

'What did you expect? It was more of a recce than anything else. I'm quite happy with what I've got, pic-wise. Plus, we've got some kind of handle on who McGregor deals with.'

'Yeah. I suppose so. But still we don't know who the hell he is.'

Rosie reflected on Adrian's phone call after he had followed the man who'd exchanged bags with McGregor in Utrecht. As planned, he had managed to tail him until he arrived in Amsterdam just under an hour later. Adrian stayed with him discreetly while he parked his car in the city and met up with another man in a cafe close to the town centre. He even took the chance of sitting a couple of tables away from them. From what he could gather, the man he'd followed spoke with what he thought was a Scottish accent, but it could have been Belfast. He wasn't sure.

The other man, he said, spoke broken English, and Adrian thought he was Moroccan or Turkish. Definitely didn't look Dutch or Spanish. He watched as the man who'd been with McGregor went into the holdall and handed him a wedge of cash. They stayed in the cafe less than half an hour, then Adrian followed him again as he took a taxi to Schiphol Airport. He almost lost him as he tried to park his car, but he'd sprinted into the departures area and caught up, staying far enough behind until he saw him checking into a flight for Malaga. That was when he phoned Rosie and asked what she wanted him to do. Take the flight, she told him. She would tell McGuire when she got home. But the flight had been full, and Adrian was now on his way back to Sarajevo. At least they had a picture of the dealer, whoever he was. But it wouldn't make McGuire happy.

Rosie's mobile rang, and she recognised Liz's number.

'Hi, Liz. How you? I'm on my way back. Just crossed the border.'

'Rosie, listen. Can you talk?'

'Sure. What's up?'

'You'll never believe this but I've just had a call from Wendy.'

'What? You're kidding.'

'No. Can't fucking believe it myself! Wendy's alive, Rosie! She's alive!' Her voice went up an octave. 'I'm still shaking thinking about it.'

'Oh my God!' Rosie covered the phone with her hand and turned to Matt. 'Wendy's phoned Liz.'

'You there, Rosie?'

'Yeah. Was just telling Matt. This is amazing! What happened? Where is she?'

'She's in Spain. Costa del Sol. She's told me everything. About the rape. That bastard McGregor. He threatened to kill her if she told anyone what he did. Said he would hunt her down and make her disappear. She felt there was nothing else for it than to do a runner.'

'Christ!' Rosie said. 'But what about her parents? Jimmy? Has she been in touch with them?'

'No, not yet. Listen. She doesn't want to tell anyone. She's still scared. McGregor might be looking for her.'

Rosie thought for a moment.

'Yeah. Better if she says nothing right now. Especially to Jimmy.'

'What time will you be back in Glasgow?'

'Should be there in just over an hour. Can we meet?'

'Yes. But I'm going away. I'm going to Spain to join Wendy. Fuck it! I want out of this place after what happened to her and with McGregor sniffing around to see where she is. He's the only one who knows she's still alive.'

'I'll meet you in that coffee shop at the top of Byres Road at seven. We'll talk then.' The line went dead.

'What in Christ's name is happening, Rosie? Has Wendy really turned up?'

Rosie shook her head and puffed.

'According to Liz she has. Says she phoned her and she's in Spain. Did a runner.'

'Jesus!'

'But she doesn't want anyone to know. I'm meeting Liz at seven. She says she's going to Spain to join her.' She looked at Matt. 'That might well be useful for us.'

CHAPTER TWELVE

Liz's face lit up when Rosie walked into the cafe.

'Hi, Rosie,' she said brightly. 'What a great day this is.'

'Well, it's a right turn up for the books.' Rosie slid into the booth.

She ordered a skinny latte from the waiter, and Liz asked for the same.

'I'm still kind of numb with shock,' Liz said. 'I spoke to her again an hour ago and she's really glad I'm going out to see her.' She lowered her voice. 'I haven't told anybody, as you said. Nobody. I haven't even mentioned that I'm going to Spain. I've only just booked the flight.'

'Liz,' Rosie asked, 'how did Wendy get out of the country? The police said her passport was still in her house.'

Liz gave her a furtive look. 'I can't tell you that right now. Okay? I need to talk to her first.' She put a hand up. 'Don't ask.'

Rosie didn't like the sound of it, but she nodded in agreement.

'Okay. But good for you, Liz, getting the hell out of here for a while. Wendy will be delighted. I'm really glad she's all right.' She paused. 'But I'm still wondering why she needed to go away. I know you said she was scared of Eddie and he'd threatened her. But what about Jimmy? Was she not really keen on him?'

Liz sighed. 'Well, yeah, she is. But the thing is, Jimmy's all mixed up with this UVF crap now. She knows that, and thinks he's in too deep. She doesn't want that to be her whole life, because that's what happens when you end up with a guy like that. She hasn't said much about it, but I'm sure she'll tell me how she feels when I get there. Maybe she'll get in touch with him eventually. But not right now.'

'What about her parents? The police?'

'She's going to do all that. But not for another wee while.'

'Seems awful hard on her parents. Could she not just call them and say she's safe, without saying where she is?'

Liz thought about it for a moment, then nodded.

'Actually, you're right. I think that's only fair on them. I'll tell her to phone them. Do as you say. Just don't tell them where she is.'

They sipped their coffee. Rosie had been considering all the way back to Glasgow whether she trusted Liz enough to tell her what they were planning to do in Spain. The truth was, she didn't really have a plan yet, just a few ideas how they could bring it all to a head when they got there – if that was how the trip panned out. Bringing Liz in on it now was risky, and she didn't even know Wendy. But the two of them in Spain with so much hatred against McGregor could be useful, so she decided to test the water. She went into her bag and brought out a photograph of the man they'd seen in Utrecht with Eddie McGregor. Matt had gone to the office and run off a print when they arrived back in Glasgow.

'Liz, do you have any idea who this character is in the picture here with McGregor, Jimmy and Mitch Gillespie?'

Liz looked at it and her eyes widened.

'Oh yeah! You bet I do.' She folded her arms, looking pleased with herself.

'Really?'

'Aye. Do you not know him?'

'No,' Rosie said, hoping she'd done the right thing asking her. 'Who is he?'

Liz took the print in her hand.

'His name's Jackson.' She looked from the picture to Rosie. 'His first name's Alex, but everyone calls him Flinty. Something to do with him setting fire to people. He's from Belfast but he's one of the biggest coke dealers on the Costa del Sol. A real bastard. Don't know if he's actually UVF. I heard he was at one time, but they got rid of him. He must have done something bad if *they* got rid of him. Well, not quite rid, but they got him out of the country. He runs a pub down near Fuengirola. Scottish pub. But it's a Rangers pub, full of Scots or Northern Irish. Anyone who's a Rangers fan. Tourists go there too . . . not Celtic tourists though, obviously.' She glanced at Rosie as though she could see she was impressing her. 'But coke's his business. No doubt about that.'

'How do you know that?'

'Sure, I was there. I told you me and Wendy were in Spain for a while. We got mixed up with the coke scene.'

'Dealing?'

'No, no. Just using. You get to know who all the players are.' She waved her hand dismissively. 'But never mind all that. What I'm saying is I know who this guy is. And if big Eddie's with him then that's who's supplying him.' She frowned. 'But I'm surprised to see him in Utrecht though. I'd have thought he'd have sent someone else. Or maybe he was there for the match?'

'No,' Rosie said. 'He left after the meeting. Got a flight to Malaga.'

'Well, maybe he didn't trust anyone else. Depends on how much coke it was, I suppose – how much money was involved.' She shrugged. 'Yeah. Actually maybe the supply was coming from Holland. Amsterdam. As far as I can remember, Flinty mostly dealt with the Moroccans, but maybe sometimes the line comes from Amsterdam. He could have had to go there for some other reason. Maybe he was doing another big meeting as well, tying it all in. Paying off some dosh he owed. You can't really keep track of these guys.'

'Yeah,' Rosie agreed. 'That might explain it. What else do you know about him?'

'Only that he lives in a big villa somewhere down past Estepona. Near a port ... Let me think ... San Pedro or something like that. No ... Puerto de la Duquesa. That's where a lot of the villains live. People think the big gangsters live around Fuengirola but that's crap. The real money and gangsters are further down the coast.'

'And he's been getting away with it for years? Nobody ever catch him?'

Liz shrugged. 'Who knows? Maybe he's a grass as well?' She half smiled. 'Though I wouldn't say that to his face.'

The waiter came over but they waved him away.

'Do you think I could get anywhere near this Flinty guy? So we could blow the whole thing open?'

Liz shrugged again. 'Maybe. I don't know enough about how he operates to tell you that, if I'm honest. But I know he's got plenty of heavies around him. Goes with the territory. There are a lot of Eastern Europeans and Russian gangsters muscling in on the drugs scene down on the Costa now, so people have to protect their turf.'

Rosie nodded. 'And my next question is this: if you're in Spain, what's the chances of you and Wendy helping us?'

Liz rubbed a finger across her bottom lip.

'I had a feeling you were going to ask me that.' She puffed. 'Dangerous, Rosie. Very dangerous.'

'But in the end, we might get Eddie McGregor nailed.' Rosie hated it when she'd to do a sales job on people. But it had to be done. 'That's what you want isn't it? At the end of the day?'

Liz nodded. 'Definitely. And Wendy would want that too. But I don't know. I'll need to talk to her about the whole shooting match when I get there.' She raised her eyebrows and looked at Rosie. 'I don't want to do anything too daft though. What have you got in mind?'

'I don't know yet. I just want to know on principle if we have you and Wendy on the same side as us.'

'Of course we're on the same side. We all want that bastard to get his balls chopped off. But we don't want to get killed in the process.'

'Me neither. Listen. I'll have people helping me. I'll have a plan, but some of it will have to be improvised. I'll need someone a little close to things helping me with an inside track.' Rosie looked at her. 'What do you think?'

'I'll see.' Liz sounded noncommittal. 'I can't be sure of anything until I have a good long talk with Wendy. But if it's possible at all, then I want to help you. I'm glad you're doing this. Honest.' She got up to leave. 'I need to go now and get organised. I'll have a Spanish mobile by tomorrow so I'll phone you.'

'Thanks. I hope you'll help.'

Rosie watched as she went out of the door, then sat down again and ordered another coffee. She didn't feel like going home to her empty flat just yet.

*

Jimmy didn't go into the Tavern for a last pint when the bus dropped them off outside. The troops were in good spirits as Rangers had drawn one all with Eindhoven, and as far as they were concerned that was nearly as good as a win away from home. Roll on the Seville match, was the general roar as fans left Holland. But the bus journey home had been long, and Jimmy could see that his father looked done in.

Deep down he was also glad he'd said he would walk home with his da. He'd had enough of Eddie and Mitch, having been joined at the hip with them for the last three days. He spotted Eddie going towards a waiting black Merc when he got off the bus, and presumed he'd be dropping the gear off.

During the journey back from Utrecht and over dinner after the Rangers match, Eddie had told them a little more of how he always dealt with the guy they'd met. His name was Alex Jackson, but his nickname was Flinty – after setting fire to a guy years ago when he was over in Belfast on a UVF job. He was also known to be handy with a blowtorch, especially on anyone who had difficulty answering questions under interrogation. Flinty was the son of a notorious Belfast UVF man who had been linked with the Shankill Butchers back in the seventies; a bloodthirsty bunch who murdered and mutilated more than thirty Catholics, and whose savagery shocked even the most hardened Loyalists. Police never had enough to charge Flinty's father along with the others who were eventually convicted. The Shankill

Butchers period was one of the darkest times in UVF history. Flinty had lived on and off in Glasgow as his mother was Scottish, but he was used by the UVF for punishment beatings. The man he'd set on fire in Belfast was front page news for days, and the Belfast command summoned him over. It wasn't the fire that was the problem – just that Flinty had set fire to the wrong guy. They couldn't have him working for them again, so they gave him a way to make himself scarce but still be useful. He'd been in Spain since, on the Costa, dealing coke. The UVF knew about it but left him to it, as long as they got a kickback and could launder their money through his bar. But it had been made clear to him that he was on his own. If he got caught, they'd do nothing to help him.

Jimmy had thought he was a cold-looking bastard all right, and he didn't show much respect to himself or Mitch. He'd barely spoken to them and directed any conversation towards Eddie. He obviously thought of them as some kind of gofers, which Jimmy had to admit they probably were. But he'd made his mind up fairly quickly that he didn't like him, and Mitch had told him later when Eddie wasn't there that he didn't like him either.

Sleep wouldn't come for Jimmy as he lay in bed with his hands behind his head, staring at the ceiling. He pushed thoughts of Wendy from his mind. He couldn't go on tormenting himself with this. If only she'd get in touch to say it was over, he'd be fine. But all the time was the niggle that Eddie had done something to her. In Eindhoven he'd gone to a bar with Eddie and Mitch late into the night and they ended up in a whorehouse. Eddie thought it would be a good idea for him to get his mind off Wendy. Mitch paid for a girl and went upstairs to one of the rooms like a rat up a drainpipe, and Eddie was taken into a room at the back. Jimmy had sat at the bar as a beautiful girl sidled up to him. He bought her a drink, but when she offered herself, he simply told her not tonight. When Eddie and Mitch emerged they ribbed him big time about it. Mitch said he was turning into a poof and it was time he got himself sorted.

'I don't pay for sex,' he said quietly. 'Never have and never will.'

Eddie glared at him sarcastically.

'We all pay for it, son. One way or another. Trust me on that one.'

CHAPTER THIRTEEN

Every time Rosie's mobile rang, she cursed that it wasn't Liz. Five days had passed since she went to Spain, and nothing. Not a word. She didn't even know if she was in Spain at all – she only had Liz's word that she was going. She could be anywhere.

Rosie sat at her desk and listened to Declan Flannagan opposite her, furiously taking notes as he spoke on the phone. It sounded like another drugs call. There had been several over the last couple of days since a sudden spate of cocaine deaths. This morning's *Post* had a picture of the latest victim, a twenty-four-year-old salesman who died following a massive heart attack at a nightclub in the city. Off the record, the hospital insider had told Declan that in simple terms the guy's heart had exploded. The cocaine he'd used was either too pure or had been cut with something toxic, or both. It had caused a rapid arrhythmic heartbeat – common with cocaine users – to go completely off the scale. Declan had spoken to his parents, who had no idea their son even had a coke habit. Poor bastards. They'd been proud of how well he'd been doing in his job and had been celebrating his promotion to area manager with a champagne party. He was the third person to die in four days, and a police statement warned that there might be a bad batch of cocaine circulating.

Don had later given Rosie an inside track on the initial tests on the victims. They indicated that the levels of cocaine in the bloodstream were actually quite small, but it had been cut with something lethal which they were still investigating. Whatever it was, he'd said, it would fell a horse at fifty paces. Worse still, now that regular coke users would become wary of the supply, the bad batch would probably end up in the crack cocaine market at the lower end – opening up all sorts of horror scenarios.

Rosie's desk phone rang and Marion told her that the editor was waiting for her.

'So much for the high-flying salesman.' McGuire looked up from his screen as Rosie walked into his office. 'Flew a bit too high. Stupid bastard.'

'Yeah,' Rosie said.

She shared his lack of sympathy for anyone who used coke, and hoped the younger journalists in the office, whom she'd seen using at parties, would waken up to the dangers. But she wouldn't hold her breath.

'That was a good interview Declan did with the parents,' she added, sitting down. 'You've got to feel for them. So proud one week, then burying their boy the next. Hellish.'

'Yeah,' McGuire said. 'Good piece. He's a good lad, that Declan. I might make him the crime reporter in due course, now that we've got rid of Reynolds. You rate him, don't you, Gilmour?'

'I do,' she said. 'He's got a lot of talent. He's young, keen and making good contacts with cops and villains, without pandering to any of them. I like the boy's style. He's honest.'

'Well. Hope he stays that way, though. It can be very seductive for a youngster, hobnobbing with cops and robbers.'

'It was never very seductive for me, I have to tell you,' Rosie said flatly.

McGuire smiled then got up from his desk and sat opposite her on an armchair.

'So what's happening? Tell me something exciting. Has that mad bird Liz got in touch yet?'

'No,' Rosie sighed. 'Not yet.' She bit the inside of her jaw, doubt beginning to niggle. 'Can't understand it. Maybe the Wendy girl isn't keen and they've just shut down completely. But my gut feeling is that she'll phone. She might be taking a few days to get her bearings back over in Spain.' She crossed her fingers and held them up. 'Let's hope.'

She changed the subject. 'But tell you what, Mick, this dodgy coke that's causing the problems – it's only happened since Eddie McGregor came back from Holland with his holdall full of something. Maybe it's the stuff he brought back.'

'Yeah, but it could have been Dutch cheese in that holdall, for all we know. Or tulips from Amsterdam.' He gave her a mocking look. 'We haven't a clue what was in the bloody bag.'

'Aw, come on. You knew before we went that this was more of a watching brief. How were we going to find out what was in the bag? No way could we have done that. Look, we're not in court. But consider the circumstantials here. McGregor, a known coke dealer, goes to Utrecht to meet this Flinty character – a known coke dealer and they exchange bags. I'd be very surprised if he's home on the Rangers bus with a holdall full of tulips.'

'I'm winding you up, Gilmour.'

'I know you are. But seriously, the fact that these people are falling like flies tells me one thing – or it makes me suspect one thing. It's McGregor's coke that's killing them.'

'You might be right. But we're probably never going to know.'

Rosie's mobile rang, a number she didn't recognise flashing on the screen.

'I'd better answer this.'

'Rosie?'

'Liz! How you doing? I've been waiting for your call.' She gave McGuire a thumbs-up.

'I've been really busy. Just getting settled in and sorting some things out. I'm staying with Wendy. She's all right, but she's been in a bit of a mess over everything. She's getting better though.'

'Liz.' Rosie glanced at Mick. 'How about if I take a quick run over to see you and Wendy? I'd really like to meet the two of you and talk. What do you think?' She would have preferred to have this conversation out of McGuire's earshot, then he wouldn't have known who made the suggestion to go to Spain.

McGuire folded his arms and gave her a surprised look. Silence.

'You there, Liz?'

'Aye. I'm with Wendy just now. I was just saying to her what you said. Actually we spoke about that last night. She's okay with it. She doesn't want to make any decisions until she meets you.'

'Right,' Rosie said. 'Great. I'll get a flight tomorrow. Just tell me where and when.'

'Really?' Liz sounded surprised and a little relieved.

'Of course. No problem.' Rosie was aware that McGuire was glaring at her.

'Okay,' Liz said. 'We're staying in a place near Fuengirola.' She paused. 'I know a wee bar in the middle of town that only Spanish people go to. La Bodega. We could meet there.

When you get to Malaga, phone me and we'll make an arrangement.'

'Perfect. See you tomorrow.' She hung up.

Rosie looked at McGuire and couldn't help smiling.

'Oh, so you're making executive decisions now, Gilmour?' McGuire said sarcastically. 'You might want to try my chair out while you're at it. You could even take the morning conference.'

'Come on, Mick,' Rosie laughed, but she knew he was only half joking. 'You know what it's like. That might have been my one shot at talking to her and I had to go with the flow. And I *am* an assistant editor, in charge of investigations.'

'Yes. *Expensive* investigations.' Mick shook his head and went back behind his desk. 'Right. Get Marion to book you a flight. You'll need to take Matt, just in case.'

His phone rang and he answered it.

'Really? Fuck me!' He chuckled. 'I like the sound of that . . . Right. Get Declan to see what he can find out from the cops. I've got Rosie in here.'

'What's happening?' Rosie stood up.

'Fucking hell,' McGuire said, sitting back with his hands behind his head. 'Jamie Coleman. You know, the guy who plays the teacher in that school TV soap, *The Academy*? He was rushed to hospital after a cardiac arrest last night. He's only thirty-four.' His eyebrows knitted. 'Did you know he was a cokehead?'

'No, Mick. I don't move in celebrity circles. Doesn't surprise me though.'

'Wait. It gets better. Details are sketchy but apparently he took ill during some kind of kinky sex session with two men!' He grinned. 'Fucking love that! He's married, isn't he?'

'Jesus,' Rosie puffed. 'Yeah, he is married. Couple of years ago, remember? Married a model at a swanky reception somewhere in Perthshire. All the luvvies were there.' She paused, her mind racing. 'You never know what might come out of this, Mick, if he's got a kinky secret. He'll want to keep that quiet, so he might be worth a door knock.'

'Took the words out of my mouth, Gilmour. We have to try to get to him. See who his dealer is and if it leads anywhere. It must be that dodgy cocaine.'

'Is he out of hospital?'

'Yep. Released this morning. You'll need to move fast if you're away to Spain tomorrow.'

An hour later, Rosie was driving slowly along leafy avenues in the West End admiring the magnificent old three-storey sandstone houses as she looked for Coleman's street. In days gone by this would have been an old-money enclave, the plush homes of Glasgow merchants or shipyard owners handed down for generations, with rows of tenement flats – all identical – a couple of streets away, purpose-built as homes for thousands of workers back in the day when the city was a thriving industrial metropolis. Now the posh houses were occupied by the nouveaux riches – lawyers, drug dealers, footballers. And the workers' flats were bedsit-land where students lived on junk food and cider preaching against the bourgeoisie. But give them a few years and they'd be living it up around the corner, sending their kids to private schools just as their well-heeled parents had done with them.

Rosie's mobile rang in the passenger seat and she saw it was Don. She pulled in to the kerb to answer it.

'Hello, Don. What's happening?'

'Did you hear about Jamie Coleman?'

'Yeah. We're working on it. The editor's loving the secret double life of the soap star.'

'And how!' Don replied. 'What is it with these guys? He's married to a babe and he's out fucking around with rent boys.'

'Rent boys?' Rosie didn't think she should tell Don she was almost at Coleman's house. 'I heard it was some kinky sex game, with a couple of men, and that he had a cardiac arrest. Is he a cokehead?'

'Big time,' Don said. 'Did you not know? But it's worse than that. He's been doing crack cocaine lately.'

'No way! You're kidding. How can he do that and hold down a job?'

'He's on a couple of months' break, apparently. Told to rest. TV bosses know he's got a coke habit.'

'Christ! How do you know all that?'

'I'm a cop!' Don said a little sarcastically. 'It's my job.'

'So the cardiac arrest was cocaine-induced?'

'Crack cocaine-induced. He was doing crack. Been on a crack binge for nearly two days. His wife's abroad on a modelling assignment.'

'Jesus! Could it be this pure cocaine that's been on the go for a few days?'

'That's the thinking. He's lucky he's alive.'

'Have you spoken to him?'

'No, but my DI has. He's admitted it.'

'Wonder where he gets it.'

'Anyone can get it, if you know the right people. A guy like him will have a regular, trusted dealer. Someone discreet.'

'What about the rent boys? You talked to them?'

'Not yet. They've gone to ground.' He paused. 'Coleman didn't exactly have their addresses. Or if he has, he's not telling us.'

'So what do you think?'

'I'm sure we'll get to one of the boys. They all gossip. My guess is they brought the crack with them. But you know what's more worrying?'

'What?'

'The fact that it was crack which got Coleman. Because this means it's been shifted downmarket. Rent boys are well down the food chain. Put it this way. We've already had a few people dead, but not from crack – just from the coke. So whoever is supplying their usual customers with coke has moved this batch elsewhere to get rid of it. To the schemes, where they'll do any crap as long as it's cheap. The scumbag dealers probably had a closing down sale, punted it at a reduction just to get rid of it, and it's now used to make crack cocaine. That would be how the rent boys got hold of it – if it was theirs.'

'That's bad.'

'Yeah. But it also opens up a worse scenario. We've already got crack cocaine in the city, which is bad enough, but we're now going to have *more* casualties if this batch has been sold widely. But we don't know exactly what's in it because we haven't been able to get our hands on any. All we have are the blood results from the stiffs which only show that it was this coke which caused the heart problems.' He paused. 'What you doing later?'

'Not sure yet. Still working. I'm going out of town tomorrow on a story. But will be back in a few days.'

'Okay. I'll keep you posted.' Don hung up.

Rosie phoned McGuire's direct line and relayed what Don had said about the crack cocaine, in case he wanted her to hang fire on knocking at Coleman's door. But he still wanted to go ahead. Coleman will be in the horrors, he suggested, and a bit more pressure from the media might just push him into talking. Rosie told him she wouldn't hold her breath. The actor's agent had put out a statement saying he was suffering from exhaustion and was having complete rest. He'll probably be in the Priory by the end of the week, McGuire said. Same old shite.

She was surprised that there was no other press lurking near the house. Scotland wasn't awash with celebrities, and Coleman was a fairly big star. He'd landed the role in the soap after a movie career that didn't really take off following a part in a British film three years ago. The film had won him plaudits at home and internationally, but the predicted megastardom hadn't quite happened.

Rosie rang the bell and could hear it echo inside. No answer. She waited a few seconds then rang it again, this time pressing it three times in quick succession for a bit of urgency. She listened at the huge front door and thought she heard movement behind it.

'Who's there?' A reticent male voice.

'Jamie?' Rosie said more in hope. 'It's Rosie Gilmour. I'm from the *Post*. Sorry to disturb you—'

'I'm not giving any interviews,' he interrupted. 'My agent has put out a statement.' There was a pause. 'I'm suffering from exhaustion. I'd like to be left alone, please.'

Rosie detected a quiver in his voice. He must be rough as hell.

She persisted. 'Yes, Jamie. I understand that. But I have something specific I'd like to ask you. Could you possibly open the door, please?'

'What do you mean?'

'Regarding the substance you were using, Jamie. The cocaine.' She stopped, glanced around her, then spoke into the corner of the door, lowering her voice. 'The crack cocaine.' Rosie waited but he said nothing. 'Look, Jamie, I don't want to be saying this on the doorstep. Could you please just open the door? Hear me out?'

'Have you got a photographer?'

'No. I'm on my own.'

'Are you bullshitting?'

'No. Absolutely not. I'm on my own. I promise.'

Rosie's stomach flipped as she heard the lock being turned and the handle of the door rotating. Showtime. He opened the door slowly and there he was. He stood in his red striped pyjamas and pale blue towelling dressing gown, his face damp with sweat and his hands shaking like a leaf as he tightened his robe across his body. His fingers trembled as he tried to tie a knot in the belt, then gave up. Dark shadows beneath his eyes gave his soft complexion a sickly pallor. Rosie had seen healthier corpses. He was wrecked. Totally out of the game. His bottom lip trembled.

'Come in.' He stepped back. 'But this isn't an interview.'

'Okay.' Rosie raised a hand reassuringly. 'Just a chat. If you decide you want to give an interview, we can talk about that.'

'So?' He swallowed, tongue darting out to moisten his dry lips.

Rosie glanced quickly around the massive hallway and

up at the high ceiling, painted with some kind of tasteless, garish variation on the Sistine Chapel. You'd probably need drugs to appreciate it, she thought. A massive darkwood staircase with a crimson carpet wound its way up two levels. Hanging on the wall was a huge framed print of Jamie with his arm slung around the shoulder of a grinning George Clooney on the set of the film that he'd hoped would take him to Hollywood. Rosie took a deep breath. She'd better make this a good pitch.

'Jamie,' she began. 'Look, I might as well be honest with you. We have some very good inside information that you were on a crack cocaine binge . . . which ended with you in hospital last night.'

He flinched, opening his mouth to speak, but his lip shuddered. He looked at the floor then at Rosie.

'I know you must be feeling awful,' she went on quickly. 'But I also know that you're lucky to be alive. Very lucky.' She waited, seeing his eyes fill with tears.

'I know.' He shook his head, shifted on his feet.

'I want to talk to you, not so much about who you were with.' Rosie returned the shocked glance in his bloodshot eyes. 'I know about that too. But that's not the issue. The issue here is the crack cocaine. Did you know that there's a batch of cocaine in circulation at the moment and it's suspected to have caused the deaths of four people so far?'

He nodded. 'The hospital mentioned . . .' His voice trailed off as he wiped a tear from his cheek.

'Well,' Rosie continued. 'Looks like that may have been what you took.' She paused long enough for him to answer, and when he didn't she went on. 'More people are going to die, Jamie, unless the cops can find out who is supplying this crap.' There was no response. 'Did you get it from your usual dealer?'

Silence.

'I know you'll have a dealer. You've got a coke habit and you're a celebrity, so you'll not be buying it from some guy at the Barras.'

Silence.

'Did you get it from your usual dealer, Jamie?'

He pressed his fingers to his lips to stop them quivering and shook his head.

Rosie waited. She couldn't believe she was getting away with this. She was taking advantage of him in a vulnerable state. But it was a means to an end.

'One of the lads brought it.' His voice was barely audible.

'One of the lads?'

He nodded. 'The boys. I've used them before. I know one of them quite well.'

Rosie nodded slowly.

'I don't know where he got it. I've no idea.'

'Can you give me a number for the boy?'

Jamie ran his hand through his thick blond hair and looked away.

'It's important, Jamie. He'll never know it came from you. But it's important we can get to him.' She paused. 'Honestly. Whoever is dealing this shit has to stop. People are dying. As I said. You're very lucky.'

He looked at the floor then up at Rosie as tears ran down his face.

'You're not going to print any of this?'

'No,' Rosie assured him, knowing she was winning. 'Absolutely not. But if at some stage in the future you want to give an interview, talk about your life, how all this happened, then I'll be there if you want that. But right now, Jamie, I won't write anything.'

'Do you promise? What if your editor says write it?'

'He won't, Jamie. None of this will go in the paper.'

Jamie turned and walked into the front room and returned with a mobile phone. His hands were shaking so much he had trouble holding it as he scrolled through the numbers.

'Here it is.' He handed Rosie the phone. 'His name's Paul.'

She quickly wrote it down, checked it again, then keyed it into her mobile.

'Look, I need to go now. I feel sick.' He went towards the door and turned the lock.

'Of course.' Rosie backed away. She stretched out her hand and shook his clammy cold palm. 'Thanks for your help, Jamie. You've done the right thing. Good to meet you. Sorry it's in such difficult circumstances.' She gave him a sympathetic look as she turned back on the threshold. 'Listen. I hope things work out and you can get yourself sorted. I really hope you come back.'

She heard him sniffing as he closed the door behind her.

CHAPTER FOURTEEN

In the bar, Jimmy studied Eddie's expression as the nine o'clock news led with the police probe of the deaths of four people, believed to be from a rogue batch of cocaine. The newsreader said there had also been two more deaths in Amsterdam in the last twenty-four hours. The rogue cocaine might have come from a batch brought in from Amsterdam, either through London or Manchester, before ending up in Glasgow. Eddie was poker-faced. Jimmy glanced at Mitch, recalling their earlier conversation about the deaths, before Eddie had come into the Tavern.

Eddie lifted his pint. 'Let's go for a seat, boys.' He walked towards a table in the corner.

Jimmy and Mitch followed him and sat down.

'Listen.' McGregor folded his arms on the table. 'That's causing me all sorts of fucking shit.' He jerked his head towards the wall-mounted television where the story was still running.

Jimmy and Mitch said nothing.

Eddie sniffed.

'That's our coke.'

Jimmy flicked a glimpse at Mitch. *Our* coke, he thought. He didn't like it being put like that, but he had to admit to himself there was no getting away from it. He was part of it, because he was there. He was well aware what they were doing in Utrecht and he knew what they'd brought back into the country. He might not have touched it, but he was part of the smuggling operation. He'd no problem with that. He just didn't know it was going to kill people. He had already voiced these concerns to Mitch, who told him to forget about it and warned that it wouldn't be smart to bleat about it to Eddie.

'What happened, boss?' Mitch ventured.

'Fucked if I know,' Eddie sighed. 'But I'm fucking raging. It's causing me a fucking nightmare. I moved the stuff on, in the normal way, the minute I got home from Holland. And now my dealers are coming back to me going fucking mental. After the first two punters died, they couldn't shift a fucking line of the stuff. All their usual customers were flapping.' He shook his head. 'So I told them to cut their losses and shift it to the housing schemes. The junkies up in places like Possil and Shettleston will use it. They'll snort anything, inject any fucking thing, make crack with it – as long as it's cheap.' He lit a cigarette and took a long draw. 'At least I got my money. There was no problem there. I got paid up front as soon as I moved it when I brought it in. But the dealers are well pissed off, because they had to sell it for a fraction of what they'd normally get.' He smirked. 'The fucking junkies up in Easterhouse think they've been at the sales because they've got the gear so cheap.'

Mitch half smiled in agreement, but Jimmy shifted around in his chair. He lifted his pint, then put it back down again.

'But will more people not die, Eddie, if the shit coke is now getting spread around? More punters taking it?'

Eddie gave him a look somewhere between a scowl and surprise.

'What the fuck do I care? Not my problem, mate.'

Nobody spoke, and Jimmy gave a shrug, hoping he looked as though he agreed.

'I'll tell you what *is* my problem though,' Eddie said. 'The dealers I moved the stuff to might be looking for a wee kickback, a bit of a reduction, on the next stuff we bring in after the Seville match.' He shook his head. 'But they're not fucking on.'

'The news says there were two dead in Amsterdam, Eddie,' Mitch said. 'What about Flinty? I suppose he didn't know about the stuff?'

'I've spoken to him all right,' Eddie nodded. 'Put a rocket up his arse this morning once it looked like it was our coke. He's raging as well. He normally deals with Moroccans down in Algeciras. But the guy he'd dealt with this time in Amsterdam is some Turkish fucker who he doesn't know so well. He was put onto him by another mate on the Costa. Flinty was coming to Amsterdam anyway to see one of his associates, so he arranged to pick up our coke from this Turk. I don't even know if the Turk knew about the strength of the stuff, or exactly what it was cut with. But if he didn't, he should have. And if he did, then he's a cunt for shifting it on to us. Flinty says he's dealing with it.'

'I'm glad I never took any,' Mitch said, with a cheeky grin.

'I'll fucking bet you are.'

Eddie looked up as big Rod Farquhar came into the bar and made a gesture to him as though he was drinking a pint. Eddie gave him a thumbs-up.

'I'm away to see Rod,' he said. 'Big bastard owes me a drink.'

Jimmy watched as Eddie slapped Rod on the back when he got to the bar and the two of them stood with their backs to them.

'It's not right, that,' Jimmy said, looking at Mitch. 'All them people dying. It doesn't feel right.'

Mitch sighed. 'Not our fault, mate, so fucking forget about it. We didn't force them to take the charlie.'

'No,' Jimmy frowned at him. 'But they're dead because we brought the stuff into the country.'

Mitch looked at him in disbelief.

'Fuck's sake, Jimmy. Are you Mother Fucking Teresa? What the fuck you want us to do about it? Phone the polis?

Forget about it.' He handed him a cigarette. 'Eddie's right. We got our money, and that's all that matters. Come on. I'll kick your arse at pool.'

They stood up and went to the pool table, close to where Eddie and Rod were standing at the bar. As Jimmy set the balls up, he looked across and noticed that Eddie's face was suddenly like thunder, and he didn't appear to be listening to Rod any more. He watched as Eddie knocked back another whisky then slammed the glass on the bar.

'Right. I'm off home,' Eddie said.

He marched past Jimmy and Mitch without a word or a nod in their direction.

'Fuck's wrong with him suddenly?' Jimmy said.

'Don't know. He was all right earlier on.'

Big Rod sat up on a bar stool, swivelling around so he could watch them play pool.

Donna glanced up at the kitchen clock as she heard the front door close. It was just after half ten. Eddie was early. He never usually left the pub until at least closing time. She pulled her bathrobe around her naked body, feeling a little irritated that he'd arrived home before she watched the end of the film.

'You're early,' she said as he walked into the kitchen.

She could see by the look of him he was drunk. And he didn't look happy. Her stomach knotted. She'd have to humour him.

'Want a cup of tea, Eddie? You hungry?'

'Nope.'

He went into the fridge and took out a bottle of beer. He opened it and slung the bottle opener across the granite worktop, then took a swig and belched as he stood staring at her.

'What?' Donna said flatly.

He shrugged and said nothing.

'You not want something to eat?'

'I said no. You deaf?'

'No. I'm not deaf, Eddie.' She gave him a sarcastic look. 'I'm just surprised to see you home so early and thought you might be hungry.'

She turned away from him and walked into the living room, feeling his eyes burning her back.

'Like having the place to yourself, do you?' he said as she sat on the sofa. 'Like doing your own thing?'

Donna decided it was best not to answer. He'd obviously been drinking whisky. It always made him like this. He was an obnoxious bastard without it, but when he drank whisky it was like throwing a switch. He could cause a row in an empty house. Most of the hidings she'd got from him had happened after he'd been tanked up on the stuff. Best to ignore him, she thought, as she pressed the remote control, bringing up the film she wanted to watch. She hoped he would go to bed.

'So what's happening?' He came into the living room and threw himself down onto his armchair.

'What?'

'What's happening? What you been up to?'

Donna felt her mouth go dry. She glanced at him, then at the television.

'What you talking about? You've only been away for about three hours. What do you think I've been up to? I just had a bath and was just settling into a film. I thought you'd have been in at your usual time.'

'Aye,' he said, kicking off his shoes. 'As long as I keep to my usual time.'

Donna didn't like where this was going. She couldn't understand it. He was fine when he went out. He'd been on good form for the last few days, took her to dinner when they came back from Holland. He'd even bought her perfume on the boat. She'd played the game with him quite well over the last week and she didn't want to get into a fight. She thought about Andy, and how much she missed being with him. The last time they'd been together was when Eddie was away for those few days at the Rangers game. It was the first time she'd actually been with him in a bed for the afternoon, falling asleep in his arms. It had felt so tender and natural, she had longed for it every moment since. Only a few more days, then Eddie would be off to Seville.

'You're not listening to me.'

'I'm trying to watch a film, Eddie. God's sake!'

'Did you go out much when I was in Holland?'

Donna looked at him.

'What? You know I didn't go out at all. I was here all the time. I spoke to you every night. What you asking that for?'

'Just wondered. Did you not do much then?'

'No.' Donna turned towards the television. 'Now I'm wanting to watch this film, Eddie.'

They sat in tense silence, Donna feeling Eddie's glare on her. She shifted around on the couch, shoving her feet up on the coffee table. Her robe fell open a little and she pulled it across to cover her breasts.

'You're making me horny,' Eddie said. 'Seeing you like that. Just out of the bath.'

He stood up and came towards the couch and sat down close to her. He brushed his hand up her calf. She kept her eyes on the film. He pushed her robe open, exposing her legs, and ran his hand up them, caressing the skin gently. She looked at him for a second and looked away. He moved his hand up her thighs, pushing them open a little until she could feel his fingers between her legs. He opened his trousers and took her hand, pushing it into his underpants where he was already hard. He knelt up on the sofa and eased his trousers down.

'Turn around,' he said, breathing hard.

CHAPTER FIFTEEN

The little tapas bar was tucked well off the usual tourist trail of English bars and restaurants in Fuengirola, and by the time Rosie found it, she was exhausted from walking in the blistering heat. It was mid-afternoon, and only a couple of old men were sitting at one of the tables outside in the shaded cobbled side street. Most of the Spanish were sensibly having a siesta. Rosie had decided it would be best to meet the women on her own and had left Matt happily sunning himself at the poolside, chatting up a Swedish girl. He'd just sent her a text asking if it was all right if he went to dinner with the lady. She had to laugh at his opportunism.

Liz saw Rosie as she walked into the deserted bar, and waved her over to the corner.

'Better in here with the air con,' she said, smiling. 'It's out of the way too.'

'Good move.' Rosie glanced around the bar, then put her hand out towards Wendy, who looked up nervously.

'Hi, Wendy. Thanks for seeing me.' She sighed, sitting down. 'I'm really sorry for what happened to you. What an ordeal. And now, uprooting your whole life because of a man like that. Awful.'

Wendy nodded and swallowed. 'Thanks. Nice to meet you,' she said, shaking her hand self-consciously.

Rosie rubbed her forehead, knowing that just about everything she asked her would seem inappropriate to a girl who'd been raped and threatened.

'Look. I know it might seem stupid asking you how you're doing,' she gave her a sympathetic look, 'but how *are* you coping?'

'Not bad,' Wendy said, clearing her throat. 'It's a bit better now that Liz is here.' She looked beyond Rosie, then down at her hand, picking at her gnawed fingernails. 'But the first couple of weeks . . . Hard to explain really. I . . . I was just living from day to day. In the very beginning when I did the runner, it was hour by hour. Totally wrecked.'

They sat for a moment in silence. A waiter came over and Rosie ordered a mineral water, as did Wendy. She was surprised that Liz did too. The remains of the drink in front of her also looked like water, so at least they were sober. Rosie hadn't really known what to expect when she got to Spain, but she'd hoped she wouldn't find them three sheets to the wind. If they were going to help her, she needed them with their wits about them. But right now, she wasn't in a position to make demands. She felt sorry for Wendy. She seemed very different to her brash pal – softer. The large brown eyes on her lean face made her look vulnerable, almost waif-like, and younger than her twenty-two years. Her hair pulled back in a clasp emphasised sharp, high cheekbones.

Rosie took a deep breath.

'Wendy. I know this is difficult for you. But do you want to talk about it . . . About the night it happened? The rape?'

Wendy looked at Liz, who said, 'I told you she'd want to ask you about it. It's up to you.'

'Are you going to be writing this though?' Wendy asked. 'I don't want anything in the papers. I can't do that.'

'No, no,' Rosie reassured her. 'Not at all. I wouldn't be able to do that legally anyway, because McGregor is out there roaming the streets, and totally scot-free. So, unfortunately, in the eyes of the law, he's innocent.'

Wendy snorted her disdain.

'Aye. Innocent. That'll be right.' She fiddled nervously with a chain around her neck as the waiter brought the drinks to the table. 'Right. I'll tell you what happened. But it's just for your information. Right?'

'Of course,' Rosie said. 'Liz has told me a bit anyway. Well . . . that you all went back for a drink and then he drove the two of you home.'

'That's right,' Wendy said. 'Then he was dropping me off at my mum's.' She looked at Liz for reassurance. 'Will I just . . . er . . . say what happened?'

Liz nodded.

'Okay. When we left Liz's place, he should have gone down the street and turned left into the main road. But that's not what he did. I admit I had a couple of drinks in me, and I was looking through his music, so I didn't notice he had gone right. There's this place where shops are boarded up and some offices disused now, and there's never anyone around there. I asked him where he was going and he didn't answer. He just kept driving. He'd been a laugh earlier on, but he looked angry, tense. Then he drove into this dark car park and stopped the car.' Wendy swallowed. 'I knew . . . I knew straight away what was going to happen and I was panicking, but I didn't want to make him mad.' She stopped and looked at Liz, who gave her arm a supporting squeeze.

'I know this is hard for you,' Rosie said. 'Just take your time.'

Wendy continued. 'He said that he saw me and Jimmy having a snog outside the pub when I finished my shift. He said it made him horny. Then he put his hand on my thigh and touched my breasts. I said to him to stop because I wasn't interested. But he was turned towards me and leaning over me trying to kiss me. I tried to push him away and said I didn't want to and that I was going out with Jimmy and I really liked him. But he wouldn't listen. He said to me that he was Jimmy's boss and that he wouldn't mind me giving the boss one. Then . . . Then . . .' Her voice trailed off and her eyes filled with tears. 'Then he was on top of me and pushed the seat back so I was lying under him. He pinned my hands above my head and held my wrists tight with one hand as he undid my trousers and pulled them down. I was crying at that point . . .' She sniffed. 'He told me to shut the fuck up or he'd really hurt me. So . . . so . . .' She wiped her tears. 'So I just lay there and let him do it. I couldn't stop him. I was terrified.'

'What a bastard,' Rosie said, shaking her head. 'And to think he's still out there. He'll keep doing that, you know. People like him don't stop.'

Wendy nodded, wiping her tears. 'I keep telling myself I should have stayed and gone to the police. But after he did it, he sat for a few seconds before he drove me home, and he told me that if I mentioned this to anyone he would make me disappear. He said he could do that. He said that I wanted it anyway because I didn't even fight him. But that's a lie. I was too frightened, I thought he was going to kill me.'

'He's a monster,' Liz said, putting her arm around Wendy's shoulder. 'He'll get his day, Wendy. Don't you worry, pal.'

Wendy swallowed. 'Then when he dropped me outside the house, he grabbed my arm and said to me did I know who he was and just how powerful he was. I nodded to him. And he said again, if you do anything about this you're dead meat. He said he would put a bullet in me, and he might even put one in Jimmy as well just for badness. Or my ma.' She took a tissue out of her bag and dabbed at her nose.

'You must have been distraught, Wendy.'

'I was. I didn't even know what I was doing. As soon as I got into the house, I went straight into the shower and scrubbed myself red raw. I felt filthy. Then I came out and couldn't stop crying. I didn't know what to do. I put some clothes on, but I was shivering. I phoned Jimmy and started sobbing to him, but when I heard him saying he'd be over and that he'd kill Eddie, I knew he would get killed himself. Before I knew where I was, I was in the back of a taxi and heading for Glasgow airport. I sat there all night and when things opened in the morning I booked a flight to Malaga. All I had with me was the clothes I stood up in.' She looked at Liz. 'And I've been here since. Luckily, I'd been saving money up in my house and I had about five hundred quid below my mattress, so I didn't take my bank card.'

Rosie looked at her. 'Or your passport,' she said, looking at both of them.

Wendy glanced at Liz, who raised her eyebrows and coughed.

'Just tell her, Wendy. You might as well tell everything.'

'I used a false passport,' Wendy said. 'False name on it.'

'You used a fake?' Rosie asked.

'Yeah,' she said, a little sheepish. 'I've had it for a few years.'

'We've both got one,' Liz said.

Rosie puffed, taken aback. 'What are you, a couple of gangsters?' she joked, hoping it was the right thing to say.

She was glad when Wendy and Liz giggled like errant teenagers.

'Long story,' Liz said. 'That's for another time. But basically, we got ourselves in a bit of bother over here and needed to move fast. Fake passports are easy to get.'

'I see,' Rosie nodded, but didn't much like what she was hearing. She could imagine McGuire when she told him. But part of her was quite taken by their chutzpah. It took balls to turn up at an airport with a fake passport.

'I'll buy you dinner when I come over again in a week or so and you can tell me all about it.' She paused. 'So. The big question is, girls, are you prepared to help me a little while we nail this bastard McGregor to the floor?'

Wendy looked at Liz, and after a moment they both nodded.

'Yeah,' she said. 'Aren't we, Liz?'

'You bet we are. But we need to talk about it and get a bit more on what's going on. Plus, we need to know that there are guarantees for our safety.'

Rosie finished her drink and put the glass on the table.

'I'd be lying to you if I said it was without its dangers. Right now, we're not sure how this is going to pan out. But as far as you two are concerned, then I'd just want you to keep your eyes and ears open for me. Maybe watch Flinty Jackson's place in the next few days. See if you can pick any knowledge up discreetly.'

'Okay,' they both said.

'But before you go,' Rosie said, 'I need to ask you something, Wendy. You must have been tempted to get in touch with your parents. And Jimmy?'

'I was,' Wendy said. 'I am. I'm dying to get in touch with them, because I saw the appeal in the *Post*. But I've just stayed lying low until I at least get my head together. I'm kind of getting there now, thanks to Liz. So I will do something soon.'

Rosie took a deep breath and let it out slowly.

'To be honest, I think it's better not to say anything right now. Let's wait until we get this investigation under way. Until after the Rangers fans come to Spain for the match.'

She stood up and took money out of her bag and left it on the table, looking at her watch.

'I've got to see a contact down here now. I'll be in touch in the next few days, once I get to Seville.' Rosie turned and left the bar.

'So you leave me bleeding to death and now you come back here looking for my help?'

Rosie was smiling before she turned around. The voice, perfect English and full of the usual Spanish indignation, could only belong to one person.

'Javier!'

He came towards her, grinning broadly.

'You got a fucking nerve, woman.' He kissed her on the lips then wrapped his arms around her, hugging her tight.

'You've no idea how worried I was,' Rosie said, her face

pressed against his neck. 'Honest. I cried all the way home on the flight.'

Javier released her and gave her a sarcastic look.

'Oh, yeah, sure. That's why you bombarded me with visits in the past few months. Phone calls about my welfare.' He put his arm around her shoulder as they walked outside of the hotel. 'Come on. Let's go.'

'I was in Kosovo, Javier. Up to my eyes in all sorts of shit, then just back from Belgrade a few weeks ago,' Rosie blurted, even though she knew he was winding her up.

'I know. I saw the paper. Don't you ever get tired fucking people up all over the world?' He frowned. 'They're gonna get you one of these days. You know that, don't you?'

'That's why I need your help.' Rosie gave him a playful dig. 'They won't get me when you're here.'

'Fuck they won't,' he snorted. 'They nearly did the last time. Bastards got me instead.'

He stopped next to a car and pressed a set of keys, clicking the alarm off.

Rosie looked up at his face, a little thinner than when they'd last worked together here a few months ago, but still a handsome bastard, and he knew it.

'You saved my life, Javier.' Just saying it brought a flashback of the night in Fuengirola when he took a bullet as they tried to escape the Russian gangsters. She was surprised at how choked she felt. 'I'll honestly never be able to thank you enough. No bullshit.' He hugged her again and they stayed like that for a moment.

'It was a scary time, Rosie,' he said, his face serious. 'The whole trip. When I think back, I'm surprised sometimes we made it out alive – what with Morocco and all that shit.'

'Me too.' She stepped back. Enough of the sentimentality. She looked at his car. 'Nice wheels. New?'

'New to me.' Ever the gentleman, he opened the door for her. 'Your paper paid for it.' He grinned as he went around and got in the other side.

'Oh, the insurance,' Rosie said as she sat in the passenger seat. 'Hope they didn't skimp on you.'

'No fucking way. I wouldn't have let them. They paid me decent compensation, I'll give them that. Wounded in the line of duty. Should have got a medal – and that's just for working with you,' he chuckled. 'But they took care of my hospital bills and compensated me while I wasn't able to work.'

He drove out of the street and down towards the seafront – a mile-long stretch of high-rise hotels and English pie and mash bars serving everything but Spanish food.

'Are you okay now, Javier?' Rosie said, touching his arm. 'Seriously.'

'I was.' He gave her a sideways glance. 'Until Rosie Gilmour got into town.'

'I've got a lot to tell you,' Rosie laughed, rolling down her window to relish the setting sun twinkling on the water.

'Good. You can tell me over a very expensive dinner then. I'm taking you to my favourite restaurant and you're paying.'

'I'll be glad to,' Rosie said, and meant it.

After dinner they sat on the terrace with coffee and brandies and Rosie watched as Javier gazed out at the yachts moored in the harbour. He had listened while she went through chapter and verse of the investigation so far, constantly interrupting her, as he always did, to point out the various pitfalls. As she expected, he was already ahead of the game. She had sent him a photograph of Flinty Jackson last week after she'd called to give him the bare bones of the investigation, and to ask him to come on board.

'I've seen this *coño*,' he said. 'I had a look at him a few days ago, and I talked to a couple of trustworthy Brit friends I have out here. People in the know. Not some of the pricks you see around here in bars who think they are hardmen, I mean real gangsters.'

Rosie decided not to argue with him. This was Javier. If he wasn't running the show, then the show wasn't running. Or at least he had to believe that. They'd clashed many times before because his strident ways brought out the fire in her, and for some reason she brought it out in him. One time, after a blazing row during an investigation, she'd left Spain without even saying goodbye. But things had changed last year when she'd come down to the Costa del Sol in search of the missing toddler, and all of them had been too close to death to be concerned about egos. She loved working with him, but she knew the next few weeks would be challenging.

'So, overall, Javier. What do you think?' She put her hand up. 'I want to nail this guy to the floor before they leave Spain.'

He nodded slowly, then half smiled.

'Of course you do. You're Rosie Gilmour. I know you like to kick doors in.' He handed her a cigarette and flicked the lighter under it.

'You know what I mean. Ideally, we get them here, with the drugs, red-handed. Plus . . . don't forget the kind of monster McGregor is. He raped that girl. He's probably raped more girls and threatened them the way he threatened Wendy.'

'Rosie,' Javier leaned forward and squeezed her arm, 'I'm on your side. Of course I am. For the rape of a young girl alone, I'd cut his *cojones* off. But these people are UVF. You know the risks. They don't take prisoners.'

'I know that.'

'And if they are connected to people here, like that Flinty *coño*, then it will make this tough. I don't want us to end up at the bottom of the ocean with a UVF brick tied around our necks.'

Rosie nodded. 'Me neither. Adrian will be here too.'

Javier pursed his lips and puffed.

'Jesus! Much as I like your big Bosnian boyfriend, he is one crazy *bastardo*. I still can't believe he actually threw that paedo *coño* down the well in Morocco.'

They both laughed, remembering how justice was meted out to the murdering paedophile who had used children for snuff porn films.

'I know. But he got what he deserved.'

'Yes. But we were in the middle of nowhere. Here on the Costa del Sol, there are more gangsters than sun loungers. And many dealing drugs, coke especially. You put the heat on one, it affects them all. We need to be careful. We need to think this through.' He took a long drag of his cigarette and let it out slowly. 'Maybe we should get the cops involved here.'

Rosie put a hand up. Javier was a former detective with the Guardia Civil, but she wanted him thinking as a journalist, not as a cop.

'I don't fancy that, Javier. Spanish cops? They'll not let us anywhere near it. I want to be close if they are getting busted. Cops won't let us do that.'

'We'll see. Let me think.' He wagged a finger. 'And before you say anything, of course I won't make a move on the cops until we speak about it and decide. Anyway, changing the subject. What time is your flight tomorrow?'

'Late afternoon.'

He drained his glass and stood up.

'Good. No need to rush back to your hotel. Come on. I'll

take you to a very nice bar and buy you a drink. You can tell me about Kosovo.'

Rosie finished her brandy and got to her feet, glad Javier was up for the job, but slightly annoyed that she found herself traipsing behind him like the hired help.

CHAPTER SIXTEEN

Predictably, McGuire was less than impressed by the fake passport story when Rosie gave him the lowdown on her return from Spain. She had to keep a firm grip on them, he stressed. But for the moment he was more interested in putting the squeeze on the rent boy who supplied the crack cocaine to Jamie Coleman. Do whatever you have to do, he told her, but the *Post* wouldn't be paying him one brown penny for his information.

The telephone conversation between Rosie and the rent boy had been brief, and she was a little surprised that her bluff had worked. She told him she knew all the details of what he did for a living, and a lot more about the dangerous coke he was pushing. Either he met her or she would pass the lot to the cops and he'd be in the pokey before nightfall. But she wasn't that confident that he'd turn up for the meeting, as arranged, at the Clydeside.

She stood watching the Broomielaw traffic, her eyes

peeled for the red Ford Fiesta he said he'd be driving. Matt was positioned around fifty yards away in a doorway on the edge of the River Clyde for a snatch pic. He would need to wing it, Rosie told him. She'd no idea if the boy would even get out of his car. After a few minutes, a red Fiesta came towards her and slowed down. She inclined her head a little so she could get a look at his face behind the sun visor, and he seemed to nod in her direction. The car pulled in just a few yards up the road. Rosie walked to it, and the passenger window slid down as she approached.

'Paul?' she said, looking in.

'You Rosie?' He barely looked at her.

'Yeah. Want to come out and we can have a seat over here at the water?'

She didn't want to get into the car.

He didn't reply, but opened the door and got out. A stick-thin figure in faded tight jeans and a pair of black and white baseball boots, he looked like a reject from a boy band. He tossed a foppish blond fringe away from his eyes as he came towards her with a stride that could only be described as defiant.

'Right. What the fuck's this all about?' He stood squarely in front of Rosie.

She looked straight at him, and for around eight seconds she didn't speak, just stared him out. It worked. He shifted his feet and looked away from her.

'Do you want to have a wee seat over here?' she said,

calmly, turning her back on him and going towards the wooden benches.

Her gut instinct told her he would follow. He might have thought he was Marlon Brando with his skintight T-shirt and fag packet stuffed under the bicep, but she could see he was a kid, or he had been, before the cesspool he swam in now had all but swallowed him up. He still had the big blue eyes of a sweet little boy who at one time would have stared innocently out of a school photograph. Now his eyes were hard and intense on a skinny face with the razor-sharp cheekbones of someone who has long since lost the urge to eat. He was a cokehead all right, and Rosie figured he'd just had a line, hence the big-shot exterior. But inside he'd be shitting himself.

Rosie sat down and he sat beside her on the bench, facing the river.

'So, Paul,' she began. 'I want to talk to you about your dealer. Where you got the crack cocaine that you took to Jamie Coleman's house.'

'Did Jamie tell you that?' He stared straight ahead.

'Jamie's in the Priory. Went in two days ago. He's wrecked. But at least he's alive.' Rosie turned her body towards him, crossing her legs. 'That stuff you gave him nearly exploded his heart.'

Silence.

'Did he tell you I gave him it?'

'Paul. Wake up. Guys in your line of work talk like budgies. You must know that. I'm surprised nobody's dobbed you in to the cops yet.'

Silence. Paul stared at the murky water, his eyes unblinking. She saw his Adam's apple slide up and down in his scrawny throat as he swallowed.

'Nobody can prove anything.'

'Not yet,' Rosie said.

Silence.

'What do you want?' he said, glancing from the corner of his eye.

'It's quite straightforward, Paul. I don't care what you do or who you do it with. That's your business. I'm not writing about you or Jamie.' She paused. 'I want the name of your dealer. I'm working on a specific investigation.'

'What do you mean?'

'You don't need to know what I mean. Who did you buy the crack cocaine off?'

He folded his arms and his mouth tightened.

'Are you paying me money? If you pay me money, I can tell you stories that would make your toes curl. And not just about Jamie Coleman. Plenty of people. Celebrities, lawyers, judges even.' He gave her a sideways glance and smirked.

'No. I'm not paying,' Rosie snapped. 'Let me tell you something, son. You've been paid. You'll get paid again. You'll make enough money to buy as much coke and crack as you need. Until one day, some bastard punts *you* dodgy stuff and

that'll be your last line. Like the four guys already dead with
that shit you're passing around.'

There was a little tremor on his bottom lip.

'I'm not passing it around. Fuck's sake! I didn't fucking
know.'

'Well how come you're not dead from taking it?'

'Because I didn't take it. I don't take crack. I just sometimes move it on.'

'So you trying to tell me you didn't take coke that day
with Jamie?'

'No. Fuck's sake! I didn't take it, because there wasn't
even fucking time to take it, even if I wanted to. I'd already
had a few lines of coke at my mate's house before we came,
then at Jamie's we got some champagne and then . . . we
got . . . well . . . you know . . . He was paying us to be with
him. So we were getting down to business. Doing a game.
He wanted crack. I told him I just got this stuff. He insisted
we used it. He had none in the house. He was smoking it.
But in about five minutes, he just collapsed.' He turned to
Rosie and his face suddenly looked wizened. 'I didn't fucking know, right? I'm telling you the truth.'

'What did you do with the stuff?'

'What do you think? My mate flushed it down the toilet.
Then we phoned an ambulance and fucked off.'

'Fucked off and left him dying.'

Silence.

'So, Paul. Let's not mess about here. If the cops get hold

of you, this is all over. Tell me your dealer's name. That's all. The cops will only be interested higher up the chain.'

'Will you tell the cops about me?'

'No. Cops aren't interested in you. They're not even really interested in who you bought the stuff off. It's who your dealer bought the stuff from. It's who brought this deadly shit into the country that the cops are after. That's what I want to know.'

'But I don't know that.'

'What *do* you know?'

'I just know that my dealer gets his stuff from someone bigger. I don't know who it is but he's one of the big boys. I heard he's UDA or something. UVF. Fuck. I don't know. I don't ask. And if I did know, I wouldn't go throwing these guys' names around.'

'UDA? UVF?'

'I don't know.'

'But who do you deal with, Paul? Just a name. That's all.'

He pulled a cigarette out of his sleeve and lit one, leaning forward with his elbows on his knees.

'His name's Wilson. Tam Wilson. He's from Govan. That's all I know.'

He shifted around, his leg shaking like a piston. Rosie could see he was itching for another hit.

'Look, I need to go. I've got to work. I don't know any more.'

'Sure,' Rosie said. 'Thanks.'

He stood up.

'You'll not write anything I said, will you?'

'No.' She looked up at him. 'I hope I never have to write about you. I feel sorry for you, son. You've wasted your life.'

He looked down at her, his eyes suddenly moist and his mouth hardened as though he was biting back tears.

'Hard to waste something that was already fucking wasted.'

Before Rosie got a chance to speak, he turned away from her and went towards his car. The swagger had gone from his stride.

Donna lay with her head resting on Andy's naked chest. She could hear his heartbeat – calm and steady as he stroked her hair. She wished they could lie forever like this, under the setting sun.

'I feel like a teenager.' Donna reached across and clasped his other hand in hers. 'I didn't even do this kind of thing when I was a teenager.' She giggled.

It was Andy's suggestion they go for a drive in the country when Donna told him Eddie had a meeting and wouldn't be home until after ten. He'd taken her to the Campsie Hills to watch the sunset, and they'd walked to a secluded spot on the fells and lay on the grass as the light faded.

He sat up on one elbow, buttoning his shirt.

'We'd better be getting back. Just in case Eddie lands home early and you're not there.'

'Okay, I suppose so,' she said, adjusting her skirt and looking at her watch. 'But I told you, he thinks I'm at the gym after work.' She knelt up and took Andy's face in her hands. 'I miss you so much when we can't be together.'

'Me too,' Andy sighed. 'We'll find a way. I promise.' He stood up.

They made their way down the hillside hand in hand and in silence. She dreaded going back to Eddie, and the stolen moments like this made her feel even more depressed when they ended.

'Andy,' she said, as they got to the car, 'this isn't just about sex for you, is it?'

'Don't even say that.' He came round from the driver's side to where she was standing and put his arms around her. 'Don't even think that. You know how I feel about you.'

Donna looked into his eyes.

'It's just that sometimes . . . Sometimes I feel that after we have sex, you want to get away. And it makes me feel . . . well . . . Just a feeling in the pit of my stomach.'

'If I want to get away, it's because I'm thinking of you. I'm worried all the time that Eddie will find out.' He gazed out across the countryside. 'I don't like this sneaking around any more than you do. But I need to protect you, make sure we don't get caught.' He opened the car door. 'Come on. Get in. I shudder to think what would happen if Eddie suspected something.'

The cars were thinning away from the car park at the

gym by the time they arrived back to where they had left Donna's car. But it was still busy. And as she got into her own car checking the phone for messages, she looked up and just for a second she thought she saw a blue Mercedes like Rod Farquhar's leaving the car park a couple of cars behind Andy's. Christ. She was really getting paranoid.

CHAPTER SEVENTEEN

Don was standing at the bar reading a copy of the *Post* when Rosie came up behind him.

'Top paper, that.' She gave him a nudge.

'Don't know so much,' he replied without taking his eyes off the newspaper. 'I hear some of the journalists are well suspect.' He looked up and smiled. 'How're you, Rosie? What you having?'

She surveyed the wine bottles behind the bar, and did a sharp intake of breath.

'I'm very tempted to have a glass of good red, but I've got such an early start tomorrow. So make it a mineral water.'

'Christ. Would that be a sparkling mineral water or still?' He frowned. 'You're a real lightweight.'

'Sparkling. With rocks.'

Don ordered another bottle of beer and they went across to sit at a table.

'So, what are you up to that means you can't even have a glass of wine?' He looked at his watch. 'It's only half seven.'

'I know. But I'm going out of town tomorrow. Early doors. I like to be alcohol free, clear head and all that.'

'Where you off to?' Don clinked her glass. 'Or is it top secret?'

'No,' Rosie said, 'I'm going to Spain. Hooligan watch with the Rangers fans. Champions League match.'

'Jesus. Do they not normally send one of the younger lads on that?'

'Sometimes. But the editor wants me to go this time. We're having a serious look at the troublemakers. There's been a few rumblings that the mad casuals are back in action, and we want to get a handle on it.' Rosie shrugged. 'I'm not complaining about a few days in Seville, that's for sure.'

'You're not going on one of these buses, are you? They're full of nutters.'

'No. Thankfully, we're flying. Going with a photographer. Just people-watching.'

Rosie felt a little guilty not telling Don the truth, because over the years he'd become more than a valuable police contact. They were close friends. But he was still a cop, and they had a mutual understanding that they used each other and both of them benefited from the relationship. But knowing

Don, he probably didn't believe she was going on hooligan watch anyway.

'So,' he looked at her inquisitively, 'you said you had information? I'm all ears.'

'Right,' Rosie said. 'I have a name for you. Don't know if it's right, but I think it might be. You guys are all over the place chasing down the dealer who's punting this heart-bursting coke, aren't you?'

Don sighed. 'You bet. That's five deaths now. And the latest one is from Cranhill. So it's already in the schemes. None of these fucking junkies seem capable of listening to the warnings. But yes. We're still trying to track who's moving it, and we're not having much luck.'

'Okay. The name I've been given is Tam Wilson. From Govan. Ring any bells?'

Don looked at her.

'Tam Wilson?' He pursed his lips and puffed, disgusted. 'Wee fucking toerag. He's a coke dealer all right. But our drug boys have already been onto him, and he's adamant he's got nothing to do with it.'

'He's hardly going to admit it.'

'I know. But he says he was away for a few days and knows nothing about it. He's got alibis.'

'Alibis? A drug dealer? Christ,' Rosie said, disappointed. 'And there was me thinking I was giving you good information.'

'Where did you get it?'

Rosie raised her eyebrows and said nothing.

'Oh. Right. You can't tell me.' He looked away, then back at her. 'Okay. Can you tell me, without naming anyone, how good the information is? A hint?'

'I got it from someone who buys from him. Lower down the food chain.' She shrugged. 'So I don't know, to be honest with you. But I think, given the circumstances I got it in, the person who told me the name wouldn't have lied.' She paused. 'Sorry for being vague, Don. But you know how it is. I'm protecting my source even if I don't like what they do.'

He took a deep breath and let it out slowly, as though he was pondering Rosie's information.

'Have you seen Jamie Coleman?' He looked her in the eye.

'He's in the Priory, is he not?' Rosie hoped her face showed nothing.

'Aye.' He lit a cigarette, putting the packet back on the table when Rosie declined. 'He is now.' He took a long draw and swallowed the smoke. 'So you haven't seen him?'

'Don!' Rosie said sharply, then smiled. 'I couldn't possibly comment. But if you're asking did the name come from Coleman, then the answer is no. All I have is the name Tam Wilson.'

'He says he's not guilty.'

'So did Harold Shipman. And you wouldn't have wanted him anywhere near your granny's eightieth birthday party.'

Rosie went into her pocket and took out a piece of paper. She pushed it across the table. 'My contact gave me his mobile phone number. That's the number he gets his coke from. You can tap his calls. He said he got bad coke from Wilson, but got rid of it. Dumped it.' She felt uncomfortable that her lie was getting deeper.

'I don't believe that crap for a minute. Dealers don't get rid of coke because it's dodgy. They don't think that way. How did he know it was bad?'

Rosie sighed. 'Don't ask.'

Don nodded and put the number in his jacket pocket.

'Well,' Rosie looked at her watch, 'That's all I know. Might be crap right enough, as you say. But if I was you I'd be giving Wilson another pull. Or watch him closely. Who is he anyway? Is he a big player?'

'Not the biggest. He's one of these UVF arseholes. That's what the word has always been, but you can never pin these bastards down to that. But he's definitely a player, and a reasonably big one. Drives a big car and got a bit of money in property these days, like a lot of them.'

Rosie changed the subject. 'Oh. Talking of UVF. That reminds me, Don. How are things going with the hit at the quarry? Those two dealers who got shot. Any news?'

'Not a fucking sausage. Totally watertight – if you'll pardon the pun.' He chuckled at his wit. 'I told you though. It's some kind of Loyalist hit. That was the word at the time, which means we'll probably never find out who the fuck did it. But it's got all the hallmarks of a paramilitary-style execution, especially with nobody saying a word.'

Rosie got up as Don finished his drink. They walked to the door and outside into the warm night.

'Who needs Spain in this weather?' he joked.

'What the hell,' Rosie smiled. 'A few days away and some tapas.'

'Yeah.' Don gave her a long look. 'Hooligan watch.' He smiled sarcastically. 'Hooligan watch, my arse.' He made a gun gesture with his hand. 'But hey, Rosie. Good luck with whatever you're after. I hope you find it.' He grinned. 'But for fuck's sake give us an early heads up if it's anything decent that I should know about.'

Rosie blew him a kiss as she walked away.

Donna put steaming plates of roast beef and gravy on the table as Eddie yanked the cork out of the bottle and poured red wine into both their glasses.

'I'm starving,' he said, placing the bottle in the middle of the table as he sat down.

'Long journey for you tomorrow.' Donna didn't look at him as she spooned potatoes and vegetables onto his plate, then hers. 'Best to get some decent food. You might be eating all sorts of crap on the journey.'

She hoped she was playing the doting housewife well, having spent most of the afternoon in the kitchen cooking Eddie's favourite meal. But she couldn't wait to see the back of him. Four whole days on her own, to relax around the house without waiting for him to come in and having to tiptoe around him in case he was in a foul mood. Four days when she could spend quality time with Andy. Just get through the night, she told herself, and blow a kiss as his arse is striding down the path. She smiled to herself as she watched him wolf down the food. Christ! He didn't half eat like a pig.

'So, any plans, darlin', while I'm away?' Eddie didn't look up from his plate. 'Just pampering yourself at the beautician's?'

Donna flashed a smile.

'You mean I'm not lovely enough?' She swallowed a mouthful of wine. 'No plans at all. Probably just relax around here. Bit of gardening. Boring really.' A fleeting image of her and Andy rolling around the Campsie Hills flashed across her mind and she felt herself blush.

Eddie sliced a piece of beef and stabbed a potato, mopping up the gravy before stuffing it into his mouth. Then he put his knife and fork down and went into his back pocket. He took out an envelope and held it up, then slid it across the table towards her.

'Wee surprise for you,' he said, looking pleased with himself.

Donna picked up the envelope, a little bemused. Once or twice in the past he'd given her a voucher for one of the big fashion stores before he went on a football trip with the Rangers fans. But that was years ago. She slit the envelope open and pulled the piece of white paper out, then turned it around. Her stomach dropped to the floor. It was a ticket for the match. Holy fucking Christ!

'Are you kidding me?' She tried to put on a face that was a mixture of shock and delight. 'The Rangers match?'

'Yep,' Eddie beamed back at her, licking the gravy off his knife. 'You're coming with us.'

'B-but . . . Eddie . . .' Donna stammered, trying to stop her brain from going into total panic. She put the card down as she felt her hands tremble. 'But I don't go to football matches. I don't even watch Rangers on the telly.'

'You used to.' He looked a little crestfallen.

'Oh, I know. But that was twenty years ago, when we were taking the kids to Ibrox.' She gulped down a mouthful of wine. She had to salvage this or she would end up with a sore face. 'I mean. Of course, it's fantastic. I'm so excited,' she gushed. 'But I haven't even got a thing done. How am I going to be ready for the morning? It's half eight already.' She picked up her knife and fork and put it down again, her appetite suddenly gone.

'Don't be daft, woman. You've got more clothes up there than the House of Fraser. Just chuck a few things into a bag.' He grinned. 'You can hit the shops when you get there. It'll be great. I've booked a fantastic room in the hotel for us, and I've got a wee bit of business to do, so you can relax and get some sun by the pool. It'll be magic. You'll love it.' He swigged his wine and raised a finger to her. 'And if you're really nice to me, I might even let you come with us the next time.'

Donna's head swam, but she hoped her face was smiling. She was utterly steamrolled, her mind a blur of terrifying scenarios, wondering if he'd found out about her and Andy. He was such a scheming bastard, this was just the kind of elaborate gesture he would do to screw her up. She knew she couldn't make an excuse not to go. She wasn't due back to work until Thursday and he knew that. The ticket sat on the table staring up at her. Sevilla v Rangers. Row E. Seat number twenty fucking two.

Eddie cleared his plate and pushed it away from him.

'So?' He looked at her, grinning and rubbing his hands. 'Am I not just the guy who's full of surprises then? That's what keeps our marriage together. The element of surprise. I'm your man for that, all right.'

Donna's lip twitched and she covered it with her finger.

'I love a surprise,' she said through gritted teeth, 'but I wish you'd told me yesterday.' She stood up and took her plate to the sink, collecting his on the way. 'Jesus! I'll need to get moving and get my bag packed.'

Eddie stood up and drained his glass. He smiled triumphantly and gave her a playful slap on the backside as he walked out of the kitchen, calling over his shoulder, 'Yes, piss off and get packed. And make sure you bring that lacy underwear I bought you for your birthday. Drives me crazy, that.'

Donna scraped the remains of her food into the bin and stacked the plates in the dishwasher, biting back tears of shock and resentment. Snared like a rat in a trap.

CHAPTER EIGHTEEN

Jimmy was already irritated at the job and it hadn't even started. The last thing he needed the night before the trip to Spain was for Eddie to send him on a job. As he stuffed his balaclava into his pocket, he caught a glimpse of his reflection in the hall mirror and reminded himself that this was who he was now. He was UVF. Eddie was his commanding officer. When Eddie says jump, you ask how high.

'Where you going at this time of night?' his father muttered, coming out of the kitchen carrying a mug of tea.

'I won't be long, Da. Just have to sort something out.'

Jimmy avoided his father's eyes, knowing they'd see right through him. When he was packing his bag for the trip in the afternoon he'd told him he was staying in tonight as it was an early start in the morning. His father would know that if he was going out then it was UVF business, but he also knew not to ask. Jimmy's phone buzzed with a text message and he pulled it out of his pocket as he opened the front door. It was Mitch. He was already at the meeting place with Johnny 'Psycho' Bentley. Jimmy's stomach did a little flip. Eddie hadn't told him Psycho was on the job, but if he was involved, somebody was getting hurt big time.

'Awright, Johnny man?'

Jimmy stooped to look inside the rolled down window of Mitch's car and acknowledge Psycho in the passenger seat. It was some face. Like two faces had been moulded into one to create a huge moon topped off with a shaven head that had various battle-scar clefts gouged out. Probably from those who had tried and failed to knock the big beast unconscious.

Johnny raised his chin slightly but stared blankly out of the windscreen.

Mitch shot a 'fuck me' glance at Jimmy and said nothing. Johnny Bentley wasn't called Psycho for nothing. He was also known as 'the chiropractor' on account of how expertly he could snap a neck – like a twig – killing his victim in an instant. He was as mad a bastard as you got, too much of a nutter for most ordinary punishment beatings because he didn't know when to stop. And he was too unbalanced for a routine hit. Torture was Psycho's stock in trade, and he relished every agonising moment of it. His capacity to inflict pain and find new ways to do it was legendary, and there were stories of him cutting ears off and ripping out eyes. One famous tale was where the interrogation victim was found with his castrated scrotum stuffed into his mouth. Psycho was only used when someone had grassed and had to be made to own up, or in other cases where the subject would learn a particularly harsh lesson that he'd be able to see in his nightmares and his disfigurement for the rest of his life.

'What's the plan then, lads?' Jimmy slid into the back seat.

Mitch looked at Psycho, then at Jimmy, then at his watch, and stroked his chin, seeming to enjoy being the senior man here.

'When the guy comes out of the bakery, you jump him and get him into the boot of your car. We're just here for back-up, in case he can handle himself. Then we take him to Johnny's garage for a wee chat.'

'Who is he?' Jimmy asked.

'You'll find out soon enough, Jimmy. He'll be coming off the back shift in the bakery in about five minutes. I was told that he usually comes out with a guy who'll get on a bike, then our man will walk to the car park. He lives near here. I've got a snap of him.'

He took a photocopied picture out of the side pocket of his door and handed it over his shoulder. Jimmy looked at it in the semi-darkness. A slim thirty-something guy with fair curly hair. He looked like a church minister or a school teacher, Jimmy thought. He'd be easy to handle. He sat back in his seat and waited.

'There's some movement now,' Mitch said after a few minutes. 'A few guys coming out of the side door. Shift must be finished.'

They watched as the men went to their cars and drove off. Jimmy got out and walked beyond the door where the men had come out, so he could see when they left and where they were headed. He stood in the shadows, feeling the tension pick up in his guts. He looked back down to the car where Mitch and Psycho sat with their headlights off. Then the side door opened again and out came two men. He could only see them from behind as they walked away from the building, so he waited for the signal from Mitch who could see them face-on. Mitch's window opened and Jimmy saw his hand stick out for a split second with the thumb up. He watched as one of the men went to the end of the building and fiddled with the lock on a bicycle before mounting it and riding off, waving to his friend, who started to walk towards the car park close to the leafy lane that led to a quiet street. Jimmy moved swiftly and silently behind him, pulling down his balaclava. He had to jump him before he got to his car. As he was approaching the lane Jimmy was right behind him, and suddenly, as though sensing his presence, the man turned around. His mouth opened slightly as though he was going to speak, but before he had the chance, Jimmy lashed out a lightning punch and he staggered backwards. The man looked surprised as he put his hand to his face and touched blood coming from his nose.

Jimmy was quick as a flash and rained in two more blows to the head and body, bringing him to his knees.

'I've no money, pal,' the man whimpered as Jimmy dragged him to his feet, his face now a bloody mess. 'Take my wallet. Take anything I've got.'

'Shut the fuck up. Just keep your mouth shut.'

The man was barely conscious and wobbling on his feet as Jimmy roughly dragged him towards his car. He pinged the boot open with his key and pulled him towards it.

'Wh-what's this all about? What do you want?'

'Shut up and get in there.' Jimmy pushed him so he was half in the boot.

'But why? Wh-why? I haven't done anything. What's going on?' the man croaked as Jimmy slapped his face, pushed him inside and slammed the boot shut.

He got into his car and saw Mitch come up alongside him and his window come down.

'Well done, Jimmy boy. Fucker didn't know what hit him. Just follow us.'

Jimmy could hear the muffled cries from the boot as he sped out of the car park behind Mitch's car.

The steel shutter door of the garage slowly rose like a stage curtain. Jimmy followed Mitch's car inside and watched as Psycho quickly jumped out and pushed the remote to bring the shutter back down. It rattled as it dropped and for a few seconds they stood in the pitch black until it closed completely. Psycho switched on a dim light, and Jimmy glanced at Mitch as Psycho went across to a bench and carried over a car battery. He placed it on a workbench and plugged it into the wall, connecting wires to the points. They watched as he worked around like a well-organised surgeon, ready to perform an operation. He rolled up his sleeves. Then he lifted a heavy jemmy from a cupboard and stood looking at them before laying it on the bench. Something resembling a smile spread over his face, and it gave Jimmy the creeps. He exchanged a fleeting glance with Mitch.

'Right. I'm ready. Get him out of the car.' He jerked his head towards the boot.

Jimmy and Mitch moved towards the car as Psycho worked, laying out various tools and utensils and filling a bucket with water.

'He's a fucking nutjob,' Jimmy whispered to Mitch as their backs were turned.

'I know. I've never worked with him before, either. But I heard the stories. He's fucking well named.'

'So what's this all about? Any idea? I only got a call from Eddie tonight. Do you know what this geezer is getting done over for?'

Mitch ushered Jimmy towards the boot and whispered, 'Eddie didn't tell me either. He just gave me the name of the guy and where I'd find him, and said Psycho would meet me. All he said was that this is personal. He told me two days ago about the job. Didn't say why, but I think I know what it is.'

'So what is it then?'

'Remember that night in the pub, big Farquhar came in and then Eddie left with his face like thunder?'

'Aye.'

'Well, I think Eddie's wife has been shagging this cunt in the boot, and big Farquhar told him about it that night.'

'Christ! How the fuck do you know that?'

'Because big Farquhar's a complete tit and he got drunk and told one of my mates. That's how thick he is. If Eddie finds out he's blabbed, he'll be next.'

'So do you think it's true, Eddie's wife shagging this guy? Jesus. She must be brave.'

'Yeah. Well I don't know the ins and outs of it, but if Eddie's brought Psycho in and told me it's personal, then I think it's probably true. Donna works at the bakery. Maybe she works beside this guy and that's how it all started.' He grinned at Jimmy. 'She's not a bad looking bird. I'd pump her, if she wasn't who she is.'

'Fuck!' Jimmy stifled a laugh. 'You're nuts. I'm surprised Eddie's not just getting him bumped off.'

'Knowing Eddie, he'll want to make the bastard suffer. Make sure he knows that he'll not be sniffing around Donna any more. Not by the time big Psycho's finished.'

'Hurry up, guys, for fuck's sake,' Psycho said, pushing

some coke from a bag onto his tongue and up his nose. 'I've got a bird to meet later.'

Mitch made eyes at Jimmy and they both tried to keep their faces straight.

'Fuck me,' Mitch said. 'Open the boot. Let's get this done.'

They all pulled on their balaclavas, as Jimmy pinged the boot open. The guy's eyes were just about visible behind the bloodied face that had begun to balloon. He curled into a ball as Mitch reached in.

'Stop fucking about. You'll just make it harder for yourself.' Mitch grabbed him by the shoulders and yanked him up.

Jimmy hauled his legs out and they got him to his feet, but his legs buckled as soon as he stood up.

'Sit him on that chair.' Psycho threw a piece of rope towards them. 'Tie him up. And stuff something into his mouth. I don't want anyone to hear the cunt screaming.'

Jimmy and Mitch did as he said, feeling the guy's whole body trembling as they tied his hands and feet. Mitch pushed an oily rag into his mouth and he gagged and struggled.

Psycho stood with his arms folded, a glazed look in his eyes as he stared down at his victim. He scratched his chin, then put a sponge into the bucket of water.

'Pull his trousers down a bit. I should have told you to do that before you tied him up. Just pull them down so I can see his tackle.'

The man writhed and struggled as they pulled him to his feet and Mitch pulled down his trousers and underpants. They pushed him back into the chair.

Psycho stepped towards him, then wrung out the wet sponge, soaking his naked genitals and thighs. Jimmy and Mitch stood back looking at each other, their faces twisted with the prospect of what was going to happen next.

'You've been a bad boy, son.' Psycho threw the sponge in the bucket. He turned to the box that was connected to the battery and turned the control up to medium. The clips on the sensors made a crackling noise, sparking when he put them together. He took one in each hand then approached the man.

'Now this is going to hurt a bit.' He gave a little snigger at his wit.

The man struggled and moved in the chair and Psycho snorted.

'Hold him still, for fuck's sake. Open his legs a bit.'

Jimmy and Mitch held his shoulders and each pulled a leg open.

Jimmy had looked away just as the electrodes were almost touching the man's scrotum, but he could tell by the sudden thrashing and jerking that they were attached. He glanced down and said 'oh fuck' under his breath. Psycho went to the box and switched the control up until the needle was nudging high. It was probably only on for a few seconds but it seemed like an age and Jimmy smelled singeing flesh. Muffled screams came from behind the rag and the man's face looked fit to burst. Veins stood out on his head and neck as he screamed and jerked. Then he passed out, his head slumping on his chest.

Nobody spoke.

'That'll learn him,' Psycho looked pleased with himself. He lifted the bucket of water and threw it over the chair, startling the man back to consciousness, the water washing away some of the blood from his face so that Jimmy could see the damage he'd done with his own fists. For a split second he felt ashamed of himself.

'Right,' Psycho said. 'That takes care of that end. Untie his hands.'

Mitch looked at Jimmy and they both went behind him and undid the ropes. Psycho brought over a small table and sat it in front of the chair.

'Spread his hands out on that.'

The man promptly pulled his hands off the table when Psycho approached him with the jemmy.

'Fuck! Keep his hands straight on the table. Palms down.'

They held his arms stiff so his hands couldn't move.

'So you're a master baker, are you?' Again with the creepy smile. 'Not any more, you're not.'

Jimmy closed his eyes tight as he heard the gut-churning dull thud of the jemmy come down hard, and the smashing sound of bones. He opened one eye and saw the man's right hand mutilated with one blow, bloody and torn. Again the screams behind the rag, as the jemmy came down on the left hand so heavily that it burst open the thumb area, nearly slicing through it. Pieces of bone and flesh were splattered on the table. The man passed out again, his legs jerking violently. Then silence. They stood looking him.

'Stand back,' Psycho said, lifting the jemmy again.

'Fuck's sake, Johnny. I think he's had enough,' Mitch said.

'No. Eddie says he's to get one on the head too. For even thinking about messing him around.'

Before Mitch had a chance to protest that he was the senior man here, Psycho had already swung the jemmy, splitting the man's head like a kipper.

'Fuck me, man. You're not supposed to kill him.'

'He's not dead,' Psycho said. 'He'll just no' be baking any cakes for a while. Or nobbing anybody's wife.' He put the jemmy back in the cupboard. 'Right. Just take him and dump him somewhere.' He looked at his watch, grinning. 'But hurry up. I need to get home and changed before I meet this bird. I'm as horny as fuck after that.'

Jimmy lay on the top of his bed, one hand behind his head and the other in his underpants, as though he was never more grateful to feel his tackle still there. He couldn't get the image out of his head of Psycho attaching the electrodes to the man. And the crunching and smashing of the bones in his hands. Jesus Christ! There was no need for that. Whatever the guy did, even with Eddie's wife, all they had to do surely was give him a warning, a sore face, and a threat that he'd get shot. But the torture? Something well sick about that. Jimmy even felt nauseous when he got into the house, and he was glad his father was in bed. He took a deep breath and let it out slowly. This is what he was now, he told himself. This is how the UVF did business. He knew that long before he swore the oath. And somewhere, despite his niggling reservations after the brutality he'd seen tonight, there was something powerful about being able to have that much clout over people. He closed his eyes, hoping sleep would come.

CHAPTER NINETEEN

They'd been at least a day and a half ahead of the bus –
time enough to hook up with Javier and Adrian and make
some kind of plan. To Rosie's surprise, big Eddie hadn't been
alone when he turned up for the supporters' coach from
the Tavern at five a.m. He had his wife in tow, tottering on
high heels and tight jeans, her face like fizz. A two-day bus
journey with a bus load of blootered, farting football fans
was clearly not her idea of fun. Rosie and Matt had watched
the bus wind its way out of the street, then they headed for
Glasgow Airport for their flight to London and on to Seville,
where they were now sitting.

'This has to be one of the most beautiful cities in the
world.' Rosie looked out across the piazza at the imposing
skyline as the sun slipped behind the mighty Giralda tower
of Seville Cathedral.

'Probably was until this bunch of knuckle-trailing arseholes invaded.' Matt nodded at the posse of raucous Rangers

fans emerging from the meandering streets of the old town. 'Christ! Listen to them. The folk here must think we're a nation of pisshead thugs. It makes me affronted to be Scottish.'

Rosie glanced at Javier who was gazing wistfully at the sea of royal blue football jerseys. The gang of around thirty hooligans were led by a shaven-headed fan draped in the Union Flag, who stopped and turned towards his army to conduct the vile chants:

'Hallo! Hallo! We are the Billy Boys,' they all sang. 'Hallo! Hallo! We're out to make a noise . . . We're up to our knees in Fenian blood, surrender or you'll die . . . Cos we are the Bridgeton Billy Boys . . . Haaallo . . . Haaallo!'

They grew louder as they marched past the cathedral in the direction of a bar on the corner.

Javier shook his head in disgust. 'You know, this city has had more than its share of invaders – none more violent than the Moors who came rampaging in, destroying and murdering everything in their wake. I think they would have made very short work of guys like them.' He looked at Rosie and Matt. 'You're right though. They do embarrass your nation. I would be embarrassed if Spanish football fans behaved like that.'

'It's not all Scottish football fans.' Rosie felt the need to defend her countrymen, even though she'd never been patriotic in her life. Of course, Javier was right, but insulting the Scots was like insulting who you were. Especially coming from him, with that air of superiority that he seemed to have about being Spanish. 'In any case, I'm sure there are plenty of hooligans among your own fans,' she added petulantly.

'You don't have to be so defensive, Rosie.' Javier gave her a wry smile.

He was digging her up. Worked every time.

Rosie emptied the last of the bottle into their glasses – except for Adrian who covered his glass with his hand, blinking his refusal in the minimalist way he had of expressing himself. He had an early drive to the Costa del Sol in the morning to pick up Wendy and Liz.

'Anyway, Matt,' Rosie said, shooting Javier a sarcastic look, 'hooligans aside, talk us through what you saw of McGregor and co. earlier on.'

Matt and Adrian had been dispatched by Rosie to the hotel in the centre of Seville where the Rangers bus from the Tavern had pitched up. Young Declan had managed to find out from contacts in Glasgow which hotel the fans would be staying at.

'It's a surprise McGregor bringing his wife. I wouldn't think many guys take their wives to matches like this. I always assumed most of the lads just got pissed and visited strip clubs and whorehouses. And especially bringing her on a drug run?' Rosie said.

'It's a good cover.' Javier sat back, stretching out his long

legs. 'Everyone around him will think he's on a little roman-
tic break.'

'To a football match? And they say romance is dead.'
Rosie rolled her eyes to the sky.

She waved the waiter over and Javier asked for another
round of drinks, then ordered the restaurant's house speci-
ality of assorted starters with a mixed paella to share.

'So how were the happy couple, Matt?' Rosie asked. 'Did
big Eddie and his wife look all loved up?'

'Well, everyone was mostly just listening while McGregor
held court. The other two – Mad Mitch and Dunlop – were
having a couple of beers, but McGregor and his wife were
drinking champagne. She didn't look a barrel of fun though.
Looked like she was just laughing at the right bits, but as
you'll see from a couple of shots, she was a bit glum.' He
called up the pictures on his camera and handed it to her.

'Hmmm. Looks miserable. No wonder. Tied to a pure bastard like him,' Rosie said. 'But I'm still surprised to see her
on the trip at all. Something not right about it.'

Javier's mobile rang and he spoke in Spanish for a couple
of minutes as Rosie turned to Adrian.

'So if you leave very early in the morning, you could be
back here with the girls by lunchtime?'

He nodded. 'The road is very good. Should be no problem. Maybe some fans coming up from the Costa del Sol
for the football, but if we leave early enough we miss a lot
of the traffic.'

'Great.'

Rosie was looking forward to seeing Wendy and Liz again. Since she'd flown over to meet them last week, they had been feeding her more information about Flinty Jackson. As Liz had told her from the start, he was the biggest dealer in the Costa with several smaller fish working with him, making drops for customers all along the coast. He ran his operation between his Rangers pub – Blue Heaven – in Fuengirola, and the palatial villa he owned close to de la Puerto Duchesa further down the coast. In the few days before she arrived, Rosie had Javier and Adrian take a discreet look at his house and at de la Puerto Duchesa, and Javier reported that they'd seen him a couple of times in the port with various Moroccans and a couple of Dutchmen.

Javier came off the phone and sat forward, pushing his fingers through his lush, greying hair.

'That was my *amigo*, the detective inspector I told you about. From the Guardia Civil.'

Rosie felt a little uneasy. They had discussed bringing in the cops and trying to make a deal that would allow the newspaper investigation to be part of the police operation, but Rosie knew it would be fraught with all sorts of problems. Dealing with any cops was hard enough when they were on a live operation. Expecting any serious cooperation with Spanish cops was just wishful thinking.

'Javier . . . I . . .'

He put his hand up. 'Before you ask, Rosie . . . No. I haven't agreed to anything. You are the boss. It's your call.'

Rosie almost smiled at his bullshit. He even managed to look like he believed she was the boss.

'As you know,' he said, straight-faced, 'I have discussed the basics without going into any names or detail. But if you ask me, having the cops with us is our only way to nail your man. If we don't involve the police this end, then you must do it at the Scottish or UK end when they land. But, by that time, anything could have happened to the stash of cocaine. That's the risk. Once McGregor and his friends get on that bus and leave Seville we have no way of tracking them. How do we know, for example, that two of the guys are not going to get off in France and drive the stuff home? Or take a private boat? I think we have to involve the police now. But, Rosita, it is your call.' He glanced at the others then back to Rosie.

'But how do we know the cops will deal us in?'

'We talk to them about it.' He lifted his phone. 'Why don't you meet him? Just a chat. See how you get on.'

Rosie felt a little pressurised but she knew he was right about losing track once they left Spain.

'What's the guy like? This inspector mate of yours?'

The prospect of another strident Spaniard in the mix didn't fill her with confidence. Especially one who had the clout to take over her entire investigation and leave her waiting on the end of a phone line for a press release.

'He's like me.' Javier grinned, blowing out a trail of smoke. 'Only not so charming.'

'Yeah. You need to work on that self-belief. But seriously, Javier, what's he like?'

'We worked together when I was here many years ago. And as I told you, in theory the Guardia Civil does not handle drugs cases as such. That is the remit of the Policia Nacional. Both forces are separate and they dislike each other intensely. It's tradition. We used to call the Policia Nacional the *madero*. It means "woodenheads". So that is the kind of rapport we had with them – none. To be honest, I wouldn't trust them with this kind of case where nothing is certain or straightforward. So if we speak to my friend Juan, then he can find a way to make the case Guardia Civil business.'

'How?'

'Well, for a start, the people who are behind this are UVF – an illegal terrorist organisation. The Guardia Civil have the responsibility for control of national borders and security. They are the anti-terrorist brigade, if you like. They can find a way to make sure that this is their case. Perhaps by saying they were involved because intelligence has come to them that the bus is carrying weapons – explosive devices, even. But you don't have to worry about how they make it their case. You just have to decide if you want to involve them.'

Rosie nodded, processing his information.

'And how close are you with your friend these days? How much do you trust him?'

'We worked together on some big investigations when I was with the Guardia. Then when I left and moved away to become a private detective, I kept in touch with him. I gave him some assistance and good information that helped him crack a major case around four years back, so he owes me a little. I haven't seen him for a while, but I trust him and he trusts me.'

Rosie looked at Matt whose face said go with it. Adrian gave what seemed to be a nod of approval. But it was ultimately her call.

'Okay. Let's meet him and we can talk. See where we go from there. Phone him back, Javier, and let's see him after dinner.' She gave him a look. 'But don't pressurise me.'

'As if,' Javier replied, punching numbers into his mobile.

The champagne had lifted Donna's spirits just enough to get through the meal in the hotel's rooftop terrace restaurant. But now, as Eddie was ordering brandies with their coffee, she had to find some excuse to get back to their hotel room so she could phone Andy.

From the moment they'd left Glasgow at five in the morning, she'd been watching her mobile for any texts from him. But nothing. Not even a single one-line answer to say that he understood the situation, that Eddie had simply presented her with a ticket for the match and made the decision for her. She felt sick throughout the journey, agonising that he had decided to call it a day. Perhaps he thought she was using him and never had any real intentions of leaving Eddie. But she convinced herself he wouldn't believe that. Not after the last few weeks they'd had, and the promises they'd made to each other. Surely he would understand. But why no answer? After Eddie had given her the ticket, she'd gone straight upstairs to pack, but quickly phoned Andy, hoping to get a word with him. His mobile rang out and she left a short message saying she had to go to Seville for the match, that she'd no choice. She hoped he would understand. When he didn't get back by the morning, she sent him a furtive text from the bathroom before they left for the bus. But still no reply. It was nearly two days on the road, and still nothing. She couldn't understand it. She knew that when he finished his shift the night before she left, he had a couple of days off. They'd had plans together. Now, with the humidity in the air and her stomach churning with nerves, she felt uncomfortable and panicky. She excused herself from the table and went to the bathroom.

'So, this is the life, lads, eh?' Eddie swirled his brandy around the glass. 'This is how the big boys roll when they know what they're doing.'

He raised his glass towards Jimmy and Mitch who responded and clinked glasses with him.

'Aye,' Mitch said. 'Let the good times roll, boss.'

Eddie lit a cigar and sat back, blowing a thick cloud of smoke up to the sky.

'You guys did a good job the other night, by the way. Psycho told me. That's what I like to hear. I like my boys to be on the ball; ready to respond as and when they're needed. You did well.'

Jimmy and Mitch nodded.

'Where did you dump him?'

'Just at the Calton. In the street. He wasn't in very good shape. He was unconscious. Psycho gave him a right tankin',' Mitch said.

Eddie glowered from one to the other, scanning their faces in silence for a moment before he spoke.

'Psycho was doing what he was told,' he said flatly. Then he snorted with a bit of a snigger. 'For once, that crazy cunt did what he was fucking told. Thing about Psycho is once he starts he can't stop. Stuff I've seen him do to guys would make your hair stand on end. But that's what he's there for.'

Donna came back to the table and sat down, hoping Eddie wouldn't see through her frozen smile.

'All right, darlin'?'

'Just feel a bit hot, Eddie – probably tired after the long journey. I think I might go up to the room and have a lie down.' She stood up.

Eddie got up and walked away from the table, his arm around her waist.

'Go and have a wee rest, darlin'. I'll take the lads for a couple of drinks, see a few of the troops, then I'll come and help you relax. I'll not be late.' He pulled her towards him as he gave her a dirty smile.

CHAPTER TWENTY

Inspector Juan Garcia of the Guardia Civil embraced Javier with a manly back-slapping bear hug, trotting out what sounded to Rosie like a tirade of Spanish expletives, the kind normally reserved for great friends. Rosie watched as Javier prodded Juan's podgy stomach, grinning as he said something back. It must be a male thing, she thought. You'd never get a woman greeting another woman friend by hugging her and declaring she was a fat bastard.

Javier towered above the stocky policeman, and slung a comradely arm over his shoulder, then turned him towards the table and introduced everyone, again speaking in Spanish.

'I hope you're saying only good things about us, Javier. I'm listening,' Rosie joked.

'*Por supuesto*, Rosita! Of course!' He laughed, ruffling her hair, and translated what she'd said to Garcia, who gave a sly smile.

As Garcia shook everyone's hand, his glance flicked up

and down each of them, sizing them up. He gave Rosie a firm and lingering handshake.

'*Mucho gusto*, Rosie,' he said, with the husky voice of someone who smokes at least two packets of cigarettes a day. Hazel eyes fixed her. 'How you like the beautiful Seville?'

'I love it, Juan. It's fantastic,' Rosie replied, then quickly added almost apologetically, 'It's a little noisy with the mad football fans though.' She waved a hand in the direction of a rowdy crowd in a nearby bar who had spilled outside singing, one of them banging incessantly on a drum.

Garcia shrugged. 'Is the football. Is no problem for us. They are all the same.'

Rosie shot a told-you-so smile at Javier, who shook his head and pursed his lips in denial.

'Sit here, Juan.' Javier motioned him to sit next to Rosie. 'You wanna beer?'

Garcia nodded and drew a hand over three-day stubble then rubbed his face as though he'd just woken up from an afternoon nap. He pulled a cigarette packet from his top shirt pocket and tugged one out with his teeth, then stuffed the packet back.

'So you are old friends, Juan,' Rosie asked, feeling she should take control of the conversation.

Garcia looked at her and hesitated. Rosie inclined her head to Javier.

'Am I speaking too fast?'

'I speak English,' Garcia said lazily. 'Is not great but I can understand if you speak slowly. Javier will translate if we have any problems. But yes, the answer is, yes, Javier and I, we are old friends.' He looked at Javier as though wondering if he'd told Rosie about his former life as a Guardia Civil.

Javier spoke to him in Spanish, and from what Rosie could pick up he was saying that he had told her the history. Garcia nodded, pushing a hand through his shock of thick curly black hair, a bit too long and dated for current trends, Rosie thought. His little beer belly hung over his jeans, and where his denim shirt was open at the neck, she could see some kind of pendant on a thick, short silver chain that was bordering on a choker. He might have been attractive in a macho kind of way back in the eighties, and she guessed he wasn't the kind of guy who liked taking orders from women.

'So.' Garcia drew deeply on the cigarette and held it for a split second before exhaling, hidden behind a cloud of smoke as he spoke. 'Javier tells me you are trying to . . .' He paused . . . 'how you say . . . er . . . expose . . . yes, expose some very bad people here.' He wagged a finger. 'And very dangerous men, I think.'

Rosie looked at Javier, then at Garcia.

'Yes. That's right.'

'And you want the help of the Guardia to trap these people.' There was a hint of swagger to his demeanour.

She had agreed with Javier that he tell Garcia the bones of the story, but she didn't want to give any more detail away until she could be assured that there would be some mutual cooperation.

'Yes. I think you know that already,' she said, deadpan.

It might have been Rosie's eternal chip on her shoulder, but she felt a little dig of irritation in the way Garcia was speaking to her, as though it was her first big investigation and he was trying to talk her through it. Patronising. She saw Javier glance at her, and was aware that he knew the signs of her cage being rattled. Suddenly he interrupted.

'Juan. If I could just say, Rosie and myself, and everyone on the team here' – he waved his hand indicating Matt and Adrian – 'we have discussed the best way to get the result we want. Which, as you know, benefits us all. We all want to see these bastards behind bars for a very long time, yes? So what we would like' – he glanced at Rosie – 'may I?'

Rosie nodded. She was irked that Javier was trampling on her pitch, as she was perfectly capable of putting her point across without his help. But the sensible part of her knew that Garcia, if he was the Spanish macho male he appeared to be, would respond better if it was put to him by Javier – even if he *was* aware that Javier was working for and being instructed by Rosie. It was annoying, but when in Spain, Rosie told herself.

'We may be in a position to give you the names of the main players,' Javier said to Juan.

Rosie nodded, assuming that Javier would have already gone through this with Garcia, and the detective had probably already made up his mind. But she had to play the game.

Garcia took a swig of his beer, then sat the bottle on the table, licking his lips, gazing into the distance for a silent moment.

'I hope we can assist each other,' he said finally.

'By that, Juan, I hope you mean that we will be able to get good access to the operation.' Rosie couldn't stop herself.

Garcia flashed her a stern glance then another at Javier.

'To some extent,' he said, scratching his stubble. 'But you are not suggesting you can be part of an official operation by the Guardia Civil, Rosie?' He raised his eyebrows for emphasis and puffed, a little pompously, then looked away.

Silence. Javier gave Rosie a pleading look, and she sat back. She would let him take it from here. But she had to let Garcia see she was no pushover.

'No, Juan. What I think Rosie means, and of course we all want, is for us to be given reasonable access to the operation. Not kept in the dark as you usually do with operations like this. We want to be able to play a part in this. We are able to give you names and players, but we need to know that once the bust happens – if it's successful – that we are the first to know and are able to be on it within seconds. We would need to be tipped off so that we can be there for pictures. Of course, we would be far enough away so as not to interfere with your work.'

Another silence.

'My bosses will never wear that, Javier. You know that.'

Rosie shifted in her seat. She looked at Matt and Adrian, then glared at Javier.

'Juan.' She looked straight at him, trying to control her irritation. 'We need some solid guarantee of cooperation. We need to be there, or close as we can get. We can help you trap these people. But we need to know we are in.'

Garcia put his head back and sighed as though he was bored.

'As I said, Rosie. My bosses wouldn't wear it.'

He stubbed his cigarette out and there was an awkward silence while Garcia stared at the table. Eventually he looked up and spoke, his face straight. 'But I will be the officer responsible for the controlling of the operation on the ground. Everything goes through me. So they cannot object to something they have no knowledge of.' His mouth almost cracked a smile. 'If you get my meaning.'

Rosie looked at Javier who gave her a quit-while-you're-ahead wink.

'Okay.' She nodded. 'So let's talk. I want to run some ideas past you that we have discussed here, and you can tell me if you think they are workable.'

She crossed her legs and was aware of Garcia's glance roving from her ankles to her chest. He gave Javier a wry smile. She wished she could be a fly on the wall when these two were having a conversation about her alone.

She was about to speak when her mobile rang. She lifted

it impatiently. It was Don. She excused herself, saying she had to take the call.

'Don. Howsit going?'

'You still in Spain, Rosie?'

'Yeah. Here for at least a few more days.'

'Aye. Hooligan watch.'

Rosie detected the sarcasm in his voice.

'Uh-huh. So what's happening?' If Don was phoning her when he knew she was abroad, it wasn't for a social chat.

'Can you talk for a minute?'

'Sure.'

'Listen. We're working on a very brutal assault back here. Torture. Very gruesome. The guy's in some nick.'

Rosie couldn't figure why he'd be phoning her about a brutal attack. It's not as though they were unusual in Glasgow.

'What do you mean, torture? Is it a drugs beating?'

'Don't know yet, Rosie. But it's not looking like it. The guy was a pretty nondescript kind of fella. A baker. Worked in that big place over on the south side. No history of drugs, no form. Nothing. He was in a coma. He only regained consciousness this afternoon, so I've not been able to get much from him. Only that he was kidnapped and bundled into the boot of a car. Then taken somewhere and tortured.'

'Tortured? How?'

'Electric shocks to his balls.'

'Really? Bet that hurt in the morning.'

'Yeah, makes me shut my legs just thinking about it. But that's not all. They smashed up every bone in his hands. Like they were giving him a lesson. He's had to have emergency surgery, but he won't get much movement in them again. Plus, they fractured his skull. Split him wide open. Then left him for dead.'

'That's grim.' Rosie wasn't sure what to say, still guessing at what a gruesome torture like this would have to do with her, especially since she wasn't in Glasgow. 'So what can I do? Have the cops not put out an appeal yet?'

'Not yet. We're making discreet inquiries before we release it. But a couple of things came up on the radar and that's why I phoned you. The guy wasn't married. Lived on his own and worked at the bakery for years. He was their top baker there. A master baker, I think they call it. Kind of like a masturbator but not as much fun – but he'll not be doing any of the two of them for a very long time.'

Rosie smiled at Don's black humour. 'Good that you've kept your compassion despite years at the frontline.'

Don chuckled. 'But seriously. The reason I'm phoning you is this: remember we had that talk about big Eddie McGregor, the UVF man?'

'Yeah.'

'Well. Word is – and it's not confirmed, but we got it from a decent source – word is that this guy was shagging McGregor's wife Donna.'

'No kidding. He must be very brave – or have a death wish.'

Rosie tried to keep her reaction as flat as possible, but her heart was doing double time. McGregor's wife having an affair, and while she turns up here on this trip, her boyfriend gets the hiding of his life.

'So have you talked to her? To McGregor's wife?' she asked. She felt a pang of guilt holding out on Don, knowing she already had pictures of McGregor and his wife in a restaurant just a stone's throw from where she was sitting.

'No. Apparently she's in Seville with McGregor for the match. It was a surprise he sprung on her. She phoned one of her pals to tell her that big Eddie had given her a ticket at the last minute. The night before they left.'

'So you think McGregor took Donna out of the way so he could get her boyfriend done over?'

'Definitely. But of course I've not got a scrap of evidence to back that up. Not a fucking thing.'

'Which makes it a perfect job from where McGregor's sitting.'

'Exactly. He's an evil bastard.'

'Do you think it's true that McGregor's wife would be shagging a guy when she knows what her man's capable of? She must know how easy it is for him to make someone disappear.'

'I know. That's the bit I can't understand. And this guy

Andy. Word is that he's a really decent mild-mannered bloke. He must be off his nut to get mixed up in all that.'

'So what you want me to do, Don?' Rosie could see the intrigue on the faces of Javier, Matt and Adrian, who were only hearing her side of the conversation.

'Don't know really. Just keep an eye out for McGregor. I know there are a lot of fans there. But you never know. You might see him.'

'Yeah, but I can hardly approach him about that. Or her, for that matter.'

'I know. Just saying. Look, I need to go. But I'm going to have a better talk with the guy tomorrow if he's more *compos mentis*, and I'll see what comes up. If it's anything interesting, I'll give you a shout.'

'Sure. That'd be great.'

'And don't drink too much of that sangria pish.'

'I never touch it, Don. You know me.'

'Aye. Right.' He hung up.

Rosie put her phone on the table and let out a long slow breath, shaking her head.

'Sounds like a fascinating conversation,' Javier said.

'Not half.' She looked at everyone, speaking slowly so Garcia could understand. 'That was a cop contact of mine in Glasgow. Some guy has been brutally attacked back there. Tortured. And the word is that he was having an affair with McGregor's wife.'

'Fuck me!' Matt said. 'He must be mental.'

'Yep. That's what I said.'

'When did it happen?' Javier asked.

'Night before they left for Seville. The guy wasn't found till the early hours of the morning.'

Javier raised his eyebrows. 'So McGregor brought his missus here not just to fuck her up so she couldn't see the boyfriend, but so he could get someone to beat the shit out of him?'

'That's what the cops think. But they can't prove it. He was just telling me because we'd had a conversation about McGregor a while ago, after Wendy vanished. McGregor was the last person to see her, and we know that he raped her. But of course the cops don't know that.'

'So what now?' Javier said. 'It doesn't change what we are doing, does it?'

'No. Of course not.' Rosie paused for a moment. 'But when McGregor's wife finds out what has happened to her lover, then things could change. Depends on how keen she was on him.'

'What, like you mean she might be willing to stick McGregor in for the shit he's done? She's not that daft. She'd get bumped off.' Javier looked at the others.

'I'm just thinking. If she was in love with the guy, she's going to be in a right old state.' Rosie glanced at her watch, then lifted her mobile and dialled Don's number. 'Give me a minute, guys.'

Don answered on two rings.

'What's up, Rosie?'

'Listen, Don. I've been thinking. I need a line about that Andy guy getting battered. I want to get something in the *Post* for tomorrow.'

'But we haven't released it yet.'

'Yeah, but that doesn't mean to say it's not out there. You know how it is. Someone – anyone – could have phoned the papers about the beating. Someone from the hospital, or the guys who found him, even one of his workmates. I need it in the paper tonight.'

'What's the rush?'

'I'll tell you as soon as I can. I promise. Just give me the name and address and a bit of detail that won't affect your inquiry. I won't mention the details of the torture.'

'Fuck's sake, Rosie. You'll get me sacked.'

'They can't sack you. You know where all the bodies are buried. And, listen. I promise, I will return this favour big time very soon. Just trust me.'

'Okay.' He reeled off the details and Rosie wrote them down on a napkin. 'But you didn't get it from me.'

'Course not,' Rosie said. 'Who are you, anyway?' Don hung up.

She phoned McGuire, who would be at the back bench putting the paper to bed. She just needed five paras on the front page.

CHAPTER TWENTY-ONE

From where Jimmy was sitting outside the bar with Eddie and Mitch, he could just see his father through the noisy throng of Rangers fans that had spilled out of the crammed bar into the sultry night air. Most of them were staggering around, as they belted out 'Derry's Walls'. He thought of a few weeks ago, and how proud his father had been, leading the sing-song at the fundraiser night. Now he looked hunched over, suddenly old and tired.

'Guys, I'm going over to see my old man for a wee while. Maybe take him for a pint and a bit of a walk.' Jimmy stood up.

'On you go, mate,' Eddie said. 'Where is he? I didn't see him here.'

'He's over there.' Jimmy pointed. 'It's been a long couple of days for him on the bus. I just want to make sure he's all right and not getting too pissed.'

'Right enough,' Mitch said. 'You wouldn't want him to

fall down around here with these Spanish cops. The fuckers are on every corner, and they look like they're just itching for somebody to make a wrong move so they can set about them.'

'Cops are cops the world over,' Eddie said, puffing on a cigar. 'Only difference here is these bastards are all swaggering around because they've got a gun in their belt.' He lifted his shirt a little to show the small pistol in a pouch attached to his belt. 'Well, they're not the only ones tooled up.'

'Fuck's sake, Eddie. Hope you don't get caught with that.'

'No chance, son. But I never leave home without it. Never know when I might need it. I've got one for each of you. You'll get them tomorrow.'

'Are you coming back?' Mitch asked. 'It's just starting to liven up here.'

'Yeah. I'll not be long. Just want to get him out of here for a bit.'

Jimmy walked away from the table and squeezed his way through the sweaty bodies until he found his father, the only guy at the table not guffawing at whatever joke had just been cracked.

'C'mon, I'll take you for a drink, Da. Just you and me,' Jimmy said as cheerfully as he could.

His father's face brightened and he stood up.

'Good idea, son. Could do with a wee walk.'

'Well, mind you two don't get pissed and end up in one of these chapels,' one of his dad's mates shouted after them as they pressed through the crowd and onto the street. 'Place is fucking full of them. You might get kept in, Jack. Especially if you went to confession.'

They took a left up a side street off the main square, away from the noise, and within a minute they were in what could have been a different city. Tourists strolled among the elegant, well-dressed Spanish couples in the cobblestone alley. Not a football jersey or a fan in sight. Candles flickered on restaurant tables strung side by side and the strains of a Spanish guitar drifted from inside one of the cafes. Jimmy saw his father's glance fall on an older Spanish man around the same age as himself who reached across the table to gently touch the face of the woman he was with. For a moment he caught the loneliness in his father's eyes, and he fought the urge to put his arm around his shoulder.

'Some place, this,' his father said, as if to snap himself out of the gloom. 'The only 'Gers fans you'll find here will be the mega-rich bastards running the club.'

'Aye,' Jimmy said. 'It's pretty classy though. And peaceful.' He pointed. 'Look, there's a wee bar at the end of the street. C'mon, we'll go in there and try one of the local drinks.'

They walked along in silence, and Jimmy couldn't help the heaviness in his chest, knowing that they would never walk this way again, just the two of them on a warm summer's night; not in a place like Seville, anyway, and probably not in Glasgow, or anywhere else, because there was so little time left.

They got to the bar and sat at a table outside where two old Spaniards sat with drinks in front of them. A waiter appeared at their table.

'What you want, Da?' Jimmy said.

His father shrugged and sighed. He looked at the waiter.

'What's that, son?' He pointed at the two old men. 'What's that they're drinking?'

Jimmy smiled. 'I don't think they speak much English in Seville, Da. He'll not understand you.'

The waiter smiled.

'Ah! *Los hombres están bebiendo pacharán.* They are drinking *pacharán.* It is Spanish liqueur. Very good. You like?'

'Aye, all right, son. We'll have two of them. With ice.'

'Christ,' Jimmy said. 'This is all we need on top of everything else we've been drinking.'

'Fuck it! You're a long while dead,' his father said, and they both looked at each other, the words hanging in the air like a prophecy. Then he puffed, 'Christ, Many a true word spoken in jest, eh?'

Jimmy was surprised at the tears suddenly stinging his eyes. He looked at the ground.

'I wish I could do something,' he managed to say.

His father looked at him, his expression somewhere between helplessness and compassion. He reached across and squeezed Jimmy's shoulder.

'You're doing it now, son.'

Jimmy sniffed and blinked away the tears as the waiter put the drinks on the table.

His father lifted his drink and they clinked glasses, then gestured to the old men, who smiled back as they raised their drinks in salute.

'No Surrender!' Jack declared.

Jimmy had seen him utter that mantra many times from as early as he could remember. As a little boy he'd got a clip around the ear from his mum after he mimicked him at breakfast the morning, lifting his mug of tea and declaring 'No Surrender'. The night before he'd watched from the top of the stairs as his father had come in drunk from a wedding and poured himself a large whisky, then knocked it back with 'No Surrender'. Jimmy could see through the crack where the door was slightly open, his mother sitting on an armchair with a look of disgust on her face, but he knew she wouldn't dare say a word. No Surrender. It's what they were. It's what he was, and as a kid he couldn't wait to be big enough to drink like his da and say it before he knocked back a stiff whisky. But watching him now, Jimmy thought the way he'd just said it was more from habit than conviction. They fell into silence for a while, then his father spoke.

'So what's the score with big Eddie bringing his wife on the trip? Never seen him do that before.'

Jimmy shrugged, swirling the ice in his glass, and said nothing.

His father pressed. 'I suppose it's a bit of cover for all the fucking drugs he's going to be bringing back.' He shook his head. 'Scumbag.'

Again, Jimmy didn't answer. They were silent as his father gazed at the dying flame of the candle on the table.

'You know something, Jimmy? See when I looked at you that night at the fundraiser, and you were walking round the hall with your UVF tie on and looking the part? I was dead proud of you, so I was. Proud that you'd grown up and you were one of us. Queen and country, and all that. A proud Loyalist. But see now? I look at you and the drugs and stuff and, I'll be honest with you, son, it's not what I wanted for you.'

'Aw, Da. Don't say that. It's just the drink talking. I was always going to be one of us. I wanted to be like you all my days. Don't start that now. You know that's what you wanted for me.'

'Aye, I did. A proud Loyalist for my laddie. But not a fucking drug dealer. Not this pish you're doing with Eddie, sneaking around and bringing drugs back. There are decent, hard-working Rangers fans on that bus with their weans. Good men. That's not what we are. That's not what the UVF's supposed to be. We're not drug dealers. We didn't fight these Fenian fuckers down the years to become drug dealers just like them parasite bastards in the IRA.'

Jimmy sighed. 'I don't make the decisions, Da. You know that. I have to do what the commander tells me.'

'Commander, my arse. He couldn't command a bus load of weans going on a school trip. And it's not just him, it's how a lot of them are now, guys like him, in positions of power. Some of the lads are even prepared to deal with the fucking IRA when it comes to drugs. Can you believe that? After all we've been through? When I was in Belfast a few months ago I was with the brigadier and a couple of other older men, and they hate all that shite too. They're like me – old school. We don't want drugs.'

'But Da, they take the kickback in Belfast from the money big Eddie makes. I know that for a fact.'

'So does that make it right? Peddling all that shite in the streets?'

Jimmy shrugged. He knew his father was right, but he had no control over anything the UVF did. There was a stab of disappointment that after all these years he had spent working towards the honour of being taken over to Belfast and brought into the ranks, his father, who he'd admired all his days for the hardman hero he was, now seemed to be preaching against the very ideals that had shaped his life.

'Why are you saying all this, Da? What's got into you?'

His father said nothing and sat with his lips tight.

'Ach.' He shook his head eventually. 'I just don't like what I see these days. The last few weeks, since I've been told I'm on the way out, I feel different about a lot of things. I've a lot of regrets, Jimmy. That's what I'm saying.' He sighed and put his glass on the table. 'Sometimes I wish I had made our lives different. Your mother asked me to move away. Go abroad, anywhere but Glasgow, when I came out of the jail that time. But I was enjoying the big-shot status too much. I was the local hero. And for what? When I look around now, sometimes I wonder for what.'

'For the cause, Da.'

'Aye, and the cause is now run by fucking drug dealers like that polecat Eddie McGregor.' He looked at Jimmy. 'Tell me. Is that where you went the other night before we left, when you went out in a hurry? Were you going to pick drug money up for him?'

Jimmy sat back and lit a cigarette, inhaling deeply then blowing smoke upwards as he looked at the black sky, remembering the scene.

'No. I was on an ordered job. Guy needed seeing to. I was with Mitch. And Psycho Bentley.'

His father's face fell.

'Psycho Bentley? You were with him? Fuck's sake! Somebody must have got a right tanking. Is the guy dead?'

'No. But he's not in good shape.'

'Who was he?'

'Don't know. Some guy who works in a bakery.'

'What's he done? Welsh on a drug deal?'

Jimmy looked at his father, then at the table. He shouldn't be talking about this and he knew it. But this was his da, he was a bigger UVF hero than McGregor or any of the rest of them in Glasgow.

'Don't know for sure. But the word is that he was shagging big Eddie's wife.'

His father laughed out loud. 'Donna? Fuck's sake! Good for her. She's got more balls than him.'

'Well, Psycho gave the guy a right hiding.'

'What did you do with him?'

'We dumped him.'

'Christ. I hope there's nothing that can link it back to you.'

'No. No way.'

'Now I see why Donna's on the trip. So that her boyfriend could get battered while she was away. If that was me and my wife, I'd have run the guy right up to my front door and confronted the pair of them. Then I'd have given him a sore face and kicked the two of them right out of my life. That's what a real man does. Not send his boys. But that's obviously why he brought Donna over here.'

'Looks like it.'

'Arsehole.' He paused, looked at Jimmy. 'Still no word on that wee lassie of yours? Wendy?'

Jimmy's stomach tweaked at the mention of her name. 'Nothing.' He swallowed.

'He's done her in. I'm telling you.'

'Don't say that, Da. I don't even want to think it.'

'Listen. If a pure bastard like McGregor can rape a defenceless wee lassie, he can do her in.'

CHAPTER TWENTY-TWO

Donna went into the bedroom and stood for a moment with her back pressed against the door, glad to be alone. She flipped up the air conditioning and kicked off her high heels, then yanked her dress over her head and stripped off her underwear, leaving everything on the floor. She crossed the carpet and lay down on the bed, relishing the freedom of being naked and cool. She thought about Andy and automatically her hands went to her breasts, imagining his caress. She turned her head towards the massive window, gazing at the full moon brightening the night sky and her hand drifted downwards.

The ping of her mobile signalling that the battery was dying crashed in on her reverie. Then it rang. She jumped out of bed and fished it out of her bag, hoping it was Andy.

'Donna?'

She was disappointed to hear the voice of her best friend Lisa.

'Hey, Lisa. How you?' Her phone beeped again. 'This battery's knackered, so it might cut out any minute.' She didn't feel like chatting.

'Donna. Listen. I've got some bad news.'

A wave of panic lashed across her stomach.

'It's Andy,' Lisa said, before Donna had a chance to speak.

'What? What's wrong?' Her legs turned to jelly and she sat down on the bed.

'He's in hospital. He's in a pretty bad way. Got beaten up really bad. He . . . he was in a coma.' Her voice trailed a little and she sniffed. 'I'm sorry. I can't believe anyone would hurt Andy.'

Donna could feel her heart pumping and her hand shook so much she could barely hold the phone. She tried to speak, but her throat was tight and her mouth dry. Eddie had done this. It had to be him. Jesus! He knew all about them. Now it was blindingly clear why he'd brought her here.

'You there, Donna?'

'Y-yes,' she managed to say. 'Oh God, Lisa! Is he . . . is he going to die? Oh Christ, please tell me he's not going to die . . .'

'I don't think so. He was in a coma but he's out of it now. Fractured skull. The boss went in to see him. He said he didn't recognise him, his face is such a mess. And . . . And . . .' Lisa started crying again. 'His hands. They smashed his hands to a pulp.'

'Oh, Christ! When? When did this happen? I was trying

to phone him the night before I left and got no answer. I've been frantically waiting for a text or something from him since I left Glasgow.'

'It happened that night. Before you left. He got attacked at the bakery coming off his shift. Nobody saw anything. Whoever it was dumped him and left him for dead. Can't believe anybody would hurt him. How could anybody do that to somebody like him? He's . . . he's . . .' Lisa's voice broke. 'He's the kindest man I've ever known.'

Silence. Donna knew exactly who was behind this, and most likely so did Lisa. They'd been close friends since she started working at the bakery, and Lisa had watched her friendship with Andy grow to the runaway train that it had become. Her friend had warned her many times that she was playing with fire, but Donna had told her she couldn't stop herself.

'You know who's done this, Lisa, don't you?'

'I think so.'

'It's Eddie. That's why he wanted me here, to get me out of the way. He must have found something out. Somebody must have told him.'

'Not me,' Lisa said quickly. 'You know I'd never breathe a word.'

'I know that. I know it's not you. But somebody has.' Donna's mind reeled with possibilities. Did someone see them? Did Eddie have them followed? How long had he known? Christ almighty! She felt sick.

Her phone pinged again, then went dead. She looked at it in her trembling hands and the console was black.

'Shit! Shit!' It suddenly occurred to her that she hadn't brought her charger. She lifted the landline phone on the bedside to call Lisa back, but couldn't remember her mobile number – she'd had it on speed dial for so long. She racked her brains but couldn't recall her home phone number either. She lay on the bed, curling herself into a ball, terrified of what was going to happen next. Eddie would be watching her like a hawk over the next few days to see if she'd found out. How long had he known? Her head spun, trying to figure out how he'd found out. They'd been so careful – Andy even more so than her. He was the one who'd tried to hold back in the beginning, not only because she was married, but because of who her husband was. They'd tried to keep it as a close friendship but it had spiralled out of control. It was all her fault. She could have stopped it at any time. Now Andy was lying suffering in hospital because of her. The tears came, trickling down her cheeks as she lay on the bed imagining his agony as they'd smashed his hands. Then she buried her head in the pillow to stifle her sobs as over and over again she whispered, 'Oh Andy! Andy! I'm so, so sorry.' She sobbed until she drifted off to sleep.

She was woken by the sound of the key in the door, and immediately was awake. She leapt out of bed and dashed into the bathroom, catching sight of her makeup-smeared face in the mirror. She quickly applied some cleansing lotion and wiped it clean, splashing water and dabbing it with a towel. She couldn't afford to let Eddie know she'd been crying. She took a deep breath and stiffened up. She would act normal. Nothing would make her go to pieces over this, she vowed to herself. Nothing. She looked in the mirror as she heard the bedroom door close. The face looking back was weary and blotchy, her eyes red-rimmed from crying. But she could do this. She had to. For the sake of Andy, lying in a hospital bed beaten to a pulp, she had to find the strength. She at least owed him that. She rubbed on moisturising cream and sniffed back her tears as she heard Eddie calling out to her.

'I'll just be a minute, sweetheart.' She swallowed hard and looked herself in the eye.

She was surprised at the resolve that suddenly came over her. Fuck him. She would fix the bastard good and proper. She'd find a way. Then it came to her. The bank card. She'd given it to Andy. Just let me get home to you, she told herself, still looking in the mirror. Then she painted as cheery a smile as she could muster and opened the bathroom door, trying to look sleepy and sexy at the same time.

Rosie had come back to her hotel room to talk to McGuire and send over a few paragraphs on Don's tip about the baker who'd been beaten and left for dead. He agreed with her that it looked like it had McGregor's fingerprints all over it.

'Yeah, Gilmour, but as your cop pal says, there's not a chance in hell they'll be able to connect McGregor to that.'

'I know. But if we stick it on the front page, it might just rattle things up a bit.'

'Explain, Gilmour. I'm all ears. But make it quick because I'm trying to get the first edition away.'

'Well,' Rosie said. 'I'm thinking that if you can stick the attack on the front page tonight, then I can pick up a copy of the *Post* here in the morning. Then I'll make sure a paper gets slipped under Donna's nose at her hotel breakfast table.'

'And?'

'You never know. If she's in love with the guy, she might just go off the edge and start talking.'

'Hold the fucking pony, here, Gilmour. Even if McGregor's wife does see the paper, and even if she's broken-hearted, it's a bit of a leap to think she'll then pour her heart out to you while she's on a trip with her husband. Think about it. Think what you're saying.'

'I am, Mick. I've thought about it. Obviously I'm not going to go introducing myself over the poached eggs. But if Donna is totally nuts about this guy and in an unhappy situation with McGregor – which Liz told me she was and that he beats her – then maybe this is the final straw. Maybe we could get her onside. I've got the two girls, Liz and Wendy, coming up here in the morning from the Costa and they both know her. I know it's a long shot, but what I'm saying is it's a possibility. Maybe we can make a connection with her.'

There was a pause, then McGuire spoke. 'But why would she? What would she have to talk to you about? It's not as if she'll know about all her man's drug dealing and UVF activity. She'll know bugger all. So why would she talk to a reporter about her private life and marriage problems? It's not Oprah Winfrey. And she must know if she starts blabbing about her man being an asshole husband, admitting she's having an affair, she'll be dead before she gets to Glasgow.'

'Yeah, yeah,' Rosie said, knowing McGuire was talking sense. 'But all I'm looking for is a road into McGregor and his dealings, and one way to get there is to get the wife with an axe to grind. Why not just get the story on the front page, I'll make sure she sees it, and we'll take it from there? It'll all be done very softly softly, to see if there's any reaction at all. I wouldn't make an approach unless I'm sure she's not going to flip her lid and tell McGregor.'

'Right. Okay, Gilmour. I'll stick five or six paras on the front. Write it as dramatically as you can. Mention the torture and kidnap, but not the burnt bollocks.' He paused. 'Or second thoughts, should we mention the burnt bollocks? Hmm. That might get her *really* angry.'

'My cop pal says not to. They haven't put any of this out yet.'

'Yeah, but one of the victim's pals could have visited him

in hospital and maybe he's told them about getting electric shocks to his tackle.' He paused. 'In fact, the more I'm talking about this, the more I'm thinking I'll make it a splash, Gilmour. Torture, kidnap, organised gangland beating. Yes. Let's rattle it out as a splash. Fuck it.'

'But, Mick. My cop contact . . .' Rosie protested.

'Fuck it. You'll be able to get round him. Just tell him we got it from a hospital insider or a friend or sources close to the place where he worked. Come on, I know you can use your imagination. I've seen your bloody expenses.' He chuckled.

'Yeah, okay, Mick. Jesus! You're going to get me in all sorts of shit.' Rosie knew he wouldn't back down. 'Oh. And definitely don't put my byline on the story.'

'Fine. Now piss off and write me a splash. I might hold it for the second edition, but get it done so I can make up my mind. You have twenty minutes. No more. Any pictures of this guy, by the way?'

'Christ, Mick. Hardly. I've only just heard about it.'

'You're slipping, Gilmour,' he joked. 'I need to go. Let's get moving.' He hung up.

CHAPTER TWENTY-THREE

Twenty minutes later Rosie hit a key on her laptop and sent her gritty story of the kidnap and torture of an innocent man on his way home from work. It would walk onto the splash in the *Post*, and she knew she was sailing close to the wind, giving the story plenty of topspin. She'd have to deal with the fallout from Don in the morning.

She looked at her watch and automatically scrolled down her mobile to find TJ's number. It would be late afternoon, so usually he'd be in his apartment chilling out for a few hours until it was time to go to work. When she'd been out there with him, sometimes, by the time he was finished playing at the jazz bar until nearly four in the morning, they would catch some breakfast on the way to the apartment, before crashing out for the afternoon. The turning of night into day didn't appeal to Rosie as a lifestyle, but it seemed to suit TJ who was more of a nighthawk. What she did love was watching Manhattan wake up to a new day; the early morning bustle on the streets and the little dramas unfolding on every corner. She could have sat in a cafe for hours, watching the New Yorkers dive into their day with a kind of ratty edginess about them that reminded Rosie of Glaswegians, only more extreme. She punched in TJ's number and let it ring a few times. No answer. Perhaps he was having a nap. She was about to hang up when a voice answered. But it wasn't TJ, and Rosie felt a thump in her stomach. It was Kat.

'Hello?' Kat sounded sleepy, and her transatlantic drawl was even more pronounced than before.

Rosie froze somewhere between opening her mouth to speak and almost hanging up.

'Hello? Who's this?' Kat said.

Silence. Just say who you are, for Christ's sake, she told herself. But the words wouldn't come. All she could see was the image of Kat dreamily answering the phone having been woken out of a deep sleep. Had she reached across TJ in the bed to answer it? Rosie's paranoia went into overdrive. She saw him lying next to Kat breathing softly in a deep, contented sleep, the way he used to after they'd made love. Her chest felt tight. She took a breath and almost spoke, but the line went dead. Kat had hung up. She pictured her putting the phone back down on the bedside table and snuggling into TJ. Rosie sat down on the bed. Surely to Christ she was wrong. Especially after everything they'd said to each other while she was there and the promises they made. Her gut burned with anger and disappointment, but worst of all some kind of sixth sense that she was losing him. Relationships across thousands of miles never worked, she'd told TJ, but he had insisted they could make it work. And she'd believed him because the way she felt about him left her with nowhere else to go. She stepped outside, gazing across the city shimmering in the myriad of lights and the silhouette of the Giralda on the skyline. A wave of loneliness shuddered through her. She took a deep breath. Get it into perspective, she told herself. There was probably a rational explanation. She should have told Kat it was her and asked for TJ – yet something had made her terrified of the answer. If Kat had said TJ was asleep, it would have been even worse. Stop getting all hung up, she whispered to herself. Perhaps they'd been working late and Kat had crashed out for a few hours. She didn't like the image of that either, but there could be all sorts of reasons for Kat to be there. She'd give TJ a ring tomorrow and have a chat with him. If he didn't mention Kat being at the apartment, then perhaps she'd have grounds for all this anxiety. She went back inside, picked up her bag and left the bedroom, then headed out of the hotel and back to the troops. She needed a drink.

Matt got up from the table and strode towards Rosie as she crossed the square where she'd left them earlier.

'Hey, Rosie.' His grin was from ear to ear. 'You'll never guess what's happened.'

'Something good, by the look on your face.' Rosie stopped in her tracks. 'You've got me all excited now.' Matt's enthusiasm pushed her anxiety over TJ away.

'You know the bar across the square from us where all the bears are singing and partying?'

'Yeah.' Rosie glanced across and could hear the chants. 'I see they're still at it.'

'I know. It's just livening up. But about half an hour ago, we're all sitting having a drink, and who do I see strolling over to the bar but big McGregor and his two sidekicks – Mitch and that Jimmy geezer.'

'Yeah? And?'

'Next thing is that bent cop joined him. What's his name? Thomson? The guy I snatched.'

'You're kidding! Did you get a snap of them together?'

'You bet I did. And more than that.'

'What?'

'They all went inside at one point and there's this big sing-song going on. All the 'Gers fans belting out "The Sash" and "No Surrender". So Javier slipped in and stood at the bar. Next thing is the cop joins the sing-song with McGregor and the rest of the mob. Javier stuck the video in his camera, and bingo! They're all on it. You need to see it. It's a belter. Fists pumping and chanting at all the right bits! Even if we never got another line of the drug story, we've got footage of a police inspector singing sectarian songs with Rangers fans. Even if we can't prove he's UVF, him just being there is a story in itself.'

'Not half,' Rosie said, delighted.

'Brilliant. Couldn't risk doing the video myself in case anyone got suspicious, but your man there just looked like one of the locals capturing the party atmosphere.'

They walked towards the table and sat down.

'Top stuff, Javier,' Rosie said. 'I would throw my arms around you, but I don't want to attract any attention.' She smiled. 'Consider yourself hugged.'

Javier grinned.

'Of course you must understand the video is extra – not part of my daily rate.'

'Yeah, yeah. I'm sure your expenses will reflect the amount of drink you had to buy to get the film.' Rosie signalled for the waiter. 'Let's have a celebratory drink.'

It was nearly two hours and two bars later by the time Rosie was making her way back to the hotel, accompanied by Adrian. They'd left the others still drinking in a dingy little flamenco bar that Garcia had told them was the oldest bar in Seville. Considering she'd been drinking for several hours, Rosie felt more sober than she was entitled. Must be the Mediterranean way. They spend hours over dinner, eating slowly and drinking copious amounts of wine, but you never see Spanish, Italian or French people falling about drunk. The secret is clearly about pacing yourself – unlike the stereotypical Brit abroad. She would find out when she woke up in the morning if she'd managed to master the continental drinking habits, or if she was just another hung-over Brit craving a full cooked English breakfast. Away from the buzz around the cathedral square, there was a calmness about the city and it was pleasant to stroll now that the night had lost its energy-sapping heat.

'Would you like to have a coffee with me, Rosie?' Adrian said as he stopped at the American cafe next to their hotel.

Rosie stood looking at the deserted tables inside, the walls adorned with black and white prints of Hollywood in the fifties. The decor somehow looked out of place in the midst of the ancient architectural splendour of Seville. Suddenly she was captivated by a song drifting out from the speakers and into the stillness of the night. The mellow tones of Nat King Cole and an old classic, 'Embraceable You', filled the air and transported her back to another life. It was years since she'd heard that song. She felt a catch in her throat, and blinked away the image of her mother and father dancing in their living room one Christmas Eve a lifetime ago.

'We sit?' Adrian pulled out a chair at the small iron table on the pavement.

Rosie studied his pale face. Long before she had known about Adrian's tragic past, she'd sensed that behind the hooded eyes and flat expression there was pain and loneliness. Being the shadowy figure he was, Adrian didn't invite questions, so she had never asked, but two months ago he'd allowed her to share his darkness. She looked at him for a long moment, remembering the morning he stood at the Bosnian cemetery on the hillside, his shoulders slumped as she and Matt waited nearby. Then he'd beckoned them close to a graveside and confided in them that the head-stone marked the place where his eight months pregnant fiancée lay buried with their son, torn from her womb by rampaging Serbian butchers. She had seen for the first time who he really was, and though he seemed to have dulled himself to the pain of loneliness, perhaps there were times, Rosie thought, when he just needed someone around a little longer.

'Of course,' Rosie said. 'I'll have a coffee.'

She didn't feel like going to bed anyway. She knew as soon as her head hit the pillow she would lie in the darkness pick-ing away at the phone call, conjuring up all sorts of pictures of TJ and Kat, or TJ and some other random woman in a dimly lit New York bar. She knew her troubled dreams would be a confusing mix of terror somewhere between Manhat-tan, Kosovo and the childhood trauma that never seemed to be far away when she slept. She thought of TJ as she sat down, and there was a sudden rush of clarity. It couldn't go on, she told herself. Perhaps the phone call was a trig-ger for what she felt right now, but the fact was that in the last ten days she and TJ had only spoken once. Mostly, she realised, because she was busy and hadn't had a chance to phone him. But she hadn't heard much from him either in emails or texts. Perhaps they *were* drifting apart. Having TJ in her life as a friend before they'd become so involved had been much easier to manage. The falling in love part hadn't been on her agenda, but when it happened, it unleashed in her explosive, passionate emotions she'd never felt about anyone before. But it also made her vulnerable, afraid she would lose him; it weakened her. Too often, she'd told herself she should have walked away after the first night they'd spent together, putting it down to a drunken error of judgement. But by the time she'd left his house that morning she knew it was already too late. And now, an even greater problem niggled away at her, no matter how much she pushed it away. Since Bosnia, she'd found herself thinking about Adrian. Amid the ruins of his life there, she'd seen him in a different light. Christ almighty! Why did she always have to complicate her life like this? The waiter brought them coffee – a decaff for her and espresso for Adrian. He looked like sleep was something he had given up years ago. He offered her a cigarette and lit them both.

'Are you okay, Rosie?' he said, his rich Slavic tones almost a whisper.

'Yes,' she replied quickly, surprised at the question, avoiding his eyes.

'You are sure?' Pale grey eyes scrutinised her face.

Rosie felt a little unnerved and said nothing, drawing on her cigarette.

'I was thinking that you look maybe a little sad. Your eyes. You seem sad for a while now.' Adrian still didn't take his eyes off her.

'Sad?' she said, trying to brighten. 'How do you mean . . . for a while?'

'No. Sorry,' he said. 'Maybe I shouldn't say. I mean tonight. You went away to the hotel, and then came back, and you look different.'

Jesus, Rosie thought. How can he see that? How can he see the angst behind my eyes? I hardly know him. When she'd come back from sending her story to the paper, they'd been laughing and joking about Javier's video and then moved to the other bar, where they drank more and listened to Javier and Garcia tell stories of their old days together. She thought she'd been in good form, given that her insides were in turmoil.

She let out a tired sigh, feeling she had to say something. 'Oh, you know how things are, Adrian. I'm always a bit jaded. Lot of travelling and working. Sometimes it catches up with me and I start to puff a little bit.' She gave him the most reassuring smile she could muster. 'But I'm fine. Thanks for asking.'

She reached across and patted the back of his hand in a friendly way, and to her surprise he slipped his hand in hers. He held it for a moment and looked at her.

'Okay, Rosie, if you are all right. You are my friend. Probably the best friend I have in the world – next of course to my comrade Risto.' His eyes smiled at the mention of his friend that he had fought alongside in the Bosnian war. He opened his mouth to speak and hesitated for a second, seeming to struggle to find the words. 'You . . . you mean a lot to me, Rosie. I am upset if you are unhappy. I care for you very much.'

Rosie allowed him to hold her hand, feeling the softness and warmth in hers, and the instinct to squeeze it or reach across and touch him was almost overpowering. But she knew she couldn't. This was Adrian, her friend, her minder, the man who had saved her life not once but twice. She looked away and then at him, his eyes still engrossed in her face.

'Thank you.' She lightly took her hand out of his and pushed her hair back a little self-consciously.

They drank their coffee in an edgy silence. Rosie wondered if she should say something, gently stress that they were good friends and could never be anything else. But what if she'd read it wrong? Perhaps Adrian was just trying to be caring. She caught herself looking at the soft underside of his muscular, suntanned forearms and again had the urge to touch him.

'I should get to my bed, Adrian,' she said, more abruptly than she meant to, and saw him lower his eyes to the table. 'I have this meeting with Wendy and Liz tomorrow. I need to be sharp. And you have a very early start.' She went into her bag for some money.

'No.' He shook his head, his expression somewhere between flat and disappointed. 'I pay. I will stay a little longer.'

She said goodnight and walked away, knowing she could not afford to look back.

CHAPTER TWENTY-FOUR

Rosie was woken by the sound of her own crying. The dream had been so real she could still hear the song as the images faded. 'Embrace me, my sweet embraceable you . . .' She wiped the tears as she groggily tried to grasp at the dream again.

Christmas Eve. She was seven. A whiteout. In her bedroom Rosie was enthralled at the plump snowflakes falling like feathers on the windows then instantly melting as they slid down the glass. The pavements thick with fresh snow, twinkling under the street lamps and fairy lights from the Christmas trees dotted around the various tenement windows. She was wearing her new pyjamas and had been carried to bed by her father who had told her Santa Claus wouldn't come until he was sure she was asleep. She'd thrown her arms around him as he tucked her in, clinging tight and telling him it didn't matter. He was here. That's all she cared about. He stroked her hair as she drifted off. A little later it was the music that had woken her, and she recognised the song. 'Embraceable You'. Her mother had told her the story many times as they'd waited for her father to come home from his travels. Rosie could sing every word of it and sometimes she and her mother would sing it together on quiet winter evenings. It had been the first song her mother and father had danced to back when they met. More times than she cared to remember, Rosie had to reach in and lift the arm off the record on the turntable on the old radiogram after her mother had fallen asleep drunk, listening to their tune. But that night, one of the few when her father actually kept his promise and came home for Christmas, she'd got out of bed as she heard the music, and peered through the crack in her door. Then she saw them, dancing slowly in the living room, swaying to the music, her mother's eyes closed as her head rested on his shoulder, her father's strong arms around her waist, holding her close.

'Embrace me, my sweet embraceable you . . .'

But in her dream, her mother and father had melted like snow until there was nothing there, just the hiss of the fire and the scratching of the needle on the LP. And the sound of Rosie's crying bringing her back.

She lay staring at the ceiling, trying hard to shake herself back from the pointless gloom of dwelling on the past. She should have stopped missing them by now, but the thoughts just kept coming. She missed running home from school at lunchtime to eat porridge for lunch because that was all her mother could afford. She didn't really care that her mum was drunk, just as long as she was there. Jesus, she even missed the hellish, crushing poverty of it all. She thought of her father and how they'd finally reconciled a few months ago, and that miserable afternoon in the cafe when he'd told her he was dying, then weeks later holding his hand as he slipped away. You'll drive yourself crazy, woman, she told herself. Sighing, she sat up on the bed, throwing the sheet back as though casting out the melancholy. She stood up and walked naked to the balcony and opened the door.

Seville was baking and it wasn't yet ten. She stood for a few seconds outside, watching the massive bell tower at the Giralda begin to ring out, one huge bell sleepily tumbling over, then another, and another until all fifteen chimed at the same time, signalling a frenzy of bells ringing out in churches across the city. It was an awesome sight and sound, a feat of engineering from centuries past, and Rosie wished she could lie down to the sound of church bells and go some place where her heart didn't hurt.

She rubbed her face briskly. Adrian would be almost in Seville by now, having picked up Wendy and Liz early doors. At least she assumed he would be. There had been no phone call to the contrary. Her mind flicked back to the awkward moment last night at the cafe, and she immediately dismissed it. No room for that. She had to get her mind focused on the day ahead. She had told Liz a rough idea of what she had in mind. If they knocked her back, she had no plan B. The niggle in her gut at what lay ahead forced her to head for a cold shower to bring her back to life.

Her mobile rang as she came out minutes later wrapped in a towel. She picked it up from the bedside table.

'I have the two ladies,' Adrian said. 'We just come into Seville. Where will I bring them? To the hotel?'

Rosie thought for a second. Did she detect a brusqueness? No, it's just how he was.

'Yes. Bring them here, Adrian. Matt said the place is fairly empty at this time of the day, so we can maybe get a little table for lunch and have a chat. I'll be down in ten minutes.'

Javier had organised a two-bedroom apartment in one of the backstreets in the old town for Wendy and Liz to stay for the next couple of nights so they could meet away from the crowds.

Rosie went into the coolness of the atrium bar overlooking the swimming pool where Adrian sat well away from the couple of tables that were occupied. Liz and Wendy sat beside him and she was glad to see them all looking reasonably relaxed.

'Hello, girls . . . Adrian.' Rosie took a deep breath, smiled and walked towards them. This had to be a good pitch.

Adrian nodded, and Liz and Wendy both smiled back.

'Hi, Rosie.' Liz stood up and embraced Rosie as though

they were old friends. She seemed confident, her usual strident self.

'Hello, Rosie.' Wendy hugged her surprisingly tightly.

'How you doing, Wendy?' Rosie asked, looking at the dark shadows under her eyes. 'Are you okay?'

Wendy nodded. 'I am, thanks. But I feel a bit nervous.' She looked at Liz. 'I'm not really sure what I'm doing, and I'm a bit scared.'

Rosie glanced at Liz who gave her an understanding grimace.

'She didn't sleep much last night,' Liz said. She patted Wendy's arm. 'We're going to try to relax this afternoon, once we get settled in.'

'Good,' Rosie said. 'I have a little place organised, so we'll go there as soon as you like and you can chill for a bit.'

She sat down, and when the waiter arrived they ordered soft drinks and some sandwiches.

'So,' Rosie said, looking at both of them across the table. 'I want to run some things past you, Wendy. But listen, if you don't want to be part of it, then I understand. But whatever you decide, I need you to be aware that what I'm going to say to you takes you completely into my confidence, and I'm placing a lot of trust in you by telling you this.'

Wendy nodded, biting her bottom lip.

'I trust you.' She looked nervously at Liz.

'She's all right,' Liz said. 'It's just been a hard time these past few weeks.'

'Okay.' Rosie sat forward. 'I want to ask you this. How do you feel about meeting Jimmy? I mean, just surprising him out of the blue. Telling him you're here.'

Wendy swallowed. 'I thought you would ask me that.' She looked at Liz. 'We talked about what you might want. And we kind of thought you would want me to meet him.' She took a deep breath and lifted her glass to her lips and sipped a little water. 'Rosie. Are you going to ask me to set him up with the cops or something? Because I don't think I could do that.'

They sat in silence for a moment. Rosie glanced at Liz who raised her eyebrows almost in apology.

'No. I wasn't thinking of getting you to set Jimmy up,' Rosie said truthfully. 'I was thinking of how you want to meet him, and wondering how much influence you think you would have over him.' She paused. 'Ultimately, Wendy, I'd like to get McGregor nailed for what he's doing here, smuggling drugs and everything else. But I'd also like to nail him for what he's done to you. That's what I'm thinking. And I was hoping that if you could talk to Jimmy and let him know that you're alive, then maybe his whole perspective would change.' She shrugged. 'To be honest, I'm not even sure if that would happen. I don't know the kind of guy Jimmy is. I only know what I've been told by Liz of how crazy he is about you and how much he's hurting over you.'

'I know.' Wendy picked at her nails. 'I know he's hurting. I'm sure he thinks I'm dead. I feel terrible that I phoned him that night and then just upped and left. I haven't even told my parents that I'm alive. I've just left everyone hanging and it really upsets me, what I'm putting them all through.' Tears came to her eyes. 'I just want to find a way to get out of this. I want my life back.'

They sat in silence, and Rosie stole a glance at Adrian who sat with his arms folded, his face impassive, as if he was somewhere else. She watched Wendy as she wiped her nose with a napkin, and Liz put her arm around her shoulder and gave her a sisterly squeeze.

'You'll get through this. You will.'

'Do you think you would have any influence over Jimmy, Wendy? Like, if you met him and he knew you were alive. Do you think he would do anything for you? And, also, do you really want to be with him?' Rosie asked.

Wendy nodded, tears spilling out of her eyes.

'I do. I love him. But I don't know how he would feel about me now that big Eddie has done what he did to me. He might look at me different. It's not my fault, I know that. But what if, somewhere in his head, Jimmy thinks I'm even a wee bit to blame? I don't know if we can ever be together again.' Tears ran down her cheeks. 'Jimmy was the best thing to happen to me. He respected me. From the first night. He didn't just want to use me.' She sniffed. 'Other guys have used me like that. I was so stupid. I don't know what I was looking for. I just wanted them to like me.' She shook her head and buried her face in her hands.

A little pang of guilt tugged at Rosie's gut. Wendy was vulnerable, and she was putting her at risk for her own ends. She could hear McGuire in her head, telling her to get on with it, stop being a bleeding heart. It wasn't just for her own ends. It was for what McGregor had done to people like her, and for what he'd been getting away with for years. She reached across and touched Wendy's hand.

'You don't have to do any of this, Wendy. Honestly. It's up to you. I can't tell you how Jimmy will be with you when he sees you. Only you can have a feeling about that. But I don't want to drag you into something. It's up to you. If you don't want to, we leave it here.'

Her words hung in the air and they sat in silence. Eventually, Wendy swallowed hard and looked at her, her lip quivering.

'What do you want me to do?'

Rosie took a deep breath then let it out slowly. She poured water into her glass.

'I want you to phone him. This afternoon. Tell him you're here, but that he's not to say a word to anyone. Ask him to meet you.'

'Just like that?'

'Yes.'

'And then what?'

'Then maybe get Liz to come in as well and the two of you talk to Jimmy.'

'Talk to him about what?'

'Well. You tell him everything you told me about what Eddie did. Then once you've had some time to yourself, Liz and you can both talk to him.' Rosie looked at Liz. 'This is where you come in, Liz. I want you to try to talk Jimmy into coming onside with us.'

'What? You mean stick big Eddie in?'

'Yeah.' Rosie lowered her voice, looking at both of them and leaning closer. 'Listen. We're working with the cops over here. McGregor is getting done, one way or another, with these drugs. He's finished.' Rosie knew it was more hopeful bluff than fact, but she could see by the looks on their faces it was working. 'If Jimmy's got any sense he should get out now while he still can.'

'But it's UVF,' Liz said. 'You can't just hand your resignation in. Jimmy knows that. He'll get bumped off.'

'That's up to Jimmy. He'll need to cross that bridge when he comes to it. But if he stays with McGregor right now then he's getting locked up for a long time.'

Liz shook her head.

'Jimmy won't grass Eddie up. No way.'

Rosie looked at Wendy for a long moment before she spoke.

'If you want to be with him, Wendy, ask him to make a choice. Believe me, he's running out of options.'

Wendy played nervously with a pendant and chain around her neck.

'Jimmy bought me this,' she said, her eyes filling up again. 'The week before it all happened.' She sniffed. Then she looked Rosie in the eye. 'I'll do it.'

CHAPTER TWENTY-FIVE

From where she was sitting, Rosie had a clear view of Donna
in the cafe across the pedestrian precinct. She could see her
dabbing her eyes and blowing her nose. A copy of the *Post*
lay on the table.

'No wonder she looks wrecked,' Rosie said to Matt and
Javier, as she reread the story splashed all over the front
page.

KIDNAP TORTURE, the banner headline screamed. Then
below, a smaller strap headline, *Victim Had Electric Shocks
to Privates*. And another smaller headline: *Hands Smashed In
Vicious Beating*.

Rosie's mobile rang and this time she knew she had to
answer it.

'Fuck me, Rosie! Fuck me!' It was Don, his voice several
octaves higher than normal.

'I've just seen the paper, Don. I didn't want to return your
call until I'd seen it.'

'Christ almighty, Rosie! The shit's flying all over the shop here. I told you not to use the line about his bollocks getting electric shocks. They're going apeshit here.'

'It didn't come from you, Don. Calm down. Listen. It came from the newsdesk.' Rosie lied – there was nothing else for it. 'When I phoned the tip, the night news editor came back to me with a line about the electric shocks. He said it came from one of their hospital contacts.'

'Pish!'

'That's what he said, Don.' Rosie was beginning to believe it herself. 'So, as far as you're concerned you say nothing. Honestly. Look, I know you're not happy, but these things always leak out. There's always some hospital porter or someone on the ward or a friend of the victim who lets a line like that go for a few quid. So don't worry.'

'Oh. Do I sound worried? Sorry if I alarmed you. I'm just keeping my head down. I didn't even talk to you. But fuck's sake, Rosie!'

'Okay, Don. I get the picture. But apart from that, Mrs Kennedy, how was your trip to Dallas?' Rosie tried to lighten the mood with the standard joke journalists used when the shit was hitting the fan.

'Aye. Very fucking funny. You should be in here. It's hysterical.'

Rosie could hear his tone relax a little.

'Just keep your head down. Seriously, though, anything

new on the story itself? Any new lines? It must be the talk of the steamie by now.'

'Nah. Well, nothing I can talk about.' He hesitated. 'In terms of who did it, I don't think we're going to get a lot of people lining up to spill their guts. It's got all the hallmarks of a punishment beating, so the guy must have done something pretty bad.'

'But you must have an idea who specialises in shocks to the bollocks and stuff? It's like something out of the Krays.'

'You'd be surprised the kind of shit your average middle-ranking gangster gets up to. They get their ideas from the movies. *Pulp Fiction* and all that stuff. We've got wee neds from the schemes who think they're in *Goodfellas*. Thing is, they're so coked up all the time, they're actually playing out the roles of these fuckwits in the movie, and we have to pick up the pieces.'

'I know. But has the victim not said anything helpful?' Rosie chanced her arm. She'd known Don long enough to sense that he was holding out on her. 'Anything at all?'

'Not really. All he can tell us is that he was taken to a garage somewhere in the boot of a car. He was blindfolded but he said he heard what sounded like a roller shutter going up, and then he was dragged out of the boot by two guys in balaclavas. Said he could smell oil and stuff. Like he was in a garage.'

'Does that not give you any ideas?'

Don hesitated. 'One or two. But I'm not about to tell you that right now. Can't do.'

'Okay, I understand. But I'm guessing you've a good idea whose fingerprints are all over this, if you know what I mean.'

'Aye. We've an idea. But not a scrap of fucking evidence. And we never will have, if it's who we think it is.'

'You mean you have a face?'

'Jesus. You don't give up, do you? I mean we've got a shit-load of work to do yet. C'mon. Give me a break.'

Rosie was silent for a moment while she decided, then she spoke.

'Listen. Totally between you and me, the next couple of days out here are going to be crucial for me. You know what I'm saying?'

'Er . . . Well, what I *think* is that you're not on hooligan watch and never were. You got something big on the go out there? If you have, I hope you're going to give me a heads up if it's something we need to get involved in.'

'That depends.'

'Depends on what?'

'Are you holding out on me over the tortured baker guy? I feel you're not telling me something.'

'The last thing I bloody told you was all over the fucking front page this morning.'

'Come on, Don.' Rosie paused and glanced at Javier and Matt. She took a deep breath. 'Right. I'll tell you something.

I'm not on hooligan watch, as I'm sure you know. I'm on something mega. And I promise you, that as soon as the time is right, I'll let you know. In fact I might even need your help. And believe me, this is something the police will want to know about. But I can't say any more.'

Don went quiet. Rosie knew that he wouldn't be able to resist getting a tip-off that would impress his bosses.

'Right, okay. I'm going to tell *you* something, and I know that this can't come from any other source but me, so if it ends up in the *Post*, then you and me are finished. You understand?'

'Come on, you don't even have to say that.'

'Yes. But if this goes in the paper, you will fuck up a major murder investigation.'

'A murder investigation?' Rosie was bursting to hear it. 'To do with the tortured guy?'

'Yep.'

'But how?'

'Christ! If this comes out, I'm right in the shit. But we've got a real mystery here. Remember the two drug-dealing wankers dragged out of the quarry?'

'Of course.'

'Well, we found something in the baker's wallet that links him to one of them.'

'You're kidding? How? I mean, what did you find?'

Don's voice was almost a whisper.

'A fucking bank card belonging to one of them.'

'Jesus!'

'Yep. It all checked out. It's definitely the card belonging to that little toerag bastard – not that he'll be needing it. But what is a fucking quiet-as-a-mouse baker doing with it? That's the mystery. Okay, we have it from a good source that he was shagging McGregor's wife, but not a hint about drugs or anything else. Guy's never put a foot wrong in his life. He's got no real money to show, and has worked hard all his days. So how the fuck has he got the bank card of a small-time hood? He must have been leading some kind of double life. But that notion just doesn't add up. He doesn't fit the profile, and there's nothing else in his life to suggest it.'

Rosie's brain went into overdrive.

'Could it have been planted on him by the guys who kidnapped him? Make him look guilty?'

'Possible, I suppose. But right now, he's barely wakened out of the coma and we're about to tell him that he's now a suspect in a double murder inquiry.'

'Have you asked him about the card? And the affair with McGregor's wife?'

'Of course. He's saying fuck all. Won't talk about it. Says he doesn't know how the card got there. And won't open his mouth about the wife.'

'Is that not worse for him? Makes him look guilty?'

'Yeah. It does. My gut feeling is that he's got nothing to do with the murder. But right now, he's the only suspect we've got, and the longer he says nothing, the more chance there is of him ending up getting charged. Plus it means that we're going to have to take a look at McGregor's wife. So her little secret is about to be blown.'

'Christ! Some story!'

'Don't start. You'd better not write this. Seriously.'

'Of course I won't. Don't worry. But it's intriguing.'

'I know. But I'd say we'll get the truth out of him eventually – once he can sit up straight – the DCI will put the frighteners on him.' He paused. 'Look, I need to go right now, I'll give you a shout if anything comes up.'

'Cheers, Don. Same here.' Rosie hung up.

She looked at Matt and Javier and puffed out her cheeks.

'My cop pal is not a happy bunny about this morning's paper. Sounds like he's got a red-hot poker up his arse.'

'Now there's a surprise,' Javier said.

Rosie looked across at Donna who had picked up the newspaper again, scrutinising it.

'But I'll tell you what, guys, he's just told me something amazing that might give us a bit of leverage here.'

'What?' Matt said.

Rosie relayed the information that Don had given her, filling Javier in on the story of the two drug dealers.

'Cops would be very surprised if he has anything to do with drugs. They think maybe it was planted by the kidnappers.'

The three of them sat for a moment, processing the information.

'Or maybe the wife gave him the card,' Javier suggested, spreading his hands.

'What?' Rosie said, confused.

'Think about it,' Javier said. 'Two drug dealers are murdered and dumped in a quarry. Chances of them being shot and beaten by a mild-mannered baker are very remote, don't you think?'

Rosie and Matt nodded.

'So,' Javier continued. 'Unless McGregor's wife is also a hitwoman when she's not working at the bakery or fucking the baker, then who else just might have been behind the murders?'

'McGregor?'

'He's had plenty of practice,' Matt chirped.

'Okay,' Rosie said. 'But how did the card get into the wallet of the baker? And how did the wife come by it – if she had it?'

Another silent moment as they all looked at each other, then across at Donna who sat staring straight ahead.

'Only one way to find out.' Rosie looked at Javier and Matt and smiled.

'Shit, Rosie,' Matt said. 'What if she flips?'

'I'll cross that bridge when I come to it.' Rosie sounded confident but nerves were coursing through her.

'It's dangerous, Rosie. Matt's right. Could blow everything.' Javier puffed.

'You got a better suggestion?' Rosie asked, a little defiant.

'No, I don't. I agree with you. We're going to have to put our heads above the . . . what do you call it?'

'The parapet,' Rosie smiled. 'Above the parapet.'

'Aye, well let's hope we don't get them shot off,' Matt said.

'Okay,' Rosie said. 'But before I do that, guys, talk me through what happened this morning.'

As planned, Matt and Javier had gone early to the hotel where McGregor and Donna were staying and staked the place out. Understandably, there was no movement in the foyer or anywhere else, as Rangers fans would still be sleeping off last night's partying.

'We were beginning to think we'd missed them, then we saw her coming down for breakfast. I left a copy of the *Post* at the entrance to the dining room, and she stopped and I saw her look at it. She stood for a moment and looked around her, pretty shocked. Then McGregor came and joined her and they went into the dining room together,' said Javier. 'I had a table far enough away, and could see she didn't eat much, just picked at the food. He ate everything in sight. Then his mobile rang after a while and he went back upstairs, talking on the phone. He didn't come back down. So I just sat until she was finished.'

'What then?' Rosie asked. 'Did she not go back upstairs?'

'No. She just came out and crossed the street to the pedestrian area and walked in the direction of the shops. She wandered in and out of a few shops, then in a mobile phone shop she came out carrying a bag.'

'Did you get snaps, Matt?' Rosie turned to Matt who was stuffing a *bocadillo* into his mouth.

'Mmmm, course,' he said, throwing back some coffee. 'That's why I'm starved. I didn't get a chance to eat this morning. But plenty of pics. They don't mean much though. She's just walking around.' He looked at his watch. 'I saw McGregor before I left, sitting with those other two, Dunlop and Mad Mitch. Them two looked like they were just up and eating sandwiches. I'm going back round there now, as we need to keep tabs on them.' He drained his cup.

When he left, Rosie and Javier sat for a quiet moment and she was aware he was watching her. She sipped her coffee and psyched herself up.

'So what you going to do, Rosie?' Javier squinted in the harsh sunlight. 'You got a plan?'

Rosie felt her chest tighten and tried not to take a deep breath. She didn't have a plan. She had a gut instinct. From what Liz had told her, Donna McGregor was a decent enough woman, long suffering by all accounts, with a brute of a husband. It would be too much to hope that she'd just spill the beans on her man, but Rosie had to find a way to get close enough to her.

'I don't know exactly. I'm just going to go over and sit down at that table next to her, and start talking.'

'And say what?' Javier looked incredulous.

Rosie stood up, pulled her hair up a little to get some air

on the back of her neck. She looked at Javier and smiled, knowing that he'd seen through her gung-ho exterior.

'That's what I don't know. But tell you what. I'm about to find out.'

'Fucking hell.' Javier lit a cigarette. 'You want me to come with you?' He grinned. 'I can bring my charisma.'

'No thanks,' Rosie chuckled. 'Keep your charisma fresh – I'll give you a wave if I need you.'

'Okay. But if this gets fucked up, let me know soon enough so I can get the hell out of here before I have to take any more bullets.' He shook his head. 'Good luck.'

'Trust me, I'm a journalist.' She squared her shoulders and walked away.

CHAPTER TWENTY-SIX

The cafe was no more than seven different-coloured tables crammed onto a patio outside the main bar, and Rosie squeezed past a Spanish couple sitting with their kids. She got a table within touching distance of Donna and saw her glance in her direction when she took the *Post* from under her arm and put it on the table. The waiter approached and she ordered a mineral water. Donna sipped her second coffee. She removed her sunglasses briefly, and as she was cleaning them with a napkin, Rosie caught a glimpse of the anguish etched in her face. Her eyes were red-rimmed and puffy and her skin a little blotchy. She pushed her glasses back on, and ran a finger across her bottom lip. Rosie's water arrived and she swirled the ice around it, holding the glass for a moment then placing her cold hand on the back of her neck. Even in the shade, it was too hot to sit outside for very long. She took a mouthful of water, then made her move.

'Donna?' Rosie's voice was quiet, but by the startled look on Donna's face you'd have thought her name had come over a loudspeaker.

'Donna McGregor?' In a seamless movement Rosie was out of her chair and at Donna's table sitting opposite her.

'Sorry?' Donna said behind her shades. 'Do I know you? Can't place the face.'

Rosie pulled her chair a little closer and slipped off her sunglasses.

'You don't know me, but I'd like to speak to you for a minute.'

It was hard to tell what Donna was thinking as Rosie couldn't see her eyes, but from her body language she looked like she was jangling.

'Me? How do you know my name? Sorry. I don't know who you are. What's—'

Rosie interrupted. 'Donna, give me one minute while I say something . . . Please listen to me. I promise you'll want to hear what I'm going to say.'

'What the fuck? Are you one of these Jesus freaks or something?' She was rattled.

'Andy Brown.' Rosie let the name hang in the air for two beats. 'The front page of the *Post*.' She pointed to the newspaper on the table. 'I've got something to tell you about this. You need to hear it.'

'Look.' Donna glanced over her shoulder. 'I don't know

what the hell you're talking about. But I need to go. You some kind of weirdo? I've got to meet my husband.'

She pushed her seat back.

'Donna. Listen to me. Andy's in trouble. Not just what's happened, I mean he's in big trouble. The cops are looking at him as a murder suspect.' She paused, seeing the information sink into Donna's head. 'I know you know him. I know you're having a relationship with him, and so do the cops. They're looking to speak to you.'

Donna took off her glasses and for the first time Rosie could see the sheer panic in her eyes.

'Who the fuck are you?' she rasped, her mouth tight. 'Who are you?'

'I'm Rosie Gilmour. I'm a journalist with the *Post*. That's my story about Andy.' She pointed to the front page. 'I've got an inside track on this, Donna.' Rosie rushed her words, sensing she wouldn't get much longer. 'The police have found a bank card on Andy that belonged to a drug dealer who was murdered along with his mate a couple of weeks ago. Right now, unless the cops get anything else to go on, Andy is a murder suspect. And they know you are having an affair with him. So . . . you're also a suspect.'

Silence. Rosie watched as Donna's lip began to quiver and whatever fight she thought she was going to put up seemed to evaporate. She put her hand up to her mouth, and Rosie thought for a second that she was going to collapse. Her whole body shuddered.

'Oh God! Oh God no!' She shook her head. 'I can't do this. I need to go.'

'Donna.' Rosie reached across and touched her arm. 'Don't go. Please. Let's go inside to the air conditioning and sit for a few minutes. You need to hear me out.' She stood up, lifted Donna's coffee. 'Come on. Let's go inside. Trust me. I might be able to help you.'

For a few seconds Rosie didn't know if Donna was going to get up and sprint away. She stood watching her, glancing over her shoulder at Javier, who was engrossed. Then slowly, Donna got up, steadied herself on the back of the chair and walked into the cafe with Rosie behind her.

'Here,' Rosie said. 'It's nice and cool back here. And we can talk. Just try to relax a bit. I know you've had a shock, but you need to try to keep it together.'

Donna sat down and buried her face in her hands, trying to speak through sobs.

'Oh God! You don't know what I'm going through.' She looked at Rosie, wiping her nose with the back of her hand. 'What do you want from me? What are you doing here?'

'Donna.' Rosie handed her a napkin and watched as she dabbed her eyes and blew her nose. 'I've been working on an investigation involving your husband Eddie McGregor for a while now. I know who he is, his connection with the UVF. I know exactly what he is in that organisation. And I know he's over here bringing in cocaine and ecstasy in the

Rangers supporters' buses. I don't know if you know about that, but the UVF have been doing it for years, and the fans know nothing about it. The football matches in Europe are a perfect cover for what Eddie does.'

'I don't know anything. I don't ask. Why are you telling me this?'

'Because I also know that you've been having an affair with Andy Brown, and that he was tortured and beaten the night before Eddie brought you here. Police are convinced Eddie was behind it, but they've no proof. And Andy can't tell them because he doesn't know who did it either. And he won't talk to them about you – but someone else told them you were having an affair.'

Rosie hoped the mention of Andy would be enough to break her. It was. She suddenly looked up.

'What do you know about Andy?' she said, then bit her lip, shaking her head. 'Tell me. Is he all right? Is he . . . Is he going to die?'

'No. I don't think so, but he's been really badly beaten and tortured. But as I told you, that's only the half of it. They've got this card on him, and it opens up a whole new line in the murder investigation.'

'Andy wouldn't hurt a fly. It's just stupid to think that. The police must know it.'

'But he's got a murder victim's bank card on him, and they don't know how he got it.' She paused, sensing she was winning. 'I take it you do, Donna?'

Silence. Then Donna put her head back, looked at the ceiling and nodded slowly.

'You do know?'

Donna nodded again.

'Did you get it from Eddie?'

'Yes,' Donna said, tears streaming down her cheeks.

'Tell me, Donna.'

'It . . . It was . . .' She broke down. 'I can't . . . I'll get shot. Eddie will get me done in.'

'I can help you. The cops will help you. They won't let that happen.' Rosie handed her another napkin. 'Donna. You know that barmaid who went missing – Wendy Graham?'

Donna looked a little confused, then it registered and she nodded.

'Eddie raped her. That's why she ran away. He raped her the night of the Rangers fundraiser in the pub. He was taking her home, and raped her in his car.'

'Jesus Christ!' She shook her head, her expression distraught. 'My God. But I've got family. My kids are grown up. I can't. I can't do anything.'

'Donna. Think about it. How long are you going to put up with Eddie's brutality?'

Donna looked at her, surprised.

'I know about that too. Someone has told me that he beats you up. Look, Donna. How long are you going to put up with this? Eddie's a killer. A murderer. A rapist. He's been organising killings and beatings for the UVF and gangsters for years. That's how he got where he is.'

Donna nodded. 'I know what he is. But I couldn't ask him about anything. I have to do what he tells me.'

'So what about the card, Donna? Where did it come from?'

She shook her head. 'I can't.'

'Donna. The cops will be asking you the same thing as soon as you get back. Only you'll be in custody. Talk to me and I'll talk to them. They'll find a way to get you away from Eddie.'

'How? How can they do that?

'They can deal with things like this. They can make you a protected witness. You can go somewhere else, start a new life with Andy when he gets better. But right now, when you go back to Glasgow, the cops will be knocking on your door with a murder investigation.'

'Oh God!'

'Donna. Where did you get the card? Did Eddie give you it?'

She shook her head again. 'It was in his trouser pocket. The night he came back.'

'What night?'

'I don't know. The night he came back with Mitch Gillespie and Jimmy Dunlop. They'd been on a job. I . . . I just took things out the pockets and burned the stuff in the garden the way I always did. But I didn't know they'd killed somebody.' She started crying again. 'I didn't know. But even if I had known, what could I do?'

'So you kept the card?'

'At the time, I didn't think anything of it. I found it below the bed the next morning when I was hoovering and I just put it away in a drawer. It was only a few days later when the bodies came out of the quarry and the name came up that I vaguely remembered. I looked in the drawer and thought maybe that was it. I was terrified, but . . . but . . .'

'But at last you had something you could pin on him.' Rosie hoped her face showed empathy rather than criticism.

Donna started crying again.

'Look. I'm not a bad person. I just brought up my kids and got the shit beaten out of me by him. Then I met Andy and I realised what it was like to be loved by someone decent. All I've done wrong is fall in love with someone who was good to me,' she sobbed.

Rosie watched and waited for her to compose herself, part of her feeling sorry for the shitty life she had with McGregor, and part of her full of admiration that she had the wit to hold on to the card that might incriminate him. But she had to admit guiltily to herself that her overwhelming feeling was one of delight that Donna was sitting here telling her all this.

'So you gave Andy the card?'

She nodded. 'We talked about how we could get away and be together. We wanted to start a new life somewhere away from Eddie. And I told him about the night Eddie came back with Mitch and Jimmy, and about the card. Andy asked me to give it to him. I don't know what he was planning to do with it. I suppose he was going to make sure the cops got it, but we hadn't even got to the planning of that yet. We were going to be talking about it this weekend, then Eddie came in with a ticket for the match and told me to get my things packed – that I was going. I had no choice.'

Rosie wanted to say to her that she did have a choice. She could have got up and left and kept on running with Andy, but she would have had to give up the money, the lifestyle and everything that went along with being the wife of a gangster like Eddie. But she said nothing and nodded.

'You think maybe I had a choice?' Donna asked.

Rosie felt she'd better say something.

'I think your choices were limited, Donna, given who Eddie is.'

'Exactly. You think he wouldn't hunt me down? Get me murdered? You think I'd ever be able to close my eyes in bed at night without knowing that it may be my last sleep, because believe you me, I know the kind of bastard Eddie McGregor is. He would use every last penny and resource at his fingertips to find me, and I'd be dead meat. Look what he's done to Andy.' She paused for a moment, and seemed to compose herself. Then her mouth tightened and she looked more angry now than distraught. 'And to think he's been with me these past couple of days, eating and drinking and he's known everything that's gone on with me and Andy, and he knows what he's done to him. That's the kind of evil bastard he is. I knew he was evil. I shouldn't have underestimated him.'

They sat saying nothing for a moment, Rosie watching her, waiting to see what was coming next.

Eventually it was Donna who broke the silence as she swallowed and looked at Rosie.

'But this time *he* has underestimated *me*. What do you want me to do?'

CHAPTER TWENTY-SEVEN

It didn't take more than a few minutes of strolling in the blistering afternoon heat before Jimmy could feel his shirt sticking to his back. No wonder there was hardly anyone out in the streets. He stopped at a cafe and went inside, glad to feel the blast of cold air. He sat down and ordered a coffee, looking at his watch. Eddie was organising a meet with Flinty around five, so he had a couple of hours before he had to be back at the hotel. He was fed up listening to Mitch's graphic details of last night at a whorehouse with two Ukrainian hookers, so he was glad to be away from it all, on his own.

His mind drifted back to last night with his father and the conversation they'd had about the drug dealing. His old man had a point, and the truth was he didn't much like the drugs either, but he wasn't going to get all worked up about it. Jimmy had never even snorted a line of coke in his life, unlike Mitch and most of the other lads who always had a stash on a night out. He'd never needed it, as long as there was plenty of beer and Jack Daniels on the go. Even if he felt strongly about the drug dealing, he wasn't in a position to do anything about it. It was clear from what Eddie and other UVF men had told him that drugs were part of the organisation and even if old traditionalists like his da objected, they still stood by and watched the UVF get more weaponry, grow bigger year in year out, a lot of that due to the money they made from drugs. It wasn't worth fighting over. But his father's words – 'this isn't what I wanted for you' – were still ringing in his ears. He tried not to think of that. The UVF was his life now, and he was making good money carrying out whatever job he was asked to do. Best not to think about it too deeply. He was more worried about his father's health, and resolved to spend as much time with him as he could when they got back home, doing all the things his da wanted to do. They'd make a list. Face up to the future, however short it was going to be. The very thought brought a catch in his throat.

His mobile rang but no number came up. He put the phone to his ear.

'Hello?'

Silence.

'Hello? Who's this?'

'Jimmy?'

For a moment he thought he was hearing the voice in his dreams.

'Jimmy . . . It's me . . . Wendy.'

'Wendy?' It came out as a gasp. He glanced over his shoulder. 'Wendy?' he whispered, his head swimming.

'Aye, Jimmy. It's me.'

Her husky voice was unmistakable.

'Jesus, Wendy! Jesus Christ almighty! What the fu— Where are . . .?' His heart thumped in his chest and he could feel the telephone shaking in his hand.

'I'm here. In Spain. In Seville.'

'What? Fuck! Where are you? Jesus Christ! I can't believe this!'

'I'm so sorry. I'm so sorry.'

He could hear her voice crack.

'It's okay. Wendy, don't cry. It's okay. I . . . I . . . I don't know what to say.' He could barely get the words out. 'I thought you were . . . I mean . . .'

'Dead,' Wendy sniffed.

'Christ! I didn't know what to think. Where are you? I need to see you. Why did you go away? It's been all over the papers. Everyone's looking for you. Oh shit! I can't believe this.' Jimmy's words tumbled out and he had to put his finger and thumb across the bridge of his nose to stop the tears. 'Oh, Wendy. I'm so glad you're alive . . .'

'Jimmy, listen. I don't want to talk long—'

'Where are you? I need to see you.'

'Listen. I ran away because of what Eddie did.'

'You shouldn't have run away. Not from me. I'd have

protected you.' He swallowed his tears. He hadn't protected her when he needed to, when Eddie was raping her. 'I'm so sorry for what that big cunt did.'

'I want to see you. I need to see you.'

'Where are you? What you doing in Seville? Have you been here all this time? Oh, Wendy, I've so many things to ask you. So much to tell you.'

'Sssh. Me too. Where are you just now?'

He looked around. He had no idea, only that he'd walked for around fifteen minutes from the hotel. His mind went blank. He couldn't even remember the name of the hotel. Shit! He got up and dashed to the door, looking for a landmark.

'Er . . . I'm in a cafe, not that far from the hotel where we're staying. In a pedestrian precinct. It's . . . It's . . . There's a big archway. Where are you? I'll get a cab. I'll come to you.'

'I'm in an apartment in the centre of the old town. I'll give you directions. Can you get a pen?'

Jimmy rushed to the counter and made a scribbling gesture to the waiter to borrow his pen. He grabbed a napkin.

'Okay. I'm writing it.' He wrote down the address as Wendy reeled it off.

'Take a taxi in case you get lost.'

'I'll be there in five minutes.' He swallowed to stop the tears again. 'Wendy. Don't go away. Please. Promise me you'll stay there till I get there. Please.'

'I'm here, Jimmy. I'm waiting for you.'

The line went dead.

Jimmy took some coins out of his pocket and scattered them on the glass table top. He handed the waiter back the pen and raced outside as if his clothes were on fire, then sprinted to the end of the precinct and spotted a taxi rank. He jumped in and sat in the back, sweat pouring out of him, as he showed the taxi driver the napkin.

Rosie and Adrian sat inside the bar in the side street next to the entrance to the apartment where Wendy and Liz were upstairs on the second floor. They had a table at the window so they could spot anyone going in or out of the building. Adrian had just come to meet her in the cafe, having been with the women in the apartment as they settled in, while Rosie had her showdown with Donna.

'So we wait here until Wendy or Liz calls you and asks for you to come up?' Adrian said, his eyes on the street.

'That's about it. Fingers crossed.' Rosie cut up a tuna sandwich and wolfed down half of it. She was ravenous after her meeting with Donna. It was always the same after she'd done a highly charged interview where she was firing on all cylinders. Sometimes, she'd come out of an interview and be so hyped up with nerves that her hands would be trembling. Her GP told her it was a blood sugar drop from using too much energy too fast and always to be ready with a bite to eat. It had become one of her little obsessions, and her handbags were a stash of peanuts and anything she could nibble on when the drop happened. She was conscious of Adrian watching her.

'You not hungry, Adrian? I'm starved.'

Adrian almost smiled.

'No. I don't get so hungry like you,' he said. 'I remember you in Bosnia. Hungry like a puppy all the time.'

'I know,' Rosie smiled, drinking a mouthful of tea. 'Always the same.'

'So you think this boy . . . this Jimmy boy will see you?'

Rosie puffed. 'Who knows? We have to wait and see.'

'It could be dangerous too, though, as Javier said. If the guy goes crazy.'

'I know.'

After Rosie had spoken to Donna, she and Javier discussed what to do next. They'd agreed that he should go and see Garcia the cop and fill him in. Javier's view was that they'd got lucky Donna had buckled as soon as Rosie had spoken to her, but he bet Jimmy wouldn't be so willing. Rosie told him to let Garcia know what she was up to now, in case they needed his help. Her mobile rang.

'Gilmour. What's happening?' It was McGuire.

'Oh, hi, Mick. I was going to give you a buzz later.'

Rosie looked at her watch. She'd meant to call him after her meeting with Donna but things were moving fast, after she'd got a call from Liz saying Wendy had spoken to Jimmy and he was on his way to them. She'd toyed with the idea of running her intention to approach Donna past McGuire, but decided against it. She knew he'd say no.

'Well, it's already later. Anything new I should get excited or worried about? You know I get stomach pains when I don't hear from you.'

Rosie hesitated. 'Er . . . couple of things, Mick. I'll have a talk with you in a few hours when I get the chance.'

'Tell me now, Gilmour. Christ almighty! Tell me something. I *am* the fucking editor.'

His indignation made Rosie smile.

'I know, I know.' She took a deep breath. 'Okay. To fill you in. Some good stuff: I got a call from my cop pal to say they found a bank card belonging to one of those drug dealers from the quarry. You'll never guess where the bank card was?'

'Yeah, you're right, I'll never guess where. Just tell me the story and don't piss around.'

'In the wallet of the kidnapped baker.'

'Fucking joking!'

'Nope. In his wallet.'

'Is he involved? Is he a drug dealer? The baker?'

'No. Nothing to suggest that. Cops think it may have been planted there, but they just don't know. The baker's saying bugger all. They want to speak to McGregor's wife Donna.' She paused. 'So I thought I'd get a word with her first.'

'Hang on, Gilmour. That could blow everything out of the

water. You don't know how she'll react. We need to think this through.'

Silence.

'You there, Rosie?'

'Yeah. Er . . . It's too late.'

'Too late for what?'

'For Donna. I've already—'

'Oh fuck me, Gilmour! You mean you just waded in without even running it past me? How many times do I have to—'

'Wait, Mick,' Rosie interrupted. 'Listen. Wait till you hear. I talked to Donna and she opened right up.'

'You serious?'

'You bet I am. It was a bit hairy in the beginning, but I threw the kitchen sink at her and she buckled. The poor woman's in a right state. She told me everything – even that it was her who gave the card to Andy . . . She—'

'How do you mean? How'd she get the card?' he interrupted.

'If you let me talk I'll tell you. Jesus, man! She told me that the card was in the pocket of the trousers McGregor was wearing when he came home one night along with Mitch and Jimmy Dunlop. She said they'd been on a job together and she was to burn their clothes . . .'

'Holy fuck!'

'Exactly! She says she didn't know they'd killed anyone, but it was normal that when McGregor was out on a job she'd get rid of his clothes. She just did what she was told.

She took everything out the pockets and when she found the card she shoved it in a drawer, not even thinking about it. Then one night she's watching the news and the guys are fished out of the quarry. The name rang a bell and she twigged. So she knew she had something on him at last.'

'She's not as daft as she might seem then. Scheming like that.'

'Scheming? I'd call it survival. The woman's been getting the shit kicked out of her for years by McGregor and she finally met a guy who made her feel what it was like to be loved.'

'Christ, Gilmour. I can hear a violin. I'm filling up. She told you all this?'

'Yep. And I've got it all on tape.'

'You're a crafty bastard. But I do love you.'

Rosie was glad to hear him chuckling.

'She's onside now, Mick. She'll do whatever it takes to bring McGregor down.'

'Fucking brilliant! Well done! But my instinct tells me things are going to get tricky from here in. What are your plans?'

'I'm not entirely sure. I'm waiting to see if something develops.'

'That's a bastard lie and you know it.'

'No it's not.' Rosie stifled a smile. 'I'll know in a little while what my next move is. But you're right. It might get a bit tricky.'

There was a pause and Rosie waited anxiously, hoping McGuire didn't just call it off from there and summon her home. They already had plenty of material – a policeman fraternising with the UVF at meetings and singing on video, and now McGregor's wife about to help nail him and his cohorts for a double murder.

'Right. Tell you what—'

'I know what you're thinking, but I have to see this through.'

'Christ! Stop telling me what I'm thinking. But yes, I was considering bringing you back. We have loads of stuff. We could address the drugs run another time.'

'No, Mick. Come on. We address it now. We're more than halfway there, we can't give up.'

Silence.

'Come on, Mick.' Rosie looked at Adrian who stared blankly out at the street.

'Right. Have you got the cops over there in this with you?'

'Yes. Javier's got them with us. And Adrian's with me now. It'll be all right.'

'Okay. But seriously, Gilmour, I don't want any fucking around or any caped crusader stuff from anyone. Not you or Matt. Not the big Bosnian, and not that Juan guy who got shot the last time in Spain. I want you backing off and getting the fuck out if anything looks like it's going tits up.'

'I will. And his name's Javier.'

'Aye, fine. And if that means leaving Wendy, Liz and

Donna to pick up the pieces then so be it. I can't protect everyone. But I want you out of there as soon as possible.'

'I know, I know. I hear you.'

'Okay. Well, good luck. And call me tonight. I'll be waiting.'

'Sure, Mick. Will do.'

The line went dead.

CHAPTER TWENTY-EIGHT

In the heavy city traffic, Jimmy was getting increasingly anxious in the back seat of the taxi, wishing he'd gone on foot. They only seemed to have crossed the city's one-way system and ended up at the top of the old town, which he could probably have walked to in ten minutes. The taxi driver eyeing him in his rear-view mirror seemed to sense his anxiety and mumbled something in Spanish that Jimmy didn't understand. But from his hand gestures, he gathered he was moaning about the traffic. Eventually, after cutting up a maze of side streets, they came to a halt.

'*Aqui*,' the driver said, half turning around.

'What?' Jimmy said.

'*Aqui*,' the driver said again, pointing to a door at the entrance to a building in between two shops.

Jimmy got out and paid him. He glanced around at the busy street, mostly cafes and small souvenir shops packed side by side. Then he noticed the number over the doorway and checked the napkin for the address. He went towards the intercom box, pressed the buzzer marked two and held his breath.

'Hello?'

It was Wendy.

'It's me.' His mouth was dry.

'Jimmy! I'll come down.'

The security door clicked open and he stepped into the gloomy hallway. He walked tentatively towards the winding staircase as he heard the sound of a door opening somewhere above. Then he saw her. He held his breath as the slim figure in shorts and a vest picked her way carefully down the stairs and stopped on the landing a few steps before the bottom. For a couple of beats he stood there frozen. In his dreams she had come to him like this, out of some darkness, her arms outstretched, and he'd always woken up reaching for her, only to grasp at nothing. He blinked to reassure himself that she was real. Then he rushed towards her up the steps.

'Wendy!'

She fell almost limp into his arms, and he wrapped her tight, feeling the softness of her body against him for a moment he thought he'd never see. He pulled back and looked at her, his fingers gently tracing her face as though even now he was still trying to convince himself that she was alive.

'Oh, Wendy!' He buried his head in her thick black hair

as they both held each other. He could feel her body shudder as she wept.

Eventually, Jimmy pulled back and kissed her on the lips, long and lovingly and as he did every fibre of his body was alive with the scent of her and the touch of her tongue on his. They stopped and looked at each other, Jimmy wiped her tears with his thumbs then sniffed back his own and they hugged again.

'I love you, Wendy,' Jimmy managed to say. 'I'm never going to let you go again. Never. I promise you.'

He thought a slight reticence flashed across her eyes, as if she was afraid.

'I've got so much to talk to you about, Jimmy. So much.' She ran her hand over his hair.

'What you doing here? How did you end up in Spain, right here in Seville?' Jimmy said.

He wanted to ask her why she didn't make one single phone call, just to let him know she was alive. He had so many questions.

'I'll tell you everything,' Wendy said. 'Listen. First of all, Liz is here.'

'Liz?'

'Yes. I phoned her a couple of weeks ago and she came over.'

'Jesus! Liz, Wendy? You could have called me. I'd have come over.' Jimmy suddenly felt as though he'd been winded.

She eased herself out of his arms.

'Listen, I didn't call you because it wouldn't have been the thing to do.' She dropped her eyes. 'After what big Eddie did to me. I . . . I just didn't know what I was doing. To be honest I was in a pretty bad way when I got here and was really desperate.'

'Wendy,' Jimmy interrupted, touching her hair. 'You could have called me. I'd have come.'

'Jimmy. Please try to understand. You can't just do things like that, not these days. Not now that you're so tied up with Eddie and them all.'

Jimmy blew out a sigh and ran a hand over his face. He felt frustrated, left out, angry and elated all at the same time. But he knew she was right.

He shook his head. 'I'd have found a way to come, Wendy. I promise.' As he said it, he didn't even know if he believed it himself.

'Please try to understand me. I wanted you more than anything, but it wasn't the right thing to do. Trust me. Just believe that.'

For a moment they stood in silence, then Jimmy spoke.

'We all wondered about Liz going so suddenly. She said she was going to Spain. We just thought with her living here before and stuff, that she'd had enough of Glasgow. Christ! She kept it quiet all right. Is she here now? In the flat?'

'Yeah.' Wendy took his arm. 'Come on. Let's go up.' When they got to the top of the stairs they stopped and kissed again and Jimmy was slightly ashamed at the feeling of arousal as she pushed herself against his groin, his hands automatically drifting down, caressing her naked thighs.

'Oh Christ, Wendy, I missed you so much. I want you so much.'

They broke apart breathless, and Wendy smiled.

'Me too. Come on. Let's go inside.'

In the cafe next door, Rosie felt a little tweak of adrenalin as she and Adrian watched Jimmy get out of the taxi and go towards the door.

'He looks a bit agitated,' Rosie said. 'Understandable, I suppose. He probably thought Wendy was dead. Plus, he can't afford to let McGregor know that he's up here seeing her.'

Adrian nodded and said nothing.

Rosie's mobile rang. It was Javier.

'Where are you, Rosie?'

'In the cafe opposite the apartment the girls are in. With Adrian. We just saw Jimmy go inside.'

'Okay. I'm coming up there with Juan and we wait together. By the way, I told Juan about Donna. He wants to talk to her.'

'Hmmm. She might freak about that, but she did say she'd do whatever we want.' Rosie realised that they didn't have a lot of time, so she would have to convince Donna to talk to the police.

'Where is she now?' Javier asked.

'I suppose she'll be back in the hotel or shopping. She bought a phone charger and she has just sent me a text saying McGregor is organising to meet Flinty Jackson. She overheard him saying the name on the phone.'

'Maybe the drugs pickup. We need to be there.'

'She thinks it might be late afternoon sometime.'

'Good. Juan wants to talk to her about keeping us informed of McGregor's movements. But she's already doing it. So that's good.'

'Yeah. As long as she holds her nerve.'

'Why don't you call her and ask her to come up to the cafe where you are?'

'Yeah. I will. But I have to wait to see what's going to happen with Jimmy in the apartment. I'm hoping to see him and talk.'

'Okay. We will come up anyway – just in case.'

'He's not going to do anything on his own.'

'You never know.'

He hung up.

Jimmy sat on the sofa in the apartment, not quite believing what he was hearing. When he'd gone into the flat, Liz was sitting at a table by the window. She stood up when he saw her and for a fleeting moment he felt a sense of betrayal. But she was ready for him. She put her hands up. She was sorry, she told him. But her loyalty was first and foremost to

Wendy. He'd just have to understand that. When he raised his voice, insisting that she should have told him, Liz stood her ground.

'Save your rage for big Eddie,' she'd said. 'Save it, Jimmy, for what he did to Wendy.'

Jimmy had swallowed his anger and sat down. She was right. He looked at Wendy, the dark smudges under her eyes and the hollow of her cheeks. She'd lost weight. He had felt it straight away when he took her in his arms earlier. Wendy had done nothing and Eddie had raped her. He felt physically sick as he listened to her telling him how it happened. He pictured every sordid second of it, imagined Eddie's hands all over her, getting on top of her, pulling at her jeans. Bastard. He felt ashamed that since she disappeared, it had crossed his mind that maybe she had given big Eddie even the slightest scrap of encouragement. But deep down he knew she wouldn't do that. Eddie raped her. It was as black and white as that. The rage coursing through him pulsed all the way to his temples and he felt a sudden dull headache. He pressed his fingers to the side of his head, as Wendy went through her account of the night it happened. When she had finished talking they sat for what seemed like a while, and finally it was Liz who broke the silence.

'I've talked to a newspaper reporter, Jimmy. From the *Post*. We both have,' Liz said, lighting a cigarette.

'What?'

'A reporter. From the *Post*.' Liz looked at Wendy. 'Her

name's Rosie Gilmour. Me and Wendy. We both talked to her.' She folded her arms.

Jimmy looked from one to the other in disbelief. 'You're fucking joking. A reporter? What for? What's the point?'

They both looked at him in silence.

Jimmy's brows knitted in confusion.

'But why? I mean what's the point? What can a newspaper reporter do?'

Silence.

'They can get him done,' Wendy said, looking at the floor.

Jimmy's mind was a blur, trying to work out what they meant. Unless Wendy was prepared to put herself on the line with the police and get Eddie charged, stand in a witness box and accuse him of rape, there was nothing they could do. If she wanted to do that, fine. He'd back her. He'd have to, he loved her that much. But he'd be finished with the UVF. His stomach felt as though someone had grabbed it and twisted it around. What would his father do if he was seen to be backing Wendy against the UVF? Judging by the way he'd been talking these past few days, perhaps he might agree with him. But when it came to the crunch, he didn't know what would happen. And how could he really put his da through that in what might be the last few months of his life? Christ! He looked at Wendy and squeezed her hand.

'Wendy. If you're prepared to go to the police and get Eddie charged with rape, it means I'm finished with the UVF if I back you.'

Wendy's head dropped to her chest and she said nothing. Jimmy lifted her chin gently and looked into her eyes brimming with tears.

'I'll be behind you, Wendy, whatever you decide. I'm with you if you want to go to the cops and get him charged,' he said.

'Oh, Jimmy!' Wendy threw her arms around him and they held each other, as he stroked her hair part of him still barely believing she was in his arms.

'That's not the only thing we talked to the reporter about.' Liz spoke.

'What?' Jimmy pulled away from Wendy and turned towards Liz.

'The reporter is working on an investigation into Eddie and the UVF smuggling drugs into Scotland on the Rangers supporters' buses.'

Jimmy screwed up his eyes, trying to take it in. His face reddened.

'What? You've talked to a reporter about that? But you don't know anything about it.'

'I do. Billy told me all about it when I was going out with him. Told me loads of stuff.'

'Billy's a fucking dick,' Jimmy said, suddenly irritated. 'Liz, whatever Billy said to you, he's an eejit for doing it in the first place, but you shouldn't have told anybody – far less a fucking reporter. Have you any idea what could happen to you?'

'I know,' Liz said, her face like flint.

'So,' he turned to Wendy. 'You've talked to this reporter too?'

Wendy nodded.

'Aw, fuck's sake!' Jimmy jumped to his feet, raising his voice. 'Listen. Fuck! If Eddie ends up in the shite over drugs on the buses, I'll be in it too. Christ! That's what me and Mitch are doing with him on this trip. He ordered us to come with him.' He paced the floor, his hands behind his head. 'This is fucking serious.' He turned to Liz. 'Who have you spoken to, Liz? How far down the road is this? Are cops involved?'

Liz nodded slowly. 'Yeah, they are.'

'Aw, for fuck's sake! I'll get done as well. Can you not see that?' He shook his head, waved his arms. 'I don't fucking believe this.'

'Not if you work with the reporter, Jimmy,' Wendy said. 'And the police.'

'What?' Jimmy looked down at her, incredulous. 'You mean grass Eddie up? You mean grass up the UVF?' He threw his hands up. 'Fuck me! I'd be as well getting a gun and shooting myself right now.'

'Jimmy, listen.' Wendy stood up. 'You need to think about this. Please. Just calm down and listen. We can be together.'

Jimmy interrupted. 'How can we be together? How? I'll be in the fucking jail, or dead!' He heard his voice go up an octave with exasperation.

'You cooperate with the police. We can get new identities and go away somewhere. The police will look after us.'

'Jesus wept! You've been watching too many movies.' He glared at Liz. 'It just doesn't happen like that. The UVF will track people down ten, twenty years after the event. We could be sitting in our house in Florida in twenty years and someone comes up and shoots you through the window. Christ, Wendy. That's what happens. You don't grass up. Ever!' He put his hand on his forehead and tried to squeeze away the thumping tension headache.

'So what do you do then, Jimmy?' Wendy's voice shook with emotion as she stood up and faced him. 'Is the UVF your whole life for the rest of your life? Is that what you want? Maybe in a few years you'll be a big man like Eddie and you'll be in charge of other young guys just like you, but that will be it. Aye. And maybe you'll find yourself one of these lassies that hang around with these boys all impressed, and that will be your whole life. Killing and beatings and drugs! That'll be it.' She paused, her voice breaking. 'But I'll not be in it. I'll be long gone. Because I can't do this. I don't want my life to be like that. I want kids . . . a proper home.'

Jimmy stood in silence, the enormity of what she was saying beating him around the head, and all the time, his father's words from the other night, when he told him that his mother kept coaxing them to go away, put the UVF behind them and start a new life. Now he was just an old, dying man, full of regret. And for what? Jimmy shook his head and put his hand over his mouth as he fought back tears. His mobile rang. It was Mitch.

'Where are you? Eddie's looking for you.'

Jimmy swallowed and tried to compose himself.

'I'm out for a walk. I'll be back shortly. You at the hotel?'

'Aye. We've a meet on at six. You'd better get back.' Mitch hung up before he could answer.

All three of them stood in silence, Jimmy desperate to put his arms around Wendy and hold her, tell her how much he loved her, convince her to stick with him. The UVF was his life now. He was making money. Soon they could have their own place, and the way things were going, he would get noticed back in the Shankill. He was big Jack Dunlop's son, and had a huge reputation to live up to. Jimmy looked away from Wendy and he could see in her eyes that she sensed she had lost him.

'I need to go. They're looking for me,' he muttered, shaking his head as he turned away from them and left.

CHAPTER TWENTY-NINE

'Uh-oh! Jimmy's coming out of the building on his own,' Javier said. 'Not a good sign.'

'Shit!' Rosie looked out from the cafe window and saw Jimmy walking away from them. 'It must have gone tits up.'

She'd barely spoken when her mobile rang, and she answered it, recognising Liz's voice.

'It didn't go well, Rosie. Jimmy walked out.' Liz was matter-of-fact.

'We saw him. We're in the cafe across from your place. We thought we'd wait here and hope for the best. What happened?' Rosie strained her neck so she could see Jimmy along the narrow street.

Javier interrupted. 'Looks like he's going into that bar just over there.' He pointed, and Rosie eased herself off her seat to get a better view while she listened to Liz.

'Obviously he was totally bowled over to see Wendy, and

she was the same,' Liz continued, 'but as soon as I mentioned we'd talked to a reporter, he freaked out.'

'It was always a risk.' Rosie knew the implications of showing their cards to Jimmy. She glanced at Javier who had one eye on the window. He made a sympathetic face back at her.

'Do you think that's it from Jimmy? How did it finish?' Rosie asked.

'His phone rang and he said big Eddie was looking for him, so he left. But he was really freaking about the idea of talking to a reporter and about cooperating with the cops. Said he might as well blow his brains out now as grass up the UVF.'

Rosie was silent, trying to second-guess what Jimmy would do next.

'I need to go, Liz,' she said suddenly. 'Stay where you are and I'll phone you in a few minutes.' She put the phone in her bag.

It wouldn't be the first rush-of-blood moment for Rosie. In the past they'd either proved to be inspirational, with her pulling rabbits out of hats when all else had failed, or they had ended in big trouble. She didn't stop to consider which one this was. She stood up.

'What are you doing?' Javier grabbed hold of her wrist.

'I'm going after him.' She slung her bag over her shoulder.

'Rosita?' Javier glanced at Garcia who looked confused.

Rosie put her arm out in a calming gesture.

'Look. I need to try something. It'll either work or it won't. But I have to try. Okay?' She addressed all three of them.

Adrian got up.

'I will come. I will stay nearby. In case.'

'I think this is not good idea.' Garcia shrugged, blowing smoke out of the side of his mouth. 'Is maybe be dangerous to approach this man.' If he was worried, he did a good impression of boredom.

'I'm going to try.' Rosie was already turning to leave. 'He won't do anything crazy. Not in a foreign country.'

Javier puffed, perplexed.

'Famous last words.' He stood up. 'I should go with you.'

'Javier,' Rosie said, touching his arm. 'I have to be on my own for this. I know what I'm going to do. Now just wait. It won't take long.'

'I know what you are going to do, Rosie.' Javier raised his eyebrows to Adrian, who gave him a reassuring nod.

'Don't go away.' Rosie flashed them a defiant smile as she left.

Jimmy was standing at the bar, already halfway through a beer that couldn't have been poured more than a minute ago. Still wearing her dark glasses, Rosie walked across to the bar and ordered a coffee in Spanish. From the corner of her eye, she caught him clocking her, then nod to the barman for a refill. She stirred her coffee and waited until he drained the sweating tumbler then lifted the new beer and took a sip. Her heart did a little flutter. Then she took a sip of coffee and made a step towards him.

'Jimmy Dunlop?'

His body flinched as though he'd been poked by a cattle prod. He half turned his head towards her.

'What?'

'I've got some information for you. You need to hear me out. This is important. You *will* want to know this.'

He towered above her, solid in a tight black T-shirt and Rosie glanced at his UVF tattoo on his muscled forearm. She gave him a your-muscles-don't-scare-me look.

Jimmy put down the glass and stayed staring at the bar for a minute, then he turned his head to her.

'Who the fuck are you?' His face was a mixture of confusion and anger.

'I'll tell you that in a minute. But first—'

'Fuck off, whoever you are.' Jimmy jerked his thumb and turned away from her, fixing his eyes on the gantry.

For a couple of breaths Rosie stood there, conscious of the hand by his side forming a fist. There was no option but to go on. She could feel the blood pulsating in her neck.

'The cops back in Glasgow have got a bank card with your fingerprints all over it . . .' Who cares if that might not be true, she told herself, astonished at how convincing it sounded.

Nothing. He stood still as a statue, but in those brief seconds she could see her words register in his brain, and the colour drain from his face. Game on.

'*Your* fingerprints, and Eddie McGregor's,' Rosie blurted. 'The card belonged to Thomas Ritchie, the drug dealer fished out of the quarry a couple of weeks ago along with James Balfour. They'd been shot.' She paused. 'But of course you knew that, didn't you?'

'Fuck off, before I smash your head off the end of that bar.' Jimmy spat the words without turning.

Silence.

'You're fucked, Jimmy!' Rosie said. 'The game's a bogey.'

Deadly silence. Rosie adjusted her feet in readiness in case he lashed out. Sweat stung the back of her neck. Jimmy kept staring straight ahead, his face grey, nostrils flaring a little as he tried to control his breathing. So far, no sore face, Rosie thought. She took a short breath.

'Cops found the bank card in Andy Brown's wallet, the baker who had the shit beaten out of him for having an affair with McGregor's wife.' She paused for effect. 'You knew that too, didn't you?' She was really chancing it now.

Rosie watched the muscle in his jaw tense and his Adam's apple bobble as he swallowed. Any minute now. She hoped Adrian was nearby. Then it happened too fast – even for Adrian. Jimmy grabbed hold of her by the lapels of her blouse and swung her around, lifting her off her feet and slamming her hard against the wall opposite the bar. He gripped the blouse so hard Rosie heard it rip somewhere at the seams and for a split second she thought he was going to headbutt her.

'I should waste your fucking face, you bitch,' Jimmy snarled. 'Listen. I know who you are. And if you've got anything other than shit for brains you'll walk out of here now and get a fucking plane out of this town. Because as of now you're dead meat. You have no idea who you are messing with.'

'Yes I do, Jimmy,' Rosie managed to say. Then she couldn't stop herself. 'I know everything. You can smash my face, but you'll still be fucked. It's over. Eddie's finished. And so are you, unless you find a way out.'

Rosie saw something like panic flicker across his eyes. Sweat broke out on his top lip. He pushed his tattooed forearm under her chin and she heard her head crack against the wall, making her dizzy for a second. Then suddenly, Jimmy buckled from a blow to his kidneys. Adrian. But Jimmy quickly swivelled around and landed an instinctive punch that burst Adrian's lip. For a second there was a look of anger and indignation on Adrian's face, then he unleashed a flurry of punches that knocked Jimmy three or four paces away, along the bar towards the toilet. Jimmy tried to fight back but he looked stunned, as he stumbled backwards through the swing bathroom door and disappeared, Adrian following, punching him all the way inside.

The barman came dashing from behind the counter and rushed to Rosie.

'I get the *policia*,' he said, his voice panicky. '*Por favor*. Sit here.'

'No police, please. I'm okay.' Rosie stayed standing, her hands trembling.

As she got her breath back, the bathroom door opened and Adrian came out, wiping blood from the side of his mouth.

'Are you all right, Rosie?'

'Yes. I'm okay. You?' Adrian shrugged, surprised at the question. 'Of course. Is nothing.'

'Is he . . . What's he doing?'

Adrian touched his burst lip with a paper towel.

'He is washing his face. He is calmer now. He won't attack you. Is okay.'

Rosie composed herself as the bathroom door slowly opened and Jimmy emerged, wiping blood from his lip, his eye already a little swollen. He squared his shoulders and came towards her.

'Whoever you are, you're as good as dead. You should know that,' he said again, blood trickling from his lip as he stood facing her.

'Jimmy,' Rosie said. 'Eddie McGregor raped your girl-friend. Wendy's got courage – more balls than you – she ran away to save you from going after him. That's the kind of girl she is.'

He said nothing, but the hardness had gone out of his eyes and he looked almost vulnerable. Rosie had stopped shaking and was on fire now, confident with Adrian at her back. She leaned towards him and whispered.

'You know what? You go back to Eddie and your UVF thugs and your coke run. You'll not see Wendy for the next twenty years because you'll be banged up for a double murder. You've got no options left, unless you listen to me.'

'Fuck off.' He turned to walk away.

'Wendy knows where I am, Jimmy. They know how to get me. This is your only way out,' Rosie called after him.

He stopped in the doorway of the bar, and for a moment Rosie thought he was going to turn around. But he didn't, and she watched as he crossed the road and disappeared from view.

She went into the toilet and splashed cold water on her face, examining the blotches on her neck and chest where Jimmy had grabbed her. There was the start of a bruise on her collarbone from the sheer force he'd used. Her linen shirt had a little tear at the shoulder. She took a deep breath and let it out slowly, looking at her pale blue eyes in the mirror, letting it sink in that this time, her rush of blood to the head might have blown the entire operation. Shit. McGuire would go nuts. Reckless, he would call it, and she had to agree, though she could defend it by pointing out the times when her recklessness had broken massive stories and gave him a front page he could brag about. She bit the inside of her jaw. She wouldn't tell McGuire, not yet.

She left the cafe after reassuring the barman that there was no problem and pleading with him not to call the police. She and Adrian crossed the street and went back to the place where Javier and Garcia waited. Javier got to his feet when he saw her come in.

'I can see by the look on your face it didn't go well.' He touched her chin and gently pulled her face to one side. 'What the fuck? The *coño* got rough?' He glared at Adrian.

Rosie took his hand away.

'I'm okay. I bruise easily. It all happened so fast. He grabbed me a bit, that's all, and shoved me against the wall. But Adrian was on him in a second.' She touched Adrian's arm. 'Jimmy's got a black eye and a burst lip to take back to Eddie.'

'Shit!' Javier said, turning to Garcia and speaking in Spanish.

'*Hijo de puta!*' Garcia replied, shaking his head. The son-of-a-bitch part Rosie understood, but she couldn't make out what else Garcia was saying to Javier.

'Juan is not happy,' Javier said.

'That makes two of us,' Rosie said, deadpan. 'And *I've* got a tear in my new shirt.'

'This could cause all sorts of problems,' Javier said.

'I know, Javier. I'm well aware of that. I knew that before I even made the approach, but I thought it was worth doing.'

She shrugged and sat down, suddenly feeling a wave of emotion. Just a bit of reaction to the shock, she told herself. Don't even think about bursting into tears in front of this cop. 'Let's have a coffee and put our heads together.'

She wished Javier wouldn't look at her that way. He knew her well enough to see through the bravado, but right now she didn't need his sympathy.

'Can I have a cigarette?' she said to him, helping herself.

He flicked the lighter and his fingers brushed intentionally against her jawline.

'You okay, crazy woman?'

Rosie drew deeply on the cigarette and held the smoke before letting it out in a long, slow stream as she smiled at him with her eyes.

'So,' she said eventually. 'Let's work out our next move.'

CHAPTER THIRTY

Jimmy was glad there was no one he knew hanging around the foyer when he arrived back at the hotel. He wanted to shower and change before he had to start explaining his black eye to people. He also needed some time to himself to digest what had happened in the last couple of hours. He had to calm down and start thinking straight, because right now he was wired to the moon.

He stood in the shower letting the cold water lash onto his bruised face, his body aching at the thought of Wendy's touch. All he could see when he closed his eyes was the look on her face when he'd said he would stand by her if she went to the police about Eddie. Eventually, he came out of the bathroom with a towel wrapped around his waist, went across to the dressing table and pulled a cigarette out of the packet. He lit it and stood for a moment gazing at his reflection in the mirror, his toned body rippling with muscles under the tattoos he'd picked up over the years. His hand automatically went to the newest one emblazoned at the side of his stomach just above his hipbone. Two hands brandishing daggers, an English rose and skull below, with the red hand of Ulster in the middle. Above it, framed in a ribbon like a family motto, the declaration, *There Will Be No Surrender*. It was his most recent, done by a former Loyalist prisoner in Belfast the morning after he celebrated taking the oath. It signalled his arrival, and as he drew deeply on his cigarette, he remembered how proud he'd been when he came home. His other tattoos were the badge of everything he cared about. On his forearm, *Rangers Forever*, with the club crest, and the letters *UVF*. And above them all on his bicep, a red heart with a knife through it, dripping blood with the word *Mother*. Christ! She'd have broken her heart the day he'd come back from Belfast after being sworn in. But she would have said nothing, just quietly worked and cooked and pretended it didn't matter. She just didn't understand, that was her problem.

Jimmy walked out to the balcony and sat down, smoking and staring out across the city as the church bells tolled. The afternoon heat rose in waves across the terracotta rooftops and beyond where the ancient buildings were barely visible in the haze. It was a beautiful city. He thought of Wendy and how he would have got such a kick just walking around this place with her on his arm, getting lost in the winding streets, stopping in bars and cafes, having a laugh at the buskers or the street performers, the two of them wrapped up in each other like the other couples he'd watched. But that couldn't happen. They would never have a life like that. His stomach sank at the realisation that it was over. He'd never see her again – he had to make that decision now and be done with it. If she hadn't run away, if she'd stayed in Glasgow, maybe they could have worked it out. If she'd decided she couldn't go to the police about Eddie raping her, he'd have spent the rest of his life trying to do everything to make her forget. But she ran away from him, and worse than that, when she needed someone, it was Liz she turned to and not him. He thought about that bitch reporter. She had some balls right enough, facing him down like that. She obviously didn't know his reputation. For all of her smartarse bastardness he admired her guts. That stuff about the bank card. Where the hell did that come from? If the reporter was being straight, that meant the card could only have come from one person – Donna. He had seen Eddie put it in his pocket at the quarry. But what could he do now? He couldn't risk telling Eddie this, or he'd have to tell him everything. And for all he knew, maybe Eddie was double-crossing them all. How did he know Eddie didn't pass the card on to the cops himself? What if Eddie was setting him and Mitch up, sacrificing them to the cops? That's what grasses did. Maybe he was on the take from the cops, had been for years, informing them and being allowed to operate. It was all entirely possible. He told himself he was just being paranoid.

And again, the image of Wendy's face. What the reporter

had said about her having more courage than him had hit a raw nerve. Maybe that was true. Because the bottom line was that Wendy had run away from him because of what Eddie did to her, and to stop him from going for Eddie as she knew he would. The only person who was innocent in all of this was her. Just like his mother had been all those years ago when his father went to jail for the bombing. And for years after that, when the cops used to burst in and tear up the house in the middle of the night looking for weapons, his mum had said nothing, protected her man, even if she knew he was guilty. She protected Jimmy too when he was a frightened little boy. She'd put her arms around him as he'd buried his head in her skirt, crying as the cops ripped up his bedroom. She was braver than anyone, his mum. Like Wendy. But the problem was Wendy had talked to this fucking reporter, and the cops. She was dead meat now and there was fuck all he could do about it. Eventually it would come out that Wendy and Liz had grassed and they'd get bumped off. He felt sick to his stomach. He thought of his da and how he'd love to be able to say to him that he'd seen Wendy and what she had suggested. But it was stupid to even contemplate that. His father would be raging at the very idea that he'd met with someone who was about to grass them up. What if he'd been seen? What if some of the Rangers fans out for a walk saw him going into the flat? He touched his face, still hot and tender. He'd have to come up with a good explanation for this. He flicked his fag end off the balcony and went back inside.

'Fuck happened to you?' Mitch looked up, grinning. 'I'd like to see the other guy.'

Jimmy gave him a look and pulled up a chair at the cafe outside the hotel. Eddie watched him intently and raised his eyebrows.

'So? What's with the sore face?' Eddie's eyes narrowed. 'Must have been somebody who doesn't know you can't take a pop at Jimmy Dunlop.'

Jimmy shifted in his seat and looked away.

'Yeah. Well. He knows now.'

'What happened? You get jumped?' Eddie asked, looking straight at him. 'Thought you were going to bed after we left you last night.'

Jimmy shrugged, trying to look blasé.

'I was. But I met this wee bird from Liverpool in a bar on the way back to the hotel. She asked me to come up and meet her for a coffee today at her flat. She lives here.'

'So did her man come in while you had her bent over the couch?' Mitch sniggered.

Jimmy rolled his eyes. 'Something like that.' He shook his head. 'She didn't tell me she had a boyfriend.'

'Fuck's sake,' Eddie said. 'That's why you're better going to the whorehouses. You pay your money and leave with a smile on your face – not a fucking black eye. And you don't have to fight your way out.'

'Aye. Well. You might have a point there. I'll know the next time.' Jimmy touched his face. 'And so will the fucker who did this.'

'So, did you not get your leg over?' Mitch sneered.

'Nah. I had to take my frustration out on the guy. And I've just had a very long, cold shower.'

'You're a silly bastard,' Eddie said. 'Never mind. We'll get you sorted tonight. Some Eastern European bird to sit on your face.'

'Sounds good to me.' Jimmy tried his best to look relaxed, but his insides were going like an engine. He thought he detected a look of distrust on Eddie's face but told himself it was his imagination. He had to hold his nerve.

'Right.' Eddie picked up a menu. 'We'll get some grub here before we go to meet Flinty.'

'Is he here?' Mitch asked.

'He's on his way. We're meeting him in some wee boozer across the river. Then back here to head for the match.'

Jimmy wanted to ask if they were doing the pickup with Flinty, but he didn't like the look Eddie had given him earlier. Christ! I'm feeling guilty and I haven't even been doing anything, he thought. He was relieved when Mitch spoke up.

'So what we going to do with the stuff when we're going to the match?' he asked. 'We can't leave it in the hotel room.'

Eddie looked at him and shook his head wearily.

'Fuck me! Good thinking, Batman! I was going to just leave it behind the reception desk.' Eddie's mouth curled sarcastically, then his face hardened. 'Just fucking watch and learn, Mitch. That's what you're here for.' He looked at Jimmy. 'The two of you. Just look and fucking learn. And do what you're told.'

Mitch's face flushed and he looked a little sheepish. They sat in silence for a moment, then Jimmy spotted his father crossing the road towards them and he stood up, glad of the distraction.

'There's my da,' he said. 'I'm going to see him for five minutes. If you're ordering, get me a burger and chips. No salad.'

'What's happened to you?' Jimmy's father stopped in his tracks when he saw his face.

Jimmy managed a smile. 'Wee disagreement with a man from Liverpool.'

'What? When did that happen?' His father walked towards the hotel entrance with Jimmy at his side.

'Couple of hours ago. Wee bird I met. I went up to see her and her boyfriend came in.'

As they got into the foyer his father motioned them towards a couple of empty sofas.

'I'm sweating like a horse, son. Can you get me some water or something?'

'Course.' Jimmy waved a waiter over as they sat down. 'You all right, Da? You shouldn't be out walking in this heat.'

'I know. I kind of lost track of how far I'd gone, then I had to find my way back.' He wiped sweat from his brow. 'That old town's lovely up there.' He gave Jimmy a long look.

'Aye. The whole city's great.' Jimmy glanced at him, then away.

The waiter arrived with the water and his father took a long thirsty drink.

'So,' he said slowly. 'What happened then? Tell me more?' His tone was gentle but emphatic.

Jimmy shook his head dismissively. 'It's nothing, Da. Just a wee punch up. I didn't know she had a boyfriend and she asked me up to her flat, then he came in.'

His father looked at him in silence as he drank some more water. Then ran a hand over his mouth, slammed the glass on the table and looked Jimmy in the eye.

'That's bullshit, Jimmy, and you know it. I can smell it from here.'

'What?' Jimmy said, startled.

'I'm your da.' He leaned forward, lowering his voice. 'I can tell when you're lying. You were always shite at it. That's why I've always hoped you'll never have to lie your way out of trouble.'

Jimmy snorted a half smile, remembering some of the

tales he'd told his father when he knew he was in for a hiding after things he'd got up to as a youngster.

'I'm not lying. That's what happened.' Jimmy looked at him seriously.

His father said nothing, just nodded his head.

'Anyway, I've got some food coming over there, so I'll need to get back in a minute. I'm going somewhere with Eddie and Mitch in the afternoon.'

'I know where you'll be going,' his father said, poker-faced.

'Da.' Jimmy gave his father a pleading look. 'Give me a break.'

Silence. Then his father folded his arms.

'I saw you, Jimmy.'

'What?'

'This afternoon. I saw you.'

'Where?'

'Up the town. Up that old town area. I was out for a walk and I was in one of them wee touristy shops and I saw you go into a flat. Just the back of your head, mind you, but I saw you.'

Jimmy said nothing.

'And I saw you when you came out. You didn't have a sore face then. So don't bullshit me, son.' He looked at him sternly. 'What's going on?'

'Da!' Jimmy said, exasperated. 'Give me a break.'

'Tell me. There's trouble, is there not? I can see it all over your face. Who gave you the black eye? It wasn't to do with some bird. I saw you when you came out of that flat and you'd no black eye, and then I watched you go into a bar. I was going to come over, then I saw a lassie go in and a big guy behind her. So I just stayed away. Then I watched you leave a few minutes later, Jimmy. And that's when I saw you with the black eye. It happened in there.' He reached over and grabbed Jimmy's wrist tight. 'So don't fuck around with me. There's trouble. Tell me.'

Jimmy sat in stunned silence. He could feel sweat on his back, even in the air conditioning. He had to stay calm because in five minutes he was going to have to go back to the table and act normal with Eddie and Mitch. He was going fucking nuts here and he'd nobody to turn to. Eventually he looked across at his father's blazing eyes and he knew he wouldn't take no for an answer.

'It's Wendy, Da,' Jimmy whispered. 'She's here.'

'Oh fuck,' his father said. 'Here? In Seville? Have you seen her?'

'Yep.'

Silence.

'That's amazing. So why the sore face? If that was her in that flat you went into, she certainly didn't give you a sore face.'

'I don't know. That's the truth. I don't know who gave me the black eye. Some big fucking minder guy. From Eastern Europe or somewhere.'

'But why? What's going on? Whose minder?'

Jimmy shook his head.

'Da. Listen. Please just stay out of it. I'm out of it now. I've dealt with it. Me and Wendy are finished. That's it. I've got work to do here.' He shook his head.

'Who was the minder with? That lassie that came in to the bar behind you? Who was she, Jimmy? What you mixed up in? I'm telling you this, son, if you're mixed up in something, I want to know about it. You're in trouble. So tell me.'

Jimmy took a deep breath and let it out slowly.

'Da, listen,' he whispered. 'This is fucking serious. Wendy has been to a reporter about Eddie. And Liz, her pal from the bar. She's here too, and they've both talked. The paper's trying to expose Eddie with the coke. They've been working on a story, and the reporter bird has talked Wendy into it.'

'So they're going to get him done while he's here?'

'They're going to try.'

'That means you too. Fuck me!'

'It doesn't mean anything, because they don't know anything. They don't know when this or that's happening. So they can't set Eddie up. They wanted me to be a part of it. To help them. To grass.'

'Fuck's sake. Have you told Eddie?'

'Are you kidding?'

'Good. Tell that fucker nothing. Because if he gets wind of it, the first thing he'll do is get you and Mitch to drive that shit home that you're picking up today. That's McGregor's style. He'll come home on the bus and he'll be whiter than white and you'll get stopped somewhere between here and Glasgow, and it's you who'll get the jail.'

'But nobody knows anything. Not Wendy or Liz, or that reporter bird. They know nothing, Da. So I'll just keep my head down and get this over with.' Jimmy tried to force a smile but didn't quite manage it.

'Who does the reporter work for?'

'The *Post*. I think she said her name was Rosie Gilmour. Cheeky bastard. But ballsy enough to take me on. She said she had stuff on me.'

'Like what?'

'You know these reporters. They'll say anything to get people to talk, to get them to admit something.'

'So what did she say?'

Silence. Jimmy swallowed.

'She must have said something, Jimmy, because whatever it was, you came out of there with a sore face.'

Silence.

'Da. She said the cops in Glasgow have got a bank card belonging to some dead guy and my fingerprints are all over it. Mine and Eddie's.'

'What guy?'

'It was a job. A hit. I was with Eddie and Mitch. We had to do over two wee pricks for someone in the town. It was ordered from Belfast.'

'Did you kill them?'

'Eddie shot them.'

His father thought for a moment, then his eyes narrowed.

'Them guys fished out of the quarry? That was you?'

Jimmy nodded. 'It was an order.'

'How in the name of fuck have the cops got the bank card with your fingerprints on it?'

'I don't know. I gave it to Eddie when I took it out of the guy's pocket. I don't know what he did with it.'

His father shook his head.

'Fucking hell. You're in big bother, son. Big fucking bother.'

'I'll deal with that when the time comes.'

'The cops will be waiting for you when you get back. You'd better watch for big Eddie dropping you in the shite.'

Jimmy knew he had to go. This conversation was making him even more nervous.

'Come on. We've got a big match tonight, Da.' Jimmy stood up. 'Listen. I need to get back. We're seeing Flinty in a couple of hours.'

'And watch that slippy-titted bastard, Jimmy. Don't turn your back on him.'

'I won't,' Jimmy said. 'See you later.'

'Right. Don't be late. I've got your ticket for the match.'

CHAPTER THIRTY-ONE

'Here they come,' Rosie said as McGregor came out of the hotel along with Dunlop and Mitch, and walked towards the line of waiting taxis.

'I see them,' Matt said. 'Your man Dunlop's got a decent shiner there.' Matt gave Adrian a playful dig on the shoulder from the back seat. 'Remind me not to get on your tits, big man.'

Adrian turned slightly to Rosie and gave her what passed for a smile. Then he switched on the engine.

'So we follow them,' he said, as though they were going for a picnic.

'Yeah. Keep as far away as we can. Donna told us which bar they're going to, so Javier and Garcia should already be there. But we'll track them just in case they go somewhere else.'

As they drove two cars behind the taxi, Rosie reflected on the fiery discussion with Javier and Garcia earlier as they ate lunch in the cafe following her dust-up with Jimmy.

Garcia was emphatic that he didn't want Rosie and Adrian anywhere near the meeting with Flinty, because if this was the drugs pickup and the exchange of money, then it was crucial that he and his team of undercover policemen were able to witness and discreetly film it to use as evidence.

Garcia was irritated as he spoke.

'Because, Rosie, you chased the man into the bar and had the confrontation with him, you should stay away from this meeting.' He waved his hand dismissively. 'As soon as you come on the scene, you may be recognised. It is dangerous and it could blow everything. The whole operation. Can you not see that?'

Rosie partly could, but resented the way he was talking down to her. She glared at Javier.

'Look.' Javier put his hand up to interrupt, and spoke to him in Spanish. Garcia blew smoke out of pursed lips and folded his arms petulantly.

'Listen,' Rosie butted in, knowing Javier was trying to keep the peace, 'I don't want to miss the handover of the drugs. Don't you understand that? okay. We won't know exactly what it is they'll be handing over to Flinty or what he'll pass them. But I need to be somewhere to witness it.'

'Why? *Por qué*? Is unnecessary!' Garcia raised his eyebrows and snorted.

'It *is* necessary, Juan. For me,' Rosie said, antagonised.

She could see that the strident woman tack didn't work for men like Garcia. She tried to soften a little. 'This is my story. I'm the one who's going to be writing it. I need to see it through every step of the way. I've been working on it since Glasgow . . . Weeks ago.'

'But Matt will have pictures, Rosita.' Javier gave her a 'calm down' look with his eyes.

'Fine,' Rosie snapped back at him. 'But I need to be there. And in any case, my gut feeling is that even if I bumped into Jimmy Dunlop when he's sitting in Eddie McGregor's company, nothing would happen.'

Garcia shook his head and rolled his eyes.

'You are being naive, *señora*.'

'Listen, pal.' Rosie felt her face flush. 'I've been doing this job for nearly fifteen years, all over the world. If I'd been bloody naive, I would be dead by now. So don't tell me I'm naive.'

Javier tried to keep his face straight as Garcia shifted in his seat and opened his mouth to speak.

'Let her finish her point, Juan. Please.' Javier put his hand up.

'Look, Juan,' Rosie said, 'let's not fall out over this, and I do appreciate the help and cooperation of the Guardia Civil . . . but try to see it this way. Dunlop's girlfriend asked him to grass on the UVF. For him to tell Eddie about that would be to sign Wendy's death warrant, and Dunlop would never do that. He loves her.'

'How can you be sure he won't tell this McGregor?' Garcia spread his hands in appeal.

'I trust my instinct.' Rosie sat back, folding her arms, and there followed a resentful silence.

In the end, they agreed that Rosie would be in a cafe close enough but far enough away, and she settled for that. It was only a small victory, but she had to win it. Garcia knew the area well. He grudgingly gave her the name of a cafe close by, then got up and went outside.

As Rosie and Javier got up to leave, he took hold of her arm.

'Rosie, it is not smart to rub this man up the wrong way at this crucial point in the investigation. Why can't you see that? Jesus, woman!'

'It's his fault.' Rosie gave him a defiant look, knowing she sounded sulky. 'He's got an attitude.'

'*He's* got an attitude?' Javier smiled, shaking his head as he walked away. 'See you at the cafe. Now be careful. Please.'

Adrian drove the car past the cafe where Javier and Garcia were already sitting a few tables away from Flinty Jackson, accompanied by two shaven-headed minders. Rosie hoped she'd made the right decision to come.

'I see Flinty's brought his gorillas,' Matt said. He tapped Adrian on the shoulder. 'How about doubling back when you can, mate, and going past again so I can get a snap of them?'

'Is that wise?' Rosie asked.

'It's okay. The traffic is quite heavy and it's a reasonably busy street,' Matt said. 'These eejits aren't going to be thinking anyone's taking their picture from a car. The minders look like they'd have trouble knowing their left hand from their right. They're probably the first generation of their family to walk upright.'

Rosie laughed. 'Yeah. You might find they've got tails when they stand up.' She turned to Matt. 'But just be careful. Don't do it if there's even the slightest risk.'

'Don't worry. They won't even know it's done.'

They drove past as the taxi pulled up and McGregor, Dunlop and Mitch got out and walked towards Flinty's table. McGregor was carrying a black holdall. Flinty stood up and shook his hand, then motioned them to another, bigger table, even though there was enough room for all of them where he was.

'They must be expecting company,' Rosie said.

A few minutes later, Adrian parked the car and they walked along the riverside where several of the cafes and restaurants on the quayside were beginning to fill up. For a moment, all three of them stood and watched the tourist boats glide down the river in the setting sun. Then they headed to the bar Garcia had told them to go to. It was two up from where McGregor sat, and the bar in between was busy enough to ensure that they were far enough out of the line of vision of anyone at his table.

'It's closer than I thought,' Rosie said, looking around for a place that would keep them out of view.

She found a table behind some tall plants and they sat down.

'The only way they'd be able to see us here is if they decide to go for a walk along this way and right through the cafe. We'll be fine.' Matt took a long look before he sat down. 'And I might just be able to squeeze a snap in from here. If not, I'll go walkabout. Nobody knows me.' He grinned at Rosie. 'You're the one Jimmy knows.'

'Don't remind me,' Rosie said. 'But I still think he wouldn't bat an eyelid if he walked up here and found me.'

'Well, don't be too sure.'

'I can see Javier and Garcia,' Rosie said, peering through the foliage. 'Do you think you can spot the undercover cops?'

Matt looked around.

'Don't think so. The restaurant's quite busy, so they could be sitting anywhere among the crowd.'

'I can see who it might be,' Adrian said, looking into the distance. 'There are three guys on a couple of tables by McGregor. I think they are police.'

'I see them,' Rosie said. 'You might be right there. How can you tell?'

Adrian shrugged and said nothing. The waiter came and they ordered coffee. Moments later, as the drinks were placed on the table, Adrian's eyes suddenly grew dark. He leaned forward, reaching across to touch Rosie's hand.

'Listen, Rosie. Do not react to what I am going to say. Please.' He took a breath. 'But your old friend Jake Cox has just come from the inside of the bar and joined them at the table.'

'Tell me you're joking!' Rosie saw his face suddenly even paler than normal. Her stomach dropped. 'Jesus! You're not joking.' She glanced at Matt.

'Oh fuck! I don't believe this.' Matt blew out his cheeks and kept his head down.

Adrian's eyes were fixed across at the bar. Rosie rang Javier.

'Rosita. We saw you arrive.'

'Javier. There's a problem.'

'What?'

'That guy who's just joined them. Can you see him?'

'Yes. The older guy. I see him.'

'That's Jake Cox.'

'Oh.' He paused. 'That *is* a problem.'

'He must be involved with them. I had no idea. It didn't even come up anywhere on the radar.'

'I suppose maybe it should have. They are all connected, these gangsters.'

'I know. But we were looking only at the UVF and McGregor. There will be other gangsters who smuggle drugs in, of course. We can't cover them all. I just had no idea Cox was at all involved with this particular mob.'

'Well. Maybe he's not involved as such. But he does live down on the Costa del Sol and he is a player back in Glasgow, so maybe he just came along to see some of his old mates. He could have come up for the Rangers match and has joined them for a drink.'

'I don't think so. Because McGregor is carrying the hold-all and Cox wouldn't be there during any kind of exchange if he wasn't involved in some way. Have you been able to see if there's any bag or anything at Flinty's table?'

'Of course, Rosie. We were here before he arrived. One of the minders was carrying the bag and he put it down on the ground next to where Flinty was sitting. Then when they moved tables, it was Flinty who carried it. If this is a hand-over, then I'd say that will be the coke. I suppose McGregor will be carrying the money.'

They were silent for a moment.

'It's dodgy for us here, with Jake Cox around. He could easily go for a walk to the river, turn around and spot me. Then we've had it.'

'I know. Well, my friend Juan did say you shouldn't have come, Rosita.'

'Javier,' Rosie said, irritated, 'I'm here. That's all that matters. No point in saying what I should or should not have done. I'm here, so let's deal with it.'

'Okay. Let's just keep it calm. I think you are far enough

away and the place is getting busier for the evening. But you might have to think about trying to leave discreetly, because the longer you are here, the more chance there is of you being seen.'

'All right,' Rosie sighed. She had to agree with him, and deep down perhaps Garcia was right that she shouldn't have been here in the first place, but she wasn't about to admit that. 'I'll talk to Adrian and Matt and we'll work it out.'

'Okay.'

'But what about you, Javier?' Rosie said, an image flashing into her mind of him the night he was shot by Cox's henchman on the Costa del Sol last year.

'Cox has never seen me before. If you remember, the night I got shot, only the minder saw me. The one who held the gun to your head. And I shot him . . . saving your life . . . not that I'm casting it up.' He chuckled.

'But there were others, Javier.' Rosie was too edgy for humour. 'The guys who ran out of the whorehouse after Adrian and his sister. What about them?'

'Rosie. I'm surrounded by five armed Civil Guards. I'll be fine.'

'And what about the handover of the drugs and money?' Rosie couldn't help her paranoia now that she was in a weaker position.

'We can take care of things here, Rosie. If there is a handover then it will be recorded.'

'Yes,' Rosie said, 'but if we haven't recorded it ourselves

we have no guarantee that Garcia will turn it over to us.' She paused. 'I . . . I just like to do things myself to make sure it's mine and I actually saw it . . . You know—'

'Rosie,' Javier interrupted and Rosie sensed his irritation. 'We will deal with that in time. Now come on. You know it isn't safe for you to stay here.'

'Okay,' Rosie said. 'Talk later.' She hung up.

She looked at Matt, then at Adrian, whose eyes were everywhere, scanning every face. She gnawed at the skin around her thumbnail as she glanced over again at Jake Cox, where she could just make out his big, ugly florid face as he threw his head back and cackled at whatever joke someone had just cracked around the table. He looked none the worse for the bullet Adrian had put in him the night he rescued his sister from the Fuengirola whorehouse last summer. The word on the street in Glasgow was that Cox was lying low, licking his wounds, and that big Al Howie was running the show for him – though after Rosie's recent exposé on the missing refugees, he too had gone to ground. She made a silent prayer that Howie didn't turn up here, because he was an even bigger psycho than Cox. But on this evidence, big Jake looked as much of a player as ever. She consoled herself with the thought that perhaps he was just up at Seville for the Rangers match, and was catching up with a few old cronies. But Rosie was certain of one thing – if this bastard got wind that she was sitting within shooting distance, she'd be dead. Her mouth was dry, and when she lifted the water bottle she hoped nobody saw the slight tremor in her hand.

'Let's get out of here,' she said, dropping some money on the table.

'In a moment,' Adrian said. 'Don't look, but there is a Merc with blacked-out windows coming along the road slowly. Could be anyone, but we stay here till it goes past.'

Rosie turned her head slightly and could see the Merc slowing up as it drove past the riverside cafes and then out of view.

'Could be anybody,' Matt said, more in hope than belief. 'I'm sure there's all sorts of people in Seville, from celebrities to Spanish gangsters. Let's not get our knickers in a twist.'

'Yeah,' Rosie said, resisting the urge to smile at the look of dread on his face.

'I think I should go and bring the car to the bar just two cafes along from here, then in a few minutes you come straight down and get in. Rather than us all leave here together.'

'Okay,' Rosie nodded, wishing she was sitting where Javier was, surrounded by armed Guardia Civil.

CHAPTER THIRTY-TWO

Rosie and Matt watched as Adrian disappeared from view, then allowed time for him to pick up the car before they left the bar. They walked briskly into the street without looking back in the direction where McGregor and his gang sat.

'It rankles me leaving something before I can actually see what I came to see,' Rosie said to Matt as they walked.

'I know what you mean. But it's better than getting rumbled by that fat bastard Cox.'

They made their way to the spot where they arranged to meet Adrian, and waited. Rosie took out her mobile phone and flicked through the contacts until she saw TJ's name. She looked at her watch. It would be around lunchtime in New York, and she thought about giving him a quick call. She hadn't spoken to him since the call the other night when Kat answered the phone in his apartment. No – leave it, she told herself. She'd wait until she got back to the hotel room, where she could think about the conversation she would have with him, see if he mentioned anything about Kat staying there. She would be able to detect if he was being cagey. Again with the paranoia. All she knew was that Kat answered the phone and TJ was asleep. She'd call him later. Put her mind at ease, or deal with whatever she had to deal with.

'Adrian's taking a while,' Matt said after they'd stood a couple of minutes longer than they expected. Then he suddenly patted his jeans pocket. 'Shit! I've left my mobile on the table in the bar.'

'Christ, Matt! Sprint back and get it. Adrian should be here in a second. Traffic's heavy.'

Rosie peered into the distance hoping Adrian's car would appear on the horizon as Matt ran back to the bar. Then suddenly she saw the Merc they'd seen earlier with the blacked-out windows. It was coming over the brow of the hill towards her in a line of traffic. Rosie turned her head away, anxious, and glanced back to where she could see Matt reach the bar. She was about to instinctively shout after him when the Merc slowed up and pulled into the kerb beside her. Panic lashed across her gut. The rear window slid down slowly. And in the back seat, his face a mask of grey, was Adrian. There was a gun at his head. The front passenger door clunked open.

'Get in.' A voice from the back seat. 'Or your fucking mate's brains will be all over the pavement.'

'What the fu—' Rosie automatically glanced over her

shoulder where she could see Matt about twenty yards away walking towards them. He stopped in his tracks and Rosie prayed he'd stay where he was.

'Are you fucking deaf as well as stupid?' the voice growled. 'Get in the car.'

Rosie's legs turned to jelly. Adrian was still as a statue, staring straight ahead. Then, when he looked up at her, there was no fear or desperation in his eyes, but there was trust.

'You've got three seconds.' All she could see was a hand, as the gun was pushed harder into the side of Adrian's head, making a red mark above his ear.

Rosie stepped off the kerb and eased her shaking legs into the front seat. As the car drove off, she could see in the wing mirror the panic and confusion in Matt's face as he punched a number into his mobile. Please let it be Javier's and not mine, Rosie prayed.

The Merc slowed down a little as it passed the bar where McGregor sat, and she saw Javier and Garcia a few tables away from them, within shouting distance if only she could shout. In the seconds it took them to pass, Rosie glimpsed Jake Cox looking straight at the blacked-out windows and she could have sworn there was a smirk on his face.

A mobile rang in the back seat and Rosie heard the voice answer it.

'Got the two of them, boss. It was no problem . . . All right . . . Hold on.'

A fist dug firmly into Rosie's shoulder and she turned her head slightly to see a mobile phone thrust towards her. She briefly saw the bloated-faced man who held the gun to Adrian's head, his thick lips curled into a sneer.

'Here . . . Mr Cox wants a word.'

Rosie took the phone in her trembling hand and put it to her ear. She cleared her dry throat.

'Welcome back to Spain, Rosie. Do you know who this is?'

She didn't answer.

'What's the matter? Lost your voice, hen?'

Rosie stayed silent.

'Well. You can just listen to me then, pal. You're well and truly fucked this time. You and that Commie bastard in the back seat. That big cunt shot me in Fuengirola that night. Did you know that? You've not forgot, have you? Did he think he was going to get away with it? I'm lucky I'm still here. But not so lucky for you. Or him. Because we're going to have a bit of fun now all right.' He paused. 'And by the way, you're not as clever as you think you are, because my driver might be a thick bastard, but he never forgets a face. And he remembered your big Commie pal from Fuengirola, and spotted him the minute he drove past as you were in the bar here. That's why you're sitting there shitting yourselves and I'm enjoying a wee drink.'

'People know where I am,' Rosie blurted out, aware of the quake in her voice. 'They'll be looking for me.'

'Aye, right. Tough shit. I'm sure they'll find you eventually.' He hung up.

The car swiftly crossed lanes and sped down the road then turned into a quieter street, pulling over at the kerb behind another car. Rosie watched as the doors opened and two burly men came out. Both had shaven heads, and one of them looked like someone had melted his face then moulded it back together in a hurry. They came towards the passenger door like hulking polar bears and yanked it open. Then, the brute with the melted face grabbed her by the hair and the scruff of her blouse and dragged her out. She didn't even get time to put her feet out and tripped on the pavement. He pulled her up and slapped her face hard.

'Get up, you stupid fuck. Stand up.'

'I . . . I can't.' Rosie's legs were giving way when she stood up and she tried to support herself on the car.

'Fuck's sake, Psycho. Just *drag* her to the fucking car then before anybody sees us,' the other guy spat.

The melted face picked her up and Rosie felt his meaty fingers like a vice around her arms and her skin bruising as he dragged her to the car and threw her in the back like a rag doll. Then both the men got into the front.

'Now don't be daft enough to move a muscle back there,' the driver said. 'Because big Psycho here is just getting in the mood for a bit of fun. And believe me, you won't like his kind of fun.'

Both cars drove out of the street and through a warren

of backstreets until they came to what looked like a row of multi-storey offices, each with underground car parking. They drove down the slope to one of them and into an almost empty car park. The tyres screeched as they sped around the tight bends taking them to the next level, then several more levels and in her panic Rosie lost count. Finally both cars pulled up sharp. The driver came out and opened the rear door and took out a gun. There were now two guns at Adrian's head as he eased himself out of the car with his hands behind his back. Rosie waited as the driver and the man called Psycho got out and opened her door. She braced herself for being dragged out, but nothing happened.

'Right. Out,' the driver said. 'And don't fuck about. Stand up.'

Rosie gritted her teeth. Her cheek was on fire and she felt her bottom lip puffing up from the force of the slap. She took as deep a breath as she could and pulled herself out of the car. She looked up to where Adrian stood and their eyes met. He blinked in that way he had of communicating without speaking, wanting to show some kind of empathy or give her a sign that things would be all right. Or at least she hoped that's what it was. Psycho grabbed a handful of her hair and pushed her forward to follow the others. They barged through swing doors and walked down a stone corridor, and along the way, through small windows, Rosie could see they were several floors up. She could make out the city and the river as the daylight faded. They hadn't travelled far. She wondered what Matt had done. He will have phoned Javier, she tried to console herself. Help would come. But they'd gone so fast out of the street, how in the hell would they find them here?

They were pushed into a tiny, stifling side room where there was only an air vent above the door. One of the men's mobiles rang.

'Yeah, boss. We're here. They're fine. Like little lambs, they're so quiet. Okay.' He hung up.

The driver looked at both of them.

'We're getting some company in a wee while, so you'll be left alone for the moment. I suggest you kiss each other's arses goodbye.'

Psycho frisked Adrian, took out his mobile phone, removed the battery and threw the phone on the floor. Then he grabbed Rosie's bag and emptied the contents onto the floor, taking the battery from her phone. He frisked her roughly, squeezing her breasts so hard the pain shot through her, and grinning as he shoved his hand between her legs.

'Can I shag her?' he said, pulling at her jeans without taking his eyes off her face. 'She's quite shaggable.'

'Nah. You'd better not,' the driver said. 'Big Jake didn't say anything about shagging, so just stick to the brief.'

Psycho pushed her against the wall, lifting her off her feet, and started grinding himself up against her.

'You don't know what you're missing, doll.'

Before Rosie could stop herself, she headbutted him, hearing his nose crack, and she instantly knew she'd made a huge mistake. Maybe the biggest she'd ever make. His face went purple with rage and he looked as though he was going to explode.

'Fuck!' he spat. 'Ya wee bastard!' Blood spouted from his nose.

The others burst out laughing.

'Fuck me, Psycho. That's the only kiss you're getting, ya daft prick.'

He slapped both sides of her face so hard she saw stars. Then pain ripped through as he punched her hard on the barely healed stab wound where she'd been operated on a couple of months ago.

'Come on to fuck, Psycho. Upstairs.'

They went out of the room and slammed the door, locking it three times.

Rosie tried to get to her feet but fell over. Adrian rushed towards her and lifted her, holding her close as he looked at her face. Tears filled her eyes.

'Bastard!' she said. 'Oh, Adrian, I'm sorry for all this.' Her face pressed against his chest.

'Sssh, Rosie. Don't worry. We will be all right.'

Rosie looked up at him.

'No we won't,' she sniffed. 'How are we going to get out of this? They're going to kill us. That Psycho bastard –

where in the name of Christ did they get him from? They're going to kill us. I know it.'

'What about Matt? What happened to him?'

'He left his mobile on the table at the bar and ran back to get it. Then as he was coming towards us he saw the car and I looked at him. I tried to signal with my hand to make him stay where he was and it seemed to work. He's our only hope.'

'He will have phoned Javier and the policeman. They will come.'

'But they don't know where we are.'

'They will come. I know they will.' He looked at Rosie and eased her away from him. 'But listen to me.' His fingers gently touched her face. 'Some bad things are going to happen here to us before anyone comes . . . before this is over. So please. You must try to be brave. To be strong.'

Rosie nodded.

'I'm scared.'

'I know you are.' He stroked her hair. 'But it happens. People suffer pain and they have to be able to stand it. You must be strong. You *are* strong, and they will hurt you. But we will get through it. We have to.'

Rosie sniffed, sliding down the wall until she was hunkered down and then sitting on the stone floor. She felt cold and shivery even though her blouse was wet with sweat. She wiped blood from her mouth.

Adrian sat watching her, then he reached down and

turned back the cuff of his trousers and tore at the material. He produced a tiny cloth and unfolded it, taking something out of it.

'What's that?' Rosie pulled herself up towards him. 'A battery? Christ, Adrian! You've got a battery!'

'Sssh, Rosie. I always have one extra, hidden, just in case. Since the war. Hurry. We don't have much time.' He slipped the battery into his mobile and switched it on, sticking it in his pocket for a second to muffle the start-up jingle.

'Here. Phone Matt.'

'Shit,' Rosie said. 'I need to think of his number. I have him on speed dial. Christ . . . 0777 . . .' Then she reeled it off, thankful she remembered. 'Right, that's it.'

Matt answered after one ring.

'Adrian. Fuck me! What the fuck?'

'Sssh, Matt, it's me. Listen. The guys in the Merc had a gun at Adrian's head. They must have got him when he went to get our car. They were clocking us. Don't know how. It's Jake Cox. I think he's coming here.'

'Shit! Wait. Javier's here. I've got him and the cops. They're on it.'

'Rosie?' It was Javier.

'Javier, I don't have much time.'

'Rosie, listen to me. Just tell me where you are.'

'I don't know. A car park – multi-storey place. They took us in two cars. We went down the main boulevard then turned right and through a load of streets. It looks like several office blocks with parking. We're up on like a fifth floor in a side room . . . Oh shit . . . Maybe it's the fourth . . . or the second. I can't remember. But I don't know where it is.'

'We came up six floors,' Adrian said calmly.

'Six floors, Javier,' Rosie relayed the information.

'It's okay, Rosie. How many people? Have they hurt you?'

'Just a slap. But there's this headcase called Psycho and they're waiting for people to come. It's Jake Cox. He's behind it. But I don't know about the others. Hurry.'

'Garcia's men are on it. We left the table as soon as Matt called us, so they are now trying to locate where you are. We'll find you.'

'They're going to kill us. For the shooting last year, they said. In Fuengirola.' Rosie felt her voice breaking.

'It's okay. Garcia has people everywhere. They're all over this.'

'I need to go. They took the batteries out of our phones, but Adrian had one hidden in his clothes. But I must go in case they come.'

'Don't worry.' Javier hung up.

Rosie and Adrian looked up at the sound of locks being turned. The door opened and Psycho walked in, followed by two gunmen.

'Right. Let's go.' They ushered them out.

'Where?' Rosie couldn't help asking.

Psycho grinned. 'Does it fucking matter?' He grabbed her

roughly and pushed her ahead of him, his hand gripping the back of her hair so tight it made her eyes water.

They were marched along another corridor and up a stone stair. Another three flights and Rosie could hardly breathe by the time they reached an emergency exit door. Psycho pushed on the bar and opened it, then shoved Rosie out onto the roof of the building. Her head swam as soon as she stepped out and could see the edge of the roof. As long as she could remember, her fevered nightmares had been plagued by falling off tall buildings or bridges, hanging on the edge of a cliff, or slipping down mountains. She was so afraid of heights she couldn't cross a bridge or even climb a ladder. Her shrink pal told her it was a deep-rooted anxiety and it was all about losing control. She felt sick rising in her throat.

'What's the matter? You're a bit white. You're no' scared of heights are you?' Psycho pulled her across towards the edge of the building and Rosie thought she was going to pass out.

There was no barrier, just a single brick lip and the sheer drop. He dragged her, still holding her hair, then he pushed her again until she was teetering on the edge of the building, the streets and the moving traffic swirling before her. If she moved a muscle, she'd be off.

'Please. Stop. I'm going to faint. I . . . I can't . . . Please.' Her legs gave way.

'Get up. Stand up.' He pulled her to her feet. 'Look. It's a long way down. That's what happens when you try to be a smart fucker.' He forced her to stand just inches from the edge and pushed her body forward so one foot was almost over.

'Please. Don't.' Rosie broke down.

Psycho pushed her to the ground, and left her sobbing as she crawled on her belly away from the edge.

Then he turned to Adrian, along with the other two men. One of them made him stand, then locked his arms behind his back while Psycho punched him in the gut, winding him. As Adrian doubled over, he punched his face and blood poured from his mouth. Then he hit the back of his legs with a pickaxe handle and he buckled to the ground.

At that moment, the door opened and Flinty Jackson walked in with a minder behind him. He stood surveying the scene then walked to the edge of the building and turned to face them.

'So,' Flinty said, coming towards Rosie. '*You're* Rosie Gilmour. Tell me this. What are you actually doing over here in Seville?' His icy blue eyes locked hers.

'Nothing.' Rosie cowered, waiting for him to kick her. 'I was just monitoring the Rangers match fans. We do it all the time. Wherever they go. It's nothing. It's in case of hooliganism.'

'Pish!' He wiped beads of sweat from his suntanned forehead. 'You're into something. What are you investigating? What are you sticking your nose into this time? Big Jake says we've to sort out your big Commie pal here for last year, and you, Gilmour, for all that carry-on in Glasgow with his cop mate, big Gavin Fox. So you're well and truly fucked.' He walked around her, and she doubled in two as he gave her a swift kick in the ribs. 'But you could make your last few minutes easier by telling us why you're here. Why were you at that cafe we were at today? Jake's driver recognised you from last year. So you're not that clever. You watching us? Because if you are, then you'll know who you're dealing with. You know what the UVF does with spies?'

'We weren't watching you,' Rosie croaked, struggling to breathe. 'We just happened to be there. We're going to the match tonight. The tickets are back at the hotel.'

Flinty snorted a laugh and the others sniggered.

'You'll not be going to the match tonight, or any other night. Big Jake's been waiting for this chance for ages. He can't believe his luck.' He jerked his head towards Adrian. 'Stand him up, Psycho.'

They pulled Adrian to his feet. Two of the men held him tight as Psycho forced Adrian to hold his arm out straight. They forced him to the very edge of the building, so that if he took one step he was off. They pulled up the legs of his trousers, exposing his naked calves.

'Keep him steady.'

Flinty's minder stepped forward and handed him a blowtorch. Flinty sparked it into action and a yellow flame appeared, then he adjusted a knob and the flame turned blue as it roared.

'Oh Christ,' Rosie said under her breath. 'Oh Christ no.'

She watched as Flinty stood close to Adrian and turned the blowtorch on his leg for a split second. Adrian jumped with pain and almost fell off the building. The henchmen grinned and pulled him back. Then Flinty turned the torch on his other leg making him jump again, to the amusement of the thugs holding him.

'Put his arms out straight,' Flinty said.

Then he turned the torch on the underside of his forearm.

'So. Now do you want to tell us why you're here with that bitch?'

Adrian didn't answer. Flinty turned the blowtorch on his arm again and held it this time for a second longer. Rosie turned away as she saw the flesh redden then turn shiny. He took the torch away and a huge blister appeared.

'This is for big Jake.'

Flinty then held the torch on Adrian's arm so long that Rosie could see the flesh crisp and blacken then drop to the floor. She felt sick. She wanted to blurt it all out, tell them everything. She was sure they were going to kill them anyway and she couldn't bear to see Adrian in such agonising pain, his teeth gritted as he tried to bear it. She caught his eye and he slowly shook his head as though reading her thoughts. Then, he screamed as his flesh burned, and she could see the colour rise then drain from his face as his legs buckled and he passed out.

'That's just for starters,' Flinty said. 'I'm going to do that all over your fucking body so that you'll actually be glad to jump off this building.' He turned to Rosie. 'Your turn.'

Rosie's heart pounded in her chest, her whole body shuddering.

'Get her up.'

Psycho and the other two pulled her to her feet.

'Oh please, no,' she whimpered.

'No? Would you rather we just shoved you off the fucking roof? It's no bother for us. You're going off anyway. We've been told to get rid of you, I'm only having a bit of fun. I get a kick out of burning people.' He sparked the blowtorch into her face for a second and she jerked her head back.

He nodded to Psycho and the others. She struggled and tried to push her feet hard against the ground as they dragged her to the edge.

'Hold her tight.'

Rosie heard the roar of the blowtorch before she felt it burn the back of her legs and she jumped, one leg hanging off the building. She glanced down and almost passed out. The thugs chuckled and held onto her.

'Hold her tight, for fuck's sake,' Flinty said. 'Get her arm out.'

Psycho held her arm stiffly out. Flinty fired up the

blowtorch and came around to the side of her. He sprayed it across her arm and she screamed.

'So why are you here?'

'Working. On the fans. I told you. Please. No more.' She glanced at Adrian who had regained consciousness and was looking up at her, his arm a blistering, gaping gash, almost to the bone.

Flinty flicked the torch again onto her arm and held it. The sudden, searing, sickening pain made Rosie utter a high-pitched scream. The last thing she saw was the raw flesh of her arm as she collapsed.

They went across to Adrian.

'Get him on his feet. He's going over first.'

But as they pulled him up, the door burst open, and they dropped him. Three armed police in uniform came in, with Garcia behind them. One of Flinty's men fired and one of the cops went down. Then a burst of gunfire, another cop got hit, and the other henchman went down. Adrian made a grab for the gun just as Flinty dived across, but Adrian got it first and fired it in a split second into Flinty's stomach. As he stumbled back, Adrian scrambled to his feet and kicked him off the roof. More gunfire as Psycho was shot in the stomach and dropped to the ground.

Garcia dashed to the edge of the building in time to see Flinty hurling through the air, as the door burst open again and Javier came rushing onto the roof along with three other armed police.

He went across to the edge of the roof where Garcia was looking down.

'That's going to take a bit of explaining,' he said, smiling at Garcia.

The detective barked instructions to one of his men about an ambulance, then he came over, crouching down beside Rosie. He touched her face.

'You are safe now,' he said.

She passed out.

CHAPTER THIRTY-THREE

Jimmy ordered another beer as he waited in the cafe across from Wendy's apartment. He scanned the front door, willing it to open and for Wendy to come walking out and greet him with the smile on her face that had haunted his dreams since the night she disappeared. But he knew deep down that wasn't going to happen. He didn't even know what the hell he was doing here, but he couldn't stop himself from making the call. He just had to see her one last time before he left.

The Rangers victory party was in full swing in the city centre with jubilant fans dancing in the streets, celebrating the narrow win that put them closer to qualifying for the next round. By the time he'd left the main square, Mitch had jumped into the huge fountain, joining dozens of other fans as they danced a conga in the water. But as every triumphant cry of 'No Surrender' echoed around the square, Jimmy's heart was sinking further. These were his people.

This was his life. But without Wendy it was never going to be the same. He knew he'd have to live with that, but he wanted to see her one more time.

Suddenly the door to the apartment block opened and she stepped out into the narrow street. She stood for a moment, bathed in the yellowy glow of the street light, and Jimmy's heart ached for her. But the face that he'd dreamed of, the eyes that had captivated him from the first time he saw her, had lost their spark. He watched her for a second as she stood, forlorn, and shame washed over him for failing to appreciate just how much she'd gone through since the night Eddie raped her. All this time, he'd been thinking only of himself, how much he missed her, how he longed to feel the touch of her body against his, yet he didn't fully consider the toll it had all taken on Wendy. She looked across and their eyes met, but her face didn't break into the smile he missed so much. She walked towards him.

Jimmy got up to greet her, but he couldn't speak. They stood looking at each other for a moment, before he stepped forward.

'I'm sorry, Wendy,' he said softly. 'I had to see you. I . . . I'm sorry.'

He waited to see if she would reach out to him, but she didn't. She sighed and sat down.

'I'm sorry too . . . I'm sorry I got raped and ruined your life.' Her eyes filled with angry tears.

The words stung and for a few seconds Jimmy was speechless as he watched the muscle on her jaw twitch.

'Aw, Wendy. Don't. Please. Don't say that.' He shook his head and looked down at the table.

The silence hung over them like a blanket, suffocating everything they'd been to each other. It was only broken when the waiter came up. Wendy ordered a glass of wine, and Jimmy hesitated before asking for a Jack Daniels on the rocks. He needed a stiff drink to get through this.

'I'm sorry, Jimmy,' Wendy said, wiping a tear from her cheek. 'I shouldn't have said that. I . . . I'm just so screwed up with everything.'

'It's okay. I deserved it. I'm so sorry for what happened to you.' Jimmy picked at his fingernails, fighting back tears. 'I'm sorry I wasn't there to protect you.'

'Oh, Jimmy.' She looked up across at him, tears spilling out of her eyes. 'I'm so sad all the time. I . . . I just want to run away, and keep on running and never come back. As if, maybe if I keep running then I can run away from that night and everything after it and maybe one day I'll be who I was again.' She wiped her face with a napkin. 'I don't know who I am any more.'

He stretched across and took her hand, relieved when she didn't pull it away. They sat in silence, and Jimmy fought the urge to pull her to her feet and take her in his arms and promise her he'd protect her, that he would never leave her and she'd never again feel the fear or pain or loneliness she had suffered. That was the man he used to be, the man he couldn't be any more.

'When do you go back?' Wendy broke the silence. 'Tomorrow?'

Jimmy nodded. 'Bus leaves at eleven. Everybody's wrecked tonight though. It'll be some trip. Not looking forward to it.'

Christ, he thought. Is this what it's come to? Small talk with the woman I want to spend the rest of my life with? He bit his lip.

'Jimmy, listen.' Wendy let go of his hand. 'That reporter lassie I told you about.'

Jimmy shook his head and sighed. 'Wendy, you shouldn't have spoken to that woman. Honestly. I'm not just saying about what we're doing here . . . okay, that's part of it. But you just shouldn't have. You're not safe any more because of that. Neither is Liz. It was stupid. If the reporter puts something in the paper, the cops will be onto her to find out how she knew. You think she's going to protect you?' He paused. 'She won't. Look . . . I'm sorry for doing my nut about it yesterday in your apartment, but I was just so shocked. I . . . I know what the UVF is capable of. But it was wrong what you did.'

Wendy's mouth tightened. 'I don't care what you say. I did what I thought was right. Anyway. It's done now.'

Jimmy nodded, blowing out his cheeks.

'That woman. That Rosie Gilmour? You know she came after me into a bar after I had been to your place? She confronted me. Took me on.' He shook his head. 'Ballsy bitch, I'll say that for her. But she's dead meat now.'

'I know what happened to you,' Wendy said. 'Rosie told me. And I know you got into a fight with Adrian.'

'Who the fuck is that guy? Her minder?'

'Don't know. He's from somewhere like Bosnia or something. He's a good guy. He protects us. I feel safe when I'm with him . . .' Her voice trailed off.

Jimmy sat tight-lipped. He glanced at Wendy and knew the dig wasn't intentional, but it was still true. He should be the one protecting her, but he wasn't.

'Jimmy. I need to tell you something.'

He raised his eyebrows at her and said nothing.

'I met with Rosie earlier on. She's been beaten up. So has Adrian. They're both quite badly hurt. Some guy burned them with a blowtorch.'

Jimmy's stomach lurched. Flinty Jackson. It had to be. But why?

'A blowtorch? When?'

'Today. Earlier on.'

'Fuck's sake. That's bad. But I did warn her she'd get in trouble, trying to take people like us on.'

'People like you, Jimmy?' Wendy snapped. 'People who use blowtorches on women? People who rape women?'

'Wendy, come on. You know what I mean. I don't know anything about what happened to that Gilmour woman.' His mind flicked back to the afternoon with Eddie and

Flinty exchanging the holdalls. There had been no mention of where Flinty was going when he left suddenly. He was supposed to meet them after the game, but he hadn't turned up.

'But it's true, Jimmy. If the guy who did this to Rosie and to Adrian was one of your mob, then that makes you the same.'

'We're not all the same. I don't even know who it was, for Christ's sake. That bird has got her nose into everything and she's rattling cages everywhere. She's bound to get hit eventually. She's a daft bastard. She wants to chuck it, because she won't win. She'll get done over.'

'Well. Whatever. The guy who burned her won't be doing it again.'

'How come?' Jimmy was curious.

'He's dead, that's how come. Cops killed him. Don't know the details really. But he ended up falling off a roof.'

'Really? Fuck me.' Jimmy's mind raced, trying to put it all together. 'Rosie Gilmour told you all this?'

'Yeah,' Wendy said. 'She was there. Look, Jimmy. I don't know if this is all connected. I don't even know what you're doing or if you were a part of that. Because at the end of the day you're UVF and that's your priority, so you're not going to tell me. But if it is all connected then you're in trouble, because the cops have got all this sewn up. Rosie is working with them. I told you that in the beginning. But you're so stupid you think you're a big man and the UVF will run the world. Well they won't. And tomorrow you'll find your-self in the pokey.'

Jimmy said nothing. He thought of Eddie and what it would mean if he got wind of Flinty being killed – if it was actually true. He couldn't work out how it was all con-nected. The guy at the table was big Jake Cox, a player from Glasgow – everyone knew that. And he was UVF through and through. But he didn't know if there was any link with him and Rosie Gilmour or with Flinty and Gilmour. He knew bugger all. That was the truth. He just did what he was told. He couldn't exactly go knocking on Eddie's hotel room door, asking him for information. And there was no way he could tell him what he'd just heard.

Wendy finished her drink and pushed the glass away.

'Listen, I need to go.' She swallowed. 'I don't think there's much more we have to say to each other.' She put her hand to her mouth as she fought back tears. 'But I just want you to know that I really thought we *had* something together – even though we'd only been seeing each other for two months. For the first time in my life I thought I'd found a mate, a best friend, someone who could make me laugh and make me feel like I was the only woman in the world. I . . . I never felt that in my life before and . . .' She paused, her voice shaking with emotion. 'And you know what . . . If I never feel it again, then that's okay. Because I know what it feels like.'

She stood up and Jimmy got to his feet.

'Oh, Wendy . . . Please. It doesn't have to be like this. I can still make you happy.'

'No you can't. You can't.'

'But I love you. I've never loved another woman in my life apart from my ma.' He blinked away tears. 'I don't want to love anyone else. I love you, Wendy. Please.'

He took a step forward and put his arms around her and hugged her tight. She held him and he could feel her body warmth and the fragility of her.

'I have to go. Please. Don't make it any more difficult.'

Wendy eased herself out of his arms and they stood there, tears blinding them. Then she walked away and Jimmy watched as she crossed to the apartment block and put her key in the door. Please turn around, he said to himself. And she did, for a fleeting, final glance before she closed the door on them both.

CHAPTER THIRTY-FOUR

Rosie was falling. Tumbling over and over again, grasping desperately for the walls as they turned to sand in her hands. High above, she could see them laughing as they stood at the edge of the building. Ugly faces with shaven heads, roaring and guffawing. And then suddenly she was soaring through the air, as her mother and father scooped her up. They fluttered, all three of them, to the ground and Rosie could smell the freshness of moist grass. Then she felt their kisses on her cheek, and they were gone. Rosie raised herself up on her elbow to look for them. But a white-hot pain cut through her arm and she let out a high-pitched howl. The banging on her hotel bedroom door brought her back and she heard herself screaming.

'Rosie. Rosie. It's us. Matt and Javier. Open the door. Are you all right?'

For a few seconds she didn't recognise the voices or the names. She didn't even know if she could sit up, such was the searing pain. Then she touched the bandage on her arm and remembered. Through her sobs, she managed to answer.

'Oh, God! The pain. I can't cope. My arm. It's on fire.'

'Open the door.' It was Javier.

She sat up and wiped the tears and sweat off her face with the sheet. Her arm throbbed to the bone. She wrapped her naked body in the sheet, and dragged herself to her feet. Every step, every movement sent an agonising throb through her. She carefully crossed the room and opened the door.

'Christ, Rosie! We thought those bastards had come back to get you. We can hear you all down the corridor.' Matt stood in his boxers, bleary-eyed.

Rosie burst into tears.

'Oh God, Matt! I can't cope with this pain. I've never felt anything like this in my life. It's like the blowtorch is still full blast on my arm.' She sniffed and turned away, trying to compose herself, as they came into the room. 'Sorry, guys. I was having a nightmare.' She shuffled across to the bed and sat down.

'It's the burn. You should have stayed in hospital overnight. The doctor told you. They could have given you something more for the pain. It's a very bad burn. Through to the tissue. It will be like this for a few days.'

Rosie shook her head and sniffed.

'Sorry. I'm such a wimp. I—' Another stab of pain shot through her. 'Oh shit! . . . It's so painful! Can you not get me something, Javier? Anything. Morphine. Heroin. I'll take anything.'

Javier smiled and sat down beside her. He put his arm around her shoulder and ruffled her hair.

'I can get you anything you like, Rosita. But you would be out of the game for the morning. And you don't want that.'

Rosie shook her head. 'I know. I'm just being a baby. But it's so sore. I'm in agony.'

'I told you. It's a bad burn. You are going to suffer a lot for quite a few days. You must go to the hospital as soon as you get back to Glasgow.'

'What about Adrian? I don't hear him screaming in the night,' Rosie said, feeling a little embarrassed now.

'I think he has doubled up his painkillers. He was also drinking whisky with me and Garcia after you and Matt left. He's probably passed out,' Javier said.

Rosie nodded, looking at the floor. She swallowed hard as she recalled the dream.

'I . . . I had a dream. That I was falling off the building. And . . . And then my moth—' She sighed, glancing at Javier and Matt. 'Never mind. It's just a dream. I have them a lot.' Her fingers touched the bandage. 'Go back to bed. I'm sorry. I'll be all right.'

'You sure?' Matt yawned, looking at his watch. 'Christ! It's four in the morning.' He went towards the door.

Javier handed her a glass of water and another two pain-killers. 'You want me to stay, Rosie? Until you fall asleep?'

His eyes softened and she felt the tears come again. Sympathy always did this to her.

'No. Thanks, Javier.' She squeezed his hand. 'I'll be all right. I'll go back to sleep now.' She stood up, feeling shivery. 'Got to be sharp in the morning.'

Javier's eyes scanned her face.

'Adrian told me you headbutted some guy called Psycho. What the hell possessed you?'

'You know me. It was done before I had time to engage my brain. Couldn't believe it myself, actually.'

Javier brushed the back of his hand against her swollen cheek.

'You are one crazy woman, Rosita. When you ever going to stop all this?'

'Who knows? It's what I do. That's all I can tell you.'

Rosie thought of TJ's constant pleas to give up. She shook her head and bit back tears, wishing Javier would go. He was one of the few people who could see beyond her bravado.

He sighed. 'Okay. Try to get some sleep.' He kissed her cheek.

As he closed the door, Rosie eased herself onto the bed and lay on her back on the pillow staring at the ceiling, her arm throbbing. Tears spilled out of her eyes and trickled into her ears.

'God help me, Mum,' she whispered. 'I can't do this any more.'

*

Rosie woke up groggy, her arm pulsating in agony as she pulled herself out of bed and went into the bathroom. She stood naked for a moment, trying to work out how she was going to manage a shower without soaking the bandage. She stepped in, wincing in pain as she raised her burned arm above her head and tried to wash. She had passed out in the ambulance from shock and pain, and only came round when she got to hospital, the doctor standing over her. The burn had gone through to the tissue, he'd said. Adrian's injuries were even worse, on both his arm and leg. The pain was bad enough, but she also had to shut out the image of hanging over the edge of the roof. Her dreams had been tormented before, so God knows what they'd be like now. Then her mind flipped into the prospect of the next few hours, and she felt a little nudge of adrenalin in her stomach. This was it. She couldn't wait to see the look on McGregor's face when it all happened.

She was halfway through her room-service breakfast when there was a knock at the door.

'It's me, Rosie. Are you up? Can I come in?' It was Javier.

Rosie put down her coffee and padded to the door, still with the towel wrapped around her.

A big smile spread across his face as he looked her up and down, then kissed her on the lips. 'You don't have to be naked every time you see me, Rosita. But it helps.'

'Jeez! So much cheeriness in the morning, Javier. How

many coffees have you had?' She smiled. His energy was infectious.

'Three. And seven cigarettes.'

'So you're just up, then?' she joked.

He helped himself to a coffee and went out to the terrace and lit a cigarette.

'Come here, Rosie. I have to tell you something.'

Rosie followed him out.

'How is your arm? You feeling a little better?'

Rosie looked at him towering above her.

'I get the distinct impression that I won't be feeling better after what you're about to tell me.'

'Okay. Listen, I've just been with Juan for the last hour, and there is a bit of a problem.'

'Shit, Javier. What kind of problem?'

'Well. The guys from yesterday. You know the Flinty guy that Adrian shot and he went off the roof? Plus the other henchmen the Guardia arrested?'

'Yeah. I'm hardly likely to forget any of them.'

'Well. It has changed things a bit. The . . .' He paused. 'How you say . . . the goalposts have moved?'

'Yes. That's right, Javier. But you're making me nervous. Get to the point.'

'Well, Rosita. Before this happen yesterday, it was Garcia's operation to nail the UVF people. That was the situation. The plan was to get them on the bus and make the raid as they are about to leave Seville. It would be Guardia as the anti-terrorist squad looking for weapons.'

'I know that. Get to the point.'

'I'm getting there. Well. The thing is, nobody expected bodies to be flying off the roof and Guardia Civil being shot and injured. Two of them were injured, you know. One of them still in hospital. Now, because of the shooting and the dead body, the Policia Nacional are involved. By law we have to share our findings with them. And drug investigations and smuggling are their remit, so they have to be in charge of the operation from here.'

'Go on.'

'Well. The big boss, the Guardia Civil captain, has told Juan that everything must be very tight now and that it has to be a closed operation.'

Rosie felt a flush of rage. 'What the hell do you mean a closed operation, Javier? There wouldn't *be* any operation if it wasn't for our information.' She banged her good hand on the table. 'Shit. I knew this would bloody happen. That little shit Garcia. Milking us dry and then ditching us.'

Javier's eyes darkened in anger.

'Rosie. Get off your fucking high horse. That little shit and his men saved your life yesterday. And Adrian's. Plus, it is not his decision. Because of what happened yesterday, things have changed.'

Rosie immediately calmed.

'Okay. Sorry. I do appreciate them saving our lives.' She sighed, frustrated. 'But you know what I mean. This is the crux of the operation now. We need the cooperation of the Guardia to be able to tell the story properly. What if McGregor gets wind of what happened yesterday and they all get away?'

'They won't. Not at all.'

'How?'

'The Guardia and the police will still get them. But it just means that you cannot be there. Or you cannot be seen to be there. I don't know. We will work that out. We'll try to think of something.' He paused, drawing on his cigarette. 'It also means that they won't give us the footage from the handover with McGregor and Flinty yesterday.'

'Shit, Javier! We need that.'

'I know, I know. I talked to Garcia and he's shitting his pants now because the captain is involved and he's already asking him how come he wasn't told enough detail in the first place. And now, with the Policia Nacional running the show, he can't just go handing over evidence to the press, because that handover footage will be part of their evidence. He'd be in all sorts of trouble. Do you understand that?'

Rosie was silent for a moment. She could nearly hear McGuire screaming from here. He would flip his lid. She hadn't even told him about the injury. But she could see that the operation they'd planned was now out of their hands. He'd be phoning her any minute for an update. She switched off her mobile.

Jimmy was surprised to find his father so organised this early in the morning when he went to his bedroom. He was sipping tea on the balcony when he came into the room, his small travel bag packed and ready on the bed.

'You must have been up bright and early, Da,' Jimmy said as he stepped onto the balcony.

'Aye, son. Couldn't sleep last night.'

'Me neither. The racket was mental. The boys were really partying big time.'

'Aye. Good on them. These are great times for the 'Gers. Long may it last.'

Jimmy felt as though they were making small talk and he sat down, waiting for his father to speak.

'So how did you get on yesterday? Did you see that Flinty bastard?'

'Yeah,' Jimmy said, 'in the afternoon. Met with him and big Jake Cox. You know him, don't you?'

'Aye. He's another arsehole. These bastards are not gangsters. They're cardboard. They can't fight. They're only brave men when they've got muscle behind them. Belfast was right to get Flinty out of the game back home. He was out of control. The things he did to people with a blowtorch. Honest to Christ, son, you don't want to know.' He paused. 'Course, he still gets his kickback from drugs. The UVF are washing their money through that bar of his down on the Costa del Sol.'

Jimmy thought for a moment, then spoke. He was running out of people to trust. He'd been awake all night since Wendy told him about Flinty and Rosie and the incident earlier on. He was seriously worried that this was all a set-up, and that Eddie would betray them all.

'He'll not be using a blowtorch on any more people, Da.'

'How do you mean?'

'He's dead.'

'What?'

'Yeah. Dead. Yesterday. Nobody knows about it yet. Not even Eddie.'

'So how do you know?'

'I met Wendy yesterday.' He then turned to his father. 'I wanted to see her one last time. I had to talk to her. And she told me. She told me something about that reporter woman I told you about. Remember? Rosie Gilmour from the *Post*? Wendy said that she got attacked by Flinty with a blowtorch and then cops burst in and Flinty got shot on the roof of some car park or office, and fell off. Right off the roof. She didn't know all the details, but she said he's dead.'

'Fuck's sake! And nobody knows this? I mean Eddie or anything?'

'No. Well he hasn't said anything to me, and I can't very well tell him. But I was with Eddie, Mitch and Flinty yesterday for the stuff we picked up. At one point Flinty went away, but when we left, Jake Cox was still at the bar we were in. There was no mention of anything. No mention of the reporter or anything. So I don't know.'

His father was quiet for a moment.

'Well, Jimmy. You know what this means, don't you?'

Jimmy looked at him without answering.

'Something is going to happen with the cops. They'll have our bus covered. Mark my words. Have you seen Eddie this morning?'

'That's what Wendy says. She says that reporter is working with the cops and they've got this all sewn up. Haven't seen Eddie, no. But he phoned Mitch and said we're to go to his room then we'll all go down and get the bus.' Jimmy looked at his watch. 'In about five minutes.'

His father stood up and looked out across the city then back at Jimmy.

'Well don't be surprised if he says he's not getting on the bus.'

'But why? If he doesn't know anything?'

'He'll have heard. He'll just not have told you. There must have been other guys with Flinty. What about big Jake?'

'Don't know. Wendy says the other guys got arrested.' He paused. 'Psycho was one of them.'

'Good enough for that mad bastard. I hope they lock him up forever. He's a fucking waster, that one.'

His father lifted his bag off the bed. 'So how did you leave it with Wendy?'

Jimmy shrugged. 'She just went away. We had a talk. It was hard. But there's no point, Da. It wouldn't work between us.'

'That's not what you thought a few months ago. You were nuts about her.'

'I know. But it's different now. I'm up to my arse in all this.' He paused. 'And when I get back, there's going to be some shit with the cops over this bank card.' Jimmy's stomach twisted at the thought. 'Don't know what's going to happen.'

His father let out a long sigh.

'Well. Let's see what happens with this bus. But if Eddie tells you he's not getting on it, then he can smell trouble. Where's the coke? Who's got that?'

'Eddie has. In his room.'

'Right.'

Jimmy looked at his watch. 'I'd better get a move on. Eddie will be waiting for me.'

'Be careful, Jimmy.'

Jimmy didn't answer as he opened the door. He glanced back as he left the room, and his da was standing staring into space.

CHAPTER THIRTY-FIVE

Rosie knew she was chancing it big time, but couldn't resist. Despite Garcia telling her to stay away, she was outside the hotel and as close to the bus as she dared. Matt was positioned above the cafe after greasing the palms of the owner to let him use his balcony for pictures.

'You shouldn't be here, Rosie. You know that.'

'What the heck, Javier. Nobody knows me. I'm just blending into the background. Don't worry.' She looked around as the fans began boarding the bus, throwing holdalls inside the open luggage compartment at the side. 'So, where's the cavalry?'

'They'll be here any minute now.' Javier moved away from her. 'I'm going to get out of the way. I suggest you do the same.'

Rosie was knackered, but the strong painkillers definitely made her feel a little euphoric. No wonder people got addicted to them. Adrian was at the cafe outside the hotel sipping coffee, his arm bandaged; he'd been limping badly. She went across and sat beside him.

'You okay?'

'I'm okay,' he said, his eyes searching everywhere. 'Is very painful, but it could have been worse.'

'I was so scared. I thought we were done for. Really I did.'

Adrian puffed out his cheeks, running a hand over his close-cropped hair. He looked past Rosie into the distance.

'You want the truth? So did I. Until the police came through that door, I really thought that was it.' He leaned across and shook her hand, then held it a little longer, his eyes soft as he smiled. 'Seems we've come a long way from the cafe in Glasgow, my friend.'

Rosie felt a little choked.

'Yeah. Bet you're glad I met you that day! It's been a bit of a rollercoaster.'

'Of course. Always. Is life. What happens, happens. Was meant to be.'

'And if we'd got thrown off that building?'

'Then that was also what was meant to be.'

Rosie looked at the dark smudges under his eyes and wondered what it must be like to be inside his head after everything he'd been through.

'I wish I could share your philosophical approach, but I'll probably be having nightmares for the rest of my life.'

Adrian squeezed her hand then he reached over and tenderly brushed his fingers across her cheek.

'The nightmares can't get you, Rosie. Always remember that. They are only nightmares.' He sighed. 'You may think you will never be free of them . . . but, you are free. You just learn to live alongside them.'

Their eyes locked for a long moment, then Adrian glanced over her shoulder.

'Look. Our friends are coming out of the hotel.'

Rosie turned around to see McGregor and Donna come out together. Then behind them, Jimmy and Mitch. Jimmy was carrying the black holdall, looking unhappy. Jimmy's father was behind them, his face like flint.

Rosie watched as they walked towards the bus, then all of them stopped.

'I'm going to get a little closer to this, Adrian. See if I can hear anything.'

She moved through the crowd and stood a few feet away where Jimmy had his back to her. She overheard them talk.

'Listen, lads,' Eddie said. 'Donna and me aren't getting the bus. We're going to have a couple of days down on the Costa del Sol, then fly home from Malaga.'

'What?' Jimmy looked shocked. 'Not getting the bus? But what about the . . .' He leaned into Eddie. 'What about the gear, Eddie?' He glanced down at the holdall.

'It's fine. You take it. It's not a problem. I'll pick it up when I get back. Just take it to your house.'

'Fuck's sake, Eddie!' Jimmy said. 'What's the score?'

Eddie glared at him, surprised, and took a step forward, his mouth tight.

'The score, Jimmy, is you do what you're fucking told. You ask no questions. That clear?'

'Is there some problem, Eddie?' Jimmy persisted. 'You never mentioned you were staying on before.'

'Oh. Do I need to run it past you?' He looked at Mitch who was shifting around on his feet, looking at the ground. 'Listen to him, Mitch. What the fuck is this?'

'It's just that you never mentioned it, boss,' Mitch said a little sheepishly.

'Well I'm fucking mentioning it now. Right! I call the shots here. Now get the fuck onto that bus. Take the gear with you and watch it. Because if you turn up in Glasgow without it you're going to have to find a hundred grand. Got that?'

'I don't understand,' Jimmy protested.

'You don't need to understand. Until you're big enough to give out orders, your job is to obey them. Right? If you've got a problem with that, then you've got an even bigger problem than you think.'

They stood in silence.

Rosie stepped back and went around the front where she knew Jimmy would see her. His face was ashen and he looked humiliated as a few of the fans stood around watching the altercation. His eyes met Rosie's and he quickly looked away. Rosie's mobile rang.

'It's showtime, Rosie. Stand back out of the way, for Christ's sake.' It was Javier.

'Okay. I'm doing it.' She backed off a little, into the crowd.

As she did, two Guardia Civil cars screeched up next to the bus, sirens blaring. Then a Policia Nacional van drew up behind it. Fans and tourists stopped in their tracks, bewildered at the sudden activity. Police armed with submachine guns piled out of the van and the cars, surrounding the bus. Garcia emerged from the front seat of one of the squad cars, along with two of the other detectives she'd seen with him. Four armed guards went onto the bus and ordered everyone onto the pavement. Then they emptied the boot of the bus and told everyone to stand by their own bags. Rosie watched the commotion and buzz of conversation among the passengers.

'What the fuck's going on?' one fan snapped to a Guardia Civil officer. 'What's this all about?'

'Wait where you are. We are searching the bus.'

'What the fuck for? We're football fans.'

'You don't want to be arrested, you will keep your mouth shut.' He made a zipping gesture across his mouth.

'Aye, what for, like? Arrested for what? I've got fucking civil rights, ya dago Tim bastard.'

Garcia and three other detectives pushed through the fans to where Eddie and the others were standing.

'Hand over your bags,' one of the officers barked.

Rosie watched as Jimmy froze. He looked at Eddie who

handed over his small rucksack, and Donna her little travel case. Mitch looked at Jimmy then at Eddie.

'Boss?' Jimmy said.

Eddie said nothing.

The detectives took the bag off Jimmy and opened it up, nodding to Garcia.

'This your bag?' the officer said to Jimmy.

He looked at Eddie, who still said nothing.

Then he glanced at his father, whose face was grey. Jimmy opened his mouth to speak as Eddie glowered at him.

'No, it's not his bag.'

Everyone looked around.

It was Jimmy's father.

'It's *his* bag,' he said, stabbing a finger towards Eddie.

'Da,' Jimmy said.

'It's not *my* bag, officer.' Eddie gave the cop a stunned look.

'It's *his* bag,' Jimmy's father said again, this time louder. 'He's a lying, slimy bastard.' He pushed out of the crowd and punched Eddie square on the face. 'You're a fucking disgrace to everything you're supposed to stand for. A cheap, lying, cheating, grassing bastard.' He punched him again. 'And you're trying to stick my laddie in to save your own skin.'

For a second Eddie looked dazed from the punch, then he wiped blood from his nose.

'Fuck you, Jack! You're in fucking trouble for this. You're a dead man walking.'

'Aye, you're right, you prick. I *am* a dead man walking. But I'll go to my grave with my conscience clear. Not like you. You're nothing but a fucking user. And you're a rapist.' He glanced at Jimmy then back to Eddie. 'Well your number's up. You're finished.' He nodded to Garcia who was standing a few feet away.

Eddie was white as a sheet. He glanced at Garcia then at Jimmy's father.

'What? You grassed me up? You're a dead man.' He turned to Jimmy. 'That's your da, Jimmy. He's a grass. A UVF hero all his days and look at him now. A fucking grass.' He spat blood on the ground. 'Shoot him, Jimmy. Do it now. Do it now or face the consequences.'

Jimmy did nothing. Eddie turned to Mitch.

'Mitch! Shoot him!'

Mitch didn't move. He looked at Eddie, then at Jimmy and his father. He said nothing. The police moved in to arrest all of them.

Jimmy's da turned his back, and as he did, a shot rang out. He sank to his knees. Eddie stood with the gun in his hand, and within a split second two officers grabbed him from behind and forced him face down on the ground.

Jimmy wrestled free from the officers who had grabbed him and rushed over to his father.

'Oh Da!' He knelt on the ground, cradling him in his arms as blood gushed from his stomach and spread across his shirt. 'Oh Da. You shouldn't have got involved.'

'I did the right thing, Jimmy. For the first time in my life, I did the right thing. Now you do the same.'

'Get an ambulance!' Jimmy screamed as he tried to stem the blood with his hand.

'It's too late, son. It's too late for me. But not for you. Now go and get that lassie and have the life I didn't have. Because I failed, son. I failed your mother and I failed you.' His breathing quickly became shallow as a pool of blood spread across the ground. 'There *is* no cause now, it's all a fucking lie. Just save yourself.'

'Da, please.' Tears streamed down Jimmy's face. 'I love you, Da. I'm sorry.'

His father's eyes stared back at him blankly as his head dropped to the side.

Two police officers pulled Jimmy roughly to his feet. His arms were forced behind his back as he was handcuffed, and he stood weeping as his father was taken away on a stretcher. Rosie caught Jimmy's eye and he looked back at her, his face etched with pain, as he was frogmarched past her and into the back of the police van.

'I feel a bit sorry for him,' Rosie said to Javier as the police pushed them back.

'Don't,' Javier said. 'They are all bastards. They deserve everything they get.'

'I think Jimmy will stick Eddie in,' she said. 'I'd take a bet on it.'

Eddie struggled with the officers as they dragged him

to his feet. His mouth was bleeding from being pushed face first onto the ground. As they hauled him towards the police car, he turned his head to where Donna stood yards away with Rosie.

'Donna. Get a lawyer for me. Now!'

Donna looked at him, the years of contempt written all over her face. She shook her head slowly.

'What the fuck, Donna?' he spat. 'You fucking whore. You better never show your face again in Glasgow.'

Rosie put a comforting arm around Donna's shoulder as she broke down.

'Who the fuck are you?' Eddie growled as he came face to face with Rosie.

'I'm Rosie Gilmour.' She gave him a defiant look. 'I'm from the *Post*, Eddie. You wouldn't have a wee comment for the newspaper, would you?' She tried to keep her face straight.

'Fuck you! You're dead.'

'That'll do.' Rosie allowed herself half a wry smile.

She motioned Donna to a table at the cafe, and she sat down, wiping her tears with a tissue.

Rosie patted her shoulder. 'It's over now, Donna.'

Donna nodded. 'Not for me. Not yet. I still have to go back home.'

'But Eddie won't be there. He'll not be there for a very long time. You don't have to stay there. Listen. I can make a call right now, talk to the cops about the bank card and you won't see Eddie for the rest of your life. That's if he ever gets out of jail here.'

'But what if they track me down?'

'They won't track you down. You can go to the other side of the world. You just tell me when you're ready.'

Donna sniffed and sobbed.

'You know, my whole life has been about covering for him, Rosie. Everything he's done, the people he beat, the money he hid. Everything. And I got my face punched twice a week into the bargain. If it wasn't for my kids . . . Christ! How am I going to tell them?'

'You might be surprised. They might be on your side.'

'They've watched the abuse for years, that's why they all left home as soon as they could.'

'Just let me know when you're ready.'

She sat for a long moment, dabbing her eyes. Then she looked at Rosie, her face set.

'I'm ready.'

CHAPTER THIRTY-SIX

Rosie watched as Adrian loaded up the hired car for his journey back to Bosnia. He'd decided to drive rather than run the risk of being stopped at the airport. Garcia had told Javier that the Policia Nacional wanted to talk to him about the small matter of shooting Flinty Jackson with one of their guns. Adrian wouldn't be in trouble over it, he assured her – they just needed to tie up the loose ends of the investigation. But Adrian wasn't waiting around to be scrutinised by the police, and Rosie had to agree with him.

'So.' He turned to Rosie as he closed the boot. 'I get started now. It's a very long way.'

There was an awkward moment as they faced each other, Rosie not quite able to read the expression in his eyes.

'I will miss you, my friend.' He rolled up the sleeves of his khaki shirt, exposing his bandaged arm.

'Me too, Adrian.' The image of both of them on the roof flashed through her mind. She didn't really know what to say, so she just stepped forward and hugged him. 'I wouldn't be here without you.'

He held her tight. 'Of course you would. You are the lucky reporter.' He eased himself away, little lines appearing at the sides of his eyes as he smiled.

'So what now? Do you think you will stay in Bosnia?'

He pursed his lips. 'I don't know. Nothing much there for me, apart from my mother, and . . . my sister has her own life now. I like Spain very much, but I think I must stay away from here for a while after this.' He gazed beyond Rosie. 'I like to come to Scotland again maybe. But I need to find a real job. Not like I was – working in the biscuit factory or as concierge in the hotel. I want to have proper work, maybe some kind of life there. You know what I mean?'

'Yes, I do.' She made a mental note to talk to her private-eye friend Mickey Kavanagh, whose work often involved shady places and even shadier people. He could use a guy like Adrian.

He hugged Rosie again, then kissed her briefly on the lips.

'I see you sometime, Rosie.' He squeezed her hand, then turned away from her and got into the car without looking back.

Two hours later, Rosie and Matt got out of Javier's car at the departure area and unloaded their gear. Seville Airport was busy with hung-over Rangers fans making their way to the check-in desk.

'Well. At least I didn't get shot this time, Rosie,' Javier joked, lighting a cigarette.

'Yeah. You can't say I don't look after you,' Rosie replied, but she knew it sounded half-hearted. The downside of painkillers this strong, as any junkie will tell you, is that when they begin to wear off, your mood drops like a stone.

'What's the matter, Rosita? You look down. What's the problem? The bad guys lost – and your boyfriend Adrian even managed to do the world a favour by shooting the bastard who burned you. You don't think you've had a successful trip?'

Rosie sighed. 'Nah. It's not that. I feel a bit sorry for Donna with everything that's happened and now she's sitting back there on her own in the hotel.' She touched her arm. 'Plus that little high from the painkillers is wearing off. I feel a bit strung out, actually.'

Rosie had already told Don about the bank card. Two officers were on their way to Seville to bring Donna back to Glasgow, where she'd be a protected witness. Rosie had been quick to point out to him that the last guy she handed over to police protection was the Kosovan refugee Emir, and he ended up shot dead while in their care. Not this time, he promised. Special Branch would take over from here, as Donna might be able to provide much more information about the UVF dealings of McGregor. Don said she would be placed somewhere far away from Glasgow and given a new identity, along with Andy, if that's what she wanted.

'I feel sorry for that girl Wendy too,' Rosie said. 'Everything's been done to lock McGregor up for drugs and the murder. But he raped her, and there's no justice for her.'

'She could report it to the cops now,' Matt said. 'It's open season on McGregor. A rape charge is the least of his worries.'

Rosie had met with Wendy and Liz earlier at their apartment. She said she wouldn't pursue the rape and would learn to live with it. The one phone call Jimmy had been allowed to make from custody was to her, and she'd already been to see him at the police station where he was being held. He'd promised her if they extradited him to Scotland, he would turn Queen's evidence against McGregor. He had already spoken to the Spanish police about his intentions and was waiting for a visit from the British Embassy. It was a long process and he could be in custody in Spain for months. He told Wendy his father's dying words were for him to do the right thing, and he was determined to try.

Liz was already planning to move to a Greek island and look for a job in a bar. She was never going back to Glasgow.

'I already talked to my cop contact in Scotland about Jimmy spilling the beans on Eddie and the UVF,' Rosie said. 'They're keen to get hold of him. They're making the legal moves to see if they can get all three of them back home to face trial in Scotland. But it's quite complicated.'

'So why are you so down?'

'Just knackered, I suppose, and stressed with all the shit

that happened. So much adrenalin and stuff. It happens sometimes. I just want to go home now.' She thought about TJ, and knew when she got back she'd have to talk to him.

Matt shook hands with Javier and they had a backslapping man-hug, then he walked to the doors with his camera gear.

'Wait, Rosie.' Javier went into the boot of his car and took out his jacket. 'I have a present for you.' He went into the pocket and handed her an envelope.

'What is it?' She opened it, and saw a DVD. She looked at him, confused.

'Is the video. From the handover of the drugs.'

Rosie smiled, incredulous.

'You're kidding me. But how?'

'How do you think, Rosita? I stole it, of course.'

'Shit! How?'

'Listen. I know Garcia a long time. I know he would give it to me if he could, but he didn't dare. So when he went for a coffee and I was making translation notes from your statement on his computer, I went in and took it.'

'Christ, Javier! What if he finds out?'

'I think Juan would be very surprised if I hadn't stolen it.'

'So I can use this?'

'Of course.'

'No comeback? What if they find out?'

'I don't think the police read the *Post* in Seville.'

'Brilliant! Thanks.'

'Just put it on my bill.' He gave her a sarcastic look. 'You're not feeling so sorry for everyone now, Rosita? You've got your front page pictures.'

He handed her another envelope.

'What's this – Christmas Day?'

She tore open the envelope and pulled out the photographs. There were three of them. Two of them were of a holdall pulled open and inside what looked like bags of sugar wrapped in cellophane stacked alongside each other. Another was of the holdall open on a bed in what looked like a hotel room. She gave a little gasp of shock.

'Please tell me this is McGregor's coke.'

'You bet it is.'

'My God! How in the name of Christ did you get that?'

'If I told you I'd have to kill you.'

'Come on, Javier. I'm nearly dizzy with shock here.'

'Okay. But strictly for us. I knew about this last night, but was sworn to secrecy before the bust. Garcia's undercover men were watching McGregor closely and when he and Donna were out of the hotel room having dinner after the match last night, the police moved in. When Garcia and his men were in the corridor, they were approached by an older man. He introduced himself as Jack Dunlop. He said he could help them.'

'Are you serious?'

'Yep. Garcia is the only one who spoke English, and he halted the operation and took the old guy to the side for a talk. I don't know the ins and outs of what was said, but I gather from Garcia that the old guy told them McGregor was the drug dealer and was bringing coke back to Scotland on the fans' bus. He told them his son was mixed up in it, and that he could tell them more if they would cut some kind of deal for his son. Garcia obviously wouldn't make the deal, but he said they would look at it. The old guy said he would go into the witness box and put McGregor away if they did something for his son.'

'God almighty. Jack Dunlop? Grassing the UVF?'

'To save his son. Though I'm not sure it would have worked.'

Rosie studied the pictures again and let out a low whistle.

'Amazing! Wait till the editor hears this. What can I say?'

'As I said. Put it on my bill.'

Rosie laughed. 'Still can't believe you didn't tell me though.'

'My decision.' He put his hand out. 'You want me to take them back?'

'Yeah, that'll be right,' Rosie said as she carefully put the pictures back in the envelope and slid them into her rucksack.

'So your day just got better.' Javier put his arms around her and kissed her on the lips, then hugged her tight, for a long time.

'Thanks. I *will* miss you, Javier,' she said, and meant it.

'Yeah, sure you will.'

'And one more thing, Rosie,' Javier said, as she slung her rucksack over her shoulder and walked away.

'Yeah?' She turned around.

'Do me a favour. Next time you come to Spain? Don't call me!'

She blew him a kiss, then added a two-fingered salute as she went towards the airport doors.

CHAPTER THIRTY-SEVEN

Rosie's mobile rang as she and Matt went through passport control at Glasgow Airport. It was McGuire. She'd already spoken to him last night when she finally got out of the police station in Seville after spending three hours giving a detailed statement about the blowtorch attack and her investigation into the drug smuggling. It took a bit of explaining. She knew McGuire would be pacing his office, desperate to get the story in the paper before the Scottish cops waded in, attempting to charge anyone. On top of that, the Rangers fans who had witnessed the arrests and the shooting outside the hotel would already be tipping off the newspapers.

'Where are you, Gilmour?'

'I'm on my way, Mick. Just getting out of the airport. I'll be there shortly.'

'Great. I need you to get all this copy together asap. Have you written anything up yet?'

Rosie hadn't told him about the blowtorch injury. There was too much going on and she didn't want to go into all the detail. But she hadn't been able to write because of the pain.

'I haven't written anything yet.'

'No? Why not? Were you out on the skite with the fans last night?'

'No.' Rosie paused. 'I've got an injury to my arm. It's a bit better today, but it was too painful last night. I wasn't in good shape.'

'What's happened? You managed not to mention this last night. What the fuck's going on?'

'Long story. I'll tell you when I get there.'

'What kind of injury? Did you get shot? Stabbed?'

'No.' Rosie looked at Matt. 'It was a blowtorch.'

'A blowtorch? Fuck me, Rosie! Someone used a blowtorch on you? Who?'

'One of the hoodlums. A bad lot. Anyway. He's dead now.'

'Oh shit! I don't like the sound of that. Are the Spanish cops going to turn up at my office any time soon?'

'No, no,' Rosie chuckled. It was good to be home. 'Don't worry. It's all sorted. But I need to go to the hospital soon as possible. It's pretty bad. Can you get Marion to sort something today? I can write, but I need to maybe take a day or two to get it done. I'm a bit slow.'

'Shit! Don't worry. Marion will get an appointment this

afternoon. But come here first so we can see where we are in all this.'

In the taxi, Rosie's mobile rang again. This time it was Don.

'Hi, Don. Have you arrested that big cop down in Ayrshire? Your very own UVF man?'

Don paused. 'Er. Not yet. Listen. You around later?'

'Don't know. Going to be up to my eyes. Plus, I have to go to hospital. Got a problem with my arm. What's going on?'

'Well. The UVF man you told me about – the cop? I've checked it out here, and, after a lot of fucking around, they're telling me he's working undercover.'

'Bollocks! I just don't believe that.'

'Neither do I. But that's what the top brass are saying. When I told them I'd had a tip-off and that the press were on it – obviously not mentioning any names – they went to his house with a search warrant. Then it all went quiet. They didn't tell me any more, but I heard through the grapevine they got a load of weapons. Sawn-off shotguns, handguns and AK-47s . . . and two fucking submachine guns! Fuck me! But they've all clammed up now. I know they're lying – the last thing they'll want is one of their own turning up in the UVF. It's totally mental. How the Christ did you dig that one up?'

'Pure chance, and that's the truth. We'd been on this UVF drugs smuggling for a few weeks, and we saw this smart-looking guy with one of the bosses after a UVF meeting in

Glasgow. We just got the registration of his car and tracked his address. Then he walked out of the bloody place in uniform. Couldn't believe it myself.' Rosie paused. 'I suppose he *could* be working undercover. I have another source who'll be able to get some intelligence on that. But I don't believe it for a minute.'

'Me neither. Oh, and by the way, that Tam Wilson asshole you gave me over the shit cocaine. He folded under pressure from my DCI, and told us he got the coke from McGregor when he came back from Eindhoven. That was a real result.'

'Great, Don. We'll drink to that.'

'Sure. If you get a chance, give me a shout and we'll have a drink. If not tonight, then tomorrow.'

'Okay. Are your guys on their way to Spain to get Donna?'

'Yep. Went this afternoon. They'll bring her back here. And they're looking at dealing with Jimmy Dunlop. He's told the Spanish cops he wants to talk. He's already spilled a few things. So much for the *omertà* code between these bastards. Every man for himself when backs are to the wall. Don't know about Mad Mitch though. He's a bad bastard.'

'Okay. But I hope they take care of Donna – because she's the innocent party in all this.'

'Don't worry.' He hung up.

Marion looked up from her desk when Rosie walked into the office.

'Jeez, Rosie. That's a bit of a slap you've had.'

Rosie touched her swollen cheek. She'd been so absorbed in the burning pain in her arm, she'd forgotten about her face. 'I know. But that's not the worst.'

'I heard,' Marion said. 'You've got an appointment at the Nuffield at four. Burns specialist. Is it really bad? Can I see it?' She came from behind her desk.

'Don't think I can take the bandage right off. But it's pretty bad. Through the skin and flesh. Never felt pain like it in my life. I was crying like a bloody baby.' She peered into McGuire's empty office. 'Where is he?'

'Here he comes.'

Rosie turned around as McGuire came briskly across the editorial floor and through the open door to Marion's adjoining office.

'In you come, Rosie. Did you enjoy the match?'

'Oh aye. Brilliant.'

Rosie followed him into his office.

'Bring us some tea, Marion, will you? You hungry, Gilmour?'

'I'm always hungry.'

'And some sandwiches, please.'

They stood for a few seconds as McGuire quickly studied Rosie's face, then glanced at her arm.

'What the fuck happened?' He moved to hug her.

'Careful, Mick. It's bloody killing me. Honest to God. I've never known such pain.'

'Christ! Sit down.' He motioned her to the sofa and sat on the leather armchair opposite. 'Tell me.'

Rosie recounted the full horror of the attack, from the moment she was forced into the blacked-out car, with Adrian at gunpoint. When she got to the part about dangling over the roof, she stopped and sat back, shaking her head.

'I feel physically sick even talking about it. The worst thing you could ever do to me is to put me high up someplace where I might fall off. It's been a recurring theme of my fevered nightmares all my life. It was awful. I don't know how the hell I'm going to get it out of my mind.'

She told him about the Spanish cops bursting in and saving their lives, and about Adrian shooting Flinty.

'Fuck me! That big Bosnian's never happy unless there are dead bodies everywhere.' He laughed. 'He's a spooky bastard.'

Rosie smiled wistfully, thinking about Adrian getting into his car and driving off.

'He's actually a really good guy. You'd like him. But he doesn't take any prisoners.'

'Okay, so tell me where we're at.'

Rosie reeled off the full story. McGuire punched the air with delight when she told him that Javier had stolen the video of the handover of the drugs from the cops, plus the pictures inside McGregor's hotel bedroom. It was copper-bottomed.

'Fucking beauty! So we're all set,' he said. 'Right. I want full chapter and verse of our inside story. Everything from the secret UVF meeting place to how we tracked these bastards from Glasgow to Eindhoven to Seville; the dodgy coke that caused the deaths of seven people here; the innocent fans on the buses who know bugger all about them being used as a vehicle for smuggling drugs. And especially the great line that this police inspector is their weapons man – the quartermaster inspector. I fucking love that!'

'Well. There's a problem with that, Mick.'

'What?'

'Cops are saying he was undercover.'

'Undercover, my arse.'

'I know. But what can we do? We can't disprove it. Undercover is just what it is. Only a select number of people are aware of it.'

'It's a load of fanny from the cops because they don't want it to come out. Have you any other source you can go to who'll tell us the truth?'

'Yeah. I have a guy with good Special Branch connections. He's into everything. He'll at least be able to make some discreet inquiries and give us a steer.'

'Right. Well get on it. I want that story as much as anything. Bastards are lying to us. I hate that.'

'Sure.'

'So, what about your arm. Can I see it?'

'I can take the bandage off a bit, but it's sticky.'

She peeled it back a little, wincing in pain as the gauze tugged at the wound, and McGuire screwed up his face when he saw the ripped, angry flesh.

'Oh fuck, Rosie! That's bad. You must have been in agony.'

'I was. They said they'd keep burning us until the pain was so bad we'd jump off the building ourselves.' To Rosie's surprise, tears came to her eyes as she had a flashback of the horror of that moment. She looked at the floor, trying to compose herself.

'Christ.' McGuire reached across and touched her hand. 'You need to stop taking chances. You said that Spanish cop Garcia told you not to go to where these guys were meeting. Sometimes you should listen to people and not be so hotheaded.'

'I know. I'm going to change.'

'Yeah. Sure you will.'

Marion brought tea.

'Okay. Get to the hospital and go home tonight. Just have a rest, get this treated and work out the stuff in your head. It won't take you long to write once your mind's clear and you've had a decent sleep. We can hang onto it for one more day. We've already had a few calls from punters on the bus, and there's been a snap of it on the telly. We're going to puff it on the front page tomorrow – read the *Post* on Thursday for the full exclusive investigation. We'll get at least two big days out of it. Plus, it's the kind of story that will run and run.' He stopped and looked at her. 'Are you sure you're okay? You look wrecked.'

She nodded. 'I am. I'll be fine in the morning.' She didn't tell him that as knackered as she was, she dreaded putting her head on the pillow tonight.

Later, in her flat, Rosie ran a bath and sat in it with a glass of red wine. When she came out she wrapped her bathrobe around her very carefully. The consultant told her she would need several skin grafts and there would probably be some permanent scarring.

She flicked on the television and stared, catatonic, at the screen. After a few minutes she picked up her mobile and dialled TJ's number.

He answered after three rings.

'Hey, scoop? Where the hell you been? I haven't heard from you in a week.'

'I was in Seville, TJ. I told you.'

'I know. But I thought you might have called me. Howsit going anyway? Did you get all the bad guys?'

'Yeah. Most of them.'

'You sound a bit down. What's wrong? Was it bad?'

'Yeah.' Rosie felt a sudden wave of emotion, wishing that he was here on the sofa beside her so she could offload everything. 'I'll tell you about it when I see you. Don't know when that will be though.'

'Tell me now, Rosie.' He paused, then said softly, 'I miss you, sweetheart. More than you know.'

Rosie allowed the silence to hang between them. She wanted to say she had called him, and that Kat had answered the phone, but she couldn't bring herself to do it. She wanted to confront him, but was scared of the consequences. It was stupid, she knew. But right now she couldn't deal with it if he said – or even hinted – that he wanted to finish.

'So what you up to, TJ? Anything happening?'

'Not much. Just working. Bit of practice with Gerry and Kat some afternoons.'

Rosie's stomach jumped a little. She took a sip of wine and then it was out before she could stop herself.

'TJ,' she swallowed. 'I did call you a few days ago.'

'When?'

'When I was in Seville. Would have been late afternoon your time.' She paused. 'Kat answered the phone.'

Silence. She could hear TJ breathing, and the sound of her own heartbeat.

'She didn't tell me.'

'I didn't speak. I just hung up.'

'Why?'

Silence.

'Why, Rosie?'

'What?' Rosie was still picturing Kat in TJ's apartment. 'Well, to tell you the truth, I was a bit taken aback.'

She could hear a long intake of breath and then a sigh.

'Rosie. How many times do we have to go through this?'

'You didn't say. About Kat being there, that's all. I was wondering if she was staying at your place. Is she?'

'No. Well. Yes. She was for a few days last week. She's moving to a new apartment and had to be out by the weekend, so I put her up. That's all.'

'You didn't say.'

'I didn't say because I hadn't spoken to you. And anyhow it's not important. I might not have said anyway. Jesus, Rosie. Stop all this crap. Have you any idea how much it irritates me to be questioned about stuff? You know I wouldn't do anything to hurt you. I told you, I love you. If you can't accept that because I'm away, and you're paranoid at every turn, then this is seriously not going to work. Honestly. Come on, sweetheart. Get a grip.'

Rosie was silent for a moment. She hadn't expected him to be so strident.

'I'm sorry,' she said eventually. 'I . . . I'm just knackered. It was a hard trip. Some bad things happened.'

'Are you injured? Did something happen?'

'Yeah. But I'm okay. Listen I don't want to talk about it now. When you coming back? Any ideas?'

'Two more months. They haven't said anything about staying on, so I suppose I'm out of here in two months. Unless . . .'

'Unless what?'

'Unless something else comes up here and I get offered more work.'

'But I thought you were coming home?'

'I am. I mean I will be. I want to come home. Really I do. And be with you. I don't think there will be any more work in the pipeline right now anyway. So I should be back when this contract is up.' He paused. 'Rosie. I want to be with you.'

'Good. I can't wait to see you.'

'Me too. And stop with the paranoia, for Christ's sake. I need to go. I'll call you in the morning.' He paused. 'I love you, Rosie.'

She sensed an edge to his voice. Something was missing. They were saying the right things to each other, but there was a little twinge in her stomach that didn't feel right.

'Yeah. I know,' she said, a little choked. 'I love you too.'

CHAPTER THIRTY-EIGHT

Rosie was wrecked with tiredness and it was only two in the afternoon. She'd flaked out on the sofa, the combination of painkillers, exhaustion and red wine knocking her out. But she woke herself screaming, in a nightmare that she was falling off the edge of a cliff. She'd gone to bed, and when she wakened again at six she knew if she lay there any longer she wouldn't get up at all. She'd got out of bed, had breakfast and started working at her laptop. The main story for the first day's spread and splash was done, and she pinged them across to McGuire before the taxi came to her flat to take her to the hospital.

Her mobile rang as she was on her way back to the office. It was Don.

'Hi, Don. How you?'

'Better than some people, I'd say,' Don replied.

'Why? What's going on?'

'The cop. Your UVF man. Thomson. He's just been found dead.'

'You're kidding me?'

'Nope. Hooded and shot in the back of the head. Some cyclist down the Kilmaurs road found his car and looked in.'

'Christ almighty! That was quick.'

'I know. All the hallmarks of a paramilitary killing.'

'Or made to look like one.'

'What do you mean?'

'Maybe the cops bumped him off.'

'Fuck's sake, Rosie. You've been watching too many movies.'

'Stranger things have happened.'

'So you think Strathclyde's finest did one of their own in, paramilitary style, to make it look like he had been rumbled by the UVF because he was working undercover?'

'That's exactly what I mean. Either way, even if it was the UVF bumping him off before he started to spill his guts now that he'd been rumbled by us as well as the cops, then it's still a brilliant story. What's the word on it at HQ?'

'They're saying bugger all. Don't even know how they're going to handle it with the press.'

'Well they'll need to get something sorted fast, because this will be our splash tomorrow. Guaranteed.' She paused. 'I need to go. I'll give you a buzz later.'

Rosie went straight to McGuire's office, knocked the door and walked in. McGuire was behind his desk with a cup of coffee at his lips.

'You'll never guess what, Mick.'

McGuire looked up from the cup.

'Ah, that's better, Gilmour. You look more like your old self today. Somebody important has obviously either been bumped off or given themselves up. Which is it?'

'Got it in one. The UVF copper's been found dead. Bullet in the back of the head. Hooded and shot, paramilitary style.'

'Oh fuck me! What a result!'

'I'm sure his missus doesn't think that.'

'Fuck him. He was as dirty as they come.'

'Well, technically we don't know that for sure. I'm waiting on that pal to give me the absolute lowdown on it. But I'm sure you're right. No way was he undercover.'

'I wonder who did it though.'

'Has to be the UVF.'

'Don't be too sure. The cops are just as capable of doing this.'

'I thought that at first, but now I just don't think they would. They could ride a storm of a cop being dirty, even being involved with UVF. It would be a huge scandal, of course, but it's a bit of a leap for the cops to go bumping people off to make it look good. What if that ever came out? I talked to a cop pal, and he says no way would they do that.'

'Well, we might never know, but one thing's for sure. That's our splash tomorrow. That and all the pics we have of him and what you've been told about him being the weapons man. Fuck him. At least he can't sue us. You can't libel the dead.' He grinned at Rosie. 'Looks like you've got at least an extra day out of this. By the way, the stuff you sent over is great. But we need to rush it into the paper by tomorrow because my instinct is that the cops will be all over this now and working towards getting McGregor charged.'

'If they do, then it's great background for the trial. But that won't be for a long time – depending on how they go bringing him back here. I'm told there's all sorts of legal stuff to go through because he's also being held in a foreign country for murder and drug smuggling. It'll take a while to sort that out. But we'll have loads for a trial.'

'Fuck the trial. If it's left to that, everyone will get it if it comes out in court. I want it now. To ourselves.'

Rosie's mobile rang. It was Mickey Kavanagh.

'Hi, Mickey. Guess who's just been found dead.'

'It has to be our UVF cop.'

'Got it in one.'

'Jesus. They didn't waste much time.'

'I know. So what do you hear intelligence-wise on the undercover line?'

'Not a snowball's chance he was undercover. That's complete crap from the cops. If they say that officially they will be in big trouble.'

'But would your people admit it anyway? I mean, if he was undercover?'

'No. Technically they would not admit it. But I have connections who are always straight with me, and I just talked to one. He checked things out and made a few enquiries. Nobody's even heard of this bastard. He's a rotten cop. End of. And I'll tell you something else that will never come out. This is why I know you're right. They found weapons in the basement of his house – an arsenal: rifles, pistols and a couple of short-stocked AK-47s, which are fairly standard in paramilitary territory, plus some small submachine guns. He is who you say he is. Well done. But the cops will never admit it. Put it this way, they can't afford to.'

'Brilliant. Thanks, Mick. It's an amazing story,' Rosie said, delighted Mickey had confirmed Don's line about the weapons being found.

'Not half. It's a safe bet that UVF will have wasted him. They'll know by now about McGregor and the other guys being arrested. And about that Flinty fucker getting killed. They had to mop up as much as they could. What exactly happened to Flinty, by the way?'

'Long story. I'll tell you over dinner in the next few days.'

'Fine. I have to go. But listen, Rosie. Don't believe anything the cops tell you if they try to say this guy was undercover. Trust me.' He hung up.

Rosie put the mobile on the desk and looked at McGuire.

'My contact. He says no way was the cop undercover. Not a chance.'

'Terrific. How sure can he be?'

'Copper-bottom sure, Mick. He knows everyone from London Road cop shop to the corridors of MI6. Don't ask me why, because I don't know. But he's very connected. He says nobody's even heard from this guy. In theory he could have been working undercover in a broader way for the UK serious crimes agency. They collaborate with forces across Europe and use key police figures. But this guy wasn't one of them.'

'That'll do for me.' Mick was already roughing out a page plan on his desk. 'Are you okay to write the story, with your bad arm? I can get Declan to do a bit of work for you. He's already done a big background piece on the UVF and the Scottish connections down the years. Dunlop's father was a player, as you know.'

'Yeah. It won't take long to get the story done. I'll go and have a coffee with Declan now and fill him in.'

Rosie stood up and went towards the door.

'And Rosie?'

She turned around.

'We need to be careful. These bastard UVF will go apeshit when this hits the papers tomorrow. So pack your bags.'

'Aw, Mick.'

McGuire put his hands up. 'In fact, don't pack your bags. I'll send someone to the flat. You're not going back there today. Maybe not for a while – at least not without an entourage of heavies.'

Rosie's stomach tightened. She knew he was right.

'Okay.'

'I'm getting you out of the country. Before the day's out.'

'Where am I going to go?'

'Go to New York. See that JT bloke.'

'It's TJ.'

'Well. Go there then. Have a holiday for a few weeks.' He paused. 'Or anywhere you like. Anywhere but here.'

'We'll see.'

Rosie went downstairs and into the canteen for a coffee. She sat for a few moments staring into space, her heart thumping like an engine as it began to dawn on her that this was the most serious threat she'd ever been under. She could go to New York. TJ would be delighted to see her. Or would he? But right now, the thought of being over there in the bustle of a big city wasn't what she needed. She needed open spaces, fresh air, some place far enough away and so obscure where nobody would even think about looking for her. She had a rush of blood to the head.

She took out her mobile, and dialled Adrian's number.

ACKNOWLEDGEMENTS

With this novel's thorny subject of bigotry and sectarianism, I wanted to show that behind the mask, they are ordinary men and women, no different from the rest of us, who love and lose and hurt in the same way. I hope people will see beyond the subject matter and understand just that.

As the author, I get the good part. I disappear to the wilds of Ireland, or the warmth of the Costa del Sol to lose myself, creating the characters in here. But wherever I am, I'm grateful to have many people at my back – too numerous to mention.

Here are a few I want to thank.

My sister Sadie, who inherited all our mother's kindness and our father's fire, my brothers Desmond, Hugh and Arthur who contribute to my life in so many different ways.

And all their children and grandchildren who make me feel loved.

My nephews Matthew Costello and Christopher Costello who I bounce some ideas off, and their sister Katrina

Campbell, my PR guru and occasional fashionista advisor! Also nephew Paul Smith who takes care of my website along with Matthew.

My close friends, Mags, Ann Frances, Mary, Phil, Helen, Louise, Donna, Babs and Jan, as well Betty, Kathleen and Geraldine, Simon, Lynn, Annie, Keith and Mark, for the way we pick up where we left off, no matter when we meet. And Thomas, far away in Australia.

The Motherwell Smiths and their banter around my kitchen table in Dingle, and cousin Mhairi who walked the Camino de Santiago with me this year.

My cousin Alice Cowan and Debbie Bailey in London, and Ann Marie Newall.

In Spain, the force of nature that is Franco Rey, whose background and advice – particularly on this novel – is invaluable, even though he drives me nuts with his meticulousness, and being irritatingly right most of the time.

In Ireland, Mary and Paud, Sioban, Sean Brendain, and everyone in TPs who make me feel at home.

My wonderful editor Jane Wood who carefully steers me through every book, and Katie Gordon who calmly answers all my daft questions. And, of course, my agent Ali Gunn, who was taken from us too young and too soon. She was a tour de force with a big heart, who believed in me, and I am privileged to have known her. Ali's phone call to me three years ago changed my life and put me on the road to where I am now. For that I will always be grateful.

**As good as Martina Cole . . .
or your money back**

We're so sure that you'll love *Betrayed*
as much as Martina Cole's books that we'll give
you your money back if you don't enjoy it.
If you do wish to claim your money back, please send
the book, along with your receipt and the reasons for
returning it to:

Anna Smith money back offer
Marketing Department
Quercus Books
55 Baker Street
London W1U 8EW

We'll refund you the price of the book, plus £1.50 to
cover postage. Offer ends April 2015

Quercus
www.quercusbooks.co.uk